Please turn to the back of the book for
an interview with Bonnie MacDougal.

More praise for
Angle of Impact

"Bonnie MacDougal's *Angle of Impact* is a stylish, fast-paced thriller with a number of top-shelf qualities. The characters are well drawn and realistic, the action quick and clever. But where it really excels is in capturing the details both of air accidents and high-stakes litigation. MacDougal's novel breathes authenticity on every page. It is written with verve and confidence and is an altogether impressive effort."
—JOHN KATZENBACH
Author of *State of Mind*

"Electrifying...The explosive growth of liability lawsuits forms the fascinating core of this riveting thriller. Attorney-turned-author Bonnie MacDougal deftly explores the powerful factors that bring out the best and worst in both individuals and our legal system. Don't miss out! Add *Angle of Impact* to your list of must-read legal thrillers."
—*Romantic Times*

"One of the best of the new legal-thriller authors is Bonnie MacDougal....Based on a real aviation disaster, [*Angle of Impact* is] exciting, plausible, and well written."
—*The Washingtonian*

*Please turn the page
for more reviews....*

D0037195

By Bonnie MacDougal:

BREACH OF TRUST
ANGLE OF IMPACT*

*Published by Ballantine Books

ANGLE OF IMPACT

Bonnie MacDougal

BALLANTINE BOOKS • NEW YORK

A Ballantine Book
Published by The Ballantine Publishing Group
Copyright © 1998 by Bonnie MacDougal Kistler

All rights reserved under International and Pan-American Copyright Conventions. Published in the United States by The Ballantine Publishing Group, a division of Random House, Inc., New York, and simultaneously in Canada by Random House of Canada Limited, Toronto.

www.randomhouse.com/BB/

Library of Congress Catalog Card Number: 98-93451

ISBN 0-345-41446-2

Manufactured in the United States of America

First Hardcover Edition: April 1998
First Mass Market Edition: January 1999

10   9   8   7   6   5   4   3   2   1

For my daughters,
Alison and Jordan,

who are more than I'd hoped for
and better than I deserve.

Certainty generally is illusion,
and repose is not the destiny of man.

OLIVER WENDELL HOLMES, JR.,
The Path of the Law (1897)

1

The landing gear lowered and locked as the red-eye from Los Angeles eased into its final approach to Philadelphia. The sun was rising over New Jersey, and rosy liquid light poured over the Delaware River like an iridescent oil spill. Slowly the dawn backlit the heavens to reveal a cloudless sky.

Dana Svenssen all but pressed her nose to the window to see it. There'd been no California sunshine for her: for a month she'd gone from courtroom to conference room to hotel room without a glimpse of the light of day. But she was home at last, flush with victory and eager to gather up her children for two weeks' glorious repose at the shore.

The giant who sprawled over both armrests in the seat beside her had already found his repose. He was a lawyer past thirty, but he slept as soundly as a little boy, even as the plane taxied to the gate and chimed dismissal.

Dana leaned over and whispered, "Travis, wake up. We're home."

He came awake like a piece of earthmoving equipment, instantly ignited and all systems go. "I wasn't asleep," he said in his usual deep-pitched slur as his head levered up on an eighteen-inch neck. "Just resting my eyes."

"Right. For the past two and a half hours."

She got to her feet and rose to a full five-foot-ten. She was an eye-catcher still, with hair a pale blond and eyes a clear sharp blue like the hot point of a flame; but with her fortieth birthday approaching, no one was going to mistake her for a Swedish model anymore. Lately the racial typing had taken on a new angle. A Valkyrie, she was dubbed in a recent bar journal story, with an illustration that portrayed her in full Viking armor complete with a cow horn helmet.

Great Dana, Travis and her other young associates called her when they thought she wasn't listening.

He lumbered into the aisle and stepped back to block as they joined the line shuffling off the plane. A former all-American football player, her second chair and right-hand man, he'd been guarding her back for a month.

"I got my car here," he rumbled. "Can I give you a ride to the office?"

Only a young lawyer bucking for partner would go straight to the office after an all-night flight and a monthlong out-of-town trial.

"I have my own car," Dana said. "Besides, the office can do without you today. Miss Texas can't."

Travis's wife was a former beauty queen, and though she never actually held the state crown, that was the way he liked to refer to her. He had a standing line: "You can't marry Miss Texas and drag her north and expect her to live in an apartment"—or drive a used car or shop at Sears or whatever new category of expense he was about to incur in her name.

"What are *you* going to do?" he asked, careful never to lose an inch in the contest of single-minded sacrifice to the god of billable hours.

"I have to go to Pennsteel this morning. But it's straight home after that, and you won't see me again for two weeks."

"What's going on at Pennsteel? Debriefing?"

She rolled her eyes. What were they, spies? "Just a short meeting with Vic and Charlie."

Travis stopped to shake hands with the receiving line of pilots and flight attendants, then jogged to catch up in the jetway. "I'll say it again, Dana," he called. "You kicked some major butt out there. Those weenies never knew what hit them." He added, "And they were *really* caught off guard by that motion *in limine* I did."

She hid a smile as she hoisted her bag over her shoulder. "You know, Travis, there're two schools of thought as to the best path to partnership: shameless sucking up and shameless self-promotion, and—"

A broad grin split his face. "And I subscribe to both!"

She couldn't help laughing. No one wore his ambition more appealingly than Travis Hunt.

They reached the terminal and followed the signs to long-term parking, and a solid wall of heat hit them as they came through the revolving doors. August in Philadelphia was always stifling, but this heat-wave-cum-drought was so severe it made the news in Los Angeles. Forty-five days without rain, forty days with highs above ninety. Dana was wearing a form-fitting sheath of ivory silk—a welcome change after a month of dark suits—but she could feel the fabric wilt the moment it hit the air.

Travis paused when their paths diverged in the garage. "I was thinking—Austin'll want some kind of blurb on the verdict to put in the next newsletter. How 'bout I draft something up?"

Clifford Austin was the chairman of their firm, and a premier practitioner of law-as-business. Under his regime, victories mattered less than profits, and not at all unless they could be quickly translated into grist for the firm's marketing mill.

"Would you *please* go home?" She took him by the shoulders and turned him on his way. "You can't marry Miss Texas and drag her north and not go straight home after four weeks away."

Sheepishly, he peeled off for his level.

Dana found her car and drove to the gate to pay the ransom to free it. One of these days, though, she thought as she dug out her money, she'd let it take its chances. The Mercedes was a constant source of embarrassment to her, especially in the view of people like the acne-troubled boy who ran covetous eyes over it as he took her money for minimum wage. She pictured herself more comfortably in a minivan like the other moms, or maybe a little red Miata to show she was still frisky. Anything but this rolling paean to self-importance. But it had the best sound insulation of any car in its class, and as soon as she cleared the concrete ceiling, she put it to good use by dialing up her home number on the speakerphone.

Kirstie won the race to pick up first, but Dana waited for the inevitable second click of the extension before she called out, "Morning, girls! Guess where I am?"

"Philadelphia!" her daughters cheered.

"Yes! And I wanted to say hello before you leave on your field trip. When's the van coming?"

"In five minutes," Trina said.

"Do you have your lunch bags and water bottles? And plenty of sunscreen?"

"Uh-huh. Mom, will you be here when we get home?"

"Absolutely, positively. Did Daddy give you some spending money?"

There was a second's hesitation before Kirstie said, "Well, it doesn't matter, we don't really need any."

"He's not there?"

"He's sleeping," Trina piped up. "And we shouldn't wake him 'cause who knows *how* late he got home last night."

The roadway blurred into gray mist as a rush of tears came to Dana's eyes. "I see," she murmured.

"We don't need any money," Kirstie insisted. At twelve she could sense trouble but looked no further than the absence of ready cash as its cause, though money had never been the problem, at least not the lack of it.

"Tiptoe in and look in my jewelry box. There should be some cash there. Take what you need, okay?"

"Okay."

"I love you."

"Love you, too," they chimed.

Dana boosted her voice to a cheerful timbre. "And have a wonderful time!"

Tears spilled over her cheeks as she disconnected. All summer Whit had spent his days sleeping in and his nights going out. This was the summer he said he would finish his book, but there was no sign he'd made any progress. She didn't know what was going on, and worse, she didn't have the courage to find out. Warrior or not, there were some battles she couldn't fight. Their marriage had turned into an uneasy Cold War truce: her only options were to turn a blind eye to the treaty violations or go to full-scale thermonuclear war.

No, she thought fiercely and swiped the tears away with the back of her fist. *Don't think about Whit.*

The traffic helicopters shadowed her as she followed the expressway past Thirtieth Street Station and west toward Valley Forge. Fifteen years ago she could have driven out of the city during morning rush hour and had the road to herself, but today there was as much outbound commuter traffic as inbound. Philadelphia once had a thriving manufacturing base, but these days only bankers and lawyers worked in the city, and even the bankers' numbers were dwindling. Before long it would be a graveyard, with no one left but lawyers picking through the bleached bones in search of claims and clients.

The phone rang as Dana crossed the city limits.

"Hey, I hoped I'd catch you," her sister's voice rang out over the speaker. "Where are you?"

"Karin—hi! City Line Avenue."

"Good. Stop by on your way out of town."

"Wish I could, but I have a meeting upstate at Pennsteel."

"I'll feed you breakfast."

"It's a breakfast meeting I'm going to."

"Ha. You'd pass up my fresh-out-of-the-oven brioches for stale Danish?" Karin ran a catering business out of her kitchen; one of her specialties was French pastry.

"Please," Dana laughed. "Don't make this any harder than it already is."

"All right, never mind. Listen, are you ready for the shore?"

"Psychologically, more than you'll ever know. Otherwise, not at all. But I will be by the time you arrive tomorrow, if I have to stay up all night to do it."

"Do it. I'll be there at seven-thirty sharp."

The sun grew bright and the cloudless sky turned to robin's-egg-blue as Dana got on the turnpike and pointed the car north. Despite the drought, the countryside looked soft and green after a month in L.A., and with the air conditioner humming, the heat outside was nothing but a rumor. She could hardly feel oppressed in having to make this trip to Pennsteel—the day was too beautiful. Besides, although the meeting was billed as a session to report on the Palazzo Hotel verdict, if she knew her client, specifically its president, Vic Sullivan, there'd be champagne in the orange juice and more back-slapping than note-taking.

An hour later she was exiting the toll plaza when the phone rang again. "Please hold," a woman said. "I'm patching in Mr. Sullivan."

A minute later the connection came through, on a radio wave crackling with static.

"What the hell are you doing on the road?" Victor Sullivan barked. Around his voice sounded a vortex of roaring air. "Aren't you supposed to be in a meeting at ten-thirty?"

"I am, and I will be," Dana retorted. "Which is more than you can say, from three thousand feet up and God knows how many miles away."

He snorted. "I'll take that bet. And for your information we're only twenty-five hundred feet up."

She pulled into the passing lane and pushed the speedometer up to sixty. "Where've you been?"

"New York. Seeing the money boys again. You'll be my second breakfast meeting today."

"Except I'll probably be gone by the time you touch ground."

"Jesus Christ. One little win and you turn cheeky."

"Little?" she hooted. For the five years since the Palazzo Hotel collapsed, the auditors had been carrying the liability at a hundred million dollars. Since Pennsteel was self-insured for the first ten million, there'd been serious exposure.

"Okay, fill me in," Sullivan said.

"I thought that was what today's meeting was for."

"You know I never go into a meeting without having more information than anybody else."

"And you know I never discuss client business over the airwaves."

"This isn't a cell phone," he insisted. "I'm talking on a dedicated radio frequency to our heliport."

"Even worse. That means it's being taped on your cockpit voice recorder, and who knows who listens to that?"

He conceded the point with a groan. "Come on," he wheedled. "Give me the public version at least."

"All right." She passed two cars, then two more before a determined speeder forced her back into the right lane. "The evidence showed that the I-beam supporting the thirtieth floor of the hotel buckled because of insufficient fireproofing and not because of any defect in the manufacture or fabrication of the steel. The jury came down against the fireproofing contractor, the electrical contractor, and the poor kid who started it all when he tried to rewire his room. Pennsteel was absolved of all liability."

"God save the honorable court!"

She laughed. "Who's going to be at the meeting today?"

"The usual suspects. Haguewood, Morrison, and Schaeffer." These three were the senior vice presidents of the company; the rank and file called them the Three Amigos since there was no love lost among them. Dana had her favorite: Charlie Morrison was general counsel and an old friend. "Ollie, too," he added. Oliver Dean was president emeritus, retired now but only so far as chairman of the board. The cast confirmed her suspicion; today's meeting would be a victory party.

"What are you in, Vic—the JetRanger?"

"Yep. Finest chopper in the air."

"At a hundred miles an hour? I can beat you in my car." A traffic light intervened, and Dana braked to a stop.

"Here's your chance."

"Wait a minute! I don't know where you are. Maybe you're sitting on the helipad as we speak."

"Naaah. Ron, where are we?" The pilot's response was swallowed by the whine of the engines and the rhythmic whop-whop-whop of the rotors. "Don't give me the coordinates, who the hell knows what that means? Hold on, let me take a gander here. Hey, I see where we are. Coming up on that amusement park, I can see the roller coaster, whaddya call it, Alpine Valley."

"No kidding!" she cried. "Give a wave to the ground, Vic. My kids are there on a field trip today."

"Whaddya know. Hey, Ron, set this baby down. Let's go cruise for a couple of blondes."

Dana laughed as static filled the void of speech for a minute. The light changed, and as she crossed through the intersection, a muffled shout sounded through the speaker.

"Vic?"

The reply came as a scream of metal slicing through metal and a roar of air sucking air.

"Vic?" she repeated.

A silence, then the buzz of the dial tone.

She wrenched the car to the shoulder of the highway and stared at the phone, then picked it up and punched in the number at Pennsteel.

"This is Dana Svenssen," she said to the company operator. "I was just speaking to Mr. Sullivan on your heliport channel, and we were cut off—"

"One moment, please."

The blare of a car horn whipped past, and Dana groped for the four-way flasher and pushed it on.

"I'm sorry, Miss Svenssen," the operator returned after a moment. "There's no response."

"Would you transfer me to your aviation department?"

"One moment."

She peered up through the windshield. The sky was clear and cerulean-blue, serene and undisturbed.

"Keller," a voice answered.

Keller. She searched her memory. "Ted?"

"Yeah?"

Memory served. Pennsteel's chief pilot, he'd flown her in company aircraft a few times. "Ted, this is Dana Svenssen, with Jackson, Rieders and Clark?" It would take him a minute to remember, but she didn't wait. "I was just on the phone with Vic Sullivan in the air and—something happened." She related the conversation, and the sounds that followed it.

There was a moment's silence before Keller breathed, "Oh, my God."

Her eyes fell shut for a second before she threw on her turn signal and screeched out onto the highway again. "I'm ten minutes away from Alpine Valley," she shouted. "I'm going there now."

She flipped on the police scanner and darted across two lanes of traffic and swung left at the next intersection. The radio blipped and bleeped through a dozen frequencies before it homed in on the strongest signal, and it started crackling at once.

"Yeah, listen," a caller shouted. "There's been a hell of an explosion up there at the amusement park. There's a fireball in the sky; it looks like a comet blew up or something."

"Omigod!" screamed the next. "There's a crash! It's pouring down like a meteor shower!"

Dana's breath caught in her throat. Her children were there, under skies that were raining fire. She pushed the pedal to the floor, and the speedometer passed seventy and hit eighty. Car horns wailed behind her.

The scanner picked up a rash of dispatch calls, sending patrol cars and rescue vehicles to the park, to respond and assist in an emergency of unknown origin. But the next call to come through removed the uncertainty.

"I saw the whole thing," a man reported. "A helicopter and a small plane flew straight at each other. It was like they were in combat or something."

"Any injuries?" the dispatcher intoned.

"Jesus, lady, more than you can count."

Hot tears swam in Dana's eyes. She switched off the scanner as another call came through the car phone. It was the Pennsteel operator again.

"Hold please for Mr. Morrison."

"Dana?" he burst out. "Keller just told me—"

"Oh, Charlie." She cut herself off. She and Charlie went way back; she couldn't trust herself not to cry. She swallowed hard. "I heard the reports on the police band. There was a midair collision between the JetRanger and a small plane. It happened right over the amusement park."

"You're headed there now?"

"Uh-huh. Can you meet me?"

"Yeah, soon as I can. I guess I better notify the carrier first."

"What's your primary coverage, Charlie?"

"Same as Palazzo. A hundred million over the first ten."

"You better notify your excess carrier, too."

There was a pause as he took her meaning. "Right," he said.

2

Cars and trucks were scattered on the shoulders of the highway like dinghies dragged to shore while their drivers swarmed to the top of the hill overlooking Alpine Valley. Dana slowed and craned her neck to see. Cumulus clouds of black smoke billowed up from the park and rolled across the low line of the horizon. Orange flames pierced through the fog, and the sulfurous stench of blazing fuel and metal was everywhere.

Spectators were clustered on the roadway ahead with their hands visored against their foreheads to block the sun. Dana leaned on her horn until they parted in a wave, and she drove between them and down the long drive of the park entrance. A picnic grove flanked the drive, and it obstructed her view for a moment, but when she cleared the trees she could see the wreckage.

There it was, not on the ground, but perched atop the tallest peak of the roller coaster, two hundred feet in the air. The helicopter and a light plane were conjoined like a pair of mating birds that spontaneously combusted at coitus. Flames shot out of the ruins, and sparks and cinders showered onto the ground. Treetops were igniting, as were the gaily colored roofs of hot dog stands and carousels. A handful of police cars had arrived, and a fire engine was already pumping a stream of aqueous foam at the wreckage.

Dana grabbed her shoulder bag and sprinted for the roller coaster, her legs churning so fast that gravel kicked up from her ivory pumps. The park employees in their lederhosen and alpine caps streaked past her for the parking lot, and sneakered moms ricocheted among them with their fanny packs flapping at their waists like vestigial pouches. They screamed for their children while tears painted white lines down their soot-blackened faces.

She raced through the park, past the bumper cars and the penny arcade and the sea dragon now breathing real fire, and over the moat and past the scrambler, which was still whirling crazily with its cars empty. She called as she ran, "Kirstie! Trina! Kirstie! Trina!" but a hundred other mothers were yelling a hundred other names, and not one stood out above the din.

An arrow marked TORNADO pointed the way to the roller coaster, and she ran down that path with the acrid smell of incinerated metal burning hot in her throat and nostrils. A tree loomed ahead, scorched black and still smoking, and Dana pulled up short. At the base of the trunk lay a body, or part of one, charred beyond recognition. The molten plastic earmuffs of a radio headset were fused to his skull. It had to be one of the pilots—maybe Ron, the solemn young man who'd flown Vic on countless trips up and down the eastern corridor. There were other blackened bodies strewn on the ground, some lifeless, some shrieking with agony as rescue workers held them down. One was a child, his hair gone and his skin seared, and Dana couldn't hold down her panic any longer. She screamed, "Kirstie! Trina!" and stumbled on until she reached the Tornado.

She thought she'd already seen all the horrors the day could hold, but now she saw the worst. A roller coaster tram loaded with children was immobile on the tracks, in a valley fifty feet from the peak where the wreckage hung.

"Thank God the operator pulled the brake," exclaimed a man in madras shorts behind her. "Or those kids would have gone right into the cooker."

The cooker was still spewing clouds of smoke that obscured most of the tram and its passengers. A team of firefighters stood with their hoses blasting upward at the wreckage through the skeleton of the roller coaster. The JetRanger lay on its side on top of the rails. Its main rotor was gone, but the tail rotor was still spinning. Next to the tip of the fuselage, so close it seemed to be soldered to it, was a light plane, single-engine, high-wing, probably a four-seater. One of its wings angled skyward like a flying buttress.

A long groan sounded like a sleeping giant waking in pain, and the wreckage gave a visible shudder. There was a gasp from the crowd, a hundred breaths sucked in and held, until it found its balance on the fulcrum of the rails and went still again.

But the movement dislodged something: an arm extended from the door of the helicopter as if flung out in a carefree gesture. The rest of the body followed and it spiraled headfirst to the ground. The children in the tram screamed as the body passed them, and for two hundred feet Dana watched Vic Sullivan in a free fall to the earth.

Rescue workers rushed to his side, but rose almost at once with their heads shaking.

She stared at the ground where his body sprawled, arms and legs askew in a posture impossible in life. "Oh, my God. Vic!"

"You know him?" one of the workers yelled.

Numbly, she nodded.

The flames began to die back amid the streams of water and chemicals. A path parted through the waves of smoke, and at the precise moment when Dana couldn't imagine anything more terrible happening, she looked up at the cars pinned on the roller coaster and saw two blond ponytails.

There was a roaring in her ears, like river rapids, or her lifeblood gushing out of her. The sky went white and her head swam, but she was not so faint that she couldn't hear herself shrieking, "Trina! Kirstie!"

But they couldn't hear her. Their arms were around each other, and their faces deep into each other's necks, Katrina sobbing, Kirsten probably trying her best to comfort her through tears and a broken voice. Dana screamed their names again, but they were never going to hear her. The most precious beings in her world, and she couldn't give them a moment's reassurance, let alone rescue.

She was afraid to pull her eyes away from them, afraid if she let go of the gossamer hold of eyesight they would disappear into the smoke. With an effort she glanced to one side then the other, looking for the ladders, the nets, whatever device it would take to bring them down to safety. Two women were sobbing and clutching each other as they stared up at the coaster, and Dana shouted to them, "What are they going to do? How will they get them down?"

The women shook their heads helplessly, they didn't know or couldn't respond, but a man shouted over, "The ladders won't reach that high. They have to send climbers up to bring them down piggyback."

As he spoke, a half a dozen firefighters were strapping on ropes and harnesses at the base of the roller coaster. Dana's eyes shot to the tram; she counted heads and did the math. Each man would have to carry five passengers, one at a time. She would have given her entire net worth plus a mortgage on her soul to bribe them to bring her daughters down first. Shamelessly she ran to tell them so, but it was too late; by the time she reached the base, the climbers were already in the steel gridwork and moving up.

The grounds were now teeming with trucks and vans and men in jumpsuits and rubber coats and boots. Someone had gained access to the park's public address system and was exhorting everyone to proceed at once to the east gate. A uniformed policeman drove with his lights flashing to the base of the roller coaster and emerged with a bullhorn to his mouth. "All of ya, get back, move back," he bawled. "Them aircraft could blow any time now."

Dana didn't move, nor did the two sobbing women, and the cop pointed his bullhorn at them, though he was no more than ten feet away. "Ladies, back up, I said. Over there." With his free hand he pointed toward the Ferris wheel.

Dana shut him out of her mind and stared up at the roller coaster. The climbers had reached the first car of the tram and were buckling harnesses on children and helping them to clamber over the sides of the cars. The two blond ponytails were not among the chosen few, and her knees went weak.

The first wave of children touched the ground, trembling, soot-covered, but otherwise unharmed. They were swiftly enveloped in the arms of their waiting families and swept away past the line that was forming in front of a nearby ice cream stand, a grisly line of body bags laid head to toe.

The climbers started up again, and Dana stood rooted to watch them, but again the blond ponytails were left behind.

It was not until the third trip that harnesses were strapped over the two girls, and it was not until they were halfway down the framework that she realized she'd never laid eyes on them before.

She whirled from the Tornado and screamed her daughters' names, but the loudspeaker was still broadcasting its undeviating command to proceed at once to the east gate, and now it was joined by a dozen bullhorns all crackling at once. A river of people was flowing toward the gate, and Dana was swept up in it, still shouting and still spinning wildly in search of her children.

Two paramedics hurried by with a stretcher between them, and though the body was covered, piercing screams came through the wraps, that and the smell of burnt flesh. Behind it came a woman, white-faced, following like a zombie.

And through all the confusion and clamor of the crowd, and the wail of the sirens, and the roar of the fire engines and the rush of the water, one small voice reached Dana's ears.

"Mom?"

She whirled. There, in a sea of green Camp Discovery T-shirts, were two blond heads, neither one in ponytails, and she burst into tears as violent as she ever shed.

They broke from their group and bolted to her, and Dana fell to her knees and grabbed them in her arms, sobbing so hard that at last Trina ventured, "Mommy, did you get hurt by the crash?"

She rocked back on her heels, startled into silence a moment before she began to laugh. "No, sweetheart—no! Did you? Are you both all right?"

They nodded that they were, and she held them back at arm's length to confirm it. Their faces were sooty, and Trina's showed the tracks of tears, but they otherwise looked fine. Even the camera case dangling from Kirstie's neck was intact.

A young woman in a matching green T-shirt raced up, hands reaching out to grab each girl, but she checked herself at the last second. "Oh, Mrs. Endicott," she said. "I didn't recognize you."

Dana got shakily to her feet and thought, *Little wonder*. Her hose were shredded at the knees, her ivory silk dress was gray with ash, and the heel had broken off one of her shoes. She lifted her foot and bent back the other heel until it snapped off, too.

"We just finished our head count," the counselor said. "We're all here and nobody's hurt."

"Thank God," Dana said faintly, aware that this college girl had managed to keep a cooler head than she, for whom disaster was nearly a livelihood.

"Do you want to take the girls home with you, or should they go on the bus with us?"

"No. With me," Dana said, and clutched them to her.

"Lady—hey, lady!" a voice bellowed, and Dana looked over her shoulder to see two uniformed men loping her way.

"Yeah, that's her," said one, and after a second she recognized him as the rescue worker who'd examined Vic Sullivan.

"Would you come with us, ma'am," said the other. He wore the insignia of the state police, and did not add a question mark inflection to his words.

"What? Why?"

"We understand you can identify one of the bodies."

"Yes, but—"

"You can?" Kirstie blurted and turned up wondrous eyes.

"Officer, I need to take my children home," Dana said, at the same moment the trooper was saying, "Look, lady, we got an investigation to do here," and the camp counselor was saying, "We'll see them home, Mrs. Endicott; don't worry."

"Mom?" Kirstie said.

Dana gazed down at her daughters. They were as much like twins as two girls four years and a foot apart ever could be, with the same yellow hair and rosy cheeks and pale eyes in long cameo-oval faces. But Kirsten looked out of Whit's eyes, steel-blue and deep-set under an intent forehead, while Katrina re-

garded the world beatifically, with tranquil gray eyes and an un-
furrowed brow. Serious Kirsten and serene Katrina—if they
were the fruit of her womb, the harvest was very, very good.

She'd never been more acutely aware of her maternity than
during the last half hour, when it seemed it might be wrenched
from her. From the moment she heard the scream of metal over
the car speakerphone, she'd been running on something like
heart's blood and mother's milk. But standing here now, with
the girls safe before her, she felt layers peeling away, hide and
pelt sloughing, mother less and lawyer more.

"Listen, girls." She pulled them into a conspiratorial huddle.
"You know the helicopter that crashed? It was a Pennsteel
helicopter."

"Pennsteel your client?" Kirstie exclaimed.

"Uh-huh."

"Then you ought to stay."

"Only if you two will be all right with your camp group. Do
you think you will?"

Kirstie nodded at once, the camera bobbing around her neck,
while Trina pondered the question at greater length.

"Sweetheart?" Dana said anxiously.

"Let's take the bus," Trina said with a decisive nod.

Dana gathered them both to her in a final fierce hug. "Stay together, okay? And I'll see you just as soon as I can."

"Ma'am," the trooper said impatiently.

"Here," Kirstie said, and shrugged the camera strap off over
her head. "Take this, Mom. I hardly used any film."

The counselor folded the girls back into the group, and Dana
stood and watched with her lip trembling as they began the
march to the parking lot.

The trooper's hand was on her elbow, and at last she looped
the camera strap around her neck and started back against the
tide of people. Other men in other uniforms were nipping like
sheepdogs to keep the flock moving and hastening the strag-
glers with sharp yaps through their bullhorns. A command
center was set up beside the carousel on a redwood table requi-
sitioned from the picnic grove. One man seemed to be the designated commander, a gaunt figure in a visored cap bearing the

insignia of a distant Allentown fire company. He held a walkie-talkie in one hand and a cellular phone in the other and took turns shouting into each.

The rotors of a helicopter sounded and Dana sent a startled look skyward, for a second almost imagining that the JetRanger had risen phoenixlike from its ashes. But no, it was the medical evacuation team looking for a place to land as the commander shouted into the phone, "Jesus Christ, not fucking *here*! The last thing we need is another fucking crash!"

The state trooper nudged her toward the line of body bags in front of the ice cream stand. A young officer stood guard over them, sick-faced, looking like it was the worst detail of his career. Smudges of soot circled his eyes where he rubbed them; he looked like Rudolph Valentino in an early silent film role.

"She's here to identify," the trooper said.

The younger man nodded and squatted by the first bag and unzipped it. Dana took a breath and came closer. It was the body she'd tripped over, the one with the fused-on headphones. She shook her head and moved past it.

The next bag was only half full. "A kid," he explained, and she stumbled on.

"Here, this one's from the plane," the young officer said, and opened the next bag.

Inside lay a sandy-haired man in a plaid sport shirt. His face was burned but not badly; the fatal wounds must have been lower. Frozen on his features was a look of pain and surprised indignation. Dana shook her head, and the officer unzipped the next bag. It was a towheaded young man, a boy really, with an obvious resemblance to the plaid-shirted man. The occupants of the plane must have been father and son.

The next body bag made the gorge rise in her throat. The face was gone, raw meat in its place.

"Let me see his hands," she whispered.

One was extracted, and she knelt and held it as she had never held Vic's hand in life. It was already cold and the joints stiff, but she recognized it. The manicure was perfect but the calluses were still there, vestige of the days when Vic shoveled coal in a refractory, working his way up through every rung of every filthy, backbreaking job until he crossed from labor into management and outworked everyone with a Wharton MBA until Oliver Dean had no choice but to sponsor his rise to the presidency. A dying industrial breed, Vic Sullivan, and now he was dead.

"Yes," she said to the state trooper, and got to her feet. "His name is—" Dimly she was aware of her error in tense, but chose not to correct it. "—Victor Sullivan."

"Who's he to you?"

"My client. The president of Pennsteel Corporation."

The trooper's interest sharpened, and he flipped a notepad out of his shirt pocket. "Is that their chopper?"

"Yes."

"Where were they headed?"

"Pennsteel headquarters, from New York."

"Who was aboard?"

Her eyes wandered back to the body bag as the young officer was zipping it up again. "Victor Sullivan and his pilot. Maybe a copilot."

"Names?"

"One was Ron. That's all I know."

The trooper secured her own name and number before he finally allowed her to move away through the crowd. She drifted toward the roller coaster. The fire was out now, and nothing was left of it but wisps of smoke like contrails across the sky. The helicopter was supported by little more than one of its skids hanging over the rail. Another groan, another shudder, and the whole thing would fall to earth.

At which point, she knew, swarms of investigators would start crawling all over it in search of clues. The forensics could be critical in determining the cause of a collision like this. She once had a case involving a small plane that crashed in the desert. Visibility was fine, winds were calm, there was plenty of fuel and no evidence of engine failure, and the autopsy showed the pilot to be in excellent health. The newspapers declared it a mystery worthy of the *Twilight Zone*. But one of Dana's experts pored over the wreckage and found traces of blood and hair on a shard of Plexiglas—presumably the pilot's, but on a hunch he had it tested. The analysis came back, and the mystery was solved. The pilot was knocked out when a jackrabbit dropped from a hawk's talons and smashed through the windshield.

Here, every scrap of the wreckage would be examined and tested in search of any clues that might show engine trouble, a flight control malfunction, metal fatigue, or even just impact damage to the fuselage. But once the wreckage fell to the ground, there was one set of clues it would never give up: the relative positions of the two aircraft immediately postcollision, which might be valuable evidence of the angle of impact.

Thanks to Kirsten, Dana could at least capture it on film. She took out the camera and aimed a few upward shots at the wreckage, but the steel grids of the roller coaster allowed only broken glimpses of either craft. She needed to be higher. A little knob of a hill behind her rose to the right elevation, but it was too far without a telephoto lens. All the ground within a fifty-yard radius was level, and even lower where the Ferris wheel sat.

The Ferris wheel. Her head went back and her eyes went up. The crest of the wheel looked more than a hundred feet high, and there were no obstructions between it and the higher crest of the roller coaster. The wheel was motionless, but a slack-jawed youth loitered at the controls, and he was wearing the Alpine Valley lederhosen.

His jaw went even slacker when Dana ran up and climbed into the first gondola. It had two bench seats facing each other across a center safety bar. "Start it up," she called. "Get me up to the top."

His mouth snapped shut. This was a situation he was trained to handle. "Lady, we're closed."

"I have to get up there and take photos of the wreckage."

She reached for the safety bar, but he reached it first and pulled it back. "We're closed, I said."

She took out her courthouse ID. All it did was identify her as a lawyer admitted to the district court bar, but it had her picture on it and the seal of the court, and that was enough for the boy.

"Oh, sorry," he said. "I didn't know you was—"

"Start it up, and take it up slow. Let it stay at the top a few minutes, then bring it down. Got that?"

He nodded and sat down at the controls.

The engine cranked on with a grumble that vibrated through the spokes of the wheel. The gondola rose slow as the dawn, and a bird's-eye landscape unfolded in layers. The medical helicopter was on the ground, on a grassy hill well away from the Tornado, and the paramedics were bearing their gurneys toward it. A line of fire trucks was circled around the roller coaster like the proverbial wagon train, though this time the danger lay inside the circle. A half mile away a caravan of cars and buses was moving steadily out of the park, and she prayed the Camp Discovery bus was part of it and whisking her daughters safely home.

Firemen and rescue workers were scaling the framework of the roller coaster with tanks strapped to their backs. Two of them were at the tail section of the helicopter, and they extracted something and lowered it with ropes and pulleys over the side of the tracks. She recognized it as it dropped to the ground: it was the JetRanger's black box, actually orange, which contained the cockpit voice recorder and her last conversation with Vic Sullivan.

The boy in lederhosen remembered his instructions, and the Ferris wheel creaked to a stop at its peak. Dana stood up and waited until the gondola stopped swaying. Here the angle was exactly right to reveal both craft. She aimed the camera and clicked until she had a dozen shots of the wreckage, then closed the lens cover and tucked the camera into her shoulder bag.

"Okay! Bring me down!" she shouted toward the ground, but the wind caught her words and blew them up again. She cupped her hands and called again, but still the wheel didn't move.

Until an instant later it did move, in a violent shudder that rattled the gondola and flung her to the floor. All around it was a roar, a blast of sound and heat and light, like a giant's cry of outrage. She flattened herself on the floor and squeezed her eyes shut while the wheel shook and the gondola swung crazily.

A hiss sounded, inexplicably audible above the roar of the explosion, and she opened an eye to see a burning ember inches

from her face. She jumped up and stomped it out, then staggered, her balance lost, until she clutched the center bar with
both hands. The metal was hot against her palms, but she held
tight until finally the shaking stopped.

The wreckage and the steel rails of the roller coaster were
shattered into a million bits of metal and glass that rained over
the park like a Fourth of July starburst. On the ground burned
twin fireballs, red at their centers, unfurling to orange with
black smoke curling at the outer edges, blossoming like flowers
in speed action photography. The heat swelled up and stung her
face and the smoke burned her eyes until she had to duck down
and close them again.

It was almost half an hour later before Dana dared to stand up
again. The fire was out, the line of body bags had grown, and the
wreckage was nowhere to be seen.

She couldn't comprehend it. Fuselage with a combined length
of sixty feet, wings and rotors almost as long, a total of more
than two tons of metal—it was gone, all of it.

Another shock awaited her when she looked over the gondola again. The Ferris wheel operator was nowhere to be seen.

She screamed, "Hey! Up here! Get me down!"

Not a head looked up. She took a breath and shouted again,
with the full force of her lungs and throat, but no one heard.

No one was going to hear, not while so much activity persisted on the ground. The boy might remember her and come
back, but otherwise she was in for a long wait. In twelve hours
maybe, in the still of the night, her shouts might reach the
ground and a wandering watchman might hear her. Meanwhile,
Charlie Morrison was looking for her on the ground, and her
children were waiting for her at home, and here she was, ma-
rooned a hundred feet in the air.

She flopped down on the seat in frustration.

As she did, there was a sound like the creak of an old door on
rusty hinges. She gave an uneasy glance around her, and a
second later she heard it again. It was a low ominous groan of
metal on metal.

The cylindrical pin supporting one side of the gondola was

slowly sliding out of its slot. The nut fastening the pin to the framework was gone, probably shaken off in the explosion. Gingerly, she stood and tried to push the pin into place, but it didn't budge. Teetering on one foot, she pulled off a shoe and hammered it against the head of the pin. But the movement rocked the gondola so much that the pin slid out another quarter of an inch.

Her heart did a skip. She wasn't facing a long wait after all; she had to get to the ground before the gondola took her there. She leaned over the side. Five or six feet from the rail was the first crossbar of the spoke—an easy stretch for a woman who measured five-ten.

She tied back her hair, slipped off her other shoe and wedged them both into the camera case, then looped the straps of the case and her shoulder bag over her head and crosswise over her chest. Another big breath and she swung one leg over the side, then the other, then let herself drop.

Her arms went rigid and her hands clenched tight to the rail as she dangled over the side. She groped for the crossbar with her right foot, found it, slipped and found it again. The left foot followed, and slowly she crept down the neon ladder to the earth.

A hundred yards away a man watched her descent through a pair of binoculars powered so high he could make out the seams of her panty hose through the fabric of her dress.

He lowered the binoculars to reveal a bronzed, youthful face in startling contrast to his white hair. At his feet lay a man who'd been burned in the second blast. He shed his coat and leaned over to cover him with it. When he straightened, he had the injured man's cap under his arm. He stepped behind the open door of an ambulance and carefully tucked his hair under the cap until none of the white was visible.

He lifted the binoculars again and located the woman as she reached the ground.

3

A sheet of paper lay centered on Whit Endicott's desk, perfectly blank, unruled, without so much as a watermark on it. If he stared at it long enough and let his eyes slide out of focus, he could lapse into a sort of trance. The page would become a rectangular void, a white hole in space, and he could crawl on his belly to the edge and peer down into the face of oblivion.

But today, his twentieth consecutive day of staring at the same blank page on his desk, it wasn't oblivion that stared up from the bottom of the pit; it was a howling maelstrom, a screech of panicked frustration, a wail of defeat.

Or maybe just the roar of a lawn mower starting up in the backyard.

Whit threw down his pen, glad of the excuse to get up and go outside. Jerome was mowing along the edge of the pool surround. He wore a T-shirt wrapped around his head like a turban, and the skin on his back steamed like hot coffee in the sun.

He cut the engine when he saw Whit approach and raised an arm to slap him a high five. "Hey, bro, you finally haul your sorry ass outta bed?"

"Look who's talking. You could've been here three hours ago and saved yourself some of this heat."

"I like the heat. Helps me sweat out all that Irish whiskey you was pouring down me last night."

"That wasn't whiskey, it was stout."

"Yeah, well, it's all hooch to me. Hey, we on again tonight?"

Whit's smile faded. "Sorry. My wife's coming home today and leaving again tomorrow. So I better tend the home fires tonight."

Jerome's teeth gleamed in a salacious grin. "That what you white folks be callin' it now?"

Whit pretended to take a jab at him, and they danced around sparring for a minute until Jerome said, "Cut it out, man. I get paid by the job, not the hour."

"Help yourself to some iced tea. And take a swim before you leave."

"Thanks, I will."

Jerome started the mower with another roar as Whit crossed the sizzling flagstones of the terrace. The house sat on an acre lot cut level into the southern slope of Valley Forge Mountain. From here he could look out over the pool to the vast valley beyond, the one the local planners dubbed, cleverly, the Great Valley. It held two ribbons of superhighway, industrial complexes and office parks, megamalls and thousands upon thousands of housing units. But distance softened the effect: the view from here was of forests and rolling green hillsides that stretched on for miles. "It feels like we're on top of the world," Dana said the day they chose the site, and Whit agreed, never stopping to think that the only place to go from there was down.

He came in through the kitchen door and poured a glass of ice water. From the front window he saw a bright flash of white through the filter of the rhododendrons at the end of the drive. It was the postal truck, the one he'd been watching for all morning. The mail was deposited, the truck departed, and still he stood and slowly drained the glass. But the news wasn't going to improve with age; he gritted his teeth and went out to receive it.

Inside the mailbox was a neat stack of catalogues and flyers and bills, but dead center on the top was an envelope emblazoned with the blue-inked logo of the university. *Thomas Whitman Endicott, III, Ph.D.,* the addressee line read. He stopped in the driveway and slit it open. *Dear Dr. Endicott.* Not typed by the dean's secretary, then; she knew he regarded the titles

Doctor and *Professor* as pretentious and always insisted on a simple *Mister* instead.

But he couldn't linger long enough on his own name. His eyes were impelled to the line below, the one that began, *We regret to inform you* . . .

No surprise there, except at the stomach-churning fury he felt at seeing the verdict in clear black type. For weeks he'd been telling himself: *They will*. But now he felt like roaring out loud: *How the hell can they do this?*

He chucked the mail onto his desk in the library, then peeled off his shirt and galloped down the back stairs to the gym, where he threw one wild punch at the speed bag that sent it swinging crazily from the ceiling. He grabbed it steady and settled into a rhythmic tattoo, pummeling it bare-fisted until his knuckles stung. When he stopped, it was only to pull on his gloves and turn himself to the heavy bag, the one that felt most satisfyingly like a body. His punches landed hard, each one punctuated with a forceful expulsion of breath, until he found himself strangling out obscenities. He cut himself off and caught the bag in his arms.

His chest was heaving and sweat was rolling down the slopes of his shoulders. He went in the bathroom and splashed some water on his face, then raised his head and stared in the mirror. He was a big man, with a brawny frame few people expected to find in an English professor. Though his parents were both small-boned people from old New England stock, he had only to look at his mug in the mirror to see that he was a throwback to some different stock, and one that was probably heavily flavored with potatoes. Shanty Irish masquerading as Ivy League academic—he'd pulled it off for most of his forty-four years, but now it looked like the jig was up.

The phone rang, and he went upstairs and picked it up in the kitchen.

"Did it come?"

It was Jack Lucas, an old friend from his days at Penn, who now chaired the English department there.

"Sorry, Jack. I forgot to call you."

"Hmm. I guess that tells me what they said."

"Yeah."

"Those cretins! How in God's name can anyone at the close of the twentieth century get fired for teaching *Huck Finn* to a class of college freshmen?"

"They didn't fire me. They declined to renew my appointment. You know the drill."

"Yeah, yeah, I know. And let me guess the rest. They don't mention *Huck Finn* or the campus P.C. police anywhere in that letter."

"Nope. Due to my failure to accept the chairman's leadership, it's in the best interests of the department to let me go."

"In other words, it's because you thumbed your nose at an asinine order from a politically correct idiot who can't tell literature from his asshole."

Whit let out a rueful laugh. "Wish you'd written the letter."

"Well, as a matter of fact," Jack said expansively, "I've done better than that. I've saved you a place in our spring semester."

Whit caught his breath. A place at Penn? He'd started his teaching career there twenty years ago, but he'd been on a downward spiral ever since—his most recent post was at a state university where the most popular major was Phys Ed. "Can you do that?"

"Hey, it wasn't even a hard sell. You're a brilliant teacher, Whit. People know that."

Whit leaned against the kitchen counter, overwhelmed and speechless.

"There is one condition." A new tone from Jack, hedging, and a little apologetic.

Whit's mouth gave a wry twist. "Publication," he said.

"All you have to do is finish your Stegner book, Whit, and the job's yours."

All he had to do was what he'd failed to do for twenty years. "Thanks," he said. "I really appreciate this."

"Forget it."

"Do me a favor, though? Don't mention any of this to Dana."

"Why not?"

"Oh, you know. She'd probably want to sue them or something."

"Actually, that's not a bad idea."

"The last thing I want is to be another one of her litigants."

"Well, whatever you say."

"Thanks again, Jack."

Whit pulled on his discarded shirt and returned to the library. On his desk sat a dog-eared copy of his summer project, Wallace Stegner's *Angle of Repose*. It was the story of two good people whose love couldn't survive their disappointment in each other; the best they could do was strive for a level of comfort with each other. The title was a term of civil engineering, meaning the angle to which a bank of earth can be graded without detritus rolling down. Whit often wondered how long it took to reach that angle; he felt himself crumbling and sliding more every day.

His mind went as blank as the page on his desk when he tried to recall what it was he meant to say about this novel, and he wheeled his chair to the file cabinet and pulled out a folder. It was easy to identify his first outline, circa 1978: the pages were yellowed with age, and stapled to the top was a brief note from a university press regretting to inform him of its policy not to publish studies of living authors.

The second outline came on the heels of an April morning in 1993 when Dana looked up brightly from the morning paper and cried, "Oh, Whit! Stegner was killed in a car crash. Now you can finish your book!"

Whit could only stare at her across the table. One of the greatest voices of the century had been forever silenced, and this was her response. Try as he might, he couldn't see any trace remaining of the girl he'd fallen for twenty years ago. An alien space creature had taken over her body, and done it so insidiously he couldn't even pinpoint the moment of invasion.

Eventually, though, he hammered out a second outline and submitted it to another university press, which not only signed him up, but paid him a ten-thousand-dollar advance—a pittance in Dana's world, but a hell of a lot of money for a literary treatise. It was gone now, as were the first and second deadlines for delivery of the manuscript. His final extension ran out at the end of the year; by then the publisher wanted a finished manu-script or its money back.

He heaved himself to his feet and began to prowl the house. It was a two-and-a-half-story, stone-and-stucco house they'd built the year after Dana drew her first big partnership distri-bution. Though she spent fewer waking hours in it than any of them, it was thoroughly her house, in the same way that Katrina's dollhouse was hers: her presence was always loom-ing, all-seeing, all-powerful.

She didn't even know about the *Huckleberry Finn* fiasco, yet somehow she knew something. All during the past month, from a distance of three thousand miles, he'd felt her frown upon him. If he had tenure, this couldn't have happened. If he'd pub-lished when he was supposed to and hadn't spent his entire ca-reer bouncing from one short-term lectureship to another, this episode would never have occurred. If she knew, she would have spoken the words with her eyes: there was no one to blame but himself.

The phone rang and he ignored it through three rings before it occurred to him it might be Dana. He snatched it up a second before the answering machine could preempt him.

"Hi, Mr. Endicott!"

Not Dana. It was the voice of a former student, Sherry or Chardonnay or something.

"This is Brandi."

Ah, yes, Brandi, a student in one of his classes last semester. It was a class of fifty, but from the start she stood out. First, be-cause she had a penchant for crop-top T-shirts and thus exposed a very pretty navel all through the coldest winter of the decade. Second, because she stared at him with a look of outright adora-tion; Nancy Reagan had nothing on this girl.

Dana once looked at him that way, when she was a sopho-more at Penn and he a promising young teaching assistant. At parties she used to say, "Whit, tell about—" then sat back and listened with her adoring eyes full of wonder that he existed and was hers. But the alien body snatcher looked out of those eyes now. She never urged him to tell his stories at parties anymore; she was too busy telling her own.

"I looked for you last night at the end of my shift," Brandi was saying. She worked as a barmaid—probably her destiny from the moment her unthinking parents named her—at a pub in Norristown he'd been haunting lately.

"I had to leave earlier."

"Too bad," she said in a breathy whisper.

Nothing subtle about this girl. "It *is* too bad," he said, a meaningless phrase but one she could interpret to fit the role she seemed to have invented for him: the mysterious Professor Endicott, so tragically morose that only she could charm a smile out of him.

"I'll be there tomorrow night," she said.

There was promise in those words, of something he barely wanted, but promise was promise, and he surprised himself by making one of his own. "What d'you know? Me, too."

"All right!" she squealed. "See ya then!"

He hung up wondering if Dana had ever squealed, but of course she hadn't. Even as a nineteen-year-old coed she had too much dignity. Life lesson number one: beware of women of dignity.

When the doorbell rang, he was happy to get up and answer it, even though he had to stop and punch a series of buttons on the keypad to disable the security system long enough to allow him to open the door. The system was Dana's idea, of course, necessary to protect the array of expensive consumer products she amassed and called home. A pain in the ass, he thought, and half the time didn't bother with it.

Bells and whistles sounded, the flashing light went out, and at last he could throw open the door.

"Daddy!" his daughters cried as they hurled themselves at him.

His arms closed around them in a reflex, and it was a moment before he noticed the young woman on the doorstep behind them.

"What is it?" he asked. "What's happened?"

"Daddy, didn't you hear?" Kirsten said, pulling back to fix him with her mother's censuring eyes. "It's all over the news."

"What?"

The counselor explained, "There was a terrible accident at the amusement park, Mr. Endicott. A helicopter collided with an airplane and crashed down on the park."

"My God." He dropped to his haunches and held the girls back for inspection. "Are you all right?"

"We're fine, Dad," Kirsten said.

But Katrina hadn't spoken. She stared at him with big eyes.

"Trina, honey?"

"Daddy, people got killed!" she burst out before she plunged her face into his shirtfront.

Whit held her tight and looked up to the counselor for verification. She nodded.

"And you know the worst, Dad?" Kirsten exclaimed. "It was Mom's client in the helicopter!"

"How do you know that?"

"She told us."

He gaped at his eldest daughter. "When?"

"She was there. She had to stay, though. On account of it was her client."

His jaw clenched. "I see." He rose and reached a hand out to the counselor. "Thank you for bringing them home."

He ran their bathwater, combed out their hair, microwaved some macaroni and cheese for their dinner, then sat between them on the family room sofa and read *Little House in the Big Woods* until Katrina's eyes began to droop.

It wasn't until after he'd tucked them both into bed that he turned on the news, but he was just in time to watch the alien who masqueraded as his wife.

4

There was no calm after the storm. Dana barely had a minute at the base of the Ferris wheel to catch her breath and slip on her shoes before she was caught up in a bedlam of trucks and vans and uniforms on the run. Park security guards were stationed at each cash register as accusations of looting were shouted out. Nothing was left of the command center but a few pieces of beeping electronics on the floor of the carousel beside a crippled wooden horse. The line of body bags beside the ice cream stand had grown to twelve.

The image of Vic's ruined face came back to her as she hurried away through the crowd, and to block it out she tried to recall her last view of him. It came to her: the day his deposition was taken in the Palazzo Hotel case. Their opponents meant to harass the company into settling by forcing Sullivan's deposition; he had no relevant knowledge, and she could have moved for a protective order. But he declared, "The hell with it, bring 'em on!" and gave up almost a full day of his busy calendar to spar with a half-dozen lawyers from across the country. At the end of it he not only did their case some good, he vowed he hadn't had so much fun in years.

She let the crowd carry her around the carousel and past the bumper cars, so numb she scarcely noticed how the people jostled against her. Until suddenly she sensed a more deliberate touch, of fingers slipping under the strap of her shoulder bag, the start of a tug.

She gave a mule kick backward and heard an *uhf* of connection. She spun, but too late for more than a second's flash of a man sprinting away through the throng. Kirstie's camera case was gone from her shoulder.

"Hey!" she shouted and lunged after him. But the momentum of the crowd was too strong, and the pickpocket was out of sight by the time she broke through. Her bag still hung from her shoulder, and thanks to her confusion on top of the Ferris wheel, that was where the camera was. The thief was going to be disappointed when he opened up his haul and found nothing but an empty camera case.

She turned around and trudged on through the crowd. A flash of a familiar face appeared ahead, and she picked up her pace until she saw all of him—tall, going to paunch under stooped shoulders, his gentle eyes registering horror at the sights around him.

"Charlie!"

Charlie Morrison turned and plunged through the crowd toward her.

"Vic?" he asked.

She shook her head.

His eyes welled up, and that was all the trigger she needed to go into his arms.

For seven years they'd been attorney and client, but for fifteen they'd been friends. Their present relationship allowed only handshakes at meetings and air kisses at parties, but they'd held each other like this once before, the day Charlie lost his job at Jackson, Rieders and their lockstep climb up each rung of the firm's ladder came to an end.

He leaned back and searched her face. "Are you all right?"

"I'm okay."

He turned his horrified look back to the fairgrounds. "What in God's name happened?"

Her hair was falling in her face, and she raked it back with both hands as she spoke. "There was a midair collision between the JetRanger and a light plane, a Cessna Skyhawk, I think, flown by a father and son. Maybe a charter or a rental, but probably privately owned."

"So no insurance."

"Probably not much. Most of the wreckage got hung up on top of the roller coaster. Burning debris came down, so we have a lot of ground injuries, and a couple of deaths, too."

"God."

"Then a fuel tank caught fire, and there was a second explosion. It completely destroyed the wreckage and killed three people. All firemen."

Charlie squeezed his eyes shut and made a noise in his throat.

"Charlie?"

He shook his head while his chest heaved as if he were fighting for breath.

Dana could guess why this news disturbed him the most. Though it might be a blessing that there were no children among the second wave of victims, it would prove cold comfort at verdict time. It was a harsh reality of the judicial system that a wage earner's life was worth millions more to a jury than a child's.

When Charlie finally opened his eyes, he kept them carefully averted. "What's—What do you think the tally is?"

"Twelve dead. All five in the air, and seven more on the ground."

As she said it she realized that was the way the fatalities would be referred to for the duration of the case: the air cases and the ground cases. It was one thing for a pilot or passenger to die in a crash after having made a choice to go up in a plane; it was far worse to have a plane fall out of the sky on you.

She continued, "There're probably twice that many serious injuries. Some will be catastrophic." Burn victims had been known to win awards triple the average paraplegic award. A severed spinal cord ended the pain, but the sensors didn't shut down for burns; the suffering was excruciating, and still there was disfigurement and loss of function.

Charlie's gaze was angled up the hill to the east gate of the park. "Property damage?"

"The roller coaster was destroyed. A lot of buildings burned here in the park and probably in the residential neighborhoods outside. We've got spilled fuel and fire retardant chemicals everywhere. There'll be environmental claims for water and soil contamination, probably for miles around."

His breath leaked out in a slow hiss. "And we'll be the only ones left at the table when the check arrives."

She couldn't argue it. Even if the helicopter were as little as one percent at fault, Pennsteel would be forced to pay a hundred percent of the damages; it was the law's way of allowing victims to reach into the deepest pocket available.

"God," Charlie said heavily. "I don't need to tell you, this is the last thing we need right now."

Dana gave a grimace one part sympathy and two parts guilt. Though Pennsteel was found faultless in the Palazzo Hotel case, the company still had to foot the bill for its defense, and that included attorneys and paralegals, expert witnesses, court reporters, and hotels and airfare for all of them, not to mention the costs of commissioning a computer-simulated reconstruction of the fire and constructing a scale model of the Palazzo Hotel that stood six feet tall. By the time the final bills were in, the total would be close to three million dollars.

She looked back toward the ruined roller coaster. A well-coiffed young woman was nodding vigorously while thrusting a microphone in a fireman's face.

"Charlie, this is going to be all over the six o'clock news," Dana said. "You need to make a statement to the press as soon as possible."

His gaze was back at the east gate. "Saying what?"

"Mourning this terrible tragedy. Eulogizing Vic Sullivan, one of the nation's greatest business leaders and a fine human being whom you were privileged to know. Expressing shock and disbelief at this senseless disaster, and pledging full cooperation into the investigation of its cause. And meanwhile—" She paused and considered. "—because Pennsteel maintains the highest standards of corporate citizenship, because you pride yourself on being a good neighbor, and because you don't want to see the children of this community miss any more of their summer fun than they have to—volunteering to pay the costs of cleanup and repair necessary to reopen Alpine Valley as soon as possible."

Charlie started to shake his head, but abruptly his expression changed. Dana followed his gaze to the east gate, where Tim Haguewood and John Schaeffer were striding through. They were the other Two Amigos: Haguewood, the head of finance; and Schaeffer, the head of operations. Schaeffer wore the rumpled shirt and black-framed glasses of a back-room engineer, but Haguewood carried himself as if he were stepping off the cover of *Business Week*; he was perpetually dressed for success.

"A P.R. move," Charlie said.

"Exactly."

"Paid for out of Haguewood's budget."

She shrugged; internal accounting was none of her concern.

"And we'll apply it toward our insurance deductible."

"You'll have to negotiate that with the carrier," she warned.

But the deal was done as far as Charlie was concerned. "Can you draft something up?"

As he went off to meet Haguewood and Schaeffer, she wandered the scorched earth for a place to work. The command center had been reestablished on the rear bumper of a police van, and the commander was slumped in a posture of bone-deep fatigue. But his work was done: no more fires smoldered, all the injured victims were evacuated, and a squad was loading the last of the body bags into an ambulance for the trip to the hospital morgue.

She found an undamaged park bench and wrote out a statement on the back of a sheet of paper in her bag. By the time she finished, the Three Amigos were standing with their heads bowed together. She handed the draft to Charlie and turned to shake hands with Haguewood and Schaeffer.

"I wanted to congratulate you, Dana," Haguewood said. "Though it seems pretty damned inappropriate under these circumstances."

Schaeffer grunted agreement. "There's two suits at the gates passing out business cards to everybody who comes through."

"God," Dana muttered.

Charlie finished scanning the page. "Sounds good. Tim, Dana wrote a statement for you to read on camera."

"For me!"

"For somebody," she clarified.

"Charlie should do it," Haguewood said. "This is legal."

"It cuts across department lines," Charlie said.

"But it's legal's job to deal with the fallout," Haguewood said.

"You're the public persona," Charlie said with an edge.

The squabble would have escalated if the three executives hadn't suddenly snapped to attention. Dana followed their eyes to a white-haired man moving with slow dignity and upright carriage toward them.

"I never expected this," Schaeffer mumbled, and Dana agreed. As figurehead chairman of the board these past ten years, Oliver Dean had played only a distant role in Pennsteel's affairs.

But Charlie wasn't surprised. "Ollie," he said, striding to reach him first. "Glad you could come." He gave a thirty-second summary of the situation, then said, "Dana drafted a statement for the press."

Oliver Dean perched a pair of reading glasses on his nose before he took the page from Charlie. "Miss Svenssen," he acknowledged her. "Good to see you're onboard."

"I'm not officially retained—"

"You are now," Charlie said.

"Excellent," Dean murmured, and began to study the draft.

But Dana had to ask, "Does the insurance policy give you the right—"

"To choose our own counsel?" Charlie said. "Yeah. Like I said, we're self-insured for the first ten million. Attorneys' fees come out of that."

"Ten million," Haguewood muttered, shaking his head, and Charlie shot him a hot look.

Dean looked up from the page. "Very well. Find me some cameras and I'll read this."

The Three Amigos looked as stunned as they were relieved. "You, Mr. Dean?" Dana asked.

"Mmm, I think that's best." His glance lingered a moment on her. "And you'll stand beside me. Always good to have counsel on hand when dealing with the press."

On hand maybe, Dana thought, bewildered—not on screen.

But later, when the reporters gathered and the lights and microphones were aimed their way and the cameras were rolling, she knew that all he wanted of her was her silent, war-torn appearance, a picture worth a thousand words of the level of Pennsteel's personal suffering from this horrible tragedy.

And it was personal suffering she felt as she made the long drive home that night. Her day's work was done, but it would start again with a vengeance in the morning. Her legs hurt from the miles she ran through the park and the hundred feet she climbed down the Ferris wheel. Her throat was cracked from screaming, and her palms were blistered from the searing metal bar she clutched onto in the gondola. And her heart ached, for her children and all the children who might have been hers, for the towheaded boy in the body bag, for Vic Sullivan, gruff, brilliant, a friend.

Overhead a thousand stars burned bright in a cloudless midnight sky. It was beautiful and benign, and hard as she stared, she couldn't see any danger there. Yet somehow two aircraft with that whole big sky to themselves flew into each other and a dozen people were dead.

She drove up the mountainside lane and through the stone pillars at the end of their driveway. Though the house was in darkness, it was a welcome sight after twenty-seven days in California and about a thousand more in Alpine Valley. She pulled into the garage and entered the security code into the alarm system, then dragged herself through the mudroom and into the darkened kitchen. She dropped her bag on the island countertop and opened the refrigerator door. A pool of light spilled out as she foraged for something cold to drink.

"Twelve hours."

She turned. The face of Whitman Endicott loomed above her, Poelike, out of the darkness.

"Twelve hours," he grated. "That's all it would have taken. Twelve hours to behave like a human mother instead of a legal machine."

"They understood."

"They were traumatized. They'd just seen the most horrific sight of their lives. And what did you do, but tell them, 'Chin up, there you go, this nice lady will see you home.' "

He was wearing a paisley silk robe, tattered from long use but still his favorite, probably because it was so in keeping with his self-image as ruined poet, storm-tossed genius, noble victim of such philistines as his wife and tenure review committees.

"Whit, I had to stay. It was an epic disaster."

"Of course it was—those are the only ones you notice. Ordinary human disasters slip right past you."

She closed the refrigerator with her back, and the darkness covered them like a shroud. "Not all of them."

"Name one."

She barely hesitated. "What about the disaster of a father who leaves his children alone so he can go out carousing every night? And comes home so late he can't even wake up to see them off in the morning. How's that? Ordinary and human enough for you?"

When her jeer was met with only a stunned silence, she added softly, "Don't ever expect them to lie for you, Whit."

The air hissed as he spun away from her. A moment later the library door slammed, and the echo of it rolled down the hall.

Dana climbed up the back stairs to their bedroom and stood a long time in the hot stream of the shower, flushing the soot and ashes off her skin and down the drain. She pulled a nightgown on over her head and tiptoed down the hall. Katrina was curled up in a tight sweaty ball, mumbling in her sleep. Dana leaned over and scooped her up in her arms.

"Mommy?"

"Yes, sweetheart."

Trina wrapped her arms and too-long legs around her, and Dana carried her next door to Kirstie's room. "Move over, honey," she whispered, and Kirstie stirred long enough to shift over in the double bed. Dana lay down in the middle and pulled each sleeping bundle into the curves of her body, and closed her eyes in exhaustion.

5

An adrenaline rush woke her at dawn. Carefully, she eased herself out from between the children and stole down the hall to her bedroom.

Whit was asleep, naked on his back with the sheet kicked to the footboard. He was a big man, four inches taller than she, and he was taking advantage of her absence by stretching his legs out diagonally across her side of the bed. Even in sleep his face had a brooding, cynical look. Her college friends used to describe him as Byronic, but Dana had lost her image of what he looked like then. His face was like a portrait the artist kept revising over time. Each new layer of age and expression covered what was there before, until she had no memory left of the original.

She shed her nightgown, and as she skirted around the edge of the bed for the bathroom, Whit's hand whipped out and grabbed her by the wrist and pulled her so that she pitched full-length on top of him. The fall took her breath away, and before she could get it back, he gave a heave and rolled, and then he was on top.

They stared at each other from six inches apart. His eyes bored into hers, and a moment later his mouth crushed down. When he finally broke away, she was gasping for breath, gulping down air in a giant spasm of throat and lungs.

Startled, he reared back, but Dana lifted her hands to his head and pulled him down again.

He entered her and thrust high, and she wrapped her arms around him, so transported by the rhythm of the act that she could almost forget who they were and what troubles they had. And soon she was soaring, and the world was full of red and yellow starbursts, and she knew that everything would be all right now. They'd hold each other afterward and laugh and murmur together, and he'd tell her what was bothering him, and she'd tell him not to worry and they'd rise up from their bed, together, renewed.

She held him tenderly while he climaxed, inviting him to linger where he was, but he rolled off with a shudder and fell flat on his back again. She lay still a moment, waiting for her pulse to slow, waiting for him to pull her into his arms. In the stillness she heard his breathing go heavy and even.

She raised up on an elbow and stared at him, but after two minutes he didn't stir. Nothing had changed at all except, fleetingly, their heart rates.

The morning news was running aerial footage: Alpine Valley was smoking and cratered like London after the Blitz. A reporter appeared on-screen and bubbled out in unconcealed excitement: "I haven't witnessed such appalling devastation since the bombing of the Federal Building in Oklahoma City!"

Great, Dana thought, watching on the kitchen TV while she made a pot of coffee. Perfect fodder for plaintiffs' lawyers who couldn't dream up their own inflammatory analogies.

The phone rang and she picked up the kitchen extension before it could wake the girls.

"Dana?"

"Oh, Travis." The sound of his deep rumble was doubly welcome—not only friendly, but ready to help. "I was about to call you."

"I figured, as soon as I heard it was Vic Sullivan in the crash. What's goin' on?"

She explained with the phone pinned to her ear and one eye on the TV while she mixed up a batch of waffles. "The FAA and the NTSB Go-Team arrived on-site last night, and they're holding a press briefing this morning. I'm meeting Charlie

Morrison and the insurance reps there, but meanwhile I'd like to get a team assembled."

She heard a noise outside and peered through the kitchen window. Karin's station wagon was turning into the driveway.

"Oh, no," she groaned.

"What?"

"Nothing," she said, though she'd forgotten their vacation plans and now would have to cancel and disappoint everyone. "Where was I?"

"You said you wanted to assemble a team?"

"Right. I'm asking Austin for eight associates, you plus seven more."

"What about Maria?" he asked, naming their chief paralegal on the Palazzo case.

"Yes. And tell her to line up someone to help her."

"Got it."

"I'd like to get the whole team together in the office this afternoon."

"Heck, I'll get 'em in this morning."

"No, I'll be at the site all morning. Try for about three o'clock?"

Her children's voices sounded on the stairs, and Dana grabbed the remote to turn off the TV before they could see the film of Alpine Valley.

"You sure you don't need me at the site?" Travis was asking.

The girls came into the kitchen in their nightgowns, and Dana clamped her hand over the mouthpiece of the telephone. "Aunt Karin's at the door," she told them a second before the bell rang.

Their eyes went wide—they'd forgotten, too—before they squealed and ran for the hall.

"I'm sure," she said to Travis. "But I'll call you if anything comes up."

She hung up the phone as Karin swept into the room with her arms spread wide under a big straw hat. She was two years younger than Dana and four inches shorter, but just as blond and fair and Nordic. Dana put on a smile and went to her for a hug, but before she got there, Karin read her expression and dropped her arms.

"What happened?" she asked as the children spilled into the room behind her, Dana's plus Karin's fifteen-year-old daughter and ten-year-old son.

"Mommy's client crashed into a roller coaster yesterday," Katrina announced.

"Oh, my God!" Karin cried. "Not that awful helicopter accident at the amusement park?"

"Afraid so," Dana said. "Grab a chair, everybody. You're just in time for waffles."

The children galloped into the breakfast room.

"And you're just out of time for our vacation," Karin said. "Am I right?"

Dana lowered her voice. "Karin, I am so sorry. You don't know how much we were looking forward to this."

From the next room Kirstie heard and spun around in her chair. *"Mom!"*

"I'm sorry, sweetie, but there's no—"

A chorus of protests rose up from around the table, all of the children whining at once.

"Isn't there anybody else who could handle this?" Before Karin started her catering company, she worked as an obstetrical nurse; her experience in delivering babies for absent doctors taught her that supporting players usually performed as well as the leads. But Dana operated in a different theater. She shook her head.

Kirstie and Trina started a chant, and their cousins joined in: "We wanna go, we wanna go."

Dana turned to the waffle iron and poured the first puddles of batter into it. Karin took the plates out of the cupboard and set them down beside the stove. "Let them come," she said in a low voice.

"Karin, I couldn't ask you—"

"You didn't, I asked you. There's no reason for them to stay home just because you're working your tail off at the office."

"It's too much—"

"No, it's not." Karin deliberately raised her voice above the chanting. "Dana, I really think you should let the girls come with us to the shore."

The children heard, and there was half a beat of silence before the chorus rang out. "Yes, Mommy, please!" "C'mon, Aunt Dana." "Please, Mom, say yes."

Dana turned helpless eyes on her sister, who took the bowl of batter from her. "I'll make the waffles," she said. "You go get them packed."

A half hour later they were fed, packed, hugged, and buckled into their seats, and as Karin started to back out of the driveway, Dana stood in her bathrobe and waved an exuberant goodbye.

A sudden shriek came from Trina, and Karin slammed on the brakes at the same moment that Whit burst out of the house with his shirt flapping open around his ribs. "We have to say goodbye to Daddy!" Kirstie hollered, and they both spilled out of the car and flew into their father's arms.

They hugged and kissed and murmured their goodbyes before he settled them into their seats again. This time both Dana and Whit stood waving, but when the station wagon finally faded from sight, she turned abruptly and headed inside.

"That worked out very conveniently." Whit spoke at her back as he followed. "You finally arranged a vacation that you don't have to attend. Sort of a virtual vacation."

She didn't spare him a glance as she started up the stairs. "It's the same kind of vacation you arranged for yourself," she said. "Staying here alone while we went to the shore by ourselves."

"But the difference is, I didn't arrange it."

She turned on the landing and stood framed before the Palladian window that overlooked the terrace. "I'm afraid I've ruined it for you, in any event," she said. "Since I'll still be here."

"Barely enough to notice, I'll bet."

She ran up the rest of the way and into the bedroom and pressed her back against the door until it clicked shut. But nothing followed her except silence; the man who once pursued her across the continent didn't bother to walk up a flight of stairs.

Though if he were no longer that man, neither was she the

same starry-eyed girl who squealed when he burst into the back of the lecture hall and flung her arms around his neck like she'd never let him go. It was hard to believe she'd ever had such a romantic heart. Now when she saw a pair of newlyweds, her only thought was that the woman had just linked herself to the man statistically most likely to murder her. It was at least a dead certainty that he'd disappoint her.

6

As chairman of the firm, Clifford Austin was the man to contact for the deployment of the associates and paralegals necessary to staff a major piece of litigation. Dana reached him at home while she dressed for her trip to Alpine Valley.

"You're definitely retained?" he asked her first.

"Yes, I met with Charlie Morrison at the scene."

"Charlie Morrison," he repeated slowly. "I wouldn't go to the bank on his word."

Austin had his own history with Charlie; she'd never understood it, and she wasn't in the mood to try now. "Listen, Cliff," she said sharply, "I was retained by the general counsel of the company, and it was ratified by the chairman of the board. And if you won't take that to the bank, maybe I'll just go off and open up my own account."

It wasn't the first time she'd threatened to leave the firm, and Austin tended to treat her like the lawyer who cried wolf. "Ollie Dean?" he said, ignoring the rest of her diatribe. "All right, then. What do you require?"

"Eight associates right away, four seniors, four juniors."

"Hmm."

It was a noise she'd learned the hard way to interpret as *no*. She clamped the phone between her ear and shoulder and went to the closet for her own camera, a professional rig with wide-angle and telephoto lenses.

"Seven then," she said.

"Have anyone in mind?"

"Travis Hunt, I already have him lined up." She scanned the closet for something to carry the camera accessories in and decided on the padded laptop computer case. "I'd also like Jennifer Lodge—"

"She's starting a trial of her own on Monday," Austin cut her off. "Pick again."

"Oh, I don't know," she said, exasperated. "Just don't give me any of those marathon billers."

She meant those young lawyers who made their marks in the firm by logging more than twenty-five hundred, even three thousand hours a year, and calling it all good billable time. Either they were padding their time sheets and defrauding the clients, or they led such seriously unbalanced lives that she had to doubt their judgment; either way she didn't trust them.

"That's some of our best talent," Austin chided.

"Not in my eyes." This was a running debate they'd been having for some time, one of many, and none would be won today.

"I understand that Pennsteel promised a cleanup of the park."

"That's right," Dana said.

"You're going to need some environmental expertise."

"Yes, I thought I'd hire Bob Kopec—"

"No reason to go outside the firm," Austin said sharply. "Bill Moran has some time. I'll tell him to get right on it."

"All right."

She hung up. It was already eight-thirty, and she had to be at Alpine Valley at ten. She barely had time to stop at the photo processors and drop off the film she shot yesterday. She repacked the laptop case with the camera and lenses and hurried downstairs. Her shoulder bag was in the kitchen where she'd left it last night, and she picked it up and reached inside.

Kirstie's camera wasn't there.

She dumped the contents out on the countertop and searched wildly through the debris, but it still wasn't there.

She sank onto a stool as realization struck. The pickpocket must have maneuvered his hand into her bag and taken the camera instead of her wallet. She wished she could make that exchange now. A hundred dollars cash and a few credit cards in return for a roll of film she'd risked her neck to shoot, and one that might now be the only evidence left of the cause of the collision.

Miserably, she repacked her bag and headed for the garage.

Alpine Valley was a ghost town cordoned off behind yellow police barricades. There were no squeals of laughter or shrieks of delighted terror today. The rides stood as motionless as museum pieces, and only one of the concession stands was open; it was doing a brisk trade selling coffee and doughnuts to the investigators and reporters as they arrived.

The NTSB briefing would begin in ten minutes in the music hall, but until then a crowd was milling around the base of the roller coaster. Heat steamed up in oscillating waves from the ashes, and men pulled off their jackets and loosened their ties. Dana took out her camera and shot a few pictures, but she knew they'd be worthless, and once again she was sick at heart for having lost Kirstie's camera.

A man on the other side of the police tape looked familiar, and after a moment she recognized him as Ted Keller, Pennsteel's chief pilot. He was a small man with thinning fair hair, slim and posture-perfect, and still youthful-looking though he'd been a fighter pilot in Vietnam and had to be close to fifty. Dana started to wave to him but checked herself when he lifted his elbow and ran his sleeve over his eyes. He lost a lot in yesterday's wreck: not only his CEO, but two of his pilots, who were probably also his friends.

Another man broke out of the crowd and barreled toward the music hall at a foot speed hard to reconcile with his immense girth. He wore white shirtsleeves, a tie in deep relaxation, and a fiery red Irish complexion. Dana knew him from somewhere, maybe twenty pounds ago, and when he lurched to a stop before the fire chief who was yesterday's crisis commander, it came to her. He was Harry Reilly, head of the regional office of the National Transportation Safety Board; she'd dealt with him once in a grade-crossing case. She sidled closer, near enough to hear the chief report that the medical examiner had begun the first of the autopsies.

"Did you order complete toxicology studies?" she put in at Reilly's elbow.

He turned, annoyed but not surprised.

"Morning, Mr. Reilly. Dana Svenssen, attorney for Pennsteel."

"I remember," he said. "And I would have remembered the drug and alcohol tests, too."

"And cardiac studies on the pilots."

"Also routine. Is that what you think happened?"

The idea had more appeal to her than most: the Skyhawk pilot had a heart attack and passed out; his son panicked and crashed into the JetRanger. "I don't have any theories yet," she said.

"Just as well," he snorted. "Since there ain't much data to test 'em out on."

She felt a sinking dread. "The wreckage?"

"Blown to smithereens. We got squat."

The same theme was sounded throughout the morning's meeting: determining the probable cause of the collision would be difficult if not impossible due to the destruction of virtually all of the physical evidence.

The crowd streamed into the music hall, an ornate gilded auditorium where circus acts and country-western stars performed on Saturday nights. Harry Reilly took to the stage and introduced the members of the elite NTSB Go-Team—each a forensic aviation specialist in such fields as power plants, aircraft structure, systems, operations, maintenance, meteorology, and human performance—then turned the microphone over to the investigator in charge, or IIC, who laid out the facts as they were known thus far.

The collision occurred at approximately 1020 EDT, between a Bell JetRanger helicopter and a Cessna 172 Skyhawk fixed-wing, in Class E airspace, with visual flight rules governing. The helicopter was bound for Pennsteel headquarters from New York; a flight plan was filed with the local Flight Service Station. Its crew consisted of Captain Ronald A. Heberling, age thirty-three, and copilot Albert M. Ciccone, age thirty-five. They carried one passenger: Victor Sullivan, age fifty-six. The helicopter had been customized with a four-channel cockpit voice recorder and a Global Positioning System navigational aid; the CVR was recovered, but the GPS receiver was apparently destroyed by the second explosion.

The Skyhawk was registered to and piloted by William Loudenberg, age forty-eight, of Montrose, Pennsylvania. He had one passenger: his son, Donald, age nineteen. No flight plan was filed, and there was no black box. No information was yet available on the route or destination of the Skyhawk.

All five occupants of the aircraft were killed, probably instantaneously, though they had to await the autopsy results on that point. Seven deaths occurred on the ground: three children, three rescue workers, and a young mother. There were at least four critical burn cases, two of them children.

Dana listened from the back of the hall and watched for Charlie Morrison through a crowd that consisted mostly of reporters taking copious notes on tiny notepads. But one man was scribbling on a long yellow legal pad, a dead giveaway even if she didn't recognize him and feel the hair rise on the back of her neck.

His name was Ira Thompson, and as always, he stood with his shirt spilling out of his pants and his glasses pushed back on his head, where he inevitably lost them. He was an absent-minded, mild-mannered Milquetoast, the butt of jokes throughout the bar and one of the deadliest plaintiff's lawyers in the country. All the care and attention that were lacking in the simple details of his daily life were focused instead on his cases. He pursued clients first and defendants second with single-minded ferocity. His combined verdicts had recently passed the billion-dollar mark.

He spotted Dana in a rare moment of focus through his fog, and his glasses slid over his brow as his head bobbed in acknowledgment.

She made her way across the room. "Hello, Ira."

"Dana."

"Who are you in for?"

"Oh, I'm only a citizen today," he said. "Searching for the truth."

There were two possible truths: one, that he wasn't yet retained by anybody but was casting his net; or two, that he'd received several overtures but wouldn't decide which client to choose until he knew who had the strongest and biggest claim. She wished she knew which way he was leaning. If he ended up with Vic Sullivan's widow, for instance, they'd be allies, united in proving the helicopter crew blameless. But she knew there was zero chance of that. The best hope for the bell-ringing verdict Ira looked for was to fault the helicopter and win the key to the Pennsteel vault.

"I'm in for Pennsteel," Dana said. "I'd appreciate a heads-up before you file suit."

Thompson ran through the pros and cons in his mind and ended in a nod.

As the IIC began a chilling recitation of the names of the dead and injured, Dana started back across the room and found Charlie Morrison slumped against the wall next to the exit.

"Morning, Charlie. Are the carriers here?"

He nodded and pointed to the backs of a pair of men seated together in the auditorium.

"So's Ira Thompson," she told him.

He blinked, then cursed softly. "Who got to him already?"

"He won't say. But it doesn't make much difference. He'll lead the plaintiffs' team no matter who he has."

"Big gun," he said.

"Big target."

Charlie grimaced and held out a roll of antacid tablets. Dana shook her head, and he popped three in his mouth.

"Anything wrong?" she asked. "Beyond the obvious."

"Oh—you know." His shoulders lifted in a shrug and ended in a defeated sag. "The politicking's started already."

"For Vic's job."

"Yeah. Haguewood and Schaeffer are off currying favor with the board. While I've got this to deal with every waking minute of the day."

"No, you don't," Dana said. "You're paying me to deal with

it. That's the way it's supposed to work, Charlie. You take care
of business at home, and I take care of this."

Charlie's gentle eyes went soft and sheepish. "Still covering
for me, huh, Dana? Just like the old days."

"Not true," she scoffed.

They'd joined the firm together fifteen years before, but
Charlie's career got off to a rockier start, mostly because he was
too nice for his own good. The partners took advantage of him,
knowing he could never say no to an assignment, and as a result, he was constantly scrambling to meet deadlines and to
make up for the ones he missed. Dana helped out when she
could: she stayed late and finished the assignments he couldn't
get to; once she even covered a deposition for him and coaxed
the court reporter to insert Charlie's name for hers in the transcript. But she couldn't do enough. Eventually a handful of
partners made up their minds that he didn't fit the Jackson,
Rieders profile. They did their best to drive him out through
crushing evaluations and lousy assignments, and when Charlie
didn't take the hint soon enough, they concocted some kind of
charge against him that ultimately forced his resignation.

It was a short-term tragedy but a long-term success story.
Charlie landed the house counsel job at Pennsteel, and actually
found a place where nice guys got to finish first. He rose rapidly
through the ranks of the law department, caught the eye and
won the favor of Vic Sullivan, and crossed the great divide to
join the senior management of Pennsteel.

Anyone else would have exacted revenge by pulling Pennsteel's legal business away from the firm, but Charlie didn't
have a bitter bone in his body. He'd turned out to be as good a
client as he was a friend.

"I mean it," Dana said. "After today you step back and let me
worry about this case."

"Okay, but listen . . ." He dug into his breast pocket and came
out with a business card. MICHAEL F. PASKO, it read, DIRECTOR OF
SECURITY AND SPECIAL SERVICES, followed by a Pennsteel telephone extension. "Call on Mike whenever you need help. He's
a terrific resource for field investigations. And he reports to me,
so you got attorney work product protection."

Dana preferred to use investigators who reported to her, but she tucked the card in her bag.

Onstage Harry Reilly was returning to the microphone. "We'll take some questions now," he announced in a voice that reverberated through the music hall.

Dana shot her hand up, but he recognized the reporters first, and one of them asked her question: "Is there anything on the helicopter's voice recorder? Has anyone listened to it yet?"

Reilly shook his head and outlined the procedure. The CVR was being shipped to an NTSB lab in Washington where a committee would be formed to listen to it and create a written transcript. It might well be months before that transcript would be released.

"But what about the tape itself?"

Because of the highly sensitive and often personal nature of verbal communications inside the cockpit, Reilly explained, no part of a CVR tape was ever released to the public.

"What's your theory of the cause of this collision?" another reporter called to the stage.

"We don't have one," Reilly grudgingly replied. "We'll pursue all leads, like we always do."

"But what's the most likely theory?" the reporter persisted.

Reilly blew out his breath against the microphone, making a sound like a million sighs. "Look," he said finally. "Something like ninety-nine percent of all midair collisions occur within five miles of an airport, in the traffic pattern, on takeoff or final approach. For two aircraft to collide in-flight and nowhere near an airport . . ." He trailed off, and addressed his final comment to the wings as he left the stage: "At this point, your guess is as good as mine."

When the briefing ended, Charlie took Dana across the music hall to meet the two insurance representatives.

"Norm Wiecek, from UAC. Don Skelly, from Geisinger. Fellas, this is Dana Svenssen."

United Aviation Casualty was Pennsteel's primary insurer, and Norm Wiecek, a saturnine man with heavy-lidded eyes and a pulled-down mouth, looked appropriately downhearted.

Geisinger Underwriters was the excess carrier, insuring against losses that exceeded the amount of primary coverage, as this one certainly could, yet Don Skelly beamed affably as he pumped her arm. He was a small man in his fifties and buoyant with goodwill and energy.

"Glad to meetcha, heard lots of good stuff," he said. The hills of Appalachia were in his voice, barely eroded by thirty years in Manhattan. "What say we all take ourselves off someplace to powwow?"

They drove in their separate cars to a roadside diner built like an Airstream trailer and sizzling like a stainless steel griddle in the noonday sun. Charlie's red Porsche pulled up beside Dana in a swirl of dust. He was on the phone, but he motioned for her to wait. The heat hit her like a fist as she got out of her car and locked it. She ran her eyes over the sand-colored grass and the dusty roads, then up to the sky. Not a cloud.

Charlie came out of his car and they went inside together. Long-haul truckers mingled with the locals at the counter, and all of them were buzzing about the crash. Don Skelly took a waitress aside and gave her a big smile and a small tip, and she ushered them to a private table in the corner. "Coffee all around," he boomed, and added with a wink, "Separate checks for the food, though."

They settled into their chairs and Charlie Morrison requested one more—for Ted Keller, who would join them later.

"I'd like to hear your recommendations on experts," Dana began the meeting. She looked to Wiecek and Skelly, who between them must have monitored a hundred pieces of aviation litigation.

"I got two words for you," Skelly said, lighting up a cigarette. "Doug Wetherby."

"The reconstructionist?"

"Yeah." He inhaled with deep satisfaction. "He's the best, and we better get him before anybody else does."

Wiecek's mouth pulled down even farther. "I like to use Ed Stoltz," he said.

A debate ensued between the two men on the relative merits

of Wetherby versus Stoltz, and who was the better forensic man and who made a better impression on a jury, and during it all, Ted Keller arrived at the table.

"We're discussing experts," Charlie filled him in. "Who do you know?"

But Keller was of little assistance. In all his years of flying, he was never involved in an aviation accident, and he stayed even farther away from aviation lawsuits. He preferred to keep it that way, and immediately buried his face in the menu.

"Tell you what," Skelly said amiably. "Let's bring both of 'em in, and let Dana and Charlie here have a look-see."

"The sooner, the better," she said. "In fact, I'd like to schedule a session for Monday with every expert we can pull in by then."

"Good idea," Skelly said. "And I got another good idea. Let's do it at our place—we can put up all the out-of-towners right there in our hotel."

"In New York?" she said doubtfully.

"No, our new place. In King of Prussia."

She remembered then what she'd read about Geisinger Underwriters. Long headquartered in Manhattan, the company recently moved to a palatial new office and hotel complex fifteen miles from Philadelphia. The complex was built by Geisinger at an estimated cost of $300 million. Little wonder Skelly wouldn't spring for lunch.

They agreed to schedule a meeting for Monday morning, and as their lunch plates arrived, Dana started a list, beginning with Wetherby and Stoltz, the general aviation accident reconstructionists, and moving into narrower, more specialized fields: radar experts, metallurgists, aerodynamicists.

"I'll need a good computer simulation firm on this one," she said. "Every scenario has to have a visual to illustrate it, from every viewpoint—the cockpit of the JetRanger, the cockpit of the Skyhawk, even the viewpoint of the people on the ground."

Wiecek and Skelly looked skeptical; both were too old to feel comfortable with computer wizardry.

"Look," Dana said, "we'll be trying these cases to people

who watch TV six hours a day. They don't know how to listen anymore. But they do know how to watch a screen."

Quietly Charlie said, "Do it."

"Good," she replied, cementing the decision. "I'll get some computer people in for Monday's meeting. All of this has to be pulled together and packaged as soon as possible if we want any input into the NTSB report."

"How much do we get?" Charlie asked.

She shrugged. "We have the right to make a written submission, which they have the right to ignore. And even if they do consider it, it's hard to say how much good it does. If we can point them in the right direction in their own investigation, it can only help. But if it looks like we're whispering in their ears every step of the way—believe me, the plaintiffs' team will find out and any favorable findings will end up backfiring on us at trial."

"I wouldn't count on favorable findings whether we're whispering or not," Ted Keller spoke up. "You know the joke? If an earthquake splits the runway open a second before touchdown and the plane crashes, the NTSB would still find some way to call it pilot error."

Don Skelly hooted, but Dana was thinking past the joke. "The NTSB won't listen to lawyers during their investigation, but we are allowed to designate one party representative to deal with them. In a corporate setting, that's usually the chief pilot."

"Ted, you're elected," Charlie said, and Keller winced.

"I'll need a couple pilot experts, too," Dana went on. "One an expert on light planes and another on helicopters. Any suggestions?" No one answered, so she turned to Keller. "What about you, Ted? You must run across a lot of top pilots."

He lowered his gaze to the black pool of his coffee. "Yeah. The best I ever ran across died yesterday."

Dana stared at the Formica, mortified, as an uneasy quiet settled around the table. She'd spent her whole life breaking through gender barriers, and now she'd demonstrated that she could be as insensitive as any man. She tried to form the right words, of apology or sympathy or something, but nothing was right, and at last Keller spared her by speaking up brightly.

"I *do* know somebody," he said. "One of the best pilots I've ever known. And I hear he's interested in doing some of this lawsuit business. Andy Broder."

Her pen hovered. "What's his background?"

"He's got a degree in aeronautical engineering, and he did some design work for McDonnell Douglas. Flew fixed-wings most of his life then moved on to helicopters in the service. He piloted a Cobra gunship in the war. Right now he's in Alaska somewhere, flying smoke jumpers for the Forest Service."

She looked up from the paper, thrilled. Broder sounded like the dream expert. "How do you know him, Ted? Did you fly together in Vietnam?"

He laughed. "No. Andy's war was in the Gulf. I flew with his dad, though."

Her enthusiasm died at once. "A kid, huh?"

"Still the best."

But she knew too well that silver hair was worth gold to juries. "Well, I suppose we could bring him in—"

The rest of her sentence was drowned out by a loud screeching from the parking lot.

"Hey," somebody shouted from the counter. "Anybody drive a black Mercedes?"

Dana jumped to her feet and ran outside. The alarm was wailing in her car, and the front passenger window was smashed.

"There he goes!" Keller shouted behind her. At the edge of the parking lot a man in dark clothing was crashing through the bushes.

"Ted, call the cops!" Charlie shouted. "I'll run him down!"

Keller bolted back inside as Charlie tore off after the thief. He was gone before it occurred to Dana that she should have led the chase herself. Charlie, with his recently acquired paunch, was the last one who should have done it.

She fumbled for the keys in her bag and pushed the button on the transmitter to turn off the alarm. Don Skelly strolled around the car to inspect the damage like the insurance adjuster he once was.

"Don't look like he got anything," he said.

She peered through the imploded glass. The car phone still

sat on the console, the stereo and CD player were intact, and so was the police scanner. Nothing was missing but the laptop case she'd packed the camera in, which meant one more thief was going to be disappointed when he opened up his haul.

Minutes later Charlie staggered through the bushes, his chest heaving hard. He shook his head while he labored to catch his breath. "He—disappeared," he panted. "Not a—sign of him."

Keller came out of the diner. "I called the cops, but they said it'll take a while before anybody can get here."

Charlie went inside and drank three glasses of water in rapid succession. Dana borrowed a dustpan and swept up the worst of the glass off the seat, and a waitress came out with a sheet of plastic and a roll of duct tape and helped her cover the gaping window. They went back inside, finished the meeting as best they could, and paid their checks.

Still the police did not arrive. Charlie and Keller decided they had to get back to Pennsteel, and Norm Wiecek remembered he had a long drive to northern New Jersey and soon followed. But Don Skelly lingered at the table with Dana as they watched Wiecek creep dolorously out of the parking lot.

"Did his dog die, or what?" Skelly snickered over another cup of coffee.

She smiled. "I think all he's seeing is the UAC balance sheet minus ninety million dollars. In fact, I wonder you're not seeing something like that yourself. Did you hear about that helicopter case in Missouri? The jury awarded three hundred and fifty million. For *one* victim."

"Yeah, I heard." He lit another cigarette. "Damn juries don't get it, do they? It's all funny money to them. Some lucky stiff gets a windfall out of this world, while every other working stiff in the country ends up paying for it. But what the heck—" He blew out a cloud of smoke and grinned. "Keeps you and me in business."

"Pretty poor business, if something like that happens here. We have a dozen victims. You could have a three-billion-dollar exposure."

Skelly shook his head. "I'm not worried on this one."

She gave an incredulous laugh. "Tell me why. I'd like to save myself some worrying."

"Well, hell," he declared. "Without physical evidence, you gotta look to the common sense of the thing. Here we got a professionally trained crew with a million hours in the chopper, following procedure, filing a flight plan, doing everything right. Then over here we got a dad out showing his boy a good time in the latest family toy. Who's more likely to screw up?"

Dana regarded him across the table. He was a curious mix of savvy veteran and good ol' boy, company man and everyman. And maybe even every juror. She wondered if he might be right.

"So we just point to the lack of evidence and call it a day?"

He shrugged. "If it was up to me, that's the way I'd defend it."

"But something caused the collision. It's my job to find out what."

He stirred his coffee for a minute. "Some people might say it's your job to defend Pennsteel."

"I can't do that without knowing the truth."

"The truth?" Skelly lifted his cup and took a long swallow. "Or the available facts?"

She looked at her watch. It was almost two o'clock and she had more than an hour's drive to the office, where her newly assembled team was to meet her at three. "I guess I'm going to have to pass on the police," she decided.

"Your carrier might not pay the claim without a police report," the insurance man warned.

"It doesn't matter. I have a big deductible."

As Dana pulled out of the parking lot, she could see Skelly in the window, smoking another cigarette and watching her until she left.

7

The offices of Jackson, Rieders & Clark were in a new fifty-story, brass-and-glass tower on Market Street, eight blocks west of the grand old deteriorating building on South Broad it occupied for the first hundred years of its existence. Clifford Austin spearheaded the move across town as the first prong of his Vision for the Next Century. The second prong was to raid rival firms for their top rainmakers and lure them over with exorbitant signing bonuses and guaranteed draws. The theory was that the new rainmakers would generate enough money not only to pay for themselves, but also to pay off the heavy bank debt incurred to finance the new quarters. The problem was that the rainmakers never stayed long enough to do more than drain the firm's profits before they moved on to bigger and better bonuses. Thus it remained to existing partners like Dana to generate enough revenue to pay for the building and the bonuses, not to mention the consultants who dreamed up the Vision in the first place.

The firm occupied the top six floors of the building, along with the underground parking garage and two floors of the sub-basement for document archives. The office layout adhered to the first rule of law firm design: lawyers' offices lined up like cells along the perimeter walls, two windows wide for associates, three for partners, and six for those partners who merited the corner locations; and windowless interior space for the secretaries, paralegals, and other support staff. Also in the interior

61

were the conference rooms, windowless rectangles lined with portraits of the firm's founders. After a long day of depositions, their ancient faces seemed to morph into variations on Edvard Munch, which was often all it took for an exhausted witness to panic and scream out the truth.

Saturday afternoon Dana gazed at the faces in Conference Room 46B, dead and alive, and almost felt the same urge to scream. Her new team was assembled around the table. Travis Hunt, her good right hand, was there, of course. But to his right sat Lyle Claiborne, a scholarly senior associate who specialized in appellate briefing. He'd never tried a case, taken a deposition, interviewed a witness, nor, she imagined, met a client.

Next was Sharon Fista, also a senior associate, though she'd had a baby in the last year or two and was still maintaining a part-time schedule.

Beside Sharon was Brad Martin, a slight figure overshadowed by a boyish shock of thick black hair. He was an intense young man who magnified every task into a matter of life or death.

Finally there was Katie Esterhaus, a sweet young thing in an advanced stage of pregnancy.

Bleakly Dana surveyed her crew. It was clear what Clifford Austin had done: she'd asked for seven associates, and he'd given her five, who in combined energy and talent equaled about three. But if she complained, he'd smile smugly and say, "Oh, so you'd like some of those 'marathon billers,' after all," and declare himself the winner of their perpetual debate.

She took a breath and resolved to struggle along with this crew. Later, if she had to, she'd plead a new crisis and get more associates. Until then she'd play the hand she'd been dealt.

"Hi, Maria," she said, addressing an olive-skinned young woman seated in one of the chairs along the wall. "You found someone to help you?"

"Yes," the paralegal said, and pointed to a chubby young man beside her. "This is Luke."

"Luke, thanks for joining us," Dana said as the boy squirmed in his chair. "I really appreciate your jumping in like this."

She shifted her attention to the lawyers around the table.

"The same goes for all of you." Briefly she described what happened at Alpine Valley the day before, then said: "Our job for the next several months is to figure out *why* it happened. The magic words here are comparative negligence and joint and several liability. A jury could fix liability at ninety-nine percent for the airplane and one percent for the Pennsteel helicopter, and Pennsteel would still end up paying a hundred percent of the damages. Unless the plane was heavily insured or owned by the Sultan of Brunei, and so far there's no indication of either.

"So we don't win any points by minimizing Pennsteel's share of liability. We have to *eliminate* it. There are only two ways to do that. We prove that the accident was completely caused by the plane, or we prove that it was an act of God and therefore nobody's fault. But since juries don't seem to believe in God anymore, we'd better aim to pin it on the plane."

The young lawyers and paralegals watched her as she spoke, and she watched each of them until she had the assignments sorted out in her mind.

"Lyle, I want you to take charge of home base. All the library research and all the briefing are your bailiwick. First project: define the standard of care. What do the FAA regulations say, and how have the courts massaged them?"

Lyle pushed his glasses up the bridge of his nose and nodded. This was his turf, and he knew how to handle it.

"Katie, you'll report to Lyle. But your focus will be the documentary evidence. First, Pennsteel's own records. I want to be proactive here. We need to retrieve all the maintenance records on the helicopter, and all the training records for the pilots, along with their personnel files. Then we need to get the FAA records. The top priority is the radar data, if there is any, but we also want all their files on the Skyhawk and on Loudenberg, his medicals, his certifications, the works. And we can only do this by a Freedom of Information Act request, which means it needs to go out Monday."

Katie's pen was flying.

There. The scholarly associate plus the one with physical limitations would tend the home fires while the rest of the team was in the field.

"Sharon and Brad." Both heads swiveled her way. "I'm putting you two in charge of eyewitness interviews. Go up to the site and surrounding neighborhoods and talk to anybody who'll talk back."

They nodded, and with far more enthusiasm than the first two. For young lawyers who spent twelve hours a day poring over case reports, a chance to knock on doors and ask questions was a plum assignment.

"Travis," she said, and the hulk at the end of the table stirred in response. "I want you to find out everything you can about the pilot of the Skyhawk, William Loudenberg. Where did he live, where did he work, visit his hometown, talk to his coworkers, try to interview his widow if you can." If anyone could, it was Travis: with his allAmerican looks and aw-shucks boyishness, he could get past doors that would be slammed in the faces of most other lawyers.

"Brad," she said, and he looked up again with a furrowed brow. "I want you to get a handle on the damages from the deaths and injuries. Start by educating yourself on burns. Find out who the best doctors are, and who's willing to testify. Get the autopsy and toxicology reports and put together a list of pathologists to review them. And start gathering the medical records of every potential plaintiff out there."

With somber Brad as point man, no one could accuse Pennsteel of taking the damages lightly.

"That leaves you, Maria, and you know the drill. Every piece of paper we receive or generate in this case gets a Bates-stamp number on it. Open up a database and log in everything."

"Checkout/check-in?" Maria asked.

"Yes. And with no checkout privileges for anything designated as confidential."

"Got it," Maria said and made a note.

Dana stood a moment, scanning her memory, wondering what she might have forgotten. At the end of the table Travis still sat with his arms pulled tight across his massive chest.

"And of course, Travis, you'll work with the experts and serve as my deputy, with overall case responsibility."

His arms unfolded and he gave a curt nod.

Brad Martin's arm was flapping in the air. "But what if we can't? I mean, what if it *was* Pennsteel's fault?"

"The facts are what they are," Dana said. "But even if they point to Pennsteel's liability, that's not the end of our work: there's still damages to be determined. Maybe even litigated."

"Yeah," Travis said. "Remember that case you had against Ira Thompson a few years back?" He explained to the group: "Products liability. We represented the manufacturer, who was dead in the water on liability. But Thompson's client phonied up most of his damages, so Dana took it to trial. The jury award came in at about half the amount of Thompson's final settlement demand."

"But the newspapers didn't know that," Brad pointed out. "They gave the win to Thompson."

"We don't try our cases for the newspapers," Dana said. "And anybody who cares more about public appearances than client representation had better resign from this case right now."

There were no volunteers.

Travis's forehead wrinkled in a sudden spasm of inspiration. "You know what? Somebody's gotta have some film of all this. Right? I mean, this was an amusement park, for Pete's sake. There must have been a couple hundred camcorders running during the crash."

Excited murmurs of agreement sounded as Dana kneaded her own forehead. She pictured Kirstie's camera on the shelf of an inner-city pawnshop while the roll of film lay discarded in a trash can or a Dumpster or even a landfill. There wasn't a chance in the world the pickpocket kept it, and even less of a chance that he would come forward to produce it.

Abruptly her head came up. "Travis, that's a great idea. We'll run an ad, a big one, in all the papers around Alpine Valley, asking people to contact us if they have any film taken at the park yesterday. Lyle?"

"I'll take care of it."

That led her to another thought. "We need to contact all the TV stations and order copies of their video footage. Broadcast as well as outtakes. Any volunteers?"

Maria spoke up. "Luke used to work in editing at Channel 3 news."

The eyes of the room turned toward the boy just as he was sneaking a peek at his watch. "Yeah, okay," he said, flushing pink.

It was Saturday night, Dana realized with a guilty start. Saturday night, and these young people surely had something better to do than sit here and listen to her micromanage the case.

"Let's call it a day," she said. "Everybody knows where to begin Monday morning?"

Heads nodded around the table.

"Good. One final point. This accident is going to be on everyone's lips, maybe for months to come. There'll be a lot of speculation in the media, people will be gossiping about it constantly, and a couple dozen plaintiffs' lawyers will be listening. Once they find out we're in for Pennsteel, they're going to trail after us with their hands cupped around their ears.

"So we don't talk about this case outside this office. Period. We don't air our theories to anybody but ourselves, we don't drop names at cocktail parties, we don't engage in pillow talk, and we don't try to impress people in bars with our exciting high-profile case. For all the outside world knows, we have the dullest practice in town; it's so boring we can't even remember what we're working on when people ask us. Everybody got that? Because I don't ever want to hear anything on the street attributed to anyone in this room."

The tension hung in the air after she finished. Her young troops stared at her in wide-eyed solemnity until at last Travis drawled, "Oo-kay, Mom."

She laughed, and as the tension broke, the group dispersed into the corridors.

For the first time in a month Dana opened the door of her office. A musty odor greeted her, but thanks to an efficient secretary, the plants were all healthy and hydrated, and the papers were all neatly stacked on a gleaming desktop.

When the firm moved to the new building, the lawyers gave up their richly paneled walls and Oriental rugs in favor of a more contemporary look. Thus the Sheetrock walls were painted oyster-white and the industrial carpeting was dyed battleship-gray, and the credenzas were topped with a slab of granite that served well as a base for plants but was so cold to the touch that Dana couldn't help thinking of a mortuary table. Sometimes she had a hard time following the forward-looking, hard-edged vision her partners had embraced; she often found herself longing for the worn upholstery and cracked leather of the old offices.

She sank into the soft new leather of her desk chair. It was nearly six, and she still had a list of a dozen experts to line up for Monday's meeting.

Travis Hunt poked his head around the doorway. "So— how'd it go at the site today?"

She looked up and met his eyes. "Ira Thompson was there."

"Oh, shit," he said, followed immediately by a chagrined "Sorry."

"Hmm. Me, too."

"Tell me what to do. I'm all yours."

The list of phone calls would be done in half the time if it were split in two. She deliberated a moment, then reached for the office phone directory and started to dial. Travis perched on the edge of her desk awaiting his marching orders.

"Hold please for Travis Hunt," she said, and held the phone out to him.

He stumbled uncertainly to his feet.

"It's your wife," she whispered. "You can't marry Miss Texas and leave her home alone on a Saturday night. Tonight you're all hers."

With a sheepish smile he took the phone.

Dana's first call after Travis left was to the shore house in Avalon, but when the line rang ten times without a pickup, she wasn't surprised. The first day on the beach it was always hard to let go of the last rays of the sun. They liked to linger long, even as the air grew cool and the water went gray and the honky-tonk music drifted out to sea. By now the girls would be wearing sweatshirts over their suits and wandering the tide-pools with plastic bags dragging behind them in a search-and-capture mission for the perfect shell.

Dana wished she were with them, and held that wish through the next two hours as she placed calls to everyone in the pool of potential experts and made her pitch for each of them to drop everything and fly to Philadelphia on thirty-six hours' notice.

Most of them had been expecting a call. News of a major midair collision did not escape the notice of people who earned their livings from aviation disasters. The only question in their minds was which side would reach them first.

At eight o'clock one name still remained on the list. Andy Broder, boy pilot.

It was two in the afternoon in Anchorage, an unlikely time to reach anyone at home. Dana picked up the phone and hoped they'd discovered answering machines in Alaska.

At first she wasn't sure they'd discovered telephones, for it took minutes for the call to go through, but at last a man boomed, "Painted Lady!" Behind his voice she heard the sound of loud voices and country-western music.

"I beg your pardon?"

"No need to beg, little lady. I'm sure we can work somethin' out."

She checked the display on the telephone console; she hadn't misdialed. "Have I reached Andy Broder?"

A peal of high-pitched laughter came over the line. "No, but you got his favorite bar."

Whatever misgivings she harbored about hiring Broder qua-drupled in the space of a second. "My name is Dana Svenssen and—"

"Swanson?"

"Svenssen, with a V. I'm a lawyer in Philadelphia, and I need to get a message to him urgently."

The music cranked up louder. "Hey, boys," the voice shouted. "I got a real Philadelphia lawyer on the line. And she's a lady!"

A roar of laughter sounded.

"Look," Dana said, "do you know where he is or not?"

"Last I heard, Andy's trying to set down a chopper some-where in the middle of ten thousand acres of forest fire."

"Is there any way I can get a message to him?"

"Well, Miss Swanson with a V, if he comes back alive, I might give it to him."

Tersely, she spelled her name, recited her number, mentioned Ted Keller and explained the circumstances, and all the while Broder's bartender/answering service grunted, drew beers, and greeted customers with hoots and hollers. She hung up with little confidence that Broder would get the message, but also little regret.

She packed up her briefcase for the night and got on the ele-vator, but before she headed for the garage, she made a detour and got off on the fortieth floor.

Although the lobby was finished, the unmarked steel door was the giveaway that this floor was unoccupied. In fact, it had never been occupied, and with two million square feet of center-city office space currently sitting vacant, the landlord's rental prospects weren't good. Dana unlocked the door and swung it in on the vast unfinished space inside—ten thousand square feet of concrete floor running in an open sweep from window to window in all directions. There were no partitions except the walls around the utility core of elevators and rest rooms, and there was nothing overhead but steel beams, cables, utility boxes, and naked lightbulbs.

This was her war room, where she and her troops kept the Palazzo case files and geared up for trial. Document storage was one of the biggest problems in law firm management, and Cliff Austin had imposed elaborate procedures for warehousing and retrieving them. Too elaborate for Dana's liking, especially in the final frenzy of trial preparation. When she discovered this space sitting empty, she contacted the landlord and made a pri-vate deal, and Austin and his minions were none the wiser. The nominal rent was paid directly by Pennsteel's law department, and Dana had the only key.

She took a folder of Palazzo documents out of her briefcase

and added it to Maria's stack of filing. The war room was origi-
nally meant to be an occasional workplace for the paralegals,
but one by one the associates on the case took to working here,
too, to escape the phone calls and faxes and bothersome partners upstairs. And one by one, pieces of office equipment were
spirited down here. They were still here, lined up against the
core wall where the electrical outlets were in place: a work-
station with an unlisted telephone and a computer terminal; a
photocopier; and a TV/VCR cart for viewing videotaped testimony. Travis dubbed the space the Batcave, and gradually con-
verted it from war room to bunker, hauling in a couple surplus
army cots, a dorm-sized refrigerator, and a coffeemaker pilfered from upstairs. Finally, during those feverish weeks before
L.A., Dana joined the team there, and together they went from
long bleary nights of numb exhaustion to overcaffeinated, panicked frenzies.

Every wrenching moment of it came back to her now. It was
always a nightmare, those last days of trial preparation, but the
rosy glow of victory usually supplanted all the bad memories.
Not this time. They'd had barely a day to savor the win before a
whole new nightmare opened up.

She was turning off the lights to leave when the cellular
phone rang in her purse.

"Hi!" Karin said. "Hope you weren't trying to reach us."

"Only once. Everything okay?"

"Yeah, but there was a plumbing catastrophe at the house and
we had to move."

"Oh, no, what?"

"The water heater burst and flooded the whole house. But the
owner was great. He gave us a refund and found another place
for us, which was no easy trick this time of year."

"So where are you now?"

"Fulmer's Guest Cottages, about five blocks south and a
block in from the ocean. You have to go through the office when
you call, and we're registered under my name, so ask for me."

Dana jotted down the number, then Karin surrendered the
phone to Kirsten and Katrina. For them the water gushing over
the doorsill of the house was only one more adventure in an all-

around adventure-packed day. They squabbled over the right to tell their stories, and ended up each telling her own version, with frequent interruptions to correct the other.

The longer they talked, the more keenly Dana missed them. They'd been together only one night after a month apart, and now it would be another two weeks before she saw them again. She felt an unexpected sting of resentment toward Karin—who ran her own business but could shut it down whenever she liked, who'd never missed a bedtime or a school play, and who was basking in the sun with *her* children.

"I love you," she said, full of feeling as the girls were saying goodbye.

Ritualistically they replied, "Love you, too, 'bye!"

She locked the door and descended to the garage feeling guilty on all counts. Karin was a single mother struggling from month to month with her ex-husband's lapses in child support; nobody deserved a vacation more than she did.

But even so, Dana couldn't help a twinge of envy. She loved to cook, too, when she had the time; she could have made it her career as easily as Karin. But it was too late now. The life of a caterer was one more avenue cut off to her when she became a lawyer and turned out to be good at it.

There was a kind of curse in being talented at something that paid well: it meant you could never leave it.

8

The dress code for barmaids at the Last Call Bar and Bistro seemed to call for tight denim cutoffs and midriff-exposing T-shirts. That had to explain why Brandi was drawn to the place; she already owned a dozen variations on the company uniform. Beyond that, though, she showed little aptitude for the job. Whit had been watching her for an hour and had yet to see her serve the correct drinks to any table that numbered more than two customers. At each contretemps, she engaged in a charming little feint—"Oh, you mean *you* wanted the Amstel?"— that left the patrons looking guilty for having confused her.

But she more than compensated for her neglect of others in her attentions to Whit. She stopped by his table at five-minute intervals to see if he needed a refill, even though the level of ale in his mug was dropping only by millimeters. She came so often that he had trouble working up a sufficiently enthusiastic greeting for her, although he did enjoy watching the tight little globes of her buttocks move up and down in her cutoffs as she departed.

Saturday night was a desperate scene at the Last Call for those who didn't arrive as a couple but were determined to leave as one. Boisterous young men were doggedly cruising the bar with a beer mug in each hand, like sailors on a search-and-enjoy mission, while the girls were doing a little more sly and selective cruising of their own. A few of the boys targeted Brandi, and Whit was puzzled at how she rebuffed them. Odd that a girl who gave no hint of hidden depths wouldn't be drawn to the surface charms of these young Lotharios, for whatever they might have lacked in polish, they certainly must have made up for in potency. But to most of them she was vaguely unresponsive; to one in particular she was downright rude.

Whit studied the boy she spurned, a fit young fellow with his own buns of steel. The boys these days were no more subtle than the girls, and it was easy to read the play of emotions across his bland good looks. Crippling embarrassment, followed rapidly by a blend of hurt and anger. He knew her, then; that look came from something more than a second's attraction.

In a few minutes Brandi returned to Whit's table, this time without her tray, and she tucked her bottom onto the stool beside him. "It's my break," she said. "I thought I'd sit it out here with you."

"Then it's a break for me, too."

She gave a happy little wiggle, something like an excited puppy just before it urinated on the rug. She was a pretty girl, with attractions beyond the ephemeral ones of her body. Her eyes were wide-set and a soft velvet brown like some gentle grazing creature, and her hair was a rich auburn-brown almost luminescent with youth and vitality.

"I'm so glad you came tonight." Boldly she added, "Tom."

It took him a second to realize what she meant, and he had to swallow back a laugh. "Actually, I'm called Whit," he said. "It's Thomas *Whitman* Endicott."

"Whitman," she repeated dimly before her face lit up. "Like the candy?"

He shook his head, but suddenly he was remembering a different exchange. *For the poet?* Dana had asked. And he lied and said yes, because at that moment and many more yet to come he felt like the reincarnation of every poet who ever walked the earth.

He gazed out over the crowd and started to feel his own desperation grow. Much as he'd resented Dana's girls-only vacation, he'd been counting on another two weeks before having to resume what passed for normal life in their marriage. Now the hiatus was gone, replaced by something worse: two weeks without the children to act as buffers. It was almost eight, she'd be home soon, might even be there now, and eventually he had to go home and face her.

"Stick around till my shift's over?" Brandi asked.

Or maybe not.

He looked down at her as her expression went past promise, all the way to proposition.

He'd been teaching postadolescent girls for twenty years, and long ago learned how to immunize himself from their charms. In fact, out of thousands of girls, there was only one who'd ever infected him. A tall blonde with intense blue eyes that spoke to him from across a crowded classroom: *I understand everything you're saying, I alone in this room, and I'm happy just listening to the way you say it.* From a distance of twenty years, he could see her still.

Slowly he shook his head. "I hope it's true, what Shaw said."

"Huh?"

"That the more a man is tempted, the more he can endure. Because I have to tell you—I'm powerfully tempted."

Brandi's lips moved in her mind as she memorized his words. A throwaway line was more exciting to her than a night in bed, and for now she was content with it. "Next time maybe," she said, sliding off the stool.

"Next time," he repeated, and lifted his mug in a salute.

She treated him to another view of her buttocks as she left, and his eyes tracked her across the room until he spotted Jerome Allen beckoning impatiently from the door.

By the time Whit made his way through the crowd, Jerome was waiting in his old black Cadillac at the edge of the parking lot. He looked at all three mirrors to check that the way was clear before he leaned over and opened the door. "Sorry I'm late. I had some trouble slippin' away."

Whit slid in beside him. "You got it?"

Jerome reached under his seat and came out with a dirty plastic bag. From it he pulled a tattered paperback copy of *Reading Basics for Adults.*

"Did you circle the problem words, like I told you?"

"Yeah, I got some."

Jerome fumbled through the pages and pointed with a long finger at the word *legend*.

"Yeah, that one's a bitch," Whit agreed. "But remember we talked about hard g's and soft g's?"

Jerome's face lit up. "That's one of them j sounds?" His lips moved as he tried it out silently. He repeated it aloud, uncertainly: "Legend?" Then triumphantly: "Legend!"

"Want to try it in a sentence?"

He reflected a moment, then declared, "Jerome Allen is a legend with the ladies!"

Whit laughed and gave him a victory slap.

Jerome was a product of the Philadelphia public school system, which proudly promoted him year after year and even graduated him with honors; everyone was so happy that he stayed out of gangs and jails that no one ever stopped to notice he couldn't read. Whit noticed one day in May when he gave him bags of weed killer and fertilizer for the lawn. From inside the house he watched Jerome squint hard at the labels, then put both sacks away in the shed. When they were still there a week later, unopened, Whit invited him inside for a beer and a chat. He'd been tutoring him ever since, usually in the car like this, so that nobody else would have to know.

Daylight faded and the streetlights replaced it, and Jerome worked steadily through the book for over an hour, which was a better attention span than Whit found in most college students.

"Nice work, buddy." Whit clapped him on the knee. "You're two steps away from finishing this book."

"Then you be gettin' me a better one, right? One with maybe some sex in it?"

"Do my best." Whit opened his door and climbed out. " 'Night, Jerome."

"Hey, man, don't go." Jerome climbed out the other side. "Come on inside. I'll buy you a beer."

"That's not our deal."

"Okay, then, you buy me a beer."

Whit laughed. "Wish I could. But I gotta get home."

"Your wife . . . ?"

"Didn't leave after all."

"Oh, man." He scratched his head. "Well, there's prob'ly a few ladies be waitin' on me tonight, too."

"Try not to disappoint too many of them." Whit thumped his knuckles on the sheet metal. "See you when? Wednesday?"

"I'll be here, my man."

Whit's pickup sat forlorn and dusty under a streetlight on the other side of the parking lot. It was a disreputable old rattle-trap, rusted and dented, and with fenders painted two different colors. Dana had been after him for years to get rid of it, but the truck went back almost as far as they did. He drove it six times across the country to visit her at Stanford; they hauled their first couch home in this truck; half a dozen times they climbed in the back and rocked the springs in the moonlight.

He got behind the wheel and pointed the pickup for home, disgusted with himself for considering a sexual encounter with that girl, and even more disgusted that he allowed the ghost of Dana's girlhood to keep him from it. What a fool he was, in love with a wraith but going home to a flesh-and-cold-blooded woman who no longer bore any resemblance to it.

He turned right on the lane up the mountainside, then left on their street at the top, and immediately slammed on the brakes. Three police cars were parked at haphazard angles at the end of their driveway, and some people were huddled together on the front lawn.

Whit felt a clutch in his chest. He threw himself from the pickup, dodged an oscillating sprinkler on the neighbor's lawn, and ran with sopping feet to his own lawn. His eyes searched wildly while his thoughts whirled. *What happened? Dana, where are you? Dana, what happened?*

Until at last he saw her, in the middle of the crowd, calmly addressing the policemen and bystanders.

"What's going on?" he demanded as he broke through the circle to reach her.

"Someone broke into the house," she said. "When I got home I found the French doors open from the terrace—the glass was smashed—and there were lights on in the bedrooms upstairs."

"You went upstairs after you saw the door smashed in?" Whit shouted. "What if they were still up there?"

"I went out on the terrace and looked up," she said, over-enunciating each word to demonstrate that she would not brook being scolded, and that in any event he was the idiot, not she.

He wheeled away from her and spoke to one of the police-men. "Can I go in?"

"Suit yourself."

He went around the side of the house, unlatched the garden gate, and entered the walled backyard. The lights were on around the pool, and as he started up the steps to the terrace he saw bits of broken glass sparkling like a cache of diamonds on the flagstone. He stepped carefully over them through the French doors and stopped dead at the living room.

The sofa was upended, one pair of draperies ripped from the wall, and the coffee table art books dumped on the floor. The drawers in the lowboy were pulled out and overturned, and the display niches flanking the fireplace were swept clean. Shards of Chinese porcelain lay at his feet.

The dining room was the same, and the family room, and in the kitchen, pots and pans were scattered over the floor. He galloped up the back staircase to the second floor. Each of the bedrooms was ransacked, and in the playroom, Trina's doll-house was overturned. All her little people were sprawled amid the rubble of tiny furniture, and at the sight of it a red steam came over him, so hot he turned and smashed his fist into the doorjamb.

The pain ricocheted up and down the length of his arm like a bullet gone wild. He cursed and stomped and slowly blinked away the steam, then followed the sound of voices downstairs to the family room. Dana was there, talking to a uniformed patrolman.

"We'll need an inventory of everything that's missing," he was telling her.

Numbly Whit stared at the family photo albums on the coffee table. The pages were torn out and loose photos were strewn over the floor. One lay next to his left foot. It was a picture of Kirstie as an infant, looking minuscule in the crook of his arm.

"Drop it off at the station," the officer said as he shut his note-book and stuffed it in his pocket. "We'll put it in our file."

Whit stirred. "You're not leaving already?"

"There's no reason to think they'll come back," the officer said. "You'll be perfectly safe."

"I wasn't referring to our safety," Whit bit out. "But to you finishing *your* job. What about fingerprints? And rug fibers? You haven't done anything to investigate this crime."

The officer glanced at Dana, the kind of look that cops probably threw to each other to say *Save me from this idiot*. "This is a straightforward burglary, sir. And Mrs. Endicott tells us you *are* insured."

"What's that got to do with it? It's not a crime to rob people who carry insurance?"

"They only do those procedures for violent crimes," Dana cut in, the voice of reason. "The lab work costs too much."

Whit jumped up, seething. "Maybe instead of paying insur-ance premiums, we should all pool our money and pay for crime lab services."

"Maybe so," the officer said, inching for the door.

"What I don't understand," Dana said before he could go, "is how they got past the alarm."

"You'll have to talk to your security company about that."

Abruptly, Whit turned and busied himself uprighting the folk art carvings on the fireplace mantel.

"I'll call them now."

She went to the phone in the kitchen, and Whit retreated the length of the house to the library. His papers lay on the desk, where he'd abandoned them that afternoon. The pages were shuffled slightly out of order, though none was missing.

But other things puzzled him. His Waterman fountain pen lay undisturbed, as did a Steuben glass paperweight worth about a thousand dollars.

He retraced his steps through the house, more purposefully this time, and found the same pattern everywhere. The stainless flatware was gone from the kitchen but the sterling was un-touched in the dining room. The VCRs were still in place in their bedroom and the family room, but the one in the playroom was gone.

The police were gone now, too, and Dana sat slumped on a chair in the family room.

"We've been robbed by a bunch of incompetents," Whit said.

She didn't take his meaning, or didn't care to respond. "I called Sally," she said. "She'll come over tomorrow and help us clean up and do the inventory."

"You don't suppose Sally—"

"No." Her spine went rigid as she pushed to her feet. "I don't."

She went to the kitchen and Whit followed after her and opened the refrigerator. "At least nothing's been plundered in here," he said, and pulled out a beer.

"Feel like eating?" she asked.

"That's the last thing I could do."

"What happened to your hand?"

He turned the bottle around. Blood was dripping from his knuckles. "I don't know." He reached for a dish towel.

"Here." She ripped off a paper towel and dabbed at the split skin. "Let me get some ice on it."

He jerked his hand away. "It's okay."

Her mouth went tight. "I called the alarm company. They'll send somebody out Monday to figure out what went wrong."

"Great," he said faintly.

"I'm going to bed," she announced, and started up the stairs.

He watched her go, and now it seemed the last thing he could do was follow her.

Eight miles away a man emerged from a McDonald's and paused under the golden arches to light a cigarette. His hair was a shade so white it glowed like a beacon in the neon lights. From the parking lot across the highway came the signal— three quick flashes from the headlights of Tobiah's car. Three meant he struck out, and for the third time.

The man flicked the untasted cigarette into the bushes and strode at once for his own car. Three strikes meant it was time to start a new inning. It was time to play hardball.

Driving north, he dialed the phone and waited eight rings for a muffled answer.

"Bad news, sir," he reported.

"Tobiah got caught?"

"No. Neither did he succeed."

"Damn."

"We're prepared to escalate."

"No."

"Sir, I remind you that it's my head, not yours. Though of course it *will* be your head, if it comes to that."

The reply came stiffly. "I'm aware of that."

"Then you're aware there's little choice."

"No—wait! I think I can go inside on this." Rivulets of desperation were eroding the usual voice of authority. A subtle power shift seemed to be taking place. "I can't get in until Monday. Give me till then. That's all I ask."

Agreement was struck, a concession from the white-haired man, but all in all a small price to pay for a thumb on the scales of power. He pressed a button and terminated the call.

9

Miss Texas was still asleep when Travis carried her breakfast tray upstairs Sunday morning. It held a grapefruit half for her figure, a glass of milk for her complexion, a chocolate doughnut for her sweet tooth, and a single yellow rose to show how much he loved her. Her strawberry-blond hair lay in a silken swirl over the pillow, and her pink-tipped fingers were tucked under one rosy cheek. She looked like a confection. He put the tray down and grinned stupidly at her awhile. Every day of their married life was a new wonder to him. After a month apart it felt close to miraculous.

He hated to wake her, and even more he hated to leave her. But while the first was optional, the second was not. He had to go upstate to find out what he could about the pilot of the plane, and there were three good reasons why he had to do it today: he was more likely to catch people at home on a Sunday than a weekday; at only two days postcrash, he'd be sure to get the jump on the opposition; and since Dana wasn't expecting it, she'd have to be impressed. But it was hard to leave his wife so soon after Los Angeles. Lately he had to remind himself as often as he reminded her: only a few more months and he'd never have to work this hard again.

He decided to let her sleep, and went downstairs with his wing-tips resonating hollowly through the two-story foyer. There was an echo because they didn't have enough furniture to absorb the sound. After they bought the house—or after the bank did; the monthly payments were $2,800—he was all set to zip down to Levitz and fill the place up with Herculon and crushed velvet, but Miss Texas said no, if they couldn't do it right, they shouldn't do it at all. Soon, though, maybe next year, they'd hire a decorator and do the place up. He couldn't marry Miss Texas and drag her north only to keep her in an empty house.

He squeezed himself into the BMW and backed out of the driveway. The lease payments were almost five hundred a month, and since it was only the three-series, his head brushed the ceiling. But it was still a BMW and he was still a man on his way up. Landing the Alpine Valley case right after the Palazzo Hotel trial—it was like playing the Rose Bowl and the Cotton Bowl back-to-back.

Only eight A.M. and already hot. He pumped up the air conditioner, then slipped a CD into the changer and let Garth Brooks sing to him as he got on the turnpike and opened up the Beemer. You couldn't get any decent country-western on the radio in Philadelphia; that was one of the things they had to give up when they came north. Miss Texas gave up the most, though, and she couldn't help reminding him of it sometimes. "If only you'd stayed with football," she'd sigh now and then, whenever she was pining for something out of reach. He'd been courted by the pro scouts, he had a shot at the Cowboys, and that was her dream, to stay in Dallas and be rich enough for all their old friends to take notice. But he persuaded her that in the long run he had a better chance of making real money in the law. The only trouble was, they had to live in the short run.

It was a long drive to Montrose, even with Garth Brooks to sing the way, but at last he exited the interstate and followed a state highway into town. Woolly white bundles appeared like puffs of smoke against the hillsides, and corn in golden tassel rose up high on both sides of the road, so close to the macadam edge he could almost reach out and brush it with his fingertips. For a minute it almost felt like home.

Montrose was a surprisingly pretty town, more prosperous than most rural farm centers, with lots of big white houses on hilly, tree-lined streets. Travis spotted a coffee shop and executed a quick turn into the parking lot. The tables inside were full of people in their Sunday clothes, speaking in soft, somnolent voices with their Sunday manners on. He took a seat at the counter and ordered two ham sandwiches and a cup of coffee. While he ate he squinted over the local area map he'd pulled from the firm's library yesterday.

"You lost, son?" said a kindly voice.

A gray-haired man was reading over his shoulder while he waited at the cash register to pay his check. A tiny old woman stood peevishly behind him.

"I'm not sure," Travis said. "I'm looking for the Loudenberg place."

"You here for the funeral?"

Bad timing. Nobody would give him an interview if the funeral was today.

"It's a service, not a funeral," the old woman snapped at her husband. "They can't have the funeral till they get the bodies back."

"The service, then," her husband said mildly.

"Yes, sir," Travis said.

"Then you want to take 706 out, oh, about—"

"You're not family?" the wife cut in.

"No, ma'am. I'm—"

"You from the college?" she demanded. "You knew Donny?"

"Well, not real—"

"You look like you play some football," her husband remarked. "You on the coaching staff there?"

Travis took another bite of his sandwich and nodded as he munched. Not too much of a lie if he didn't speak it.

"That's real nice of them," the woman said, her head bobbing with approval. "Sending somebody up for the funeral. I wouldn'ta expected it."

Travis shrugged and kept on munching.

"Well, like I was saying," the man went on. "You take 706—"

His wife cut him off with a poke to the ribs. "Why are you giving him directions when we're going that way ourselves?"

10

The Pennsylvania countryside at the height of summer was a patchwork of green and gold shot through with ribbons of silvered highway and swaths of green-black forest. In a bird's-eye view soaring in from the southeast, blue foothills appeared ahead. One grew into a mountain, was crested, and suddenly the pastoral scene was recast as an apocalyptic nightmare. Fires raged and black smoke billowed out as if from the pit of a volcano. Alpine Valley was an abyss.

The screen went dark as the news team helicopter was enveloped in a cloud of smoke.

Dana watched the film roll from the back of the auditorium. The paralegal Luke was operating the video equipment in the projection booth in back, Travis was manning the door, and the two insurance reps were working the crowd. More than a dozen of the best forensic aeronautical minds in the country were gathered in the room with their heads craned back at the enormous movie-sized screen onstage. Charlie Morrison was not in attendance; he'd finally taken Dana at her word and stayed behind to tend the home fires at Pennsteel. But Ted Keller was there, slumped in his chair and watching the screen with a look of horror on his face.

Dana rose and slipped out past Travis into the fifth-floor corridor. Beside the elevators was a glass-doored telephone booth, and she went in and dialed the NTSB regional office in Parsippany. Ten-thirty, and it was the third time she'd called today.

"Oh, yes, Ms. Svenssen," Harry Reilly's secretary said. "Mr. Cutler said he would call you later."

"Cutler?"

"Jim Cutler. Mr. Reilly's deputy."

"Please tell Mr. Cutler I'll hold for him."

It was ten minutes before he took her call, but he got right to the point. "Okay, we're releasing the scene on Wednesday. You can have access at ten A.M."

"Wednesday, ten o'clock," she confirmed, and hung up and dialed again.

This time her own secretary answered. "Celeste, hi. It's me."

"You have five new messages."

Celeste spoke like a more impassive version of the computerized voice-mail system. She was a forbidding woman without a modicum of personal charm, but after five years together, Dana wouldn't trade her for the winner of a congeniality contest even if Miss Congeniality typed two hundred words a minute.

"You have an appointment at the auto glass shop at seven-thirty tomorrow," Celeste intoned.

"Okay, thanks."

"Angela Leoni called about lunch."

"Oh." Angela was an old friend, and since she was also a busy lawyer, they never saw enough of each other. But before Dana could feel any pleasure that she called, Celeste steamed ahead with the next item.

"Mr. Austin wants the final bill on Palazzo by Wednesday."

Clifford Austin kept a vigilant eye on the firm's unbilled time and he was always nipping at the heels of the partners to get their bills out promptly. But Dana had her excuse ready. "Can't. The backup detail isn't available yet."

"Also, Charlie Morrison came by to see you this morning."

"What? Why?" Dana sat up straight. "He knows I'm here at Geisinger today."

"He forgot. He went in your office and made a few phone calls, then left for another meeting."

Poor Charlie. He must have been even more frazzled by all this than she'd thought.

"Also, the adjuster for your homeowner's called. But I transferred him to Mr. Endicott."

"Oh," Dana said after a moment. "Okay, thanks."

She came out of the booth and paced the length of the corridor to the expanse of windows beside the elevators. A hundred yards away the west tower of the complex was still under construction. A giant crane stood asleep on its feet inside a deep excavation where a few steel beams rose out of the ground like the start of a child's erector set project. They were Pennsteel beams, Dana recalled; Charlie once mentioned they had the fabricating contract.

Surrounding the complex was a neatly manicured landscape that only five years before was planted in cash crops. Now it was "dedicated green space," a badly needed buffer between the hotel and conference center and the sprawl of King of Prussia below.

King of Prussia appeared every few years in listings of unusual place names like Oil Trough and Intercourse. The locals had been saying it so long and so often that they'd lost all sense of the words; it was spoken as a jumble, Kingaprussia, with a vaguely Indian sound like Kennebunk or Kankakee. Legend had it that the town was named for an eighteenth-century King of Prussia in gratitude for troops he supplied to the Revolutionary Army. The truth was a bit more pedestrian: a colonial innkeeper named his tavern after his former king in the old country, and since the only feature of the village was the tavern, the name came to designate both.

The village remained a little crossroads farming community until the 1950s when one of the farms was sold to a developer with a vision, and a mall was born. The town sprang up backward, from retail to residential to commercial/industrial. Builders put in subdivisions around the mall, people moved in, and jobs followed. More stores were built to accommodate the workers in the office parks and plant complexes, and the mall was expanded, until it was now the largest conglomeration of retail space in the country.

But the regional planners had a failure to match every success the developers achieved. The highways were a quagmire of intertwining lanes and crisscrossing ramps and mistimed traffic lights. Where two roads should have intersected, there were three or four. Lockheed's spacecraft plant sat on a hill behind the mall, and it was a local joke that it took a rocket scientist to figure out how to get there.

The auditorium door opened, and Don Skelly came out lighting up a cigarette. "Ah, there you are," he said on a deep exhalation of smoke.

"Need me?" Dana asked him.

"Wondered what you think of our crew in there."

"I'm impressed. On paper at least, their credentials are first-rate."

"I thought so, too." He was puffing fast, the mark of a man who worked in a smoke-free office. "I skimmed that packet you gave me of all of their—whaddya call it, their résumés?"

Skelly had worked too long in this field not to know that experts' résumés were called curricula vitae, but he liked to let people know he wasn't cozy with words like that. "Their CVs," Dana said.

"Right. I noticed one of them isn't here. That pilot fella, Broder."

"Yes, he's our only no-show. But that was a long shot anyway."

He took one final deep drag. "So—how're ya leaning?"

He meant as between the two accident reconstructionists, Wetherby and Stoltz, which meant that neither he nor Wiecek was backing off his favorite, which meant that Charlie Morrison would have to cast the deciding vote, which in fact meant that Dana would.

"Too soon to tell," she said, and turned and pointed out the window at the construction site. "How come nobody's working today? Did you give them the day off?"

"Naah." Skelly stubbed his cigarette out in the sand-filled saucer beside the elevator. "Some damn idiot in the engineer's office made a goof, so here we all sit while they go scrambling back to the drawing board, and everybody points a finger at everybody else."

Not at Pennsteel, she hoped. Charlie's litigation budget was already straining at the seams. "Got insurance for that kind of delay?" she asked.

"You better believe it!" He started for the auditorium door. "See you back inside?"

"In a minute."

She pulled out her flip phone and stared out the window as she waited for the connection. An open Jeep Wrangler was careening up the hill, and it cornered the construction site barely on four wheels and whipped into the parking space beside Dana's car. She sucked in her breath as the door swung open, but it missed the Mercedes by a hair. A man got out—or maybe a boy, judging from the way he vaulted to the ground—wearing blue jeans, work boots, and a white shirt. He reached into the back of the Jeep and pulled out something that passed for a sport coat and shrugged himself into it. He did a quick duck in the side-view mirror, and from five stories up she saw him give himself a grin.

The line rang four times before the answering machine clicked on, which meant Whit was out, or not answering the phone. She wasn't sure which was worse. She wasn't sure about anything anymore.

Funny that the same article that called her a Viking warrior also described her as decisive. Now she couldn't decide between Wetherby and Stoltz; she couldn't decide whether to stay in her marriage or leave it. She knew one thing, though: she couldn't survive another weekend like this past one. Whit never came to bed Saturday night, and last night they lay awake for hours, silent and careful not to bump each other. The resentment came off him like steam.

She leaned her head against the cool surface of the glass. *No, don't think about Whit.*

The elevator chimed, and she turned as the cocky young driver of the Jeep stepped out. Not a boy after all, she saw, though not quite a grown-up, either. Black-haired, brown-eyed, dimpled and devilish. He stopped when he saw her and let his eyes move deliberately down the length of her body.

"Hi." He smiled and his dimples bored deeper.

She'd trained herself twenty-five years before never to speak to a man who looked at her that way; she wasn't going to start now no matter how flattering it might be.

But he went on, "Any idea where Room 501 is?"

Startled, she pointed toward the auditorium.

"Thanks."

She waited a beat before following. Travis was leaning against the back wall with his arms folded over his chest. "Late arrival," he whispered, and pointed with his chin.

The cocky young man in blue jeans was sitting beside Ted Keller and watching the video intently.

"Andy Broder," Dana almost groaned.

"Yep."

What was Ted thinking? Airfare from Alaska was expensive, and they'd have to pay Broder at least that much before they sent him on his way.

Luke shut off the tape, and as the lights came up Dana walked to the front of the auditorium and mounted the stairs to the podium, where she introduced herself and pointed out Travis and Norm Wiecek and Don Skelly.

"Now that you've seen the videotape," she said to the group, "you know as much as we do about the circumstances of this accident. We'll get access to the site Wednesday, and we're pressing the NTSB for early release of the CVR transcript from the helicopter. We're putting in an FOIA request today to the FAA, and hopefully we'll get some usable radar data in a month or so. Until then, gentlemen, what you've seen is what we know."

Broder's hand was in the air, probably to point out that he hadn't seen much of the video and to delay the meeting by requesting a replay. But when Dana sent him a piqued look, he called out, "I hear you were at the site before the news cameras arrived."

"That's right."

"Was that before or after the second explosion?"

Her pique was growing. He arrived an hour and a half late to the meeting, but now was showing off that he'd done his homework. "Before," she answered tightly.

"Then you have to know a lot more than the rest of us do."

Certainly a lot more than you, she refrained from retorting. "Well, whatever impressions I have I'll share at the appropriate time." She continued, "Now I'll call on Pennsteel's chief pilot and director of aviation services to give you an overview on the JetRanger. Ted?"

Ted Keller climbed reluctantly to his feet as Luke dimmed the lights and flashed the first of the slides of technical specifications onto the screen. A half a dozen penlights clicked on in the audience as the experts began to take notes.

Dana beckoned to Skelly and Wiecek, and they rose and stepped outside with her and Travis.

"Time to caucus," she said.

Skelly pointed down the hall. "Got a room waitin'."

"I'll check in at the office first," Travis said to Dana as he stepped into the phone booth.

She nodded and followed the insurance reps to a small conference room at the end of the corridor.

"I still like Stoltz," Norm Wiecek insisted sullenly before his buttocks touched the chair.

"So do I," Dana said, and the first expression of something less than misery touched Wiecek's face.

"But hold on a minute—" Skelly cut in.

Their debate opened up again, but in the midst of it, Travis burst into the room.

"What?" Dana asked at the look on his face.

"Brad talked to somebody down at the Crozer burn center. He got a rundown on some of the victims."

"Let's hear it."

He sat down and read from his notes. "Two kids. A four-year-old boy who suffered burns of the torso, including extensive damage to the genitalia. And a ten-year-old girl whose hair caught fire. She lost both ears and half her face."

Dana's own face went white. Little children suffering so horribly—the pain had to be excruciating, and even when it ended, the little girl faced years of plastic surgery; the little boy might grow up without full sexual function. Skelly and Wiecek gave each other a look; they knew the implications as well as she.

"Then there's a forty-two-year-old man named David Greenberg," Travis continued. "Extensive burns to his hands and arms. The story is he came to the little boy's rescue and beat out the flames with his bare hands. And the last one we got was a park employee. He was struck on the back by burning debris."

"Go back to David Greenberg," Dana said. "Where's he from? What's his occupation?"

Travis flipped through his notes. "Local. Lives in Jenkintown with his wife and four kids. Occupation—" He flipped some more. "—dentist."

His head came up and Dana met his eyes, both of them thinking the same thing. A hero who saved a child's life, a dentist who lost the use of his hands, a husband and father who probably had a solid six-figure income, now gone. If Ira Thompson was looking for the ideal plaintiff to represent in this litigation, David Greenberg had to be his man.

"One way to find out," she said, and reached for the directory in her briefcase, then dialed the speakerphone on the table.

"Ira Thompson," an incongruently female voice announced.

"This is Dana Svenssen. Is he in?"

"Not at the moment. May I tell him you called?"

"Please." She started to recite her number but cut herself off as if she'd suddenly changed her mind. "On second thought, maybe you can tell me and save him the call back. I need to know if Mrs. Greenberg will be joining in the complaint as a plaintiff, or if it's only going to be David?"

Skelly gave a wink at her ruse.

"Oh, it's both, Ms. Svenssen," the secretary answered. "David and Andrea Greenberg."

Travis barely stifled a groan.

"Okay, thanks."

Skelly greeted the information with a whistle through his teeth, but the rest of the room lapsed into a grim daze as Dana disconnected. The one-two punch of Ira Thompson and David Greenberg would be a certain knockout if Thompson had any viable theory of liability against Pennsteel. But what could he possibly have? So far nobody knew anything about the cause of the crash.

"Here's what I want to do," she decided. "I want to retain both Wetherby and Stoltz. In fact, I want to sign up all of them. Keep them on our team, see how the evidence develops. And then decide who to use as testifying experts."

"Works for me," Skelly said.

"Me, too," Wiecek said miserably.

"All except Broder, of course," she said. "I think we can safely send him on his way."

"Why's that?" Wiecek asked.

"Well, there's no risk anybody else is going to hire him. We wouldn't even have him on our list if it weren't for the Keller connection."

"I don't know about that," Skelly said. "I like the looks of his CV. Some of our opponents might, too."

"But what about the looks of Broder?" She laughed. "Come on—he's a kid. Nobody on the jury will take him seriously."

Skelly rocked back in his chair and addressed the ceiling. "Ya know—I can remember when folks used to say that kind of thing about lady lawyers."

Travis smothered a guffaw.

"Besides," Wiecek pointed out gloomily, "if we don't hire him, he might go tell Thompson exactly who we got."

"Bright boy like him's probably in there right now figuring out everybody else's name," Skelly said.

Dana regarded the men around the table. She couldn't imagine ever putting Broder on the stand. But he might be worth an hour or two of consultation, and even if he wasn't, she could sign him up and never consult him again. Besides, with the kind of wild flying he liked to do, he'd probably be dead before they got to trial.

"All right. We'll sign them all."

Lunch was catered in, and afterward Dana met with the experts one after the other in the conference room: Doug Wetherby, a lean, laconic westerner who'd worked the USAir crash in Pittsburgh; Ed Stoltz, an energetic dynamo who'd consulted on the Lockerbie case; John Diefenbach, a radar expert; a meteorologist; a metallurgist; an aerodynamicist; two computer simulators; and experts in avionics, visibility, and human factors. Each was happy to sign on, but miserable about the state of the physical evidence.

"I need some impact points," Ed Stoltz complained throughout his interview. "That's the best way I know to calculate how the craft came together."

"We'll have to do what we can with the eyewitness interviews and whatever radar data we come up with," Dana said.

But John Diefenbach explained in his interview that even if radar data existed, once two craft came within a certain range of each other, the radar couldn't distinguish them anymore; they showed up as a single blip on the screen. "I can plot each one up to the point where they got within about five hundred feet of each other," he said. "Closer than that nobody can do."

And the expert on visibility and perspective warned against relying too heavily on eyewitness interviews. "For every ten people you talk to, you'll get ten versions of how this accident happened. Nobody could've seen the same thing unless they were standing in the exact same location and focusing on the exact same thing. It never happens."

Doug Wetherby summed it up. "It's a damn shame that second explosion had to happen. It prit near blew ever'thang to hell."

For the hundredth time Dana grieved for Kirstie's camera and the lost film that might have answered at least a few of the experts' questions. Before her final interview she checked in with Lyle Claiborne. Yes, a notice was running in ten different newspapers, requesting anyone with photos or video footage of the crash to contact their office. The proverbial operators were standing by.

She saved Andy Broder's interview for last. He swaggered into the conference room, and when she motioned him into a chair, he flipped it around and straddled it like a bar stool.

"Well," she began, taking her seat across the table from him. "All of us are very impressed with the breadth of your credentials, and very grateful that Ted thought of you."

"Uh-huh." He was trying to read her papers upside down. She folded her arms over them, and he mimicked her, folding

his arms and leaning toward her. His biceps bulged inside the
tight cotton of his sleeves.

"You work for the Forest Service, is that right?'"

"Nope."

"Oh." She picked up his CV again. "I thought—"

"I just hire out to them now and then so I can fly their
choppers."

"So what do you do with the rest of your time?"

He let a suggestive smile play at the corner of his mouth before he finally answered. "I freelance for a charter service. Bush
pilot."

"Fixed-wing?"

"So far."

"How'd you get started in flying?"

"My dad taught me. After Vietnam he went back to the
family farm in Nebraska and started a sideline doing crop-
dusting and aerial photography. I could fly before I could
drive."

That, she thought wryly, explained his poor performance in
the parking lot. "At some point you switched to helicopters?"

"Uh-huh." He gave a vigorous nod, his smart-aleckness gone
for the moment. "VTOL technology is light-years ahead of the
best fixed-wing."

"Veetoll?"

"Vertical takeoff and landing. The problem is the average
guy can't buy a chopper, it costs too damn much. I had to join
the Marines to learn how to fly one, and I had to hire out to the
Forest Service so I could keep on flying one. But someday I'll
have my own."

"And do what with it?"

He shrugged; his adolescent fantasies ran only so far. "Maybe
run my own charter service in Alaska. Ever been there?" She
shook her head. "Greatest place on earth."

This was the segue she was waiting for. "Is there an address
there where we can reach you?"

"No." He pulled his CV out of her hand and reached for her
pen. "Reach me here instead."

She squinted at what he scrawled across the page. "Where is this?"

"A private airport in Bucks County. That's where I'm keeping my plane."

"You flew your own plane here from Alaska?" Impossible; that had to be five thousand miles.

"Not exactly."

She smiled. "I didn't think so."

"The plane's only half mine." She gaped at him, and he laughed at her discomposure. "What'd you think—I flew here commercial? Anyway, a buddy of mine works at this airport, so I thought I'd crash there for a while."

She raised an eyebrow at him. "Crash?"

He laughed again, exposing his dimples beneath dancing eyes.

"Well." She busied herself with her papers. "On behalf of Pennsteel, I'd like to retain you as an expert for this case. Have you thought about your hourly rate?"

But he hesitated. "Exactly what are you retaining me to do?"

Oh, God, she thought, he wanted to parade his scruples and insist on maintaining scientific integrity. "To consult and advise as requested," she said. "And potentially to testify as an expert witness at trial."

"Potentially."

"Yes."

"I want to know now: will I be testifying?"

"We don't have to make that determination yet."

"But you have made it."

She shrugged. "I suppose we're more likely to use you as a background consultant than a testifying expert."

He shot to his feet and thrust his hands into his jeans pockets. "What's the problem here? My hair?"

Dana swiveled in her chair, tracking him as he prowled the room. "I beg your pardon?"

"It's all there and it's not gray."

She gave a smile and purposely made it condescending. "You are rather young."

"I'm past thirty."

"Barely." According to his CV, he turned thirty only the

week before, and to her eye he looked even younger. "Besides, you've never testified."

"And I never will if I keep running into lawyers like you. Hell—I didn't go into this business so I could double-check other people's work."

"I don't know that we'd ask you to do that."

"No. You won't ask me to do anything. You'll throw me a couple thousand dollars, and that's enough to make me yours and keep me from working for anybody on the other side. That's what nontestifying experts are all about, right? Well, no fucking thanks."

He swiped his jacket off the chair back and stalked to the door. "If anybody else wants me, I'm available."

Dana leaned back in her chair and called after him, "I hope the other side *does* hire you, Mr. Broder. And I hope you *do* get to testify at trial."

He stopped with his hand on the knob, sensing a trap but too curious not to probe it. "Why's that?"

"Because I can't wait to get you on cross-examination."

His face went hard for a second before he allowed a slow grin to spread across it. "I'm looking forward to that myself."

The air was hot and heavy as Dana started the drive home that night. The wind whipped at the plastic sheeting over the broken window with an irritating whop-whop rhythm, and the air conditioner pumped overtime, trying to compensate for the sweltering air that leaked in around the plastic.

The interview with Andy Broder left a bitter taste in her mouth, but something more than that was troubling her. Two aircraft with the whole sky to themselves somehow flew into each other. Don Skelly might be reassured by the lack of physical evidence, but she wasn't. Something caused the collision, something caused a dozen deaths, and she couldn't accept a "We'll never know" explanation any more than a jury would.

She dialed into her office voice mail while she waited at a stoplight. The insurance adjuster had called again, which probably meant that Whit blew him off, and which left one more chore for her to deal with herself. Finally, as the traffic started to move, she heard the message she'd been waiting for.

"Hello, Mrs. Endicott? This is Al from CastleKeep Security. We sent a team out to your house today, and they ran a complete diagnostic, and the reason the alarm didn't sound was that the system was deactivated at 7:05 P.M. on Saturday, password keyed to Whitman Endicott."

Dana stared at the phone until a horn honked behind her. With a start she gunned the engine forward.

"So," Al concluded cheerily, "you'll be happy to know your system's in tip-top condition."

Hot tears stung her eyes as she disconnected.

11

Down the length of the house Whit heard the car door slam in the garage, and seconds later Dana stood at the threshold of the library. She was wearing a pale blue suit with a white silk blouse and a skirt that was nicely tight. It was her best color, a wintry Nordic blue that made her eyes shine and her hair glow incandescently.

"You might have told me," she said. "And saved the alarm company the trouble of coming out."

Icicles formed on the ends of her words. Whit leaned back in his chair and answered mildly, "I thought it was all part of the monthly service fee."

"Then you might have saved *me* the trouble of calling them. Not to mention the embarrassment."

His gaze cut to her face, then beyond it. "I don't see that there's any reflection on you."

"You don't see it?" she exclaimed as the icicles shattered. "You go out alone on a Saturday night and deactivate the alarm before you leave and you don't see that it reflects on me?"

"No, but I expect you're about to enlighten me."

"You did it so you could sneak back in as late as you liked without worrying about the alarm going off and waking me."

His jaw dropped. He tossed his pen aside and pushed back from his desk.

"You always assume the worst, don't you?" he spat out. "Did

you ever stop to think that maybe I just didn't want to be bothered with the damn thing?"

She turned up her cold blue eyes, and they pierced him from three feet away. "Did you ever stop to think," she said, "that maybe I just don't want to be bothered with you?"

He was blown backward by the gale force of her words, across the library, knocking aside books, turning over furniture, smashing the glass, and hurtling out the window into a vortex of a scream so loud his ears rang.

After a moment he realized nothing had moved and no one had spoken.

"Did you ever stop to think," he whispered, "that maybe you'd get your wish?"

She blinked, and in the blessed cessation of that ice-blue stare, he scooped his keys off the desk and charged through the house to the garage. The security keypad flickered beside the door, and he sneered at it as he wrenched the door open.

The alarm was still wailing as he screeched out of the driveway.

He drove too fast, in a beeline for the Last Call. He was guilty by suspicion, he might as well be guilty in fact. Some misplaced notion of duty or honor made him flee from the charms of a willing girl, but no more.

He parked and threaded his way inside through the haze of smoke and dim light and made a complete circumnavigation of the bar. When he couldn't find Brandi, he started to feel a desperation growing as great as any he ever witnessed in a Saturday night crowd. He *had* to find her, he had to *have* her. He didn't know what he would do otherwise, kill himself or go home and let Dana finish the job.

A girl was bent over a table in the corner, in cutoffs so short two half-moons of buttocks peeked out below the denim fringe. He squinted at her as she turned, and something surged through his veins when he saw it was Brandi, adrenaline or testosterone, or maybe only relief that he wouldn't die tonight after all. He charged up to her and seized her by the shoulders.

"Mr. Endicott!"

"When do you get off?"

Her eyes went wide. "Eleven."

He peered at his watch through the dim smoky light. It was only nine-thirty. He looked up, panicking.

Somehow she understood. "I'll get somebody to cover for me," she whispered. "Meetcha outside in ten minutes."

He waited in the pickup with the windows open and his eyes trained on the door. The night heat seeped into the cab like toxic sludge, and it crawled close and clammy up the skin of his arms and tightened around his neck. The air was too heavy to suck into his lungs, and he felt himself starting to choke.

Until the door burst open and Brandi stood on the threshold. Her head was spinning in search of him, and he flashed the lights to mark the way. She slid breathlessly into the seat beside him and threw herself at him as literally this time as she had figuratively a dozen times before. She wound both arms around his neck and crushed her mouth against his and moaned with pleasure. Somewhere below her was the gearshift, and Whit had a passing wonder of what the exact source of her pleasure was. But she put all doubt to rest when she thrust her hand between his legs.

"Your place, my place, or right here?"

"Your place, I think," he croaked.

She kept a hand on his thigh as she directed him through the old decaying streets of Norristown. She made one mistake, telling him to turn left when she meant right—"Ooops!" she giggled as they circled the block—but in another five minutes they were there.

Or somewhere. She led him down an alleyway behind a block of old brick storefronts. "I live over the video store," she explained as he trailed after her up the outside flight of stairs. "Which is really good because they close at eleven. My friend Sharon? She lives over the bar at the corner, and that place keeps rockin' till two!"

She fished a key out of her purse, and with a pretty little moue, handed it to him. He took it and fitted it into the lock. Nothing high-tech here. The door swung free at once, and she ran in laughing.

The lights came on to reveal an efficiency apartment with a little strip of a kitchen to the left, a bathroom to the right, and a bed dominating all the rest of it. It was covered with a pink-and-white floral bedspread, but black satin sheets peeked out underneath.

"C'mere," she said, and took him by the hand. "Sit down over here."

She led him to the one and only armchair in the room, then moved to a boom box under the window and switched on a rock station. "Drink?"she offered. "I got wine."

"Great."

She kicked off her shoes and walked sinuously to the kitchen, a slow exhibition he was meant to admire and did. She poured one glass and handed it to him, then dropped to her knees on the floor beside him. "You're not having any?" he asked as she went to work on his shoelaces.

"Not yet." She slipped off his shoes and massaged his feet.

"Why don't you join me?" he asked, meaning in the chair, or the drink, or anything.

"Not yet."

Brandi rose and walked deliberately away from him and stopped halfway across the room. She looked over her shoulder under the sweep of her hair, a pose so obviously designed to be arousing that Whit would have laughed out loud if he hadn't been so aroused. Her hands moved to the bottom of her little crop top, and she shrugged out of it, revealing a bare back. The ratchet of a zipper sounded, and she shimmied out of her shorts, this time revealing almost everything in a black thong bikini. Abruptly she swung around to face him.

Her breasts were smaller than Dana's, but also perkier. She smoothed her hands over them as she sauntered toward him, and five feet away she pinched her nipples into hard little points. Whit shifted in the seat and took another gulp of wine. She let her hands run down her belly, and hooked her thumbs into the sides of the thong, and as she lowered it to her ankles, his breath sucked through his teeth: her pubic hair was shaved into the shape of a valentine.

She was naked now, but for a chain around her neck and

another around her ankle. She stood between his legs and slowly and lasciviously slithered to the floor. He put the glass down and reached for her, but she shook her head.

"You know what, Whitman?" Her fingers were on his fly, and another zipper ratcheted. "All I want to do is to make you happy."

He leaned back and closed his eyes. "By all means," he began before he had to stop and clear his throat. "Proceed."

Later, after he'd staggered across the room and collapsed on the bed, Brandi remembered the curtains. She padded to the window and leaned briefly against the glass as she pulled them shut.

One story down and a hundred feet away, a young black man sat behind the wheel in a dark sedan.

"Tobiah?" crackled a voice over the radio. "You got visual contact?"

"I'll say," he said, and lowered his binoculars with a grin.

12

Dana rolled over, and in the recesses of sleep she could feel the empty expanse beside her in bed. Her eyes came open. Daylight streamed into the room, and Whit's pillow still lay smooth and plump against the headboard. She sat up and listened for sounds of life, but the house was almost eerily silent. She threw back the sheet and padded downstairs, through the kitchen and all the way down the hall to Whit's library, but everything was as he'd left it last night. He hadn't been back.

She dressed in desultory slow motion and drove to the auto glass shop, where she had to wait endlessly for her turn at the service desk. When at last she reached the front of the line, it was only to be told that they couldn't get to her window replacement that day. It was thirty minutes later before she finally drove off the lot in a loaner, a white Taurus with a broken radio.

She arrived at the office and collapsed behind her desk, already exhausted at nine-thirty. Before she could take five minutes to flip through her mail and phone messages, Celeste staggered in with a twelve-inch ream of papers.

"Morning, Celeste, how are you?"

Though it was a month since they'd seen each other, Celeste gave her no welcome. "The Pennsteel billing printouts," she said, and deposited the stack on the desk.

"Already?" So much for her excuse to put off final-billing the Palazzo case. Here was the downside to an efficient secretary.

Celeste clutched her cardigan around her and left Dana staring bleakly at the reams of paper. Billing was every lawyer's most dreaded chore, but Dana actively despised it. She loathed the whole concept of selling legal services by the hour; it fostered inefficiency and dishonesty and created a constant tension between the interests of the client and the self-interest of the lawyer. For years she'd been campaigning for value-pricing, but nobody else seemed ready for it, clients included.

Now she had another motive for delay. The last thing Charlie Morrison needed this week was to receive the familiar thick envelope from Jackson, Rieders & Clark.

Later, she thought, and picked up the sheaf of yesterday's phone messages.

Charlie Morrison's name was on the top, but he was on his way to New York by the time Dana got through to his office.

The next message was from Angela Leoni, and instantly Dana's spirits rose. Angela was like a breath of fresh air—no, wrong analogy; she was like a blast of air from the kitchen of an Italian restaurant—hot and spicy and delicious. Dana waited eagerly for the call to go through, but when it finally did, it was only Angela's secretary reporting that she'd just left for court.

She hung up and stared again at the stack of billing printouts. It couldn't be put off any longer. She pulled the stack front and center and set to work.

Ten minutes later she grabbed the phone and punched in Travis's extension. In moments he appeared in her doorway, tugging on his too-tight collar.

"Close the door."

He blinked at her unfamiliar tone. As he turned from the door, he took in the reams of printouts on her desk and his face went red.

"Dana, wait, let me explain."

"I can't wait to hear you try," she said tightly. "Since you'd have to be Einstein to explain how you managed to work twenty-six hours in a single day."

"That was a mistake."

"Then I assume it was also a mistake when you billed twenty hours on the seventeenth? And twenty-two on the twentieth? In fact there must have been a mistake every single day, since you never billed fewer than sixteen hours the whole time we were in Los Angeles."

"Dana, I worked my ass off on that case."

"You also ate three meals a day, worked out every morning, and talked to your wife on the phone for an hour every night."

"But I barely slept! I thought about the case all the time. I sweated bullets over every procedural and evidentiary point."

"That's the life you chose!" she erupted. "You want a job where you don't have to think about your work after hours, go find an assembly line someplace."

His head drooped as if his massive neck were suddenly too weak to hold it up.

Dana's heart pinched at the sight. He was more than a valuable associate, he was dear to her, and she hated to see him suffer for this, deserved or not.

"Travis," she said more softly, "you did your best work on Palazzo, better than anything I could have hoped for." She pointed to the printouts. "Don't screw it up with this crap."

Staring at the floor, he muttered, "You're the one who's always talking about value-pricing our work. Well, we won, didn't we? We got a hell of a result for our client. Where's the harm in it?"

"The harm is it's a fraud. If we tell our clients they have to buy our time by the hour, then we damn well better sell it to them that way."

He slumped into a chair. "You know I'm up for partner the end of the year."

"And *you* know you have my endorsement."

He shook his head. "I appreciate that, I do, but it's not enough. When push comes to shove, you're only one vote. I'm up against Ben Hager, who's brought in two good clients of his own, and Mark Watley, who's got seventeen hundred hours logged already this year. And it's only August! He's gonna have close to three thousand by year-end. I have to catch up somehow."

She put her elbows on the desk and held her head in her hands. Travis was a better lawyer than Watley, and someday he'd be a better rainmaker than Hager. He deserved partnership more than either of them. But she knew better than he did that talent guaranteed nothing.

"I'm sorry, Travis," she said. "But I can't let you play catch-up on the back of my client."

He swallowed hard. "How much of the bill are you cutting?"

"A third." He blanched before she went on, "And I'm allocating it equally between my time and yours."

His eyes fell shut in relief; he was taking a hit only half as big as it could have been. "Thanks," he said, pulling himself to his feet. "I appreciate this, Dana."

But she knew he'd appreciate it a lot more if she let his time stand. He moved awkwardly to the door and stopped. They'd never had harsh words before. He didn't know how to leave, and she didn't know how to send him off.

They were both spared by the ringing of the phone. Celeste's monotone came over the intercom: "Don Skelly from Geisinger."

Dana put him on the speaker.

"Hey," he said. "I was sorry to hear things didn't work out with young Broder yesterday."

She shook her head, disgusted at the recollection. "He's got an agenda of his own. That plus a colossal chip on his shoulder."

"Too bad, though. I think you two woulda set off some sparks in the courtroom."

"I don't think so, Don."

"Well, let's just hope Thompson don't get him."

"I bet he's already on a plane back to Alaska."

She turned to Travis as the line disconnected. "Do me a favor?"

"You bet."

"Give Broder a call." She shuffled through the papers on the credenza until she found his CV. "See if he's still at this airport in Bucks County, and find out how long he's planning to stay. Tell him I want to know where to send his expense check, here or back in Alaska."

"You got it."

The house was empty when Dana got home that night. She wandered the rooms and switched on the lights, but it still seemed eerie and foreign to her, and finally she realized what it was: she'd never been here alone before.

She clutched her arms around her, and suddenly her vague wandering became an angry pacing. She couldn't believe it. He'd actually left her. She was the one who'd been turning a blind eye to his treaty violations, yet he was the one who dropped the bomb that ended the truce. It was like the preemptive lawsuit, where a lawyer who knows his client is about to be sued files his own lawsuit first, transforming himself into the aggrieved party by a simple stroke of timing. That was the same thing Whit was doing. Before she could act to end the marriage, he walked out of it.

What a stupid cliché that was—*walked out*. Unfair, too. A man always walked out on his marriage, while a woman always ran away. It was as if the man was leaving for political reasons, taking a stand on principle, or, like a labor action, striking for something better. While a woman ran away like a coward or a confused adolescent.

But then another cliché came to mind, and it was the more common one for a woman ending her marriage. *She threw him out.* What did it usually mean? That the wife ordered, "Leave this house"? Or that she screamed one final irrevocable insult?

Did he walk out, or did she throw him out?

The steam went out of her furious pacing, and she flopped down on the sofa in the family room. A pile of loose photos lay on the coffee table in front of her, the ones that were torn from the albums during Saturday night's burglary. She leaned over the table and shuffled through them, and the sight of her children's smiling faces suddenly made her ache with loneliness for them.

She picked up the phone, and at the sound of Katrina's voice she sank with pleasure into the sofa cushions.

"Hello, sweetheart!"

"Mommy—" Trina was hot with indignation. "Kirstie came right into the bathroom tonight and took a picture of me. And I was in the bathtub. *Naked*."

Dana held back a laugh. "Well, that was very unkind of her. She shouldn't have done that."

"She says she's going to show it to everybody at school!"

"Don't you worry, I would never let her do that. Tell her I want to talk to her."

She listened to their conversation, Trina gleefully announcing that Kirstie was in big trouble, Kirstie hissing that she was a tattletale. Dana smiled and tried to prepare a stern lecture.

But in the span of time it took for Kirstie's sullen voice to come over the line, all thoughts drained from her mind but one: Kirstie was taking pictures.

"Kirstie!" she almost shouted. "Do you have your camera there?"

She answered slowly, puzzled. "Yeah . . ."

"How? Did you take it out of my purse on Saturday?"

"Well, yeah. I didn't think you needed it anymore."

Dana closed her eyes with relief. The camera wasn't stolen by the pickpocket; Kirstie reclaimed it while she was upstairs packing their things.

"Listen carefully. How many pictures have you taken?"

"Six or seven."

There could have been that many left on the end of the roll. The only danger was that Kirstie accidentally rewound the film and double-exposed it. But at most that would only ruin a couple shots out of a roll of twenty-four. This was still salvageable.

"Honey, I need the camera back. I can't explain right now, but I'm going to send a messenger down tomorrow to pick it up. Leave the film inside, don't touch it no matter what. Tell Aunt Karin I'll have the courier there first thing in the morning. And whatever you do, don't take any more pictures."

"But what will I—"

"Buy some disposable cameras."

"All right."

Dana called the second-shift supervisor of the firm's messenger operations and arranged for a driver to go to Avalon first thing in the morning, then hung up, elated. The film she'd risked her neck to shoot wasn't lost after all. Tomorrow it would be on her desk. And with a little bit of luck it would supply some of the missing evidence of causation; with a lot of luck it might even absolve her client.

She lay in bed that night, wide-eyed in the dark with her mind racing through the day's events and the ones that would follow tomorrow, when unexpectedly Don Skelly's words about Andy Broder echoed in her mind: *You two woulda set off sparks*. But even more unexpectedly, another fainter echo came after it: *You two sure set off sparks today*.

A classmate spoke those words to her almost twenty years ago, after an English lit class on the poem, "To His Coy Mistress." Mr. Endicott had maintained that the poet wanted his beloved to give up her pretense at virtue only so that they wouldn't lose precious time together, and he quoted: "Had we but world enough, and time/This coyness, lady, were no crime." But Dana argued that the woman's virtue was no pretense, and that the poet was merely looking for instant gratification; she quoted back at him: "Your quaint honor turn to dust/And into ashes all my lust."

By that time she and Whit had already found their own gratification, and the only pretense was that they were nothing more than instructor and student. They were keeping their relationship a secret, as much to prolong the thrill as to avoid a scandal, and one of the thrills was debates like that one, full of hidden meanings meant only for each other. Later they took it further and developed a private language of covert gestures and signals. Complex and subtle—a lift of an eyebrow, a flick of a finger against the chin—but they spoke it effortlessly, carrying on entire conversations while the class droned on, oblivious.

Ironic. Bitterly so when she considered that now they couldn't even communicate in words.

No, don't think about Whit. She remembered her incantation, and crushed her face into the pillow to sleep.

13

The next morning Dana was back at the auto glass shop, waiting in another endless line to pay the bill and pick up her car. When she finally reached the front of the line, the service manager couldn't find the work order in his bin of papers and told her to wait.

A dozen men and women sat on vinyl upholstery watching TV in the acrylic-walled waiting room, but she remained on her feet on the shop floor. She was due at Alpine Valley at ten o'clock; Travis and half a dozen of the experts were meeting her there to inspect the ashes of the wreckage. She powered up her flip phone and was about to dial the office when the phone rang in her hand.

"Dana, thank God, I was afraid I wouldn't be able to reach you."

Brad Martin's voice came over the airwaves, edgy and intense; a non-English speaker would think nuclear war was threatened and Brad had his finger on the reciprocal button.

"I don't know how this could have happened," he said desperately. "I mean, it's totally against regulations—"

"Brad, what are you talking about?"

"You haven't seen it? Turn on Channel 6 news. They're running it again right now."

She looked over her shoulder at the TV in the waiting room. A familiar face was on the screen, and his mouth was moving soundlessly in front of a giant bouquet of microphones.

111

She burst through the door as Ira Thompson's voice filled the room. "And this tape removes all doubt about the cause of this terrible tragedy," he was saying. "This was no act of God. This was an act of extreme recklessness and callous disregard for human safety. It was no better than a gang of drunken teenagers going for a joyride in a stolen car." He paused for effect as if he were before a jury instead of a gaggle of reporters. "It was that reprehensible."

Dana clutched the phone to her ear and kept her eyes on the screen. "What—?"

"The cockpit voice recording," Brad said. "Somehow he got a copy of the tape, he wasn't supposed to—"

"Sssh," she said as Thompson began to speak again.

"Here we had three grown men, flying in a multimillion-dollar helicopter, but it might as well've been a 1957 Chevy for the kinds of games they were playing. It's all there on the tape, and I want to tell you that in twenty years of practice I never heard a more damning piece of evidence."

"My God, what is it?" she whispered.

"Listen—he's going to play it now."

Ira Thompson stepped back from the microphones and stood beside a woman who was hugging her elbows and fighting not to cry. Static crackled through the speakers, followed by the hearty boom of Vic Sullivan's voice.

"Hey, I see where we are. Coming up on that amusement park, I can see the roller coaster, whaddya call it, Alpine Valley." There was a pause, and more static where Dana's voice should have been, before Vic declared: "Whaddya know. Hey, Ron, set this baby down. Let's go cruise for a couple of blondes."

Dana stood stunned in the middle of the waiting room. "No," she said. "No, he's got it all wrong."

Thompson again bowed his head toward the microphones. "Twelve people dead. Dozens injured. At least four catastrophically. All because the president of Pennsteel wanted to go cruising for girls at an amusement park like some kind of delinquent teenager."

"That's not what happened!" Dana shouted.

The people in the waiting room began to notice her, then shifted in their seats trying not to.

"The pilots were as much to blame as Sullivan," Thompson said. "They should have ignored him, but they were as irresponsible as he was. They dropped the JetRanger down exactly like Sullivan told them, losing altitude so precipitously that the Skyhawk never saw them coming until they crashed down on top of it."

Thompson introduced the trembling woman beside him as Andrea Greenberg, and as he was beginning a description of David Greenberg's injuries, Dana ran out of the waiting room.

"Brad, are you still there?" she called into the phone.

"I'm here."

She spotted the man behind the service desk and shouted to him, "I need my car *now*."

"Excuse me?" Brad said.

"Call the NTSB— No, call Ted Keller and tell him to call the NTSB. I want a meeting with Harry Reilly, and I'm on my way to Parsippany right now."

"Parsippany, New Jersey," he clarified.

"And get a message to Travis that he'll have to handle the site inspection by himself."

She ran to the white Taurus she'd just returned to the loaner pool and jumped behind the wheel.

"No, we got your car coming," hollered the service manager.

"Not soon enough," she said, and gunned it out of the garage.

It took her two hours through rush hour traffic to arrive at the regional office in northern New Jersey, but Ted Keller was already there and waiting, having taken the shortcut five thousand feet up.

"It's a pack of lies," he fumed. "Ron never would've done that, and besides, where was he gonna land if he did? On top of the merry-go-round?"

She ignored his rant to ask the more urgent question. "Ted, what happened to my side of the conversation? Why wasn't it on the recording?"

Keller rubbed a hand over his jaw and grimaced. "There might've been a short in the wiring there."

"What?" she asked, bracing herself.

"Sounds to me like the CVR was only recording outgoing transmissions on that channel. Not incoming."

She hadn't braced herself enough, and she rocked back on her feet at the implications of this news.

"We got trouble here, too," he went on. "They say they can't talk to you unless they bring up their general counsel from Washington."

"Somehow I don't think they want to do that," she said, and charged ahead to Reilly's office with Keller at her heels.

She was right. Almost at once, Harry Reilly came out and ushered her and Keller into his office. His deputy, Jim Cutler, was already there, leaning against a bookcase with his arms tightly crossed. The shelves behind him looked like the playroom cubbies of a small boy; they were lined with model airplanes, trains, buses, and tractor-trailers.

Reilly settled his bulk behind his desk. "First off," he said, "I want you to know that we've launched a full investigation into how Thompson got ahold of the CVR tape."

"I think we all know how," Dana bit out. Ted took an inconspicuous chair in the corner, but she stayed on her feet. "The question is who and why. Or should I say how much?"

Cutler bristled. "If you're trying to suggest that one of our people—"

"I'm not suggesting, I'm accusing. And if Pennsteel doesn't get immediate reparation, I intend to broadcast that accusation, not only to your general counsel's office, but also to the FBI. In fact, maybe I'll hold a press conference of my own."

"Hold on now." Reilly held up a meaty hand. "You'll get your reparation. Jim?"

Cutler handed her a manila envelope. Inside she felt the hard rectangle of an audiocassette.

"There," Reilly said. "Now you got what Thompson's got. No harm, no foul."

But Dana shook her head. "There is harm, maybe irreparable

harm, and it's pretty damn foul that you're allowing this to happen."

"What harm?" Cutler complained, returning to his slouch against the bookcase.

"Ira Thompson got the jump on us, he got to call a press conference and put his spin on the tape before we even had a chance to hear it. He's poisoned public opinion against us."

Reilly spread his hands out. "Sullivan said what he said. The tape is what it is, no matter who got it first."

"No, that's where you're wrong, Harry. That's where Ira's wrong, too. Sullivan didn't say what you think he said. His words were taken out of context."

"What context?" Cutler scoffed.

"The context of a conversation he was having with me. I was talking to Vic from my car phone only seconds before the crash."

Cutler straightened and glanced at his boss.

"You know that pause after Vic says, 'What do you call it, Alpine Valley?' For thirty seconds you only hear static?"

Reilly squinted at her and nodded.

"I said, 'Give a wave to the ground, Vic. My kids are there today.'"

Slowly he said, "Your kids are—"

"Blondes? Yes, they are."

He fell back against his chair, and the springs squawked in protest. "Well, why the hell didn't you tell us about this sooner?"

"Ted faxed you a list of twelve people we think you should interview. If you ever bother to glance at it, you'll see that my name's first."

Reilly sent a look to Keller, who nodded, then to Cutler, who managed to avoid eye contact.

"So," Dana said, "that covers harm and foul."

"If what you say is true," Reilly said finally, "I guess I'd have to agree. But—" He roused himself and leaned forward in his chair. "—you'd have to be prepared to prove it."

That was something she'd been thinking about, too. If her side of the conversation wasn't recorded, there was nothing to prove it except her own testimony, and the rules of professional conduct precluded her from serving both as a witness for Pennsteel and as its trial counsel. Unless she found independent corroborating evidence, the price of that proof would have to be her own withdrawal from the case.

"I'm prepared," she said. "So do we talk about reparation? Or do I call my friends at Justice?"

Reilly held both palms up, helpless. "I don't know what else we could do to—"

"I'll tell you what else," she cut in. "The radar data. The FAA is sitting on our FOIA request, but I bet they don't keep you waiting long."

Cutler started to shake his head at his boss, which told Dana exactly what she'd been hoping: that there *was* radar data.

"I'd have to give it to Thompson at the same time," Reilly warned, ignoring Cutler's signals.

"I wouldn't expect otherwise," she said archly.

"That's it, then?"

"Not quite." She shot a look at Keller, but he didn't know where she was going with this and gave back only a blank face. "Give us an audience," she said. "Not just the right to make a written submission that you'll put in a circular file somewhere, but a real chance to show you how this accident happened."

Now Keller reacted, with an expression that said *How the hell are we going to do that?*

Reilly massaged his jaw awhile before he nodded. "All right. But no closed-door sessions. I won't have people saying you folks ran our investigation for us. You tell us what you think happened, you tell the rest of the world at the same time. Fair enough?"

"Fair enough."

14

Whit woke for the second consecutive morning with Brandi twined around him like a python. He lay very still—sometimes she tightened her death hold if she sensed her prey was escaping—and listened for what it was that woke him.

Not Brandi herself. She slept the sleep of the innocent, this strange womanchild with the drawer full of condoms. Since Monday night they hadn't left the apartment or each other. He'd slept more than was healthy, had as much sex as he could manage, and listened long hours to Brandi on Brandi. After twenty years he couldn't write a book on Wallace Stegner, but after two days he could write a book on Brandi.

Her mother ran off with another man when Brandi was twelve, leaving behind a bitter, withdrawn husband and a confused pubescent daughter. "I tried to take Mom's place, I did the cooking and the cleaning and the shopping. I kept myself pretty and cheerful for him, you know? But Daddy just couldn't get over his sadness. There was nothing I could do to make him happy."

Chapter Two of the Book on Brandi: into the story skulks the mysterious Professor Endicott—so much like Daddy in his core of sadness. But—the twist in the plot—Brandi learns that it's possible to coax a smile out of Professor Endicott! He responds to sexual overtures! At last—she's found a daddy she can make happy, because this one she can fuck.

Whit shifted on the mattress, and predictably Brandi's thighs tightened around him. His desperation was growing—he had to get out of here. Nothing that happened during the nights was worth the way he felt in the mornings when he rolled over to face this giggling girl acting out some fantasy he didn't want to share.

The problem was coming up with a decent way to extricate himself. A man of his age and experience couldn't leave a twenty-two-year-old girl after two nights' cohabitation without having a damn good excuse. Especially not when the girl knew his name and address.

There it was again, the noise that woke him, a belligerent bawl from one flight down. Brandi's eyes fluttered open as she heard it, too. It sounded like a furious bull calf separated from its mother, and when it came again, it spoke a word: "Brandi!"

"Oh!" She gave a little cry of annoyance and bounced out of bed to run naked to the window. "Go away, Sean!" she shouted, then lifted the sash and leaned bare-chested out of the window to shout it again. "I told you, I don't want to see your face!"

Whit stepped into his pants and looked over her shoulder. In the alley below, a boy stood bellowing, "I only wanna *talk* to you! Why can't you come down and talk?"

He was the same fit young fellow Brandi had spurned at the Last Call Saturday night. "For God's sake, put some clothes on," Whit said, and pulled her back out of view.

She pulled on shorts and a T-shirt, but continued to crane her neck for a glimpse of the boy on the ground. Whit hurried into his own clothes, too. The last thing he needed was for the boy to catch him here in flagrante, and bound up the stairs with murder on his mind.

"What's this all about?" he asked. "Who is he?"

"He's nobody," Brandi sniffed. "He has no business being here. I told him last week it was over."

Whit gazed at her, and suddenly it was as if an exit sign lit up over her head. "Did you tell him why?"

She whirled away from the window and sat down with a pout. "He knows why."

Whit squatted by her chair. "You give men too much credit,

Brandi. We're a lot denser than you women when it comes to affairs of the heart."

She watched his mouth as he spoke, lapping up his words like a kitten at a bowl of cream.

"I saw him at the Last Call the other night," he went on. "And I said to myself, 'I wonder if she realizes the power she wields over that young man.' "

"Huh?"

"The look on his face when you turned away from him." Whit placed a melodramatic hand on his chest. "It was like his heart shattered into a thousand pieces."

She cocked her head. "Really?"

"And I thought to myself, 'Amazing how a girl so lovely could be so cruel.' "

"Cruel?" she whispered, but then shook the idea out of her head. "You don't know how cruel he's been to me! He said he had to work Friday night, but then my friend Suse? She saw him down at the Riverdeck Café, and she told me—"

Whit held up both hands. "Wait. Am I the one who needs to hear this, or—" He pointed a finger at the window. "—is he?"

She got to her feet and cast a pensive look out the window. "I guess it wouldn't hurt just to talk," she said slowly.

"He deserves that much, don't you think? After all you've meant to each other?"

"Maybe you're right," she sighed. "It's been almost a month already that we been going out."

Whit struggled to keep a straight face. "See there?" he said, point proven.

"All right, I'll talk to him."

The bawling stopped as Brandi cleared the door and descended the stairs with her chin in the air. Whit stepped behind the curtain to watch. Words were exchanged, and the boy opened the passenger door of his car. She hesitated, he implored her, and at last she shrugged and slid into the seat. He dove behind the wheel and they disappeared without a backward glance.

Whit scavenged for a piece of paper and settled for the back of an envelope, where he penned a note full of gratitude and regret and all best wishes for her and Sean. He pulled on his sport coat, gathered up his keys and wallet, and finally, feeling nothing but enormous relief, let himself out.

He pointed his car for home without a clue of what he would do when he got there, and with no more sense of free will than a boomerang on its return trip.

It was close to noon, and the sun baked hot and dusty on the roadway. He drove with the windows down—the pickup didn't have air-conditioning, and it would have been broken if it did— and he could hear the engine the second it began to sputter. He glanced at the gas gauge—below empty, he must have been running on fumes. The engine coughed twice and gave a prolonged wheeze.

A mile from home and out of gas. There was a metaphor in there someplace.

A gas station appeared ahead behind a barrier garden of exuberant annuals, and Whit coaxed the truck to keep rolling long enough to reach the self-service pumps. He switched the key off in the ignition and got out and fitted the hose into the tank.

"Morning," a hearty voice said.

A man with an oversized head of curly brown hair was climbing out of a black car at the next pump. Whit gave him a nod.

"Hot one today."

"Yeah."

While the pump whined and the meter whizzed, Whit leaned against the truck and thought of what he would say to Dana whenever she got home tonight. He couldn't believe that they'd split over something as idiotic as a burglar alarm. He never bothered to put the seat down on the toilet, either, but that failing never amounted to grounds for divorce. The only difference was her crazy idea that he'd deactivated the alarm to cover up his tomcatting. It was funny to think of Dana being jealous enough to imagine he'd cheat on her.

But not so funny when he realized that now he had.

It hit him like a punch in the stomach, so hard he had to catch himself against the burning sheet metal of the fender. The pump shut off and a beeping sounded, and Whit stood oblivious to it in a wave of sudden nausea. Jesus Christ, what had he done? Dana might have gone too far Monday night, but words could be retracted and apologized for. How the hell could he undo this?

"You need to go inside," the curly-haired man said.

"What?" he said, whirling.

"You have to go in and pay for your gas. It won't stop beeping till you do."

"Oh. Yeah."

Whit hung up the hose and went into the office.

"What number?" growled the old man behind the register.

Whit stared at him like he was speaking in tongues. "Sorry?"

"The pump. What number pump?"

"Oh." Whit turned to point it out as a young black man burst into the office behind him.

"Hey, somebody just drove off in your truck!" he shouted.

Whit gaped at him, then bolted outside as the tailgate of his pickup was disappearing around the end of the block.

The curly-haired man jumped into his car. "Call the cops!" he yelled to the black man. "I'll try to keep up with him!" He shot a look at Whit. "You wanna come?"

"Yes!"

Whit scrambled into the passenger seat of the black car as the driver peeled out of the station and roared down the street.

"Son of a bitch," the curly-haired man said. "He came out of nowhere. Hopped in your truck and took off. Guess you left your keys in the ignition, huh?" Whit nodded, chagrined. "Well, hell, who doesn't?"

"But it's a wreck," Whit said. "It's close to twenty years old."

"Parts. I tell you, what this country's coming to."

They whipped around the corner at the end of the block. The truck reappeared at a distant point ahead.

"There he is!" Whit yelled.

"I see him." The man gunned the engine to catch up. "Tell you what. Let's just keep him in our sights until the cops show up."

Whit nodded. Smart plan.

"My name's Ike," he said, and reached out a hand.

Whit clasped it warmly. "Whit Endicott."

Ike hung back a respectful distance from the pickup as it led them farther and farther from the highway, out of the suburbs and into the rural back roads of Montgomery County. He trailed it like a pro, never missing a turn, never getting too close or dropping too far back.

"I really appreciate this," Whit said. "Sticking your neck out this way."

"Hey," Ike said with a shrug. "Somebody's gotta take a stand sometime."

They followed the truck around a bend to the left and down another lonely road. Ike's eyes flickered toward the rearview mirror, and Whit heard the sound of a car approaching from behind. The police, he realized in satisfied relief.

The thief must have heard it, too, for the truck slowed and pulled over to the shoulder of the road. It looked like a complete surrender. Ike came to a stop behind the truck, and, elated, Whit twisted to look back. The unmarked car was stopping behind them, and he waited for the police to emerge with guns at the ready.

But the man who climbed out of the car behind was the same black man who'd stayed behind at the gas station to call the police.

Whit turned to Ike, confused, then suspicious and on the verge of outrage.

"Slight detour," Ike said as a shadow fell.

A dull crunching pain radiated out from the base of Whit's skull. Ike faded in and out of focus, and the punch Whit threw glanced off the side of his jaw. The car started to spin and he lunged forward and grabbed for Ike's head with both hands. Lights flickered and dimmed, and Ike's head came off in his hands.

The last thing he saw as darkness swallowed him was a halo of bright white hair.

15

The courier delivery was waiting on her desk when Dana reached the office that afternoon, and she grabbed the package and tore it open. Inside, carefully swathed in bubble wrap, lay Kirstie's camera. Dana rewound the film and opened the back to extract the roll. At last, there it was in her hand. She started to buzz Celeste, but thought better of it. This she had better do herself.

A sweltering two-block walk and she had the film safely in the hands of her favorite processing shop, with delivery promised before the close of business that day.

When she was back at her desk that afternoon, Travis knocked hesitantly on the door. *Poor kid*, Dana thought, waving him in. He was afraid he was still in disgrace over the bill. She wished she could tell him to forget about it, but the truth was she didn't want him to forget. He was going to have to find some other way to redeem himself.

"How'd it go at the site this morning?" she asked him.

He sat down and gave the expected report. The few scattered bits of wreckage that survived the second explosion had already been bagged up and carted off by the NTSB investigators, and there was little else to do there. The metallurgist took a few samples of metal ash back to his lab, and the visibility expert shot some site elevations to use in his eyewitness perspective studies, and that was about it.

When he was done, Dana told him about Ira Thompson's

spin on the cockpit voice recording and her devil's pact with Harry Reilly, and predictably, Travis's face went red with outrage. It grew more thoughtful, however, as she described her ethical dilemma.

"Let me get this straight," he said. "You don't have to withdraw unless your testimony's necessary for Pennsteel's defense, right? And your testimony wouldn't be necessary if your side of the conversation was tape-recorded, right?"

"Right. But it wasn't."

He scratched his neck. "I did a little bit of reading on CVRs last night. They record the radio transmissions off the headset mikes, but they also record ambient noise off a cockpit-area mike mounted in the ceiling. The CAM picks up the engine noise and anything else that's audible inside the cockpit."

Dana looked up sharply.

"At some level, your voice was audible in that cockpit. Right? I mean, Vic Sullivan could hear you."

"Yeah, but—"

"I worked on this case a couple years ago—our guy taped the other guy making an admission, but then he forgot and recorded two hours of music on top of it. We hired a sound engineer, and he did his magic, and we ended up with a restored recording of the conversation, clear as a bell."

She stared at him. "You're saying a sound engineer might be able to find my voice on the cockpit recording?"

He shrugged.

"Travis! That's a great idea!"

His face lit with shy pleasure as she pulled the cassette from her briefcase and handed it to him.

"Can you get him started right away?"

"Do my best."

"Like always," she said with a smile that made him duck his head with embarrassment as he left.

Later that afternoon a strong aroma of aftershave wafted into her office, and Dana looked up to find Clifford Austin in the doorway.

"A moment?" he said, eyebrows rising up into his high-domed forehead.

"Sure, come in."

He sat down and crossed his legs and the knife-edge crease in his pants leg didn't even bend. He was a formal man with a haughty bearing who never once appeared in shirtsleeves in the office, not even behind his own desk at ten P.M. He didn't drop by merely to chat; she knew he had a mission.

"The Palazzo bill?" she guessed.

"Yes."

She started to formulate a defense of the one-third reduction she'd made, but he surprised her by ignoring it.

"That's a large receivable to have outstanding at the same time that we're starting to run up substantial fees in the Alpine Valley case."

"Charlie's always been a reliable thirty-day payer."

Austin pulled his lips into a thin line. "Pennsteel's always been," he said. "Charlie Morrison's never been reliable about anything. Except maybe destroying evidence."

Dana flushed hot. "That's a lie, and you know it. If there were any truth to it, Charlie would have been disbarred years ago."

"Anyone who's litigated as much as you knows that what's true and what's provable aren't always the same thing."

She came out of her chair. *"Cliff—"*

An uncertain knock sounded, and she and Austin both swiveled their heads to the door.

"Sorry," Travis said, beet-faced and already backing up. "I didn't know—"

"What is it?" she snapped.

"I finally got through to that Broder guy."

She went blank. "Who? Oh, Broder—right. Where is he?"

"He's still here. And he's planning to stick around awhile. Oh—and he says he doesn't want your money. In fact . . ." Travis gave a futile tug on his collar. "He sorta had a suggestion for where you could put it."

She stared, then let out a short, astonished laugh as he hurried away.

"Let's get back to business, shall we?" Austin said, as if it were only business Travis interrupted. "In thirty days at the present rate, what do you estimate the Alpine Valley fees will be?"

She sat back down, still furious, but did the calculations. She had seven people working at an average billing rate of about one fifty an hour. "Two hundred thousand," she said finally. "Not including my time."

"And not including our out-of-pocket costs, either."

"So how big a fee deposit do you want?"

But again Austin surprised her. "Instead of a deposit, let's push for immediate payment of the final Palazzo bill."

"What's the difference?"

"Dana, you disappoint me." He pressed his hands to his knees and levered himself to his feet. "A deposit leaves us open to fee disputes. Whereas final payment should conclude the Palazzo matter, once and for all."

She stared after him as he made his way to the door. She'd rendered a good, honest bill in Palazzo, she'd jeopardized her relationship with Travis to do so, and she didn't need to trap the client into paying it.

"Cliff, I want to add an agenda item for the next partners' meeting."

"We've all heard your view on billing, Dana," Austin said wearily. "Half of us can recite it in our sleep."

"No, not value-pricing. Associate billable hours. We need a complete overhaul of the system. Reduce the annual minimum requirement. Eliminate all credit for any hours in excess of say, twenty-two hundred. Put some balance back into these kids' lives."

He shook his head with an expression meant to pass for exasperated fondness. "You know the old adage: if it ain't broke, don't fix it."

"But Cliff, it is broke."

"Our profit figures say otherwise." He cut her off before she could launch her next argument. "You know, Dana, someday you'll realize what an ideal partnership this is for you. You may attract the clients, you may win their cases, but if the running of this firm were left to you, we'd never be able to make a payroll. This is a business. Your talent spares you from having to run it yourself, but please don't impede our efforts to run it for you."

The aroma of his aftershave still lingered in the air as Dana's phone rang. "Mr. Morrison," Celeste announced on the intercom.

"Charlie," Dana said, snatching up the phone. "You just missed your old friend Cliff Austin."

"Oh? How is the Stiff One? Rigor mortis complete yet?"

"Close enough."

"How's the investigation going? Got any bad news you can't spare me?"

"Afraid I do."

He listened without comment as she described Ira Thompson's press conference and her meeting with Harry Reilly.

"Well," he said, striving hard to be upbeat when she was through, "you got us the radar data, and you got us the right to make a presentation to the NTSB. If they give points for the side with the better lawyer, we're bound to win."

She smiled at his near-miss at optimism. "But there's the rub, Charlie. I can't be your lawyer if I have to testify about my conversation with Vic."

He sucked in his breath with a slow hiss. "Code of Ethics, huh?"

"Afraid so."

He barely hesitated. "Then you won't testify."

"And then we forfeit our presentation to the NTSB."

A long, heavy silence followed.

"Charlie?"

"Yeah, I'm here. It just never gets any better, does it?"

Her sentiments exactly, but instead she said, "Stop trying to take over my job."

"Huh?"

"Worrying. That's what you're paying me to do, remember?"

"Right."

"Besides, there may be a way out of this. Travis is lining up a sound engineer to try and pick up my voice on the cockpit recording. If it's there, I don't have to testify to anything."

Charlie let out a laugh. "Why didn't you say that in the first place, before you got me all depressed?"

"Because you need to be thinking about substitute counsel if it doesn't work out."

"Nope. I'm not thinking about anything. That's what I pay you for. Speaking of which . . ." A rustle of papers sounded from his end of the line. "I had a message from Dan Casella yesterday. Or maybe the day before."

Dan Casella was the star litigator at Foster, Bell & McNeill; he and Dana had crossed swords a few times over the years. "Casella? What's he calling you for?"

"I don't know, something about the crash. Return the call for me, would you?"

"Sure."

She hung up with one more thing to worry about. These days she and Dan Casella were crossing paths more than swords, ever since he married one of the associates in her firm, but she reminded herself now: he was first and foremost an adversary.

Of which she had far too many. She found herself gazing at Whit's face in the family portrait on the credenza, and abruptly wheeled away from it.

Late in the day a package arrived from Harry Reilly's office, a three-inch-thick ream of radar data, which she immediately forwarded to John Diefenbach, and soon after, Travis came by to report that the sound engineer was onboard and already at work on the CVR tape.

"Good. Thanks," Dana said, and bent back to her work.

Travis shuffled his feet at the door.

"Anything else?"

"I couldn't help overhearing." He cleared his throat. "When you and Cliff were hollering at each other . . . ?"

Her head came up with a guilty start.

"I was wondering, what did he mean—about Charlie Morrison?"

Dana deliberated, then said, "Close the door." He leaned back against it like a barricade. "You know Charlie used to be an associate here."

"Yeah. I always wondered why he left."

"He had to handle a document production on one of Austin's cases. It took him three weeks to comb through all of our client's files, and he ended up delivering close to three thousand pages of documents. But thirty minutes later opposing counsel was on the phone to Austin complaining that he didn't get the one document he was looking for. It was some kind of hand-written complaint log—the original, of course, and no copies made. Our client swore they'd turned it over to Charlie, and Charlie swore he'd never seen it. Austin chose to believe the client, and that was basically the end of Charlie's career here."

Travis was white-lipped by the time she finished. "It doesn't take much, does it?" he said faintly. "I mean, one day you're on the top of the world, and the next—" He broke off and stared at the floor.

She cocked her head. "Travis . . . ? Is anything wrong?" Her phone rang, but she left it for Celeste to pick up.

"With me? Nope."

"If it's the Palazzo bill, it's forgotten."

"It's nothing."

It rang again, and again Celeste didn't answer.

"Gotta get back to work," Travis said.

She watched him go, bemused, but when the phone rang for the fourth time, she realized it was after five and Celeste was gone for the day. "Hello?" she blurted, picking up before the voice mail did.

"Dana? Is it live or is it Memorex?"

"Angela!"

"Hey, I know your schedule's a bitch, but give a girl a break, wouldja? I gotta talk to you."

"I'm sorry—"

"Make it up to me. Meet me at Morgan's in twenty minutes."

"Oh, Angela, I don't think—"

"You can't miss me. I'll be the only one in the place who isn't Frenching a Dictaphone. See ya!"

Angela Leoni was a different breed of woman lawyer—loud-talking, flashy-dressing, hardball-playing, educated in second-rate schools and the streets of life. She practiced with a man named Frank Doyle—or at least she did until he went to the federal penitentiary a few years before. With the help of a heroin-addicted doctor who would sign anything for a hundred bucks, he'd run an insurance scam that netted him two million dollars. That was all gone now, as was his law license. But while he served his time, Angela not only kept his practice alive, she made it flourish. He was back now, pretending to be her paralegal while she threw him half the profits. She'd been sleeping with him for fifteen years and was the best friend his wife and children ever had.

Dana gave a wistful smile as she put the phone down. There was nothing she'd like better than a drink with Angela, but there were few enough hours in her day and no room at all for happy ones.

A squeaking wheel announced the interoffice mail cart in the corridor, and the floor messenger came in with several packages, including a hand delivery from Joplin Photos.

Dana opened the envelope with a gleeful cry. Six photographs slid out: five shots of empty blue-green water, and one shadowy picture of Katrina's outraged face. Puzzled, she turned the envelope upside down and shook it out, but that was all there was.

Clipped to the envelope was a note from Jack Joplin: "Ms. Svenssen: The rest of the film was unexposed. Did you realize that? Also, you should have used a flash for the indoor shot. If you want me to try lightening it up some, let me know."

Dana held the negative strips up to the ceiling light. He was right. All but six showed no exposure at all. Which meant that Kirstie must have loaded a fresh roll into her camera.

So where was the exposed roll?

She reached for the phone and dialed Fulmer's Guest Cottages, but Karin's line rang twelve times before the switchboard cut in. "No answer on that line, ma'am."

"Could you see that they get a message to call me as soon as they get in? It's urgent."

"Okay, but they just left for the boardwalk in Ocean City. I wouldn't expect 'em back before nine or ten."

Dana left a message for them to call her tonight, no matter how late.

She hung up and looked at her watch. It was only five-thirty; a long anxious evening stretched before her.

A quick sharp sigh and she grabbed her bag and left.

16

It was once true that the only proper building for a Philadelphia law firm to house itself in was one whose ground floor was entirely occupied by a bank, perhaps with a shoeshine and a newsstand wedged into a corner. But all that changed with the new construction in the Eighties. Lobby-level boutiques and bistros now came as standard equipment on every office building. Though they often proved to be loss leaders for the landlords, they were a real boon to the law firm tenants. Young lawyers were encouraged to patronize the on-site restaurants at lunchtime, and even to drop in for happy hour, so long as they returned to their desks before the third drink. The closer a firm could keep its lawyers to their time sheets, the better. It was the same thinking that led Jackson, Rieders to install an on-site gym: keep 'em fit, keep 'em happy, keep 'em *here*.

Morgan's was an undistinguished restaurant that served eight-dollar burgers for lunch and overcooked pasta for dinner, but it was a mecca for the happy-hour crowd. Dana was caught in a full-body press before she cleared the doorway. A throng of young men and women stretched from the entrance down four granite steps to the sunken floor and across the vast room. But for the bar and the tailored suits, it could have been the trading floor of the New York Stock Exchange.

Angela was standing on a chair at one of the few tables in the room, flapping her arms to hail Dana while a few nearby men delivered leering appraisals of her eye-level bosom. She was short and curvaceous, with a generous mouth and abundant black hair worn big, and she wore a Madonna-style bustier under a suit one size too tight. Resembling a Catholic schoolgirl from Our Lady of Stiletto, she was walking proof that you couldn't take South Philly out of the girl.

She jumped to the floor and met Dana with a hug that would have been better executed if she'd stayed on the chair; even in four-inch heels she barely grazed Dana's chin. "I already ordered. Ya still drink those wussy spritzers, right?"

"Great, thanks," Dana said, taking her seat. "How have you been? You look terrific."

Angela sat down and crossed her legs with an attitude. "Yeah, well, we can't all be tall, cool blondes, so we work with what we got. So how ya doin'? How's Whit and the cuties?"

There were times when Angela's run-on questions were a blessing. "Terrific. They're at the shore this week with my sister and her kids. So—have you seen Mirella lately?"

Mirella Burke was also a lawyer and a friend to both. The three of them met in a bar review course for new lawyers fifteen years before and formed the kind of fast and unlikely friendship that combat troops find in the trenches.

Angela shook her head, disgusted. "Cripe, she's almost as hard to get to as you. She's running some big drug investigation, and if she's not in the grand jury, she's on the road with the Feebies." Her expression changed as something caught her attention across the room. "Oh, look, there's Dan Casella. I don't see much of him anymore. Not that I ever saw as much as I woulda liked to. What a waste, huh? Him gettin' married."

"Oh." Dana twisted in her seat and located Casella at the bar. "I'm supposed to call him. Forgive me, Angela, I won't be two minutes."

"Sure," Angela hollered after her. "Dump me for the first hunk ya see."

Casella turned from the bar with a drink in his hand, and over the heads of a dozen people Dana called, "Got a minute, Dan?"

He spotted her and smoothly altered course through the crowd. When he was a young lawyer coming up in the bar, people used to call him a diamond in the rough, but now, at forty and the top of his form, his facets were pretty well polished. Impeccably groomed and conservatively dressed in navy-blue pinstripes and a rep tie, he was the walking exception to Angela's rule; there was no South Philly left in this boy at all.

"Evening, Dana. How've you been?"

"I meant to call you."

He gave her a practiced smile. "That's what the ladies always tell me."

He'd held little charm for her during his lady-killer days, and not a lot more now that he was a family man. But she took him seriously as a lawyer; there was nobody in town better at unraveling complex commercial crimes.

"No, really," she said. "Charles Morrison asked me to return your call."

"Ah. I thought you might be the one I needed to talk to. Your name's on everybody's lips this week. Can I get you a drink?"

"No, thanks, I have one coming."

A man clutching a briefcase backed into her and muttered an apology over his shoulder. Casella motioned his chin toward an unoccupied spot against the wall, and she followed him there.

"So what's up?" she said lightly. "Don't tell me Pennsteel's involved in a major fraud."

He dropped his voice and spoke in a new, ominous tone. "I sure as hell hope not."

Her back pressed against the wall. "What's that supposed to mean?"

"Last Friday the chairman of the board of Pennsteel said, and I pretty much quote—because we maintain the highest standards of corporate citizenship, because we pride ourselves on being a good neighbor, and because we don't want to see the children of this community miss any more of their summer fun than they have to—Pennsteel will take care of all the cleanup and repairs needed to reopen Alpine Valley as soon as possible. End quote."

She met his eyes and tried to hide her dread. "You represent the amusement park?"

"Yeah, and trust me, they're not amused. You have any idea

how much a week in August is worth in this business? We're talking megabucks in lost profits."

Her mind went spinning over the events of the last few days. Austin was supposed to line up their partner Bill Moran to supervise the cleanup. She'd called Moran once—Monday?—and left a message, but here it was Wednesday and he'd never followed up. But neither had she, and not only was it her case, it was her idea to promise a cleanup.

"Dan, I'm sorry. I meant to get right on it, but there's been a trillion things—"

"And there'll be a trillion more. But I'll tell you something, Dana. For our purposes it doesn't much matter who's at fault in this thing. Pennsteel *promised* a cleanup. We're past tort and into contract. The only question is who's going to move first, Pennsteel or me."

"Pennsteel," she said at once. "Don't file yet. Give us a chance to take care of this."

"Meet me Monday morning at the park with your people. Ten o'clock. We'll see where we go from there."

He left her to join a table of his partners, and she flopped back into her chair at Angela's table. "Sorry."

"Trouble?"

"What else?"

"Men," Angela snorted. "Can't live with 'em, can't litigate without 'em."

A barmaid wove an expert path to their table and set down Dana's wine spritzer and Angela's scotch on the rocks. Dana reached for her wallet, but Angela already had a twenty on the tray.

"My treat."

"No, on the phone you said—"

"False pretenses to lure you here. This is work, not play."

While the barmaid made change, Dana took a sip of her drink and wondered what it could be. Doyle & Leoni handled divorce, DUI, and minor personal injuries. In fifteen years Angela's practice had never intersected with hers.

"Okay, here's the thing," Angela said when the barmaid

departed. "I hear you represent the helicopter that crashed at the amusement park the other day."

Dana sat back with a jolt. This was the last thing she expected. "Pennsteel, right."

"Well, Frankie's kids were there, right at the scene."

Frankie was Frank Doyle, her erstwhile partner and evermore lover.

"Oh, no—were they hurt?"

"Absolutely traumatized. You have no idea."

Dana thought she had some, since her own children were there, too. "I mean physically hurt."

"They've been vomiting, they can't sleep, the psychologist says it's post-traumatic stress syndrome, for sure. They have permanent scars."

Dana couldn't help a short, astonished laugh. "Angela, it's only been five days. They couldn't even have scabs yet."

"Hey, the shrinks can tell this stuff, believe me. The kids had two sessions already. And there's a *long* course of treatment ahead. So—we need to know—what're you gonna do about it?"

"What am *I* going to do about it?" Dana repeated with deliberate denseness.

Angela made an impatient noise with her tongue. "You know—the helicopter."

"Well, I don't know. What's the airplane going to do about it?"

"We hear there's no insurance there."

"Oh, you're looking for *money*."

"Come on, Dana. Don't play cute."

"You come on, Angela. You know you can't recover for emotional injury without physical impact."

Technically this was true, though the Pennsylvania courts had been torturing that rule for about a hundred years. They carved out an exception for a plaintiff who witnessed a family member's accident, then for a plaintiff who didn't see the accident but heard the squeal of brakes, and even for a plaintiff who was traumatized when a circus elephant defecated in her lap; the court figured the defecation itself was enough to satisfy the physical impact requirement. There was no telling how the rule would be stretched and bent in this case where hundreds of children had witnessed such a horrible accident.

Obviously Angela had entertained the same thought. "I think I can dance my way around that one," she said, and tossed back a hefty gulp of her drink.

"But you haven't done the barest investigation. How can you look to Pennsteel for money when you don't have the remotest idea who was at fault? If anybody was."

"Look." Angela leaned forward with her elbows on the table. "We don't wanna have to file suit. And I don't think you want us to, either."

A blind man could read between those lines. They didn't want to file suit because Doyle needed to keep his name out of the papers; too much attention and somebody would notice that he was practicing law without a license. And Pennsteel didn't need a hundred people filing me-too lawsuits after they read about Doyle's in the newspaper.

Dana sagged back in her chair. "Do you have a demand?"

"Do you have an offer?" Angela parried. Nobody ever wanted to start the bidding in these little wars.

"Not without more information, I don't. I don't even know how many kids we're talking about, or how old they are, or where they were, or what they saw."

"I can get all that to you."

"And I'll need a report from the psychologist."

"Done."

Done? What kind of doctor wrote a report on the strength of two sessions within four days of an accident? But Dana knew what kind. The same kind who helped Doyle bank two million dollars in insurance fraud proceeds.

She put her glass down. Suddenly she was having none of it. Suddenly she wanted this to be something more than a game played with funny money.

"On second thought, Angela—you better go ahead and file suit. We'll get our discovery through the rules. You know—keep us all honest."

There was a chilly silence across the table. "You're making a mistake, Dana."

"Well, it won't be my first this week." She got to her feet. "Let's do lunch real soon, okay?"

She turned and pushed her way through the crowd in a straight line for the door. She probably was making a mistake. Doyle might back down, but it was just as likely that he'd go ahead and open the floodgates to a hundred copycats.

And they wouldn't all be frauds. She got on the elevator and slumped against the wall. She didn't doubt that many of the children there that day were traumatized. The ones who saw their friends so horribly burned, the ones who spent thirty terrifying minutes trapped on the roller coaster. And maybe even her own.

17

They finally called late that night, so full of exuberant chatter that their voices climbed all over each other in the fight for pre-eminence. They'd been to the boardwalk in Ocean City, and Katrina won a stuffed panda at the arcade, though it took an hour of squirting a water gun into a tube to do it; by Dana's calculation, the panda ended up costing fifty dollars. They'd both been careful with sunscreen, they swore it, but Trina's shoulders were burnt and Kirstie's nose was peeling. Trina sat in the surf all morning, and when she stood up, her bathing suit bottom was loaded with wet sand. Kirstie was still teasing her unmercifully about it.

"Kirstie," Dana said when they finally paused for breath. "When you took the camera out of my bag Saturday morning, was there a roll of film in it?"

"Sure. Gosh, Mom—you took the pictures yourself, don't you remember?"

"Honey, think hard now. Try to remember where you put that roll of film."

"Duh—I put it in the crisper, of course."

"The what?"

"In the refrigerator. That's where Grandpa Svenssen says you should store film. He's a chemist, Mom—he knows these things."

Dana got to her feet and stretched the phone cord all the way out until she reached the refrigerator. In the crisper drawer

between a head of romaine and a bunch of carrots lay a little orange and black cartridge of film.

She sputtered a laugh. There it was, all along, where no one
would ever think to look. Secure, untouched, and ready to be
developed in the morning. She closed the refrigerator and
sprawled out happily on the family room sofa.

"Where's Daddy?" Trina asked.

"Yeah, put Dad on."

In the space of a second Dana's happy mood evaporated.
"He's working in the library right now," she said, a glib liar
even to her own daughters. "He's been having a really good day
on his writing. He didn't even want to stop for dinner."

"Oh, then don't interrupt him," Kirstie said at once.

"No, we'll talk to him when he can't think of anything to
write," Trina put in.

"Love you both, talk to you soon."

She hung up, ashamed of herself for lying, but even more
ashamed of how ashamed she was of Whit.

The light was flashing on the answering machine, and she
leaned over and pressed the play button.

"Hey, man," spoke an unfamiliar voice in a dialect seldom
heard on Valley Forge Mountain. "Wasn't we s'posed to hook
up at eight tonight? You blowin' me off or what?"

Obviously a wrong number. She reached for the delete button
as the next message came on.

"Hey, Whit," said the same voice again. "Where's the man
who taught me how to be a legend with the ladies?"

Obviously a right number.

She stared at the phone a moment, then surged to her feet.
The darkness beckoned outside, and she opened the French
doors in the living room and stepped out on the terrace. The air
was so heavy with humidity that she felt as if she were wading
as she walked to the edge of the pool. Sweat broke out in a
sheen over her body that made the fabric of her blouse and
panty hose melt into her skin. She went to the pool house
and switched off the lights, then unbuttoned her blouse and
skirt and peeled the nylon off her legs.

The air felt no cooler to her naked skin, but when she slid off the wall and into the pool, the water flowed over her like an arctic breeze. She took a breath and plunged down into the black depths and swam the length of the pool before she surfaced again in a geyser of silvery water. The stars winked overhead and she lay back and floated, weightless at last in the heavy air.

She remembered other summer nights like this. Late nights, after the girls were asleep, when she'd join Whit on the glider and they'd share a bottle of crispy cold chardonnay, then shed their clothes and pour themselves like something liquid into the cool water. Ten feet down they'd find each other's mouths and taste the wine and the chemicals of desire, and they'd pull themselves out and make love on a nest of towels. Sometimes they'd even wake there, arms and legs entwined in the rosy glow of dawn.

She pulled herself out of the pool and stood dripping chlorinated water on the flagstones while she gazed out over the valley. A thousand lights blurred dimly below her, and the dull, distant roar of the turnpike traffic was carried up the hillside like a bundle wrapped in damp gauze and cotton.

It feels like we're on the top of the world, Whit said the day they decided on the lot.

But the top of the world was only a spot on a globe that spun so fast and so far on its axis that she no longer knew which way was up and which way was down. All she knew was that Whit was gone. Two days and heading into the third night, without a word.

She picked up her clothes and went inside and deleted both messages from the answering machine.

As she was finally drifting off to sleep that night, the bedside phone splintered the darkness.

"Listen," the voice said without introduction or preamble. "No attribution on this, okay? But I feel bad about this morning, so I'm giving you a freebie."

Dana sat up on the edge of the bed. It was Harry Reilly from the NTSB, though if he didn't want to announce his name, she wasn't going to do it for him. "All right," she said slowly.

"This is strictly need-to-know. The FBI and the BATF got their own investigation running on this one, and they wanna keep the lid clamped."

FBI? And Alcohol, Tobacco and Firearms? "My God, what is it?" She switched on the bedside lamp and a small pool of light spilled over the nightstand.

"We found something at the site. It must've flown clear, it was a hundred yards from the wreckage and barely scorched. It's got nothing to do with the cause of the crash, but it might be something you'd want to track down."

"Uh-huh." She picked up a pen and held it poised over a notepad.

"A case of MP-5Ks."

Her pen wasn't prepared for that information, nor was her voice. She stammered, "Are—Are you talking about guns?"

"I'm talking about submachine guns."

"What was Loudenberg doing with submachine guns?"

"Hey, nobody said they came from the Skyhawk."

"Come on. You know the president of Pennsteel wasn't involved in illegal arms smuggling."

"I don't know anything."

He hung up, and tight-lipped, she did the same. Nobody ever knew anything. That was what the burden of proof was all about.

18

Whit woke with a dull heavy ache at the back of his skull and a roiling nausea in the pit of his belly, like the worst hangover he ever had. So it was no big surprise to find himself slumped beside a toilet, although as he came woozily awake it did seem weird that the lid was closed and the room was in pitch-blackness.

He pulled himself up and lifted an arm in each direction to find his bearings. His fingers brushed a wall on either side, three feet or less apart. He rotated ninety degrees and repeated the move and found two more walls front and back, the same distance apart. Beginning to doubt the toilet, he groped along the floor, but that was what it was, either that or some new European-design chair.

It had to be a lavatory stall. He must have found his way this far before passing out, and later someone must have turned off the lights without realizing he was there. He didn't remember how he got in, but the important thing now was to get out.

A wave of dizziness crashed over him as he stood up, and as he lurched forward to grab the top of the stall door, his fingers met solid wall. He reached higher, but still it was a solid wall of a smooth plastic surface. He swayed on his feet until the dizziness subsided, then pressed both hands against the wall and walked them up to the ceiling. All four walls curved up seamlessly to form the ceiling.

There was no stall door, because this was no stall. He must be

143

in a portable latrine, the kind found on Parisian street corners and at outdoor wedding receptions. He could understand how he might have passed out in the men's room of a bar, but he couldn't imagine how he ended up in a Porta Potti, no matter how much drinking he'd done.

How much had he done? He had a foggy recollection of a man's head coming off in his hands, which had to mean he was totally looped.

No—he remembered now. He was wide-awake and cold sober. He was heading home—until his truck was stolen.

His truck was stolen, but the thief surrendered, and a man named Ike said "slight detour" as another man pulled up behind.

Now he understood. He was the butt of some student-orchestrated prank. Whit oriented himself to the front of the latrine and felt along the wall again, and this time his fingers slid into the crack marking the door. *Yes.* He reached for the handle and leaned his weight forward.

But there was no handle.

Maybe it was a southpaw latrine. He switched hands and reached again.

Again no handle.

He probed the door with his fingertips and felt three small bolt holes where the handle should have been.

What the hell kind of prank was this? He pounded a fist against the door and shouted, "Hey! Open this door! Let me out!"

He waited and listened and heard nothing. He hammered again and shouted louder. Still nothing.

It was suffocatingly hot. He pulled off his jacket and fanned himself with it, then climbed on the lid of the toilet and felt along the ceiling until he found an air vent molded into the fiberglass. But when he pried his fingers through the slats, there was no circulating fan there, only a barrier of mesh cloth.

Maybe this wasn't a prank. Maybe this was Brandi's boyfriend, out for revenge. He searched his memory for the boy's name.

"Sean!" he shouted and pounded again on the door. "Sean!

Open the door! It's not what you think! She only wanted someone to talk to!"

This time he heard something, a rhythmic expulsion of breath. Maybe a sob? Sean, in the grips of remorse?

"Sean, let me out! It's you she loves!"

The noise came again, louder and through the roof. An electronically transmitted chuckle, broadcast through a speaker in the air vent.

"Sorry, you guessed wrong," spoke a voice.

"Who are you?" Whit demanded. "What do you want?"

"Nothing from you, so sit back and relax. You'll be released as soon as we have what we want."

Whit stared blindly at the ceiling. Not Sean, not a fraternity prank? A memory jarred loose, an image of a bronzed, youthful face topped with a head of bright white hair.

"You're making a mistake," he shouted. "You got the wrong man."

There was a long silence. Whit pictured his captors glancing worriedly at each other as they realized their error.

"Sorry, Professor," came the voice at last. "No mistake."

19

A thought floated up while Dana slept that night, like something torpedoed to the deep that lay heavy and ponderous and undisturbed on the bottom of her mind until the tides shifted and heaved it to the surface. It burst into her consciousness with a force that woke her, and she bolted straight up in bed.

The film.

She tossed off the covers and ran downstairs to the refrigerator. There, in the light of a forty-watt bulb, was the roll of film, hidden in a place no one would ever think to look.

And someone had been looking.

She closed her fist around the film and sat down in darkness in the family room. This was the room where the photo albums were ransacked; the same day that her camera was stolen from the car; the day after a faceless purse snatcher grabbed the camera case off her shoulder and disappeared into the crowd at Alpine Valley.

Someone had been trying to get the film since Friday, and she'd been too blind to realize it. Though Whit tried to tell her— "We've been robbed by a bunch of incompetents," he'd grumbled Saturday night. Nothing of any real value was taken, because the burglary was only a ruse to disguise the search for the film. The thief wasn't after the laptop when he smashed her car window; he was after the camera he must have seen her put in the laptop case. And the pickpocket—he didn't fail to get her purse; it was the camera case he wanted.

146

She opened her fist and stared at the film by the pale moon-light streaming through the windows. The pictures might show signs of mechanical failure or sabotage; they would certainly show the damage to the fuselage and the relative positions of the two aircraft. Maybe from that the angle of impact could be calculated.

And maybe someone didn't want that to happen.

She clenched her arms around her. There could be any number of people who didn't want that to happen, starting with Ira Thompson and ending with her own client.

And there was another possibility. There might be something else on the film that someone didn't want exposed. Something related to a case of submachine guns.

She paced the house with the roll of film clutched in her hand until the gray fog of early dawn appeared through the windows. She had to get it developed, but she couldn't trust a commercial lab to do it now, not even her favorite processor. She needed an expert to analyze the photographs and tell her what they showed. She'd already met with most of the leading experts in the country; any of them could do it. But she needed someone independent, without ties to the case or the client or its insurers, and all of those experts were already on the payroll.

All but one.

When morning arrived, she dressed in the brightest clothes she could find in her closet, a lemon-yellow suit and a tropical print blouse, then got into the Taurus loaner and backed out of the garage. She stopped before she reached the street. No one was parked at the curb and nothing appeared in the rearview mirror, but she climbed out and made a show of peering at all four tires before she drove on.

The doors at the auto glass shop rolled up at 7:05, and she was there with her engine running, first in line to drive onto the shop floor.

"Morning, Mrs. Endicott," the manager called from behind the desk as she stepped out of the Taurus. "We got your Mercedes right outside. I'll get Herb to bring it around."

"Great," she said, but before he could pick up the phone, she was at the desk and speaking softly. "Actually, I don't want it back till this afternoon. Could you get me a different loaner this morning?"

"But Mrs. Endicott—"

She looked at the embroidered oval on his shirt. "I'll pay extra for it, Les."

He gave a shrug that said there's no fool like a rich fool.

"Where's the rest room?"

He pointed it out, and she went in with her briefcase and locked the door. She took off her suit and checked that the film was still securely lodged between the cups of her bra before she changed into the clothes crammed into the briefcase. She twisted her hair into a knot on top of her head and took a deep breath in front of the mirror. There: khaki shorts, sneakers, navy T-shirt, and a baseball cap. A different woman, she hoped, from the one anyone might have followed here this morning.

Les did a double take when she came out. "Mrs. Endicott?" he called. "We got that beige Buick for you."

"Thanks." She grabbed her bag and ran for it.

The airport in Bucks County was not only private but close to secret, nothing but a runway behind a perimeter planting of hemlocks, probably a secluded way station that allowed some wealthy New Yorker to visit his weekend getaway without having to expose himself to the gape-mouthed scrutiny of the locals. Dana circled it twice, doubtful. There was no radio tower, only a long flat airstrip, a corrugated metal shed, and a Quonset hut.

The Jeep was the giveaway. It was parked near one end of the airstrip beside a small house trailer that sat on cinder blocks on a dusty plot of bare earth.

Dana pulled up to the trailer, and two dogs crawled out from under it and threw themselves at her tires in a frenzy of high-pitched yelping. She lowered the window and called out in her old baby-talk voice, "Good boys! Oh, what good boys you are!" until their barking ceased and their tails started to swing. They stood watching with their heads cocked as she climbed out and knocked on the aluminum screen door. Inside, a kitchen sink was piled high with dirty dishes, and an oscillating fan on the counter revolved slowly and hit Dana with a blast of luke-warm air before it moved on.

"Hello?" she called, and knocked again.

A young woman appeared through the haze of the screen. She had short spiky hair and wore the top of a bikini and the bottom of a sweatsuit.

"Excuse me—I'm looking for Andy Broder?"

The woman unlatched the door and held it ajar. The bikini top was two triangles of spandex and a few feet of string; the sweatpants were Rocky Balboa gray. Triceps were cut into the back of her arm, and she had the kind of washboard stomach men dream of.

The woman was giving Dana the same sort of appraisal. "He didn't mention he was expecting you," she said huskily.

"He's not," Dana said, but feeling the woman deserved some kind of explanation, she added, "This is work-related."

The woman shrugged, making the deltoids stand out on the caps of her shoulders. "He's working on his plane," she said finally. "Other side of the terminal."

There was no hint of humor in her voice, so Dana took it that the Quonset hut and metal shed comprised the terminal.

"Thank you."

The screen door banged shut.

Dana crossed the field with the dogs trotting along at her heels. The sun shone hot and bright against the metal roofs of the buildings, and puffs of dust rose up from her sneakers. The grass was brown and dry, and the air was hot and heavy with the rain that wouldn't come.

But despite the heat, she felt a shiver of uneasiness. Coming here might have been a colossal mistake. For all she knew, Ted Keller was the one chasing the film, and Andy Broder his deputy. She might be doing nothing more than surrendering what they'd been unable to steal.

A metallic clanging sounded, and she followed it to the shed where a pair of barn doors were propped wide. A Piper Cub was inside, but that wasn't where the noise was coming from. She circled around the back.

A single-engine, high-wing plane stood tethered to the tarmac in the shade behind the shed. It was a Cessna 172 Skyhawk, like Loudenberg's, except its blue and white paint was peeling badly. A pair of denim-clad legs and work boots appeared under it. The clanging sounded again, from under the engine cowling.

"Excuse me?" she called.

A head protruded from under the belly of the plane.

"I'm looking for Andy Broder?"

The body followed the head and came up standing on her side of the plane. "Found him."

He was dressed the same as before, only trading the white shirt for a blue work shirt. But she wasn't dressed the same, and he gave her a blank look until she pulled off the baseball cap and shook her hair loose over her shoulders.

"Dana Svenssen," he said. There was an edge to his voice—not quite a sneer, but if he were ten years younger, she might have called it fresh.

"Could I talk to you a minute?"

"We already talked." He turned his back on her and circled around the plane.

She followed after him. "So you fly a Skyhawk, too," she said with forced casualness.

"Yeah. You woulda gotten two experts for the price of one if you hired me."

"Well, actually that's what I'm here for. I want to hire you."

"Why?" He picked up a wrench from the ground. "I'm only a couple days older than I was before, you know."

"This is for a special project."

His head and shoulders disappeared into the engine, and when he spoke again, his voice resonated against the metal. "Same deal as before. Unless you guarantee that I'll testify, I'm not interested."

"But this project may not end up in court."

"Then I'm not interested."

Her patience was straining, and her voice rose. "Would you hear me out?"

"We already had this conversation."

"Not this one, we haven't!"

Her shout seemed to bounce off the metal siding and roll down the runway. Broder pulled his head clear of the cowling as a muscle tugged at the corner of his mouth. "Well. That got my attention." He tossed the wrench to the ground. "You got five minutes. Come on into my conference room."

He ducked under the wing of the plane, and, puzzled, she trailed after him until he dropped to the ground in the shade and patted the grass beside him. "Pull up a chair."

Feeling foolish, she folded her legs and sat down cross-legged across the imaginary table from him.

"Okay, so what's this special project?"

She took a breath while she considered how to begin. "In the past week," she began, "my car's been broken into and my house burglarized. Oh, and somebody tried to snatch my purse."

"Bad run of luck."

"No, I don't think so. I think somebody's after something."

"Such as?"

Again she hesitated. He looked boyishly handsome lying there on one elbow, like a pinup in one of Kirstie's *Teen Dream* magazines. It was ridiculous to think he could help her, but suddenly it was equally ridiculous to think he could hurt her.

"I have a roll of film," she said. "Shots of the wreckage, taken before the second explosion."

He came up off his elbow, eyes going wide. "How'd you get ahold of that?"

"I took it myself."

He gave a whistle and sat up straight. "Boy, you play your cards pretty close to your vest." One of the dogs flopped on the ground beside him, and he patted it absently before he spoke again. "It'll show relative positions. Probably impact points. If there was any kind of fatigue failure, we might see some evidence of it. Or any kind of sabotage, for that matter. Jesus—you know what this could mean?"

"Of course I know. It could prove what caused the collision."

"So who's after it?"

"If I knew that," she said peevishly, "I wouldn't need you."

"Okay, back up. Who knows you took these pictures?"

"I haven't told anyone, but a hundred people could have seen me. The collision was at ten-twenty. I arrived about ten-thirty. It must've been another—God, I don't know—half an hour?" She recalled her mad dash through the amusement park, her heart-clutching vigil at the base of the roller coaster while the children were unloaded, her reunion with the girls, and finally her trip up the Ferris wheel. "Maybe even longer," she said finally. "It could have been eleven-fifteen before I shot the pictures."

"So whoever saw you was either already at the scene or arrived within the hour. And it has to be somebody who knows what caused the collision, or they wouldn't bother trying to steal the evidence."

She plucked a blade of grass from the ground and split it carefully along its spine.

"Right?" he said, watching her.

She lifted both arms and twisted her hair into a knot on the top of her head, and held it there, deliberating. "It's possible that they want the film for some reason unrelated to the cause of the collision."

"Like what?"

She dropped her arms and let her hair tumble to her shoulders again. "This is confidential, okay?"

"I assumed the whole conversation was."

She made a sound of annoyance, but not at him. She'd forgotten to give her standard expert witness confidentiality lecture. "Yes, that's right."

"So?"

"There was a case of assault weapons in the wreckage."

Broder gave a low whistle and rocked back on his haunches. After a moment he said a single word: "Paramilitary."

A jolt went down the length of her body. "No," she said, incredulous.

"That's what it sounds like to me. I ran across some of those characters in the service. In Alaska, too—nobody believes in living free of the government more than an Alaskan. And you know what their number one activity is? Well, number two, right after playing soldier in the woods. It's trading in illegal arms. That way they keep their own ordnance up-to-date plus raise some cash on the side."

It was ninety degrees in the shade, but Dana went cold. *Not since the bombing in Oklahoma City,* the newscaster had said Saturday morning while Dana scoffed at the inflammatory analogy.

"No," she said finally. "Maybe in Alaska, maybe Montana, but not here. Besides, what could the film possibly show that paramilitaries would care about? The feds already found the guns, and they already know who the plane was registered to and who its occupants were. A paramilitary troop wouldn't care about the cause of the collision. It's not like anybody's going to collect damages from them."

"Maybe not," he conceded. "Before we go speculating too much, why don't you just find out what's on this film of yours?"

That was the idea that brought her out here this morning, and hearing him speak it hardened her resolve. "That's why I want to hire you."

"Exactly what are you hiring me to do?" he said with a smirk, echoing what he spouted off during their meeting on Monday.

"To help me get the film developed, analyze the photos, review the other data, and reconstruct the accident. Then try to figure out who's been trying to steal the film." She added archly, "And with no guaranty that you'll testify."

He laughed.

"Well?"

"Hey, sign me up. I'm yours." He leaned toward her. "Where is the film? Did you bring it with you?"

She hesitated only a moment before she nodded.

"Then let's get going."

He was up and around the corner of the hangar before she could scramble to her feet to follow. "Andy, wait, what are you—"

"Lucky thing for you I know my way around a darkroom." He was crossing the field in long strides toward the house trailer. "I'll find one and wheedle my way in. Maybe tonight."

"Andy, wait." She broke into a run to catch up. "This is too important to rush into."

"Nobody could accuse you of that." He tossed the words over his shoulder as he headed for her Buick loaner. "The lady who sat on the film for a week."

"No, I mean—I only have this one roll."

He stopped. "Oh, I get it." Indolently, he folded his arms and leaned against the trunk of the car. "So what do you wanna do? Drop it off at your local Speedy Photo kiosk?"

"Of course not."

"Well, then?"

He gestured at the Buick, and she realized the reason for his mad dash across the field. He thought the film was in the car.

She turned her back to him and reached down into the neck of her shirt to extract the film. When she turned back, it was in her hand.

Broder's gaze lingered at the point between her breasts, even after he took the roll from her.

Suddenly the heat was too much. She moved to the door of the car. "I better get back to the office."

He moved with her. "Remember, the photos are only one piece of the puzzle. I need more if I'm gonna reconstruct this thing. The radar data, for one thing."

"I'll send you the report as soon as I get it." She slid behind the wheel, but it was no cooler inside the car than out.

"What about that room full of brainpower you pulled together Monday? Can I tap into them?"

"Only through me."

He showed his dimples. "What—are you ashamed of me?"

"Look," she said sharply, "I don't know who's been chasing the film. It could be anybody. Including anybody in that room."

He braced an arm against the roof of the car. "How do you know I'm not one of them?"

The sixty-four-thousand-dollar question. Dana only hoped her answer was worth half as much. "Because you walked away from the chance to be part of this investigation."

"Coulda been a ruse."

"I thought of that."

"And?"

"I decided you weren't that smart."

He laughed, a short burst of delight.

"I'll call you tonight," she said.

"Lots of luck." He gave a pointed look at the trailer.

She saw it then: no phone lines.

"I'll call you," he said.

"No. I don't want my office to know you're involved in this, either."

"I meant at home."

"Oh." One of the dogs trotted up to Broder, and he gave it a vigorous rubdown while Dana deliberated. "All right," she said finally, rooting in her bag for a pen. "You can reach me at this number."

Broder stuck his hand through the window.

"I have paper," she said dryly.

"But this way I won't lose it."

With more pressure than was required, she wrote her home number in blue ink across the back of his hand.

Both dogs reared up and thrust their noses through the car window. "Good boys," she said, and gave each one a pat, then put on her sunglasses and got out her keys. "One final thing. Your fee. Have you thought about it?"

A wicked gleam lit his eyes. "Wait a minute. You mean I get to name my own price?"

She pulled her mouth tight and started the car with a roar. "A hundred dollars an hour."

"You got it all wrong, you know."

She put the car in gear and hit the gas.

"These dogs are girls!"

He was still laughing in the rearview mirror when she peeled out onto the road.

20

She was at her desk by eleven-thirty, and she reached Mirella Burke at hers by twelve.

"What you wanna be knowin' 'bout that shit for?"

Mirella could speak like the Queen of England when she wanted, but her preferred accent was South Carolina by way of North Philadelphia. She was a fifty-year-old black woman who put herself through law school at night and reared three children alone. Today she was an Assistant U.S. Attorney and the mother of three Ivy League graduates.

Dana answered her question with vague murmurs about gun control legislation and advisory committees.

"Huh," Mirella said, unconvinced.

But within the hour she faxed over the information. Dana stood by the machine and devoured each page as it slithered out. The MP-5K was a German-designed weapon only twelve inches long but accurate up to two hundred yards. A grainy photograph came over the fax line, too, and it was clear enough to show the forward grip handle and the distinctive curve of the magazine. The gun held fifteen rounds of ammunition and could fire all of them in the space of two seconds. It was more accurate and powerful than the Uzi, making it the preferred weapon of most of the world's special forces teams. Its compact size and smooth surfaces also made it the ideal concealed weapon for criminals and terrorists.

If the worst-case scenario resulted and she had to withdraw

from this case—well, she thought as she stared in horror at the photo, maybe that wouldn't be the worst-case scenario at all.

The young faces around the conference table were grim when she convened the team meeting that afternoon. They'd all heard Thompson's press conference yesterday, and they were watching Dana with wide, wary eyes today.

"Lyle, any conclusions yet on the standard of care for the pilots?"

"Yes." He pushed his glasses up his nose and turned a page on his legal pad. "Part 91 of the Federal Aviation Regulations requires pilots to exercise vigilance so as to see and avoid other aircraft."

"What constitutes vigilance?"

"The courts have devised three different yardsticks. First, vigilance requires the pilot to see and avoid unless it's unreasonable to do so. Second, to see and avoid unless it's more than unreasonable. And third, to see and avoid unless it's physically impossible to do so."

"That last one sounds pretty tough," Travis said.

"Yeah," Sharon said. "When would it ever be physically impossible?"

"Basically only in extreme weather conditions," Lyle replied.

Dana recalled the skies on Friday. They were clear and cloudless and robin's-egg-blue. "Katie," she moved on. "Tell us what you've turned up in the Pennsteel records."

The young woman tried valiantly to rouse herself, but with her pregnancy close to full-term, she was bloated and miserable. Dully, she described the training and maintenance records she'd gathered from the aviation department. Pennsteel required its pilots to undergo refresher courses every six months, and they had to have both a college degree and four thousand hours in the air, at least five hundred in the craft to be flown. Those requirements were met and exceeded by the two pilots flying Vic on Friday. The maintenance department exceeded FAA requirements for routine inspections and overhauls. The JetRanger underwent a complete systems check only a week before the crash.

It was the best news they'd had so far in the case, but Brad Martin's panicked hand was in the air the moment Katie finished. "No offense, Dana, but so what? We're already dead in the water. Thompson has all the ammunition he needs in the cockpit recording."

"Hey," Travis growled, "you know that's not the way it happened."

"Sure, but how are we going to prove it?"

"We're working on it, okay?"

Brad blew out his breath, unpersuaded, while Travis glowered at him.

Dana gazed around the room. Half the young lawyers were leaning on the table with their hands over their brows; the other half sat slumped with their spines curved deep into their chairs. Team morale on a big case was a delicate matter. No good came of too much optimism; if a lawyer couldn't see the flaws in his own case, he couldn't very well defuse them. But a defeatist attitude was no good either. Believing a case was a loser usually became a self-fulfilling prophecy.

She cast about for something upbeat, and ended, predictably, with Travis. "How are you coming on your Loudenberg investigation?"

"As a matter of fact," he said with a grin, "I put together a slide show."

A ripple of surprise went through the room as he wheeled out a projector, pulled down a screen, and dimmed the lights.

"Bill Loudenberg," he announced as the first slide projected on the screen. It was a photograph of a photograph, but the quality was good. A sober-faced, sandy-haired man in an orange hunter's jumpsuit stood with a rifle in his hands next to the strung-up carcass of an eight-point buck.

"Born in 1947 in Montrose, Pennsylvania. And except for three years in the army including a tour of duty in Vietnam—" The screen showed a skinny young man in dress uniform, a ringer for the boy Dana saw in the body bag. "—he lived there all his life. For the last few years he resided on Rural Route 2, Montrose, in Susquehanna County." The screen flashed a photo of the main street of Montrose, followed by a map with a circle marking the spot in the northeastern part of the state.

"Married, wife Dottie. Children Bill, Jr., age twenty-three, Donald, age nineteen, Louise, age fifteen." A family photo came next, Loudenberg seated beside his wife with the three children arrayed behind them. Judging from the sizes of the children, it was taken about five years earlier.

"No real estate owned. He rented a house and barn with thirty acres." The screen showed a weather-beaten farmhouse with a sagging front porch under a painted tin roof, followed by a slide of a dilapidated barn. Planted in the yard were painted wooden cutouts of cartoon women in polka-dot bloomers.

Dana shifted in her seat. Loudenberg lived in a shabby rented house, but flew a Skyhawk? "Who held the lien on his plane?" she interrupted.

"Nobody. He owned it free and clear. Bought it about a year ago, and paid cash. About forty thousand."

"What did he do for a living?"

Travis clicked to the next slide, a highway storefront with two pickup trucks parked alongside. "Managed a local True Value hardware store."

"Any ownership interest?"

"Nope."

"So where'd he get the money?"

"Inheritance, according to his assistant at the store. There's no record of any Loudenberg probate at the county courthouse, but it could have been another name or another court. He used all of the money to buy the plane."

"Let's order a credit report," Dana said.

"Tried. As far as I can tell, this guy paid cash for everything he ever owned. He's not in anybody's database."

"Try the wife. Maria," she said to the paralegal. "Let's do a county-by-county probate search. Go out of state if we have to."

Maria nodded and made some notes while Dana made a few of her own. A man with nothing received a sudden untraceable infusion of cash and used it to buy an airplane. And maybe also some illegal arms?

"Loudenberg's best friend and hunting buddy was Jake Ziegler," Travis said. "The owner of the local gun shop."

A picture of Ziegler's Gun Shop appeared on the screen, and Dana felt a wave of uneasiness. The gun connection was turning up everywhere.

"Mr. Ziegler declined to be interviewed," Travis said dryly as a man with his sleeve over his face appeared on the next slide. "And so did Mrs. Loudenberg and the daughter Louise." Another slide of the farmhouse appeared on the screen, this time with all the shades drawn. "And so did son Bill, Jr., who lives in a trailer at the rear of the property."

The young man's face appeared, unsmiling, with a weak chin disappearing into a wattlelike neck and a furtive, fearful look in his eyes.

"However, his wife Judy was happy to talk." The next slide showed a plain young woman smiling broadly for the camera between two shanks of brittle bleached-blond hair.

"Unfortunately, Bill, Jr., returned, and the interview terminated."

Laughter burst out through the room.

"Travis! You might have been hurt!" Dana cried, though she couldn't help laughing with the rest.

"Well, I scooted off the premises pretty fast. But I think it was worth the risk."

Dana heard the deliberate suspense in his voice. "Why's that?"

A yearbook photo appeared on screen of a clean-cut and wholesome-looking young man. "I think Donny, the younger son, mighta been at the controls at the time of the crash."

She pounced. "Really?" as an excited buzz cut through the room. If they could prove that much, they probably didn't need to prove more. An inexperienced teenage pilot would be an easy hook for a jury to hang its deliberative hat on.

"Did he have a pilot's license?"

"No, not even a student license. But Judy says every time Bill went up this summer, Donny was with him. She thinks maybe Bill was trying to teach him himself."

The next slide showed a strip of pastureland mown to a

stubble. "They had a homemade runway out behind the barn. A neighbor heard the plane take off about dawn Friday morning."

Travis reached the end of his slides and turned off the projector light.

Dana asked, "What's the flying time from Montrose to Alpine Valley in a Skyhawk?"

"Depends on wind velocities, but probably a little more than an hour."

"The collision was at ten-twenty, and dawn was about five-thirty," she said. "So what were they doing for the extra three or four hours?"

"That's consistent with a training flight," Travis said.

"Okay," she said. "Let's say Donny was flying the plane that day. How do we prove it?"

"There's no way," Brad said at once. "With nothing left of the wreckage, how could anybody tell who was flying?"

Travis thought for a minute. "We can try to get Loudenberg's flight log. Figure out each departure and arrival point, then see if anybody was around—anybody who remembers seeing the kid at the controls."

"And we could talk to Donny's friends," Sharon suggested. "See if he bragged about flying the plane."

"Hearsay problems?" Dana said.

"Ought to fit into the declaration against interest exception," Lyle said. "He'd be violating any FAA regulations by flying without a license."

The room started to hum. The young lawyers around the table were making notes and consulting in low voices with one another, and Dana could feel their mental energy fueling up and building steam. This scene before her—this was the reason she'd joined a big law firm. There wasn't a solo practitioner or small firm in the country that could offer the kind of deep staffing and brainstorming opportunities that made it possible to handle a case of this magnitude. Jackson, Rieders had a lot of flaws, but this was its singular strength. Sometimes it was good to remind herself of it.

"What did Donny do?" she asked Travis. "Did he have a job?"

"For the summer he was working for his dad at the True Value. He just finished his freshman year at Bucknell."

"Oh." Dana felt a new pinch of sadness. Bucknell was a well-regarded private college upstate. The boy must have been the bright hope of the family, on the brink of a better life until it ended. "Was he a financial aid student?"

There was a pained silence before Travis mumbled, "I don't know."

"That's okay," she said quickly, to spare him his embarrassment. "It's just that you covered so much ground I was almost going to ask you how they voted in the last election."

"I don't know, but they're all registered Republicans," he declared to hoots of laughter.

After the meeting, Travis trailed Dana back to her office, and he was there when Celeste called out, "I have a secretary from Pennsteel on the line. She says it's urgent."

"Put her through." Dana picked up on the speaker as Travis filled the doorway behind her.

A silence, then the woman's no-nonsense voice. "Miss Svenssen, a man was just here, insisting on making a hand-delivery to an officer of the company. Mr. Haguewood took it and advised me to call you."

Dana felt a familiar sinking sensation. "A summons and complaint?"

"Apparently so."

"Whose names are on the top of the page?"

"David A. Greenberg and Andrea M. Greenberg, his wife."

So much for Ira Thompson's promise to give a heads-up before he filed suit. Travis made a half spin on his heel and cursed under his breath.

"What court?" Dana asked.

"Court of Common Pleas, Philadelphia County."

Not Montgomery County, where the Greenbergs resided; not Lehigh County, where Pennsteel was headquartered; not even Northampton County, where the collision occurred. Instead, Thompson filed suit in Philadelphia, where the inner-city jurors regarded the judicial system as a supplement to the Pennsylvania State Lottery. The average Philadelphia jury verdict ran three times the size of verdicts in the outlying counties.

"Fax me a copy, please?"

"Certainly."

"Thompson's a snake," Travis said bitterly when Dana hung up.

She gave a philosophical shrug. "Even if we had advance notice, it wouldn't do any good. There's nothing we could do to stop him from filing."

But Travis was unappeased. "I'm glad this happened," he said, glaring. "Now we know not to trust him on anything."

At 5:01 Celeste came in with her bag in one hand and her cardigan over her arm; in the summer she dressed in reverse, wearing a sweater against the office air-conditioning and peeling it off for the bus ride home.

"You had two mystery callers today," she said. "The first man wouldn't leave his name or number. All he'd say was for you to be sure to watch the news tonight."

If it was another Thompson press conference, Dana thought she'd pass. "Who was the other one?"

"Another anonymous man. Called three times. Won't leave his name, won't be transferred into your voice mail. Just says he'll call again."

"Salesman," Dana said, and waved Celeste on her way.

But later, when the phone rang and she saw that it was an outside call, she felt a ripple of dread in the pit of her stomach. Terrorists, paramilitaries? Three rings. After four, the call would be routed into voice mail.

She picked it up before the fourth ring finished.

"Got your message," Charlie Morrison said. "What's the crisis du jour?"

Relief flowed through her like a warm current of blood. "Well, the crisis du *hour* is that Thompson served his complaint."

"Yeah, Haguewood told me. Didn't waste a second, did he?"

"No. But that's not why I called."

She began by telling him about Harry Reilly's late-night call, but before she could finish, he said, "Whoa, hold on a minute."

She didn't realize he was speaking literally until she heard the telephone click. A moment later his voice returned. "Dana, you there?"

"Yes. Charlie, I—"

"Mike?"

"Here, sir," a third voice said.

"Dana, this is Mike Pasko, director of security and special services for Pennsteel. Tell Mike what you just told me."

She hesitated. "I don't know, Charlie. Reilly said this was strictly need-to-know."

"Yeah, well, Mike's the one we need to know. Go ahead."

"Mr. Pasko, this is highly confidential."

"I understand. It won't go any further."

"The NTSB investigators found a case of submachine guns in the wreckage."

"Make and model?"

"MP-5Ks," she said. "It's not clear which aircraft they came out of."

"It's clear to me," Charlie said hotly. "Mike, what the hell kind of people carry that stuff around?"

"The bad kind, sir. Ms. Svenssen, am I correct that the first order of business is to exonerate the Pennsteel crew?"

"Yes, I suppose—"

"Then I should go up to the heliport in New York and track down the ground crew that inspected the JetRanger before takeoff last Friday. See if they recall any cargo onboard."

"Good idea," Dana said, impressed. "If you find them, get their names and addresses and I'll send someone up to take their affidavits. But please don't suggest guns to anyone. Let them describe what they saw in their own words."

"Understood."

"Thanks, Mike," Charlie said.

He disconnected and Charlie said, "He's a good man in a crisis. Use him."

"Okay."

"Any other bad news you can't shield me from?"

Framed that way, she had to stop and think. The film, the thefts, the break-in. All bad, but she could shield him, she supposed. "No, that'll do it for today."

"Good. Hey, how 'bout a break from all this work and no play? Let's you and Whit and me and Marie get together for dinner this weekend. Maybe see a show. Been ages since we all saw each other."

Dana's eyes fell shut. She'd managed most of the day to keep Whit from her thoughts, but now that he was there again, she felt a sting like a fresh brush burn.

"Sounds like fun," she said cheerily. "Let me check calendars and get back to you?"

"You got it."

She hung up and stared blindly out the window as the sun began to sink over the Schuylkill.

21

Whit was stripped to his shorts against the heat, and his discarded clothing was rolled up and serving as a pillow on the floor where the coolest layer of the hot, stale air resided. He had a toilet—thoughtful of Ike, embassy hostages rarely had it so good—and a two-gallon thermos jug of water that was wet if not cold. Food was brought in once a day, after dark, and although he couldn't actually see the golden arches on the wrappers, he'd spent enough days on the road with two kids to recognize McDonald's when he smelled it. The food was always hot, which probably meant there was a McDonald's nearby. That narrowed his location to only a million different sites.

When dinner was announced, it was through the speaker in the ceiling. "We're going to open the door now, Professor, only wide enough to give you your food. You will back up into the corner by the john. There will be two guns trained on you as the door is opened. If you make any move toward the door, those guns will be fired."

It was always Ike's voice. There was a military rectitude to the way he spoke, no-nonsense and can-do. No malice there, neither any sympathy.

When the door was opened, Whit squinted through the crack and received a quick, dim jumble of images. A hand and a bag reaching through in the foreground, and behind it a series of vertical lines, like telephone poles or goalposts. A flash of orange at a distant point.

"Professor." Ike's voice came through the roof and jarred Whit out of his thoughts. He'd had dinner already; unless they were treating him to brandy and a cigar, he didn't know what they could want with him now.

"We have a little job for you, Professor. We're going to open the door and pass you a piece of paper. You will sit up on the john and face the door and read it out loud. Once again we will have two guns trained on you, and if you move they will be fired."

"How am I supposed to read in the dark?"

"You'll have some light."

He sat up on the toilet lid, and realizing that he would be videotaped, he called, "Wait a minute. Let me get dressed."

His shirt and pants were still sweated through. He pulled them on damp and clammy and sat down again. The door was thrown open and a spotlight blazed into his eyes, so intense he had to throw his hands up against the glare. He heard the paper come toward him, and he took it and held it up to shield his eyes. Ike was speaking in a low voice, which meant at least one other person was present. Another sound—the whir of a video camera?—came from a few feet ahead. And finally, faintly, the dull Doppler roar of highway traffic.

His pupils gradually adjusted, and he held the paper back to scan the text, curious as to what value they'd placed on his life. But what he saw there made him drop the paper and blind himself all over again.

"Who are you? What the hell does this have to do with us?"

"Just read it."

"But my wife won't know what you're talking about!"

"She'll know."

Now he understood exactly what the value of his life was—fleeting. As long as Dana had something they wanted, and as long as he possessed the dubious power to convince her to surrender it, his life was worth something. But as soon as he finished making the video, he'd depreciate faster than a new car driven off the lot.

"I better have a drink." He reached behind him and worked his fingers around the handle of the water jug.

"Hurry up." Ike's voice came from the right, about three feet from the man with the camera.

Whit hurled the jug in that direction and heard it hit, then dove forward and connected with the midsection of the cameraman, who grunted and toppled out of the way. Whit leaped over him and broke into a run.

For a minute nothing sounded but the rasp of his own lungs struggling for breath as his feet pounded across the ground. His eyes adjusted to the darkness as he ran, and he realized what kind of place this was at the same time he realized that someone was up and on his feet behind him.

A straight line run wasn't going to get him anywhere, not in this place. But there had to be some way out. As his head spun in search of it, he caught a glimpse of white hair gaining on him from behind. He whipped his eyes forward. A blank wall twenty feet high loomed ahead.

He cut a ninety-degree turn to the right, but behind him Ike shot a diagonal to intersect his path. Whit could see him coming, horizontal and airborne, his white hair marking the path of his flight like landing lights. He came in slow motion, but Whit had the same slow-motion sickness himself and couldn't get out of the way in time. Ike tackled him to the ground and Whit skidded six feet across the earth before something hard and metal rammed up against his hip. Pain screamed down the length of his leg, but he rolled and came up in a crouch as a click sounded next to his ear.

"Freeze," Ike panted, as if the sound of a gun cocking weren't enough.

But maybe it wasn't. He was no good to them dead, not until after the video was made, and a gunshot here would be heard by too many people.

Another pair of footsteps sounded—the other man was coming. Whit sidestepped them both and broke into another gallop. One of them grabbed him by the arm. He spun and threw a punch, and heard the satisfying crunch of bone against bone. But a second later he took a solid punch in the gut, and the breath left his lungs in a whoosh. The second man circled and held him from behind, and Ike delivered a few more punches to his abdomen and a final, crippling blow to his solar plexus.

Stars glittered, his body went numb, and on the edge of unconsciousness a memory jarred loose, the echo of a familiar voice on another edge of unconsciousness, shouting, *"Christ, how hard did you hit him?"*

Hard enough, he thought woozily, and toppled to the ground.

22

Late that night, Dana turned off her office lights, poked her head into a few open offices to say good night, and got on the elevator. She pressed the garage-level button and called out an enthusiastic goodbye to the cleaning crew.

As soon as the doors closed, she hit another button and got off on the thirty-ninth floor. The lights in the brokerage reception area were turned low, and no one was in sight. She crossed to the fire stairs, closed the door softly behind her, and trotted up one flight. The fire door on the fortieth floor was locked, but the same key that opened the door to the war room opened this one, too.

The plan came to her that morning after she retrieved her Mercedes from the shop and parked it in her usual space in the underground garage. Whoever was after the film knew where she lived and what she drove; it would be a simple enough task to find out where she parked. From there they could follow her to any place she tried to hide or anyone she tried to meet.

But they couldn't follow her here. Even if they got past the security guard in the lobby, even if they searched every floor, they wouldn't find her here, because she had the only key.

She closed the door behind her and turned the key in the dead bolt to lock it from the inside. The city nightscape wrapped panoramically around the windows of the war room. She could see the revolving message on the top of the PECO building, the art deco outlines of Liberty Place, the golden glow of the Bell Atlantic tower.

The rest rooms were finished except for the gender signs on the doors. She selected the nearest one as the ladies' room and went in and undressed and washed as best as she could in the shallow sink. Travis's idea of bringing in cots seemed suddenly brilliant to her, and she opened one up and spread out the makeshift bedding.

The eleven o'clock news was starting, and reluctantly she switched on the TV and sat on the edge of the cot to hear Ira Thompson broadcast his latest allegations.

Ten minutes into the broadcast the anchor cheerfully reported: "Philadelphia attorney Peter Seferis today filed a class action against Pennsteel Corporation over Friday's tragic accident at the Alpine Valley amusement park."

Dana lurched to her feet as film rolled of Seferis standing on the steps of the federal courthouse in a Briani suit, freshly shaved at four o'clock and ready for the cameras.

"We're talking hundreds, maybe thousands, of children," he declaimed, "who not only witnessed a horrific nightmare, but feared for their very lives. The emotional and psychological damage these young people suffered is beyond measure."

His complaint sought damages in an amount unknown but estimated to exceed one billion dollars.

Dana stared at the screen even after the weather map came up. She knew Peter Seferis. He wasn't an expert in aviation, or in psychiatry, or even in personal injury cases. His speciality was the threatened class action suit. He seldom succeeded in getting a class certified, and he wouldn't succeed here. The rules didn't permit a case to proceed as a class action where individual issues predominated; here, the psychological damage sustained by each child would have to be determined on a case-by-case basis. Nonetheless, Seferis made a handsome living; defendants usually coughed up huge sums to settle the claim of the named plaintiff, along with a generous attorney's fee payment, in return for which Seferis would agree to seal the record and forgo contact with any of the prospective class members. It made for good business, if bad law.

And it was utterly, screechingly *wrong*. Angela Leoni was bad enough, but this was too much. A horrible disaster was being turned into an open feeding trough for lawyers. Somehow, she would get Charlie Morrison to back her, Dana decided. No payoff for Seferis this time. This one she would fight.

She switched off the TV, but before she turned in for the night, she went to the phone and dialed her home number. One mystery man was accounted for; she hoped the other could be revealed as easily. Four new messages, the answering machine reported, and the first two were hang-ups.

The third message was from Kirstie and Trina, both talking at once. "Daddy? Daddy, pick up—let me—no—Daddy, it's us! Call us? Love you!"

She felt a skip of panic as she stared blindly at the city lights. What if someone had been in the house and picked up at the sound of the girls' voices? And asked where they were? Or traced the call during the length of time they talked on the answering machine?

The fourth message came on. Another hang-up.

She dialed again and reached the twenty-four-hour customer service line. Five minutes later telephone service to the house was terminated.

23

Whit was back in his cell when he came to, and Ike didn't wait long before he came for him again.

"We're giving you another chance, Professor," he said through the overhead speaker.

The scuffle left Whit with an aching midsection and a passing taste of blood in his mouth, but he hauled himself up as the door opened and the paper came at him again. He took his time getting ready. His memory was more like a dusty old archive than a high-speed computer database, and it took a while to find what he was after. Would Dana remember? That was his gamble.

"Professor," Ike prodded him.

"Yeah, okay." He sat up, faced the camera, and read the script.

"Dana, I'm being held by a group of armed men who will kill me if you fail to comply with their demands. You know what they want. Put it in an eight-by-eleven manila envelope and take it to the Paoli train station tomorrow morning. At seven fifty-eight, board the SEPTA R5 inbound train and sit in the third car. Place the envelope in the overhead rack above your seat. Get off at Penn Center and don't look back. As soon as the contents are verified, I will be released with no harm done.

Do not attempt to contact the police. These men will

know if you do, and the consequence will be that you and the children will never see me again."

After the light was extinguished and the door closed, Whit stripped off his clothes again, flushed himself through with water, and returned to his slump on the floor to ponder what he'd read. There were a few clues in there, and a mistake, and one major reassurance: the girls were safe.

The mistake was that Dana no longer commuted by train. She once lived and breathed by the R5 schedule, but that was before her practice reached such a fever pitch that she couldn't be out of touch even for a minute. Since she never used her cellular phone within earshot of others, she commuted strictly by car these days.

First clue: the kidnappers hadn't kept up with her very well.

Second clue: whatever the item was, it wasn't self-authenticating.

Third clue: they would know if she contacted the police. Crooked cops? he wondered. Lately the Philadelphia police were neck and neck with New York for corruption and Los Angeles for ineptness, so it wasn't impossible, but in the end he decided it was an empty threat.

The biggest clue was the one that came to him as Ike delivered his final punch: the somehow familiar voice he'd heard on the edge of unconsciousness. He remembered when and where—in Ike's car, after the black man came up from behind him and clubbed him—and he remembered what: *Christ, how hard did you hit him?* What he couldn't remember was who. He played the voice over and over again in his mind until it was acid-burned into his memory, but the name and face wouldn't come. It was like a melody without lyrics, only tones and a rhythm.

He knew that voice.

Long hours stretched before him to figure out how.

24

Friday morning Dana rolled off the cot, dressed in her T-shirt and shorts, and took the fire stairs six floors up. In the closet behind her office door hung a change of clothes, her constant habit ever since she once had to work straight through two days. The second-day fatigue bothered her less than the telltale repeating outfit. All day long her smart-assed colleagues stopped her with a leer, "Hey, Dana—where'd you spend last night?"

Now she grabbed the hanger and took it with her up two more floors to the firm's fitness center, where she showered, dried her hair, and dressed. She stuffed yesterday's clothes in a gym bag and departed in a severe black suit.

Travis was eating breakfast at his desk when she passed his office on the way to her own.

"Dana?" He got up and bolted down the hall after her with a paper napkin tucked in his collar. "I tried to reach you last night—"

"What's up?" She scooped the mail from her in-box and went into her office.

"Bunch of stuff." He sat down, and when he realized he was still wearing his napkin, jerked it off with a grimace. "There's this class action—"

"Seferis, yeah, I know. Service effected yet?"

"I don't know—"

"Call Pennsteel and find out. And get Lyle started on the class certification issues. Tell Brad I want a press release saying that

175

Pennsteel won't roll over for this kind of extortion. Our hearts go out to any child who suffered trauma at the park last Friday, but everyone should remember that Pennsteel is a victim here, too. And in any event, a class action is completely inappropriate, as Mr. Seferis well knows."

Travis was scribbling notes as fast as he could.

"What else?" she asked.

"We got another new lawsuit. Coupla kids named Doyle."

She winced. So Angela Leoni called her bluff after all. "Where?"

"Philadelphia Common Pleas, just like Thompson. In fact, all the allegations of negligence are lifted verbatim from Thompson's complaint."

No surprise there. Damages weren't awarded on the basis of art or originality in drafting; a lot of million-dollar verdicts came out of cut-and-paste complaints.

"Any press release to go with it?"

"Not so far."

That must have been the compromise Angela struck: she filed suit but would do her best to keep Frank Doyle's name out of the newspapers. It would have minimized the risk of copycats, if only Seferis hadn't gone public the same day.

Dana's mail contained a preliminary analysis from John Diefenbach, and she spent the balance of the morning trying to decipher it. He'd analyzed radio detection and ranging—RADAR—data collected from four different sources: the ARTS III sensor at Philadelphia International; the QARSA antenna at Allentown; the base antenna at the Willow Grove Naval Air Station; and incredibly enough, an Aegis cruiser sailing up the New Jersey coast on its way to Naval Weapons Station Earle. Each of those sites had an emitter shooting electromagnetic energy out into airspace, and when it hit a target, some of that energy was reflected back to the receiving antenna. The target's range was fixed by measuring the time it took for the energy to travel from emitter to target and back to receiver; its speed could be determined by calculating the change in range over time.

Diefenbach had an easy job tracking the JetRanger, because it was equipped with a transponder that replied with its own signal to all the emitters that happened to interrogate it. Since the transponder signal was encoded with a four-digit number specifically assigned by Air Traffic Control, it was as if the JetRanger wrote its signature across the sky. Plotting in four dimensions—latitude, longitude, altitude, and time—Diefenbach was able to trace the flight path of the JetRanger in a smooth line from Wall Street to Alpine Valley.

Tracking the Skyhawk was more of a challenge. The plane wasn't equipped with a transponder, at least not an operating one, and the radar hits were weak and inconclusive. Moving back from the point of collision, Diefenbach picked up a few stray signals at two thousand feet that might have been the Skyhawk. He made some assumptions and extrapolations and tentatively plotted a course for the Skyhawk from northeastern Pennsylvania to Alpine Valley.

The narrative portion of Diefenbach's report ended there. The presumed flight paths were depicted in a complicated series of charts, both on plain paper and on transparencies layered over topographical maps. Dana squinted and turned the pages upside down and sideways, but still couldn't tell what she was looking at.

She closed her eyes and rubbed her temples and tried to focus. But her brain was working like a radio scanner, flipping through a hundred frequencies in search of a signal and finding none strong enough to hold it.

She went to the vending machines upstairs and gulped down a diet Coke for her lunch. A fax was lying on her desk when she came back. It was a five-page transmission, and the cover page held a brief note from Mike Pasko at Pennsteel:

Ms. Svenssen: I located the two crewmen who did the preflight inspection of the JetRanger in New York and were in the cockpit minutes before takeoff. I took the liberty of drawing up their affidavits, attached. Original signed and notarized affidavits will follow.

Dana flipped the pages in annoyance. Pasko wasn't supposed to do the affidavits himself; she'd clearly told him that she would send a lawyer to do it. She read through the two affidavits, each one swearing that there was nothing bigger than a briefcase aboard the JetRanger when it departed New York last Friday. Each one was flawless.

She called Pasko at once.

"Dana Svenssen. Nice work," she said.

"Glad I could help. Now the question is, what else can I do?"

"I don't know. What else *do* you do?"

"My department's schooled in all forms of surveillance and investigation. We liaise regularly with law enforcement agencies. We also maintain a certain amount of ongoing scrutiny over known saboteurs, industrial spies, and select terrorist groups."

At the word "terrorist" she rose from her desk and crossed to the window where the view stretched down the silver length of the Schuylkill River to the golden Greek facade of the Art Museum. Yesterday she would never have allowed a stranger to run a freelance investigation in her name, no matter how professional and levelheaded he sounded, but today everything looked different.

"Mr. Pasko—"

"Mike."

"Mike. Now that we know where the guns didn't come from, I'd like to know where they did come from."

"I agree."

"I'd like to know what it is the FBI and the BATF think they're investigating. And why it's so highly confidential."

"I'll get on it immediately."

Late in the afternoon, Celeste came in with a scowl on her face. "There's some kid in the lobby," she said indignantly. "With a hand-delivery that he refuses to give to anybody but you."

Dana got up and took the long route around, the one that gave her a view of the reception area from fifty feet away. The messenger was easy to spot. He was sitting brazenly on the desk, forcing the agitated receptionist to crane her neck to see around him. He wore a sleeveless muscle shirt and tattered cutoffs, and his hair was slicked back over reflective sunglasses.

He jumped off the desk as Dana approached. Nervously, she eyed the envelope in his hand. Standard eight-and-a-half-by-eleven, and thin, holding no more than a page or two. Too thin to be anything more dangerous than a summons. She held out her hand, and he thrust it at her and strode for the elevators.

She opened it and a single scrap of paper slid out. It was a handwritten note: *Meet me in fifteen minutes at the corner of 16th and Market.*

"What . . . ?" She turned to look for the messenger.

He was already in the elevator, watching her bewilderment with a widening grin, and in the final second before the doors closed, his dimples appeared.

Five minutes later Dana stepped into the same elevator, and as it plunged to the lobby, she tied a black silk scarf over her hair and put on a pair of sunglasses. She emerged in the midday heat of concrete and asphalt and weaved a circuitous path south and east, cutting through office buildings and lingering a moment in the lobby of the Ritz-Carlton before she came out on Sixteenth Street and joined a line at an Italian water ice cart. An open Jeep was parked in a towaway zone on Market Street.

"What do you think you're doing, Broder?" she said as she climbed into the seat beside him.

"Me?" He threw the gearshift into first and cut out into traffic. "You're the one who went missing last night. And then when your line went dead—how was I supposed to know you weren't dead, too?"

"What?" she exclaimed. But then she remembered. She'd given him her home phone number, then not only wasn't she home, the service was disconnected. "Oh, sorry. I stayed in town last night."

"Thanks for telling me."

"Well, what's the big emergency?"

He turned the corner and gave her a look. "I just have one question: where the hell *were* you?"

"I told you—" she began impatiently.

"Not last night. When you took the pictures."

"The prints are done? How do they look?"

"Like you were hanging out of the fucking sky."

She smiled. "Not quite, but I was on top of the Ferris wheel. Did you find anything useful?"

"On top of the Ferris wheel," he repeated.

It took her a moment to hear what was in his voice. It was more than surprise; there was a kind of awed admiration, and the unexpectedness of it made her flush with pleasure.

"That was nothing," she said. "You should have seen me climbing down from there after the operator disappeared." Hearing herself boast made her flush even more. "Where are the pictures? Do you have them with you?"

"Yeah." He pulled his eyes back to the road. "Let's go to wherever you stayed last night, and we'll take a look at 'em. Which way?"

She bit her lip and watched the city buildings roll by. The war room was the only place she felt safe; it was her final fortress.

"Come on," he said. "Let's not screw around with this. We lost a week already."

"I know, but—"

"Look—are we working together on this or not?"

His water-slicked hair had dried, and it was tossing loose and free in the hot wind. He turned west on JFK Boulevard, and as they picked up speed the wind tore her scarf from her head and wrapped it around the roll bar. She grabbed for it, but it flew out of the Jeep and tumbled away through the canyons of the city.

"Well?"

She could see her reflection in his sunglasses. Her own hair was tossing now, too, pale and wild in the wind.

"Together," she said.

Half an hour later she was waiting on the fortieth floor when the elevator chimed and Broder stepped out. She unlocked the war room door, and he sauntered inside and pushed his sunglasses to the top of his head. He stopped and let his eyes move through the room.

"What *is* this place?" he asked.

"It's *my* imaginary conference room," she said archly.

He laughed and slapped an envelope on the worktable.

Inside was a stack of eight-by-ten prints. The topmost shot was of three strange girls mugging for the camera with their arms wrapped over one another's shoulders. She cleared her throat. "Uh, Andy?"

He was across the room, squatting in front of the miniature refrigerator. "Hey, I was gonna ask you."

She peered at the strange girls. CAMP DISCOVERY, their T-shirts read. "Oh—I forgot. My daughter took some shots at the beginning of the roll."

She flipped through five more pictures taken by Kirstie, all scenes of a fun-filled summer's day at an amusement park: kids whirling on rides with their hair whipping over their faces; a flustered counselor collaring a boy whose legs kicked in the air; Trina with her eyes closed and her tongue darting out at a pink cloud of cotton candy.

"Beautiful girl," Broder said, behind her now.

"Also my daughter."

"Yeah, no shit."

The next image emerged in grim and startling contrast. The JetRanger and the Skyhawk were entangled on the roller coaster in a position that looked impossible even with the photographic proof in front of them. The plane was on its side with one wing projected upward. Partially visible behind the wing was the helicopter, dangling by a skid. Around the wreckage, the skeleton of the roller coaster stood out in sharp relief. The image was so clear that Dana could make out the soot-covered faces of the rescue workers climbing up the steel grids.

A horrible image but a good photograph, especially considering it was taken with a point-and-shoot camera from a rocking gondola. There were a dozen more like it, and Dana went carefully through each one before she turned questioning eyes up at Broder.

"Do they help or hurt?"

"Can't tell yet. When are you gonna get the radar information?"

"Oh—I have it."

She pulled Diefenbach's report out of her briefcase and handed it over, and Broder straddled a chair and turned to page one.

She went to work, too, at the computer terminal across the room. She signed onto the office system and accessed Maria's database to confirm that each of the three lawsuits was logged in and the response dates calendared and tickled. She sent another e-mail message to Bill Moran, reminding him of their meeting with Dan Casella at the park Monday morning. Brad Martin sent her an e-mail draft of a press release, and she edited and revised it and sent it back with delivery instructions that would time it to make the Sunday papers.

By early evening she'd attended to everything she possibly could by modem. Her stomach rumbled angrily, reminding her that she'd fed it nothing but coffee and diet Coke all day. She looked over at Broder. He was still at work on the radar data, and now he was making notes and calculations on a legal pad.

"I'll go downstairs and get us something to eat," she said.

His head came up. "No. I'll go."

"There's no reason—"

"It's you they're following, not me."

He worked out a pattern of knocks to signal his return, and disdainfully Dana locked the door after him. Last night it seemed like a prudent thing to lie low in the war room; now that Broder was here, it was turning into a kid's cloak-and-dagger spy game.

The computer beeped and she sat down to retrieve the incoming e-mail. There were two new messages, the first from Travis.

Dana: The credit searches came up dry on Loudenberg's wife. I just called his assistant at True Value. He was real chatty the last time I talked to him, but now he's clammed up. You think maybe Thompson got to him? What should I try next?

Dana stared at the screen. In the space of a minute it didn't seem like a kid's game anymore. Travis was so eager, and so naive. Quickly she typed:

> I need you to start drafting responses to the complaints. We'd better develop a good form answer; something tells me we'll be doing quite a few. Until that's done, let's leave Loudenberg alone.

She clicked the send button.

By the time the prearranged knock sounded on the door, night had fallen and nothing lit the room but the city lights and the green glow of the computer screen. Dana whispered through the cylinder of the dead bolt. "Andy?"

"Yeah."

She turned the key, and he squeezed through the door with two bags of groceries and a pizza.

"Anybody see you get off on this floor?"

"No, I waited till I had the elevator to myself, and I punched three other floors."

He sat down and started in on the pizza while she paced the perimeter of the darkened floor. Other buildings rose in all directions, and every office with a light on was displayed like a fishbowl. Across the street she could see a young lawyer in another firm as she toiled over her desk. It was like being in an interrogation room with a two-way mirror. Anybody could have done it to her, anytime and almost anyplace.

"Come on—sit down and eat," Andy said.

She sat down and nibbled at a pizza slice, but soon got up again to unpack the groceries. Soda, chips, doughnuts—except for milk and cereal, there was nothing there but frat house party food. With a diet like this, he wasn't going to keep that muscle-boy body for long. She put it all away in the makeshift kitchen and returned to the table in a weary slump. Broder was back to the radar report, and polishing off the pizza while he worked.

Dana picked up the accident photos and studied them again,

one by one, straining her eyes for answers, but soon all she was seeing was black and yellow spots swimming in obscurity.

"You look wiped out," he said.

She leaned back and raked her hair off her face. "Take a good look." She laughed ruefully. "It's called middle age. Someday even you might face it."

"Would you get off this age thing? What's the big deal? You're in your thirties, I'm in my thirties."

"Just barely on either side."

He rolled his eyes. "Why don't you just go get some sleep?"

At the thought of sleep, the cot across the room beckoned like a feather bed. "When are you leaving?" she asked.

He bent back over his notes. "I'm not."

"Andy—"

"Forget it," he said. "I'm not leaving you."

"I hired you to reconstruct the accident, not to be my bodyguard."

"So? You get two for the price of one."

"I don't need you."

"I don't care. Look, move your cot into the bathroom if you're squeamish, barricade the door. I'll crash out here."

She raised an eyebrow. "Crash?"

He smirked and went back to his work.

She did as he said and dragged a cot into her designated ladies' room. Quietly, she closed the door and pushed the cot against it, then took off her clothes and stretched out on her back. But even with the door barricaded it made her jittery to sleep naked, so she got up and pulled on her T-shirt before she lay back down again.

Later, on the edge of unconsciousness, she wondered how Broder knew how old she was, but before she could puzzle it through, she was tumbling headlong into sleep.

25

Whit's cell was so well sealed against the light that the only way he could measure the passage of time was by the length of his beard. Wednesday morning was when he last shaved, with a disposable pink plastic razor at Brandi's apartment. Rubbing a sweaty palm over a stubbled jaw, he calculated close to three days, which probably made this Friday night. This morning's rendezvous had come and gone, yet here he sat. He had to wonder if Ike was confirming the contents of the envelope, or if Dana had simply failed to appear. *I don't want to be bothered with you,* she'd told him Monday night, and there was no denying this would be a bother.

He heard Ike's voice outside, and once again he remembered the third voice, the one he'd heard on the edge of consciousness, the one he knew he knew. He slapped his forehead, and though his hand came away dripping with sweat, it did nothing to stir his memory.

"Professor," Ike said through the speaker. "We need you to read another statement."

Another? Meaning she didn't show for the first one?

"What is this—a sequel?" Whit shouted at the ceiling. *"Lethal Toilet 2? Sweat Hard 3?"*

"Yeah, right." No room for humor in this man's army.

The mistake had to be on this end. They wouldn't bother with a second video if Dana blew them off on the first one. Somehow they'd screwed up, or they'd never give her a second chance.

It was a second chance for him.

Think, he goaded himself as he pulled on his clothes and prepared to face the camera. *Remember.* This would be the last chance he would ever get. The door opened, the page came at him, and the veins bulged on his skull as he strained to remember.

"Ready?" Ike said.

It was no use.

"Yeah," he said. "Ready."

26

Dana's eyes opened to darkness, and when she lifted her wrist and peered at her watch, the LED showed quarter to four. There—it came again: the rumble of a low-spoken voice. She rolled off the cot and tiptoed to the rest-room door and slowly cracked it open.

Broder stood across the room with his back to her and Dana's flip phone in his hand.

"Yeah, if you can get her ready for me," he was saying. "I'll be there in an hour. Yeah, I will. Sorry I woke you."

He disconnected and was turning around when he saw her in the doorway. "Oh, sorry. Guess I woke you, too."

"What's going on? Where are you going?"

He picked up a doughnut from the box on the table. "I'm doing a flyover of Alpine Valley," he said, taking a bite. "See if I can reconstruct the flight paths." He chased the doughnut with a quick gulp of coffee. "I think I got this thing figured."

Her eyes opened wide and she burst out of the rest room. "How? Show me!"

"I gotta fly it first, check out a couple hunches."

"Then I'm coming, too."

He glanced over, and this time his eyes caught all of her, from where the T-shirt ended at the tops of her thighs, down the length of her bare legs. He grinned. "Fine by me."

Blushing furiously, she backed into the rest room. "Give me

five minutes to get dressed." She shut the door, then swung it open again. "Don't you dare leave without me."

The night was still black as they drove north out of the city, and a waxing half-moon glowed a hot dusty yellow in the sky.

"Look at this," Broder said, pointing to a photograph with one hand and gripping the wheel of the Jeep with the other. "See the right skid?"

Dana opened the glove compartment and held the enlargement to the light. She could make out a line slashing diagonally across the helicopter skid. More than a line, it was a jagged tear in the metal. "Yeah?"

"Blade strike."

"From the plane's propeller?" Doubtfully, she studied the Skyhawk. "I don't know. The skid could have been cut by the rail of the roller coaster before it flipped. We can't even see the propeller to tell if it was damaged."

He snorted. "The prop's over six feet in diameter. You can't see it because it's not there."

"It could have come off when the plane hit the roller coaster."

"Take another look at the skid. See the second strike?"

She peered closer. A faint line appeared parallel to the first. This one was more a dent than a tear.

"The first blade struck the skid and sliced it open. A millisecond later the second blade hit. Not as hard, because by that time the prop's coming off the plane, and the blade only glances off the skid."

She could see it, she could almost visualize the nose of the plane coming up under the helicopter, its propeller blades cutting through everything in their path.

"Take a look at the cotton candy picture," he said.

"What?"

"That shot of your little girl."

She shuffled through the photographs until she found it.

"Look at the sky behind her."

She squinted hard and a second later gasped out loud. "I thought that was a bird!"

"Yeah, me too."

In the distance behind Katrina was the low hump of a forest-covered mountain, and in the sky above it, a plane with its nose pitched upward.

"I'll blow it up enough to read the tail number and confirm that it's the Skyhawk. But assuming it is, he's making one hell of a climb right there."

"To get over the mountain?"

Broder nodded.

"But the mountain's probably under fifteen hundred feet," she said. "Diefenbach put the Skyhawk at two thousand."

"Yeah, I know he did."

"So?"

"I think he's wrong."

She waited, but he kept his eyes on the road and his mouth closed. "Want to tell me why?" she prodded him.

"Not yet."

"How come?"

"Because if I'm wrong—" He reached over her lap to close the glove compartment. "—the last person I want to look like an ass in front of is you."

The light went out and darkness washed over his face.

The sky was turning gray and the moon was a pallid white by the time Dana climbed into Broder's plane. She stowed a thermos of coffee behind her seat, then pulled the shoulder harness around her and peered through the windshield. She'd flown in single-engine planes before, but never in the copilot's seat. The perspective was different.

Broder was different, too. She watched him outside, circling the plane as he did the preflight inspection. He'd changed out of his muscle-boy/messenger outfit into jeans and a polo shirt, and by the time he vaulted into the cockpit, he seemed more like a sober pilot than a wisecracking scamp. He ran a systems check, then unfolded his charts and calculated the heading and penciled it in on his flight plan.

Though it was obvious they were alone, he cracked the window and shouted "Clear!" then set the carburetor and started the engine with a sputter. The propeller slowly beat a circle through the air, and the engine began to whine as it picked up speed. The plane lumbered forward. At the end of the runway he turned the nose around, and while the rpms revved up, he checked the gauges and magnetos and set the instruments.

"We're a go," he shouted, and pushed in the throttle. The plane began to hurtle down the runway, shuddering wildly with the engine vibration.

"Hey," Dana yelled. "Did you fix whatever you were working on the other day?"

He showed a flash of white teeth below the dark sunglasses. "A little late to be asking now, isn't it?"

She retorted, "We're still on the ground," but by the time she said it, they weren't. The wheels left the airstrip, he pulled back on the yoke, and they climbed up into the western sky.

Ahead the moon still shone. The treetops dropped off below, and the horizon tilted as they banked slowly to the north. The sun met them as it climbed the sky in the east.

Dana was struck by the image. "Look." She pointed. "The sun's rising at the same time that the moon's setting. And here we are, trapped in the middle."

"Trapped?" Broder said. "No way." He pulled off the radio headset and let it hang around his neck. "It means the whole world is ours."

"Yeah, right."

"Hey, it is when we're up here. You know, a lot of people call Alaska the Last Frontier, but for my money, this is it. The sky. Here's where a man really makes his own way. There's no traffic lights, no stop signs, no yellow lines or medial strips. There's no road but the one you carve out for yourself. And no rules except the ones you make up as you go."

He proved his point by banking to the left and fixing on a heading to the northwest.

Dana watched the earth recede below them. The golden cornfields yielded to the silvery wheat and everything disappeared into the black forests. "It is beautiful up here," she said.

"Yep—flying's the second greatest thrill known to man."

She was afraid to ask what the first one was. "What's the first one?" she asked.

"Landing."

She laughed. "I heard that joke another way. 'Flying's not dangerous, landing is.' "

"Nah, I don't feel any danger. You know why? Because up here I'm in control."

Dana watched him as he spoke. She'd known a lot of eager young men over the years—the corridors of Jackson, Rieders & Clark were clogged with them—but never had she seen one so enthusiastic about his work. "It must be amazing to love what you do," she murmured.

She didn't mean for him to hear, but despite the roar of the engine and the rush of the wind, he did. He looked at her curiously. "You don't love being a lawyer?"

"Not very often. Want some coffee?" He nodded, and she reached behind the seat for the thermos and poured them each a steaming cup.

"What about when you started out?"

"Then? Then I loved it."

"So what happened?"

"I don't know. It's hard to explain." She sipped at the coffee until she could think of a good analogy. "Say you run an airline. Your business depends on dropping off one load of passengers and picking up another. And say a couple times a day something goes haywire in Air Traffic Control, and they won't let anybody land. So you, being a good law-abiding airline—"

"Watch out, you might lose me here."

"You circle the airport, waiting for clearance to land. But meanwhile the other airlines decide, heck, the runway's clear, the gate's clear, I'll land anyway. Their passengers cheer, all of the ticket holders waiting at your gate stampede over to change their flights, while the passengers you're carrying are staging a mutiny because you won't break the rules and do the same."

"Okay, but there's a penalty on the guys who landed."

"A slap on the wrist if it comes at all, and easily absorbed anyway because their revenues quadruple from all the increased business they get. Meanwhile, you're up there circling the airport, your passengers are rioting in the aisles, and in comes a call from your management on the radio: we need to double our fares to keep our shareholders happy, and by the way, cut down on your fuel consumption, would you?"

"Help me out here," he said. "This is relevant—how?"

She took another sip of coffee. "Our legal system's broken," she said. "The people who obey the rules get screwed, and the ones who flout the rules and exploit the cracks in the system pull ahead, every time. And justice? It's somewhere up there circling in the clouds. It never gets to land."

"Sounds pretty gloomy."

"Yeah." She drained her cup. "It is."

"But you stick with it anyway. Because the good guys don't have any chance for an even break if they don't have a good lawyer."

She gave a rueful laugh. "I stick with it because I have bills to pay, and two kids to get through college."

"Come on. You're not exactly living on the edge."

"Yeah, but you know the definition of survival wages: ten percent more than you made last year."

He was watching her, too closely. "You're a complicated lady."

"No, I'm not. I just have a complicated life."

After a minute he pointed out his window. "Take a look."

She peered over his shoulder toward the west. "What? I don't see anything."

"The moon's gone," he said. "See? You're not trapped anymore."

In thirty minutes the burnt remains of Alpine Valley came into view. Through the incinerated treetops appeared the vertical disk of the Ferris wheel and the crushed backbone of the roller coaster. It was a few minutes after six. Not a soul stirred on the ground below them, and the sky was all theirs.

Broder pulled back on the throttle and looped slow concentric circles around the amusement park and its surrounding terrain. The park sprawled over the floor of a valley, and a chain of low-lying mountains formed a rim around it on all sides but the east. He kept one eye on the altimeter and another on the charts, and every minute or so turned his head to study the ground.

After the fourth circuit he said, "Now we'll go back a ways and pick up the trail of the chopper."

He pushed in the throttle and pointed the nose to the northeast, and a few minutes later made a smooth 180-degree turn. "Okay, our altitude's twenty-five hundred. That's where the radar places the JetRanger at this point. We got a two-ten heading southwest, toward Pennsteel headquarters."

Dana reached between the seats for Diefenbach's radar report. Broder had plotted a route in pencil on the topographical map in the appendix, and now that she was flying it, she was able to follow it on the page. There were no mountains on the eastern approach, and Alpine Valley appeared clearly ahead and a bit to the right, or north.

"Now watch this," he said as they came closer to the amusement park. He banked and turned a few degrees to the north, then straightened out again. Now the park was directly ahead of them.

"The JetRanger veered to the north?" she said, following on the map. "How come?"

Broder pointed out the left window with his chin, and she leaned over him to see. Spread out in orderly rows of houses and streets south of the park was a large residential neighborhood.

"Check it out with Uncle Ted," he said. "Betcha his department has a policy of flying away from residential areas whenever they can. Cuts down on noise complaints. They probably also have a policy of decelerating over populous areas. The radar tells us the JetRanger did that, right about here."

Dana had a sudden horrible thought. "Are you telling me that the helicopter made a swing north and collided with the plane?"

"Impossible. At this point the plane was about a thousand feet below. At least according to my theory. Let's go back and fly the route Loudenberg did."

He headed northeast again, and again made a 180 turn for the approach to Alpine Valley. This time he flew a path north of and roughly parallel to the one he flew before.

"Wait a minute," Dana said, reading the altimeter. "You're at twenty-five hundred. That's where the JetRanger was. You said you put the plane a thousand feet lower."

"Not here I don't. But—" He glanced at Diefenbach's map and abruptly pitched the nose down. "—here I do."

Dana's back flattened against the seat as they descended. When they leveled off again, the altimeter read fifteen hundred feet mean sea level. She turned to the radar report again and flipped through the pages.

"I'm not following," she said. "Diefenbach puts the plane at a steady course at two thousand feet."

"That's because the only good radar echoes from the plane were picked up at two thousand feet. Diefenbach assumed a constant heading at that altitude, which is a reasonable assumption ninety-nine percent of the time. But I think two thousand was only a way station for the Skyhawk, on its way up and down between fifteen and twenty-five hundred."

"But then there'd be echo signals at those altitudes."

He grinned. "Not so, Dr. Watson. In this terrain you can't get any good echoes below about fifteen hundred feet MSL. There's too much clutter from targets on the ground."

"All right," she said, still skeptical. "But why no echoes at twenty-five hundred feet?"

"Because the plane flew so close to the chopper it came inside its radar signature. The receiver only picked up one echo."

This much rang a bell of authenticity. Dana remembered Diefenbach warning that he could track the two aircraft only to the point where they came within about five hundred feet of each other; after that they showed up as a single blip on the screen.

"Picture this," Broder said. "We're in the Skyhawk now, at fifteen hundred feet. The JetRanger's a thousand feet higher. We both have the same heading, but we're north and a little behind. I put the chopper right about there." He pointed to the empty sky above and ahead, at about eleven o'clock high. "Now watch what happens."

Broder held the altimeter steady at fifteen hundred feet, but the ground seemed to rise up beneath them.

"The mountain!" Dana exclaimed. "The one in Trina's picture!"

"Right. Loudenberg hasn't been paying attention to the ground elevation. He gets a little nervous and goes into a climb right about—" Broder pulled back abruptly on the yoke. "—here."

The nose of the plane pitched upward, and the vertical velocity indicator surged upward. "He's so steep at this point that he suddenly realizes he might go into a stall."

"What's that mean?"

"When the angle of attack of the wing gets too steep, you lose lift. Unless I bring the nose down and increase the thrust in the next thirty seconds or so, we'll fall out of the sky."

"So do it," she urged him.

With a grin he pushed forward on the yoke and pushed in on the throttle. The whine of the engine went up an octave with the increased power. When the nose leveled off, the altimeter read twenty-three hundred feet.

"There's a couple unidentified radar hits here at twenty-three hundred. I call it the Skyhawk. So—we avoided the mountain, we almost stalled, and we climbed eight hundred feet. A minute's gone by while all this was happening. It was during that same minute that the JetRanger veered to the north. So tell me, where's the chopper now?"

Dana closed her eyes and tried to see it. The JetRanger above, decelerating and banking to the north. The Skyhawk flying a parallel course north of it and suddenly climbing eight hundred feet.

"Same bearings two hundred feet above us," she said. "Almost directly above us."

Broder nodded. "Now imagine you're Loudenberg. You didn't see the chopper make that turn to the north, and you're wondering where the hell it is. Take a look."

She turned and craned her neck to the left, but that part of the sky was blocked out. She tried to look directly above, and then above and to the right. From every angle, the wing was in the way.

"This is one of the best light planes ever built," Broder said.

"But the top-mounted wing means there's not much upward visibility. Loudenberg couldn't see the chopper."

"Great," she groaned. "Loudenberg couldn't see and avoid, so he's exonerated. But what about the JetRanger crew? They should have been able to see and avoid the plane. It was a clear blue sky that day."

"Yeah, the worst possible background to detect aircraft against. With gray or white sky, you get some contrast with the dark silhouette of the plane. Not with blue. And then throw in the sun glare. At ten A.M., with the plane trailing to the east and south, the chopper crew had a full sun glare when they looked into that part of the sky. And when the plane came up underneath, there's just no way they could've seen it."

"But they'd have to hear it."

"You can't hear anything in a chopper. There's so much noise in that cockpit, you have to wear a boom mike just to talk on the radio."

"Okay, but Loudenberg would have to hear—"

"He's been hearing the rotors of the JetRanger all along. He knows it's in the sky somewhere. But in terms of measuring separation?—Here, put this on."

He handed her the headset, and she fitted it over her ears. There was a loud crackling of static and a distant babel of chatter over the radio. Broder's mouth was moving. She pulled off one side of the headset. "What did you say?"

"I said, believe me, hearing isn't a sense you can rely on in the air."

She mused as she handed the headset back to him. "But we still have two hundred feet of vertical separation. What brought us together?"

Alpine Valley was below them now. Broder banked to the right and circled it again.

"Well, here's my theory," he said. "Let's say I'm Loudenberg, and I've been shadowing the chopper for a while."

"Deliberately?" Dana scoffed.

"Play along for a minute," he said. "I was caught off guard by that mountain, I climbed too fast, I almost went into a stall. I lost my bearings a little, and I can't see the chopper anywhere. What'll I do?"

Incredulous, she said, "You climb a little higher."

"Bingo. I put my nose up, and by the time I see what's on top of me, it's too late. My propeller hits first. One blade slices through the chopper's right skid, then the second blade hits. The prop comes off, the plane goes into a spiral. The right wing pitches up and gets caught in the main rotor of the chopper."

"The fuel tanks are in the wings."

"Right. The rotor hits against the right wing and ignites the tank. That's the first explosion. Meanwhile, the main rotor's knocked off the JetRanger, and it sinks like a stone."

"With the Skyhawk tangled up under it!"

Dana pressed her face to the glass. Directly below was the amusement park. She was quiet a moment, running through the scenario again in her mind. Finally she shook her head. "That can't be the way it happened. Why would the plane deliberately fly that close to the helicopter?"

"Bad guys do it all the time. That's how they get into American airspace. They follow a craft that's flying here legitimately and get inside its radar footprint, and nobody ever knows they're there. Same thing with the low elevation. Scud-running, they call it. Fly low enough, you're invisible on a radar screen."

"But these weren't international flights," she said. "And Loudenberg didn't have any reason to hide. Nobody was following him." She shook her head emphatically. "I'd never be able to sell that theory to a jury."

Broder set his jaw and turned his eyes straight ahead. "Now I know why the legal system's broken."

"Why?"

"Because you people won't look any further than whatever a jury'll believe."

"What else should I be looking for?" she demanded.

"The truth," he said. "Figure out what happened first, and then worry about how the hell you can sell it."

They sat in silence while Broder, fuming, continued to fly laps above the park.

Dana was the first to relent. "I guess I need to know more

about Loudenberg. Maybe I should make a trip up to Montrose myself."

"Not Montrose."

"What?"

"That's not where they took off from, at least not on the last leg of their flight."

She grabbed the radar report and flipped through the pages. "Then where?"

"Place called Laporte."

"Where's that?"

Broder pulled off his sunglasses and turned to her with his eyes dancing. "Let's go find out."

27

Laporte was a small town in Sullivan County, about—Dana measured with her knuckle on the road map—fifty miles southwest of Montrose. She knew a little about Sullivan County. One of her retired partners owned a summer place there in a mountain resort town called Eagles Mere. It was the gem of the county, a Victorian-era town with tree-lined streets and three-story stone and clapboard cottages, all hugging the shore of a vast private lake. The summer residents were Philadelphians and New Yorkers whose families had been vacationing there for three or four generations and who still used grandmother's wicker on the porch. They stayed all summer, but from Labor Day until spring it was a ghost town, visited only by men from the neighboring communities who supplemented their unemployment checks with handyman wages taking care of the empty houses.

Sullivan County was one of the most sparsely populated counties in the state. Dana's partner liked to tell an illustrative story. When he bought his cottage out of a cousin's estate, the closing was presided over by a lawyer in Laporte who simultaneously represented the seller, the bank, and the title insurance company, not to mention the Eagles Mere property owners' association. He was also county solicitor and district attorney—in fact, he was the only lawyer in the county. Her partner joked with him over the settlement table, "How'd you like to hire me? Looks like you could use an associate up

199

here." To which the Laporte lawyer growled, "Associate, hell. What I need's an adversary!"

The county's sparse population was evident from the air. Dense stands of forest undulated over the mountainous terrain, broken only occasionally by an acre of cleared land revealing a house, a pickup out front, and a woodpile out back. Roads appeared even more infrequently; this country was not easy to get into or out of.

Even from the sky. Andy circled for ten minutes, alternating glances between the ground and his charts, but there was no sign of an airport, an airstrip, or even a field open and level enough to land a plane.

"This can't be the place," Dana said.

Andy made another loop that took them over a narrow, winding valley. A lonely highway twisted below, and densely wooded mountains sloped up on either side. There were a few clearings but they were only big enough to allow some meager daylight into a house or cabin.

"Are you sure you plotted this right?" she asked.

"If there's a mistake, it's in the radar data, not in my navigation."

"Must be nice to be so sure of yourself."

"Yeah, it's great." He pointed. "Take a look down there." For a few hundred yards the road traveled in a gentle curve, the closest thing to a straight run in a twenty-mile radius. "I'm guessing that's Loudenberg's airstrip."

"Where?" She pressed her forehead to the glass. "The road?"

"Yep."

Her eyes moved over the steep terrain. "But then what? He couldn't very well leave his plane parked on a highway."

"Must be a small clearing by the roadside back there. Let's go down and see."

" 'Down' meaning 'on the road'?" she exclaimed. "Broder, try to remember: this is a plane, not a helicopter."

He laughed. "You try to remember you're flying with an Alaskan bush pilot. I've landed on ice floes when I had to."

He eased the nose up and circled a thousand feet higher to scan for traffic, then waited for a lumber truck to pass before swooping down into the valley again. When the straightest stretch of road appeared ahead, he pulled back on the throttle and glided low over the road surface. Dana's hands gripped the sides of her seat as she braced herself, but the main wheels touched softly down, followed an instant later by the nose wheel.

"See?" he said. "Nothing to it."

A clearing appeared off the left shoulder ahead, and he worked the rudders and brake to make the turn. The plane jolted hard as they left the macadam surface, and the sunlight dimmed as the forest rose up all around them. Tree limbs arched overhead, and the wingtips almost touched the trunks as they rolled to a stop.

"Barely enough room in here for a Skyhawk to turn around," he said.

"Not a bad hiding place, then." Dana gazed through the window at the dark woods beyond. "Let's get out and have a look."

The clearing was made recently. The undergrowth was brambles and brush, rough-cut and fighting to come back. Three stumps remained, chainsawed almost flush with the ground. Andy went down on his haunches to study the earth.

"Any sign that Loudenberg's plane was here?" she asked.

"The ground's so hard and dry, I couldn't tell you if *my* plane was here."

She searched the perimeter of the clearing, and after a few minutes found what she was looking for: a faint trail leading through the woods up the mountainside. "Let's look up this way," she called, and started up the hill.

It might have been nothing more than a deer trail. Rocks and roots protruded and the brush swiped at her ankles and calves until she began to regret her shorts and sneakers. Halfway up, Andy elbowed past her. "Not so fast," he said in a low voice. "If this is a paramilitary camp, there'll be a lookout posted."

She couldn't believe there was any camp there. The woods were so quiet, she couldn't believe there was *anyone* there. But she let him take the lead; in jeans and work boots he made a

better trailblazer. He hiked in long strides that made no concession to the steepness of the slope except for the muscles that
clenched and unclenched in his buttocks as he climbed. Dana
followed with her eyes fixed on the treetops above.

The light started to brighten as they approached the top of the
slope, and soon another clearing appeared ahead. Andy sidestepped off the trail, treading softly to avoid the deadfall. Carefully, Dana followed him around a clump of bushes until they
had an open view of the clearing.

A low wooden building squatted in the field. It was painted a
dun brown and its flat roof was covered with evergreen branches
that almost concealed the satellite dish mounted there. Two
windows were in the rear wall, and both were closed. There was
no sign of movement inside or out.

"Check it out?" Andy whispered.

She nodded, and they rose together in a half crouch, and
circled through the woods to the other side of the clearing. A
field of parched brown grass led to the front of the cabin. There
were two more windows on this side and a heavy steel door. All
was quiet.

Andy pointed to the building and raised his eyebrows in a
question. Dana watched another minute before she nodded. He
held up a branch, and she ducked under it and stepped out of
the woods.

The dark shape of a man shot up in front of her.

Andy grabbed her around the waist and threw her to the
ground under him. They lay frozen, ears straining and hearts
pounding, but nothing happened. Slowly he levered off her, and
Dana lifted her head. The man still loomed over them, but he
wasn't moving, and after she could breathe again she saw that it
was only a two-dimensional plywood cutout.

They waited and watched, but when nothing stirred from the
building and no more plywood men rose out of the grass, they
got to their feet and circled around to the front of the silhouette.
It was perforated with bullet holes.

"A shooting range," Andy said.

Fuzzy chalk lines in the grass marked off the firing lanes, and a half-dozen more pop-up targets of human silhouettes lay in the weeds.

"Let's check out the cabin," she said.

They ran across the open field and flattened themselves against the wall, then inched to the edge of a window. Dana dropped to her knees under it and raised up long enough for a split-second glance inside before she ducked down again.

"Anybody?" he whispered.

"All clear."

They both raised up. Inside was a single room with two sets of bunk beds to the left, a Formica-topped table and vinyl chairs straight ahead, a TV and a couch to the right.

"It looks like a hunting camp."

Loudenberg was a hunter, Dana remembered, and for half a second she persuaded herself that that was all it was. Without sentries or bunkers or barbed-wire battlements, there was nothing to mark it a paramilitary camp.

But hunters wouldn't do target practice on human silhouettes, and they wouldn't try to camouflage their cabin from the air, either.

Andy's breath hissed beside her, and a second later Dana heard what he'd heard—the metallic click of a cocking lever behind them.

"You know, honey," Andy said as his hand dropped to squeeze her buttock. "I don't think this is the right place."

Her eyes slid toward his. "No," she said in a strangled voice. "He said there'd be a double bed and a fireplace."

"Hands on your head! And turn around real slow."

Andy gave a little jump of surprise, and Dana did the same. Together they rotated, palms flat on their heads.

Two men stood with guns pointed. Dana recognized the forward grips and the curved magazines, and a shiver rippled down her back.

"Hey, what's going on?" Andy asked.

"You're trespassing, buddy," spoke the one on the left, a weak-chinned man with wispy blond hair.

"Oh, Lord, Ralph," Dana cried. "What've you gone and done?"

"Look, we're real sorry," Andy said. "Truth is, we just this minute realized we're in the wrong place. We never meant to trespass on you folks, believe me."

The first man put up his gun, but the other one kept it trained. "Who are you? Where'd you come from?" he demanded.

"I'm Ralph Bellamy. From Wilkes-Barre. And this here's—well, I'd appreciate it if I didn't have to give the lady's name."

"How come?"

"Come on, she's married, all right? But we're not out to hurt anybody. We're just looking for a place to have a couple hours alone. You know how it is. A friend told me about a cabin up this way, but it sure seems like I took a wrong turn someplace."

The blond man laughed and the other one shot him a hot look.

"Come on," Andy wheedled. "I don't have a place of my own, I don't have nothin' but a truck. And look at her—you can see she's not the kind of woman to make do with that."

"Ralph, you hush."

The blond man gave her an appraising look, then waved his gun at the woods. "Go on, get outta here."

"Hold on," the other man snapped. "Better wait and see what the boss has to say about this."

"Who's in charge here, Zack?" The blond man aimed a glare at Andy. "You two didn't see nothing, you hear me?"

"I hear ya!" Andy grabbed Dana's hand. "Thanks!"

They walked stiff-legged across the clearing and didn't look back until they reached the tree line. The other man's gun was up now, too, but he was shaking his head angrily.

"Let's get the hell out of here," Andy said. "Before they change their minds."

The forest laid a cover of darkness over them as they sprinted for the trail. It was as steep going down as it was coming up, and Dana lost her footing and slid six feet over roots and rocks before Andy scrambled ahead and grabbed her. She stood up shakily, and he took the lead down the trail.

"Those guns—" he said over his shoulder.

"MP-5Ks, I know. The blond man, the one who let us go?" She'd recognized him from Travis Hunt's slides.

"Yeah?"

"Loudenberg's son, Bill, Jr."

"Jesus."

The dim light of the woods began to brighten. The roadside clearing was ahead, and Dana picked up her pace as the glimmer of metal fuselage winked through the trees.

But Andy suddenly pulled up short, and her chest met his back in a full-body press. She opened her mouth in a little cry of surprise, but he turned and clapped his hand over it.

Her eyes sparked with uncomprehending anger.

"Look," he whispered, pointing with his chin, and took his hand away.

Three men stood beside the plane, each one cradling a sub-machine gun. One of them approached the plane, and the other two brought up their guns and took a bead on the cockpit as he climbed up inside. When he came out, he had something in his hand.

Andy cursed softly. "The ignition key."

The man jumped to the ground and yelped something to the other two. There was a flash of light from the muzzles of their guns and then an explosion roared over the hillside.

Dana hit the ground with Andy on top of her. The rapid-fire bursts of bullets echoed in pings and clangs against the fuselage, and a boom sounded as a window exploded.

Andy grabbed her hand and pulled her scrambling frantically after him into the woods. An exposed root tripped her, and she lurched forward and sprawled headlong on the ground. His hands were at her waist, lifting her up and urging her on.

The gunfire ended, and in the sudden silence they dove to the ground. They squeezed together under the cover of brush and strained to listen for the faint voices behind them.

"The two guys back at camp'll describe us," Andy whispered. "And then they'll come looking for us."

Dana looked back the way they'd come. The ground was so hard and dry that their footsteps left no impression. Unless the troop included an Indian tracker, they shouldn't be able to follow.

"We could head for the highway," he said. "Flag down somebody to help."

"But that's the first place they'll look."

"Or we can go deeper into the woods and hide."

A Hobson's choice between safety in the woods and no help, or help on the highway but no safety. "Let's go for the highway," she decided.

"Okay, but we better keep to the woods for a mile or so and come out a ways down."

She nodded.

They got to their feet and ran on in a hard jog over the rough terrain. Dana forgot about her shorts and sneakers and ran without a thought for the branches that whipped at her arms and ankles. She was trying so hard to be soundless that for a minute she forgot to breathe. Her chest was bursting before she remembered to suck in air.

Andy carved a trail leading west, and after half an hour they poked their heads through a clump of bushes bordering on two lanes of asphalt.

It was a Saturday afternoon on a lonely stretch of road in the middle of one of the least populated counties in Pennsylvania. Dana didn't expect to find rush-hour traffic. But neither did she expect to wait another thirty minutes without a single car passing.

They squatted low behind the bushes, Andy watching the road in one direction and Dana in the other, and when their muscles locked up, they dropped to their knees and traded positions. She had the image of every leaf of every tree and bush imprinted on her brain, until at last the faint dull whine of rubber tires sounded.

A truck rounded the curve of the highway, an old dusty blue pickup with a cap over the bed, traveling slowly. Andy tensed up beside her, ready to spring out and flag it down, but something made her reach out and hold him still as it passed.

The truck rolled to a stop on the shoulder ahead, and out of the woods, from behind a tree she'd been staring at for half an hour, came one of the men with a submachine gun slung over his shoulder.

Andy cursed. "They got the whole fucking road staked out."

The man conferred briefly with the driver of the truck, then blended back into his post in the woods. The truck moved on, and with painstaking soundlessness Dana and Andy slithered out of their hiding place and moved back into the woods.

"They can't cover the whole road," she said. "There aren't that many of them."

"We don't know how many there are. And we don't know how far apart they're spaced, or how often the truck makes its rounds."

"They won't search forever."

"No. Only until they find us."

She walked ahead of him to think. If he were right, hiding would do them no good. They had only two choices, and one of them was to run away, as far and as fast as they could.

She turned to Andy. "We have to get back to the plane."

"The plane? It's all shot up. Even if we could get to it, there's no way we'll fly it out of here."

"No, not fly. Call for help on the radio."

"They took the key, remember?"

"Can't you hot-wire it or something?"

"Yeah, maybe. If I had an hour or so to work on it."

She trudged on a few minutes before she turned to him again. "Won't they come looking for us after a while? The FAA or somebody? Isn't that what they do when a plane goes down?"

He shook his head. "I didn't file a flight plan. For all anybody knows, I'm on my way back to Alaska."

Dana looked at him, confused. "But I heard you. On the phone this morning? Weren't you talking to somebody—"

"To Carly, yeah. But only to get her to fuel up for me."

Carly. That must have been the female bodybuilder in the house trailer. The one with no phone lines running to it.

"Wait a minute," she said sharply. "How could you call her? She doesn't have a phone."

His cheeks colored a little before he gave a sheepish laugh. "All right, you caught me. She has a cellular."

"Then why'd you tell me—"

"Hey, it's not the worst lie I ever told to get a lady's phone number."

He turned on his full-dimple power, but Dana stalked away from him in outrage. Her first instincts were right, and she should have obeyed them. He was a reckless kid with no sense of responsibility or appreciation of the gravity of the circumstances. She should have gone to Doug Wetherby or Ed Stoltz for help. They would have handled the matter professionally, and without playing adolescent, testosterone-driven games.

But another thought came to her, so fast it burned out her anger. She ran back and caught him by the arms.

"Andy! I have *my* cellular phone! It's in my bag in the cockpit!"

His eyes opened wide. But a second later he shook his head. "We'd never get past them."

"They're out looking for us—not guarding a plane that won't fly."

"And it probably wouldn't even work. I mean, what are the chances of a mobile phone transmitter tower being anywhere within range?"

She considered a moment, then said, "The best we've got."

28

One man was left behind to watch the plane. They watched from the bushes as he pulled off his cap and mopped the sweat from his forehead. It was Billy Loudenberg, pulling punishment duty and not taking it like a soldier. He leaned lazily against the wing strut with his gun slung loosely over his shoulder, muzzle pointing up.

Andy's eyes moved through the clearing and the woods surrounding it. "It's too dangerous," he said again.

But Dana could see that he was thinking it through, working up a plan. "Should I run for the plane, or you?" she prompted.

His breath came out in a puff of resignation. "I'll circle to the other side and try to draw him away. If he goes for it, you run to the plane, get your phone, and run back here and wait. But *don't move* until he goes after me."

He got up and set off in a running crouch. Dana rose up on her haunches, runners on your mark, ready to dash when it was clear.

From deep in the woods on the other side of the clearing, Andy's voice sounded. His words were indistinct but the tone was conversational and punctuated by a laugh, as if he were talking to her.

Loudenberg's back went straight and he brought the gun into position. His head rotated in a slow survey of the clearing. When Andy's voice came again, he took off at a run into the woods.

Dana waited two beats and sprang to her feet. She moved

carefully through the bushes, but when she hit the clearing she ran in a flat-out sprint to the plane. She vaulted onto the step, swung the door open, dove behind the seat.

Her bag still lay where she'd left it on the floor, beside the stainless steel coffee thermos. She grabbed it by the shoulder strap and jumped to the ground and was halfway back to the woods when she remembered Andy's manila envelope. The photographs were in it. The ones these men had been chasing for a week.

She did an about-face and ran back and jumped into the cockpit again. The envelope was in the back, next to Andy's markup of the radar report. She grabbed both and was backing out of the cockpit on her hands and knees when a metal click sounded behind her.

"Okay, lady, nice and easy, hands on your head and back out real slow."

It was Zack, Loudenberg's compatriot at the camp. Her head came up and she could see his reflection in the window in front of her. He stood rigid, with his gun pressed to his ribs and his finger on the trigger.

"Okay, don't shoot!" she cried.

She dropped her bag and the papers, and her left hand crept forward as she clamped her right hand to her head and inched backward on her knees. In the glass she saw his stance relax as she obeyed.

She kicked back against the forward grip of his gun and knocked the muzzle up, then twisted around with the thermos in her left hand and crashed it with a steel smack into the bones of his face. A dull grunt and a geyser spray of blood, and he crumpled to the ground.

Behind him the barrel of another gun loomed up, and she let out a strangled cry of fury and frustration.

The gun came down and Andy's face was behind it.

"Jeez, Dana," he said. "You didn't have to break the guy's nose."

Her breath came out in a long shudder. She grabbed the papers and her bag and slid to the ground.

Billy Loudenberg was lying in a second heap a few yards

away. "Here, take this," Andy said, thrusting the gun at her, and as she held it with trembling hands, he took a length of wire out of the plane's toolbox and bound the two men together, face-down, feet-to-feet, then lashed their hands behind their backs. He peeled off his shirt and ripped it down the center and used the cloth to gag them.

"That'll give us a little head start." He picked up the other man's gun and started for the woods.

Dana crammed the photos and papers in her bag, looped the strap over her shoulder, and, clutching the gun awkwardly to her chest, followed in a run after him.

She kept her eyes glued to the muscles of his back as he raced ahead of her. Twenty minutes passed in a hard run through the forest, but when nothing sounded behind them but the echo of her own ragged breath, she took a chance and slowed to a walk. Andy dropped back beside her. His breathing was unlabored, but sweat shone over his shoulders and chest, and his hair curled dark and damp against his skull.

She took out her phone and powered it up. The NO SVC message lit up on the display.

"Told you," he said, watching over her shoulder.

She wheeled on him with a retort on her lips, but as the antenna revolved, a weak signal blipped on the screen. They looked at each other, then at the direction the antenna was aimed.

"I vote that way," she said.

They turned and walked on.

Twilight fell and the mountains cast long murky shadows over the woods, but as a last ray of western light slanted through the trees, it struck against a brilliant liquid blue. Gleaming through the tree trunks ahead was a mountain lake.

They kept to the cover of the forest and circled it. On the western shore a hidden glade was already shrouded by the dusk. It was under a low canopy of maple trees, and the ground was a grassy circle wrapped with wild laurel.

"Safe?"

Andy scanned the shoreline and nodded, and Dana put the

gun down and flopped to the ground. Crickets were singing in the grass and frogs were croaking in the marsh reeds. She lay on her back and watched the last puffs of cloud turn gray and fade into black.

Suddenly she burst out, "Ralph *Bellamy*?"

Andy started, then looked down at her and laughed. "Hey, you're the one who named me Ralph."

"It was the least you deserved after that story you spun. I'm amazed those guys bought it."

"You know what they say—the best lies are the ones that don't stray too far from the truth."

She flushed as she deciphered his meaning. "I think I'll get a drink," she murmured.

She got up and knelt by the edge of the lake. The water smelled so cold and sweet that she bent over and plunged her face into it, then sat back on her heels and shook the droplets from her hair.

Andy was behind her, watching.

"Aren't you thirsty?"

His eyes swept the shoreline before he put the gun down and stretched out on his belly to drink.

They moved back under the cover of the maples, and Dana tried the phone again, but the signal was no stronger than before. She hugged her knees, and through the opening in the laurel she watched the play of the fading light on the water. Another shore beckoned on the other side of the lake, and beyond it the distant blue humps of the mountains. It was such beautiful country up here, and so hard to reconcile with the men they were fleeing.

Andy's expression was as solemn as her own. He sat with his chin resting on one knee up. His back was curved in a weary slump, and dark circles of exhaustion underscored his eyes.

"I'm sorry about your plane," she said. "I guess you didn't know what you were getting into when you volunteered for this, did you?"

He smiled and shrugged, and suddenly he looked very young to her. She reached out and stroked his face, and it was almost a surprise to feel the beard stubble there. "You didn't sleep at all last night, did you?"

He caught her hand and turned his mouth into it and kissed the well of her palm.

A shiver rolled up the length of her arm. Gently, she pulled her hand away. "Why don't you try to get some sleep now?"

"Dana—"

"I'll keep watch. You get some sleep."

He was too exhausted to argue. He stretched out on the grass and closed his eyes.

When she was sure he was asleep, she lifted her hand and gazed at the place he'd kissed.

29

The man turned the corner slowly and pulled up the long sweeping curve of the drive. Five stories of lights burned ahead, but the lot was almost empty. He parked at the edge of it and reached under the seat to pull out two items: a black knit stocking cap and a canvas backpack. He yanked the cap over his bright white hair and slung the pack over his shoulder.

At the tree line he stopped to strap on the goggles, and the night took on a sepia glow. He kept to the trees, a black figure moving against a black wall, until he reached the back of the fenced area and crossed the grass again. The gate was locked with a length of chain and a heavy padlock. He ran his fingers over the keyhole and followed them with an electric pick. A hinge faintly squeaked as he started to open the gate inward, and he stopped and reached for the oil can in the rucksack. A few drops and it opened soundlessly.

He kept his eyes on the ground littered with metal scrap and cigarette butts until he reached the edge of the pit, then followed the perimeter a hundred feet to the ladder. The side rails bowed and trembled under his weight as he climbed down twenty feet into the earth.

The box stood seven feet tall and turquoise-blue in the northeast corner. He opened the smaller box behind it and switched on the microphone. "Professor, you will step back into the corner by the john. There will be two guns trained on you as the door is opened. If you make any move toward the door, those guns will be fired."

"Yeah, yeah, I know all that," came the voice. "Got any other news for me?"

The man switched off the microphone and opened the ruck-sack to pull out the food and water. It was a tricky maneuver to pass it in without Tobiah's gun trained on the door, so he talked at some length to an imaginary Tobiah as he unlocked the chain wrapped around the box.

But the professor didn't try anything. "What's going on?" he demanded as the door was cracked open. "What have you done with my wife?"

The white-haired man closed the door and snapped the pad-lock through the chain again.

"KFC?" the professor called out next. "It better be extra-crispy."

The man chuckled under his breath as he packed up and started up the ladder. The phone chirped in the rucksack, and when he reached the top he pulled it out.

"Yes, sir."

"What now?"

He would keep this brief; his contact didn't know the loca-tion of the site, and he intended to keep it that way. "More bad news," he said.

"That she's disappeared? I know."

The man's eyes narrowed thoughtfully. So—his contact was cultivating a contact of his own. The power hadn't shifted as far as he'd hoped.

"Yes, sir. And in view of that, I recommend we shut down the operation."

"No!" The note of panic was back, and the man smiled to hear it. "No, listen—I'll find her."

"Keep in touch," he said, and turned off the phone.

30

A gentle murmur of water sounded, like the lapping of waves against a rocking boat. The air was still and hot, but the sound of the water was so cool and fresh, its whisper alone seemed to stir a breeze.

Dana opened her eyes and wondered how long she'd slept. The stars were out and a half-moon was rising over the treetops, but the air was still so thick and heavy that it couldn't have been night for long. It was so hot that she barely wanted to breathe.

She stretched out her arms and rolled onto her back. Littered on the ground beside her were a pair of boots, blue jeans, underwear, and socks. She sat up straight and looked through the opening in the bushes. The moon shone a pale yellow on the surface of the lake, and in the glow of it was the dark silhouette of a man.

Slowly, she rose to her feet and moved to the edge of the laurel. He was standing with his back to her, and it glistened from the slope of his shoulders to where the white curve of his buttocks disappeared into the black water. The moon was shimmering off the lake in dreamlike waves of light and dark and air and water, and the vision nearly hypnotized her. So much that when a splash sounded and he disappeared, she almost wondered if it were a mirage.

But a moment later he burst through the surface ten feet away. The lake was shallower there and reached only to his thighs. He shook himself like a spaniel, a spray of water fanned out from his head, but the hard flesh of his body never moved.

The heat crawled out of the earth and slithered up her legs and tightened like a ponderous weight around her shoulders. Her breasts were swollen and throbbing, and a pulse of blood pounded through her pelvis and between her legs. She felt heavy and engorged and ready to burst.

Andy dove under the surface again and left only silvery ripples where he'd been.

She was so hot and sluggish that when her hands moved, she hardly knew how. The shirt peeled from her skin and slipped off over her head. The shorts fell open and slid to her feet. Still too hot. The bra unhooked and her aching breasts escaped, her underwear whispered to the ground.

He shot through the surface again, facing her this time, and from twenty feet away she heard his breath catch. He didn't move, but eddies of water swirled out from his body, flowing in wider and wider circles until they reached the shore. Her feet were rooted to the earth beneath her, but the heat was so intense, she had to move. She took one tentative, awkward step toward him.

He was out of the lake and in front of her in three strides. The water streamed off his shoulders, so cold and wet that when his body pressed against hers, the steam seemed to rise off her skin with a hiss. They were the same height and everything met, from their eyes down to their toes. His hands were in her hair, his mouth was at her neck, her name was strangling in his throat.

She wrapped her arms around him and met his mouth. He felt like nothing she knew, and nothing she could have imagined. He was a solid in her arms, but so wet he felt like something liquid. Her hands splayed over his back, and she swallowed him in through her fingertips, drinking him in giant craving gulps of desire.

But he was a gas, too, combustible, and ignited. His lips ground against hers and his tongue thrust deep and hard into the recesses of her mouth. He reached for her breasts and pulled each nipple into his mouth, one after the other, sucking like a man dying of thirst. His erection brushed against her, once, and then more forcefully as he pressed for entry. Her knees went weak; the urge to open to him was all but irresistible.

She caught his head and lifted it from her breast, but he mistook her meaning and kissed her mouth again. The probing below became even more insistent. Another second and she would pull him in. With a struggle she broke free long enough to gasp, "Andy, do you have—"

"Oh—yeah." Panting hard, he hooked a foot behind her knees, and they tumbled to the ground. He groped in the pocket of his jeans until he found it, and with a cry of relief she rolled onto her back.

The water blinded her as it streamed from his hair into her eyes and mouth. He was all hard liquid fire now, and she drank him into the depths of her. Her legs came up and wrapped around his waist. She could feel him in the core of her body, and soon she could feel something else—the catch at the beginning of the climb. She moaned out loud, and his eyes lit up as his mouth swooped down over hers. The climb went steeper and harder and steeper and harder, until at last she was there, and with a cry she slid down the other side in a shower of shattering light.

He came a moment later with a groan that echoed like a mating cry through the wild, empty woods.

The night had gone deeper. A breeze whispered at the treetops, and at last, as their hearts slowed, the air began to cool. He rolled on his side and pulled her close, and they slept the night through in each other's arms.

The temperature plunged thirty degrees during the night, and Dana woke with a shiver. A ghostly white mist hung in swirls over the lake, and deep in the woods a bird shrieked a haunting, eerie cry. She propped up on an elbow, and her breath caught in her throat as a dark undulating shape appeared through the fog.

It was a deer, standing at the edge of the lake with his forelegs splayed wide and his head bent low to the water under a broad rack of antlers. Muscles quivered with tension inside his tawny hide; he knew she was there. But he held his ground and drank his fill before he bounded away through the forest.

Beside her lay the ghostly white shape of Andy Broder. He was curled toward her, with one elbow folded for a pillow and the other hand tucked between his arm and face. His hair was tousled and his lashes swept long and dark over his cheeks.

Her eyes traced the length of his body. It was nothing like the rangy, loose-limbed body she'd known best for the last twenty years. Andy's was tight and compact; it reminded her of an explosive in a container labeled WARNING: CONTENTS UNDER PRESSURE.

She couldn't quite fathom herself in this scene, here with this swaggering young man who set her teeth on edge the moment they met and whom she couldn't wait to ship back to Alaska. From the start she'd known he could make her mad, but now she knew he could drive her mad, too.

It was the cold light of morning. This was no moonlight madness, no heat-induced hypnotic trance that she could blame for her behavior. But the contractions of desire were pulsing inside her like a life force, and suddenly she understood how a million men must have felt before her. *I've worked so hard, and I've given so much. This is my reward. Right and wrong don't apply to me anymore. I deserve this. I want this.*

She closed the distance between them and woke him with a shiver of his own as she took him in her mouth. She moved with long, luxurious strokes, and when his hips began to buck with excitement, she rose up and straddled him, and all thoughts flew from her mind but this: *Yes! Yes, I deserve this. Oh, God, I want this!*

Afterward they got to their feet, beating their arms and stamping their feet against the chill of the morning. Their clothes were damp with dew, and their breath puffed out in twin fogs as they hurried to dress. Andy's shirt was gone, cut up for gags back by the plane, but Dana watched him shimmy into his jeans, and when he started to zip up his fly, she brushed his hands away and did it herself.

He gave a lazy, contented grin. "I guess now you think I'm cheap."

"At a hundred bucks an hour? Hardly."

He laughed and pulled her into his arms for a kiss. The warmth was so wonderful she let herself linger there, and it was an effort finally to break away.

"Regrets?" he murmured, holding her.

"No," she said, startled. "Why should I?"

He glanced down at her hand, the left one, where it rested on his hipbone.

"Oh." Her wedding band looked suddenly discordant and out of place on her finger, like some kind of mutating cancer. "I'm separated," she said. "I don't know why I haven't taken this off before." She twisted hard at the ring, but it wouldn't slide over her knuckle. It hadn't been off her finger since Whit put it on fifteen years before; her joints must have swollen since then.

He squatted down to lace up his boots. "How long?"

"Seems like forever." In the next second she realized he meant how long had she been separated, but she let her answer stand; it felt true enough at the moment.

"Where's he live?"

"I don't know." Another truth. "Hey." She smiled down at him. "What's with the twenty questions? You notice I've refrained from asking you anything about your 'buddy.'"

He straightened. "Who? Carly?"

"Is that her name? I thought it was Charlene Atlas."

"Yeah, she's got some bod," he said appreciatively. "We flew together in the Marines."

"She's a pilot?"

"Yeah. And if she walked out of the woods last night and saw the two of us here naked? Guess whose bones she'd jump."

Dana's jaw dropped. "She's . . . ?"

"Last time I checked. Which, believe me, I've done."

She gaped at him a moment before peals of laughter tumbled out of her.

*   *   *

They started off again with the guns slung over their shoulders, moving away from the lake and back into the woods. Slowly, the sun rose and filtered soft light through the treetops, and slowly the air began to warm.

Dana took out the flip phone and tried again.

"Decided who you're gonna call?" he asked while she waited for the display to light up.

"A friend of mine in the U.S. Attorney's office. Mirella Burke. We're out of her jurisdiction, but she'll know who to contact and what buttons to push."

The NO SVC light continued to glow.

The day grew warmer as they hiked on. Though it was still early morning, the heat was building up for a replay of yesterday and the fifty days of drought and heat wave before it. Every fifteen minutes Dana stopped to try again. But the signal didn't grow any stronger, and now she had battery power to worry about, too. She waited thirty minutes before the next try, but still it was too weak to make the connection.

"Let's try this way," Andy said, and angled off the path they'd been following.

She kept her eyes on the display as they changed direction. At once the signal started to fade. "Andy, no—that way's no good."

When he didn't answer, she looked up and saw where he was headed—up the steep face of a treeless mountain. She craned her head back. Above them towered a bald peak of rock, the highest, clearest point for miles around.

She put the phone away and scrambled up after him, hand over hand, foothold to foothold. She reached the summit panting for breath, and powered the phone up again.

They watched together as the signal bands lit up across the display, and their eyes met in triumph.

31

Mirella Burke pushed the door open with her considerable rear end and backed into the interrogation room with a tall glass of ice water in each hand. Dana gave her a look of pure gratitude and took a long drink. The local police protocol for a wilderness rescue was to wrap the victims in blankets and force hot coffee on them—even when it was ninety degrees and the victims had been feeding a roaring signal fire for hours. She'd been dying of thirst since they were brought in.

Andy, too. He took his glass and gulped it down without coming up for air. Someone had given him a white shirt to wear, fresh out of its box and a size too big. It fell from his shoulders in sharp fold lines and billowed around his ribs.

Mirella announced: "Mr. Broder, there's an agent out in the hall wants to talk to you about your plane."

He put the glass down. "They found it?"

"That's what the man says."

He touched Dana's shoulder on his way out. "Be right back."

Mirella shut the door after him and turned around with her hands on her hips. "You doin' all right, baby?"

They'd spent two hours waiting to be sighted by the rescue plane, an hour in transit via plane and unmarked car, and another two hours here in the federal building in Scranton. Scratches and bruises were starting to appear on Dana's body in places she couldn't remember injuring, there was a dull pounding in the back of her skull, and still this unquenchable thirst. "Yes, I'm fine," she said.

"How 'bout I bring you another samwich or somethin'?"

"Mirella, please. Just sit down and tell me what's going on."

Mirella's face clouded as she lowered herself into a chair. From the chin up she possessed the regal beauty of an African queen, with chiseled cheekbones and exotically slanted eyes and hair sleeked back into a chignon at the nape of her neck. But too many years' subsistence on cheap starches and fried foods had taken their toll. The government-issue chair of molded plastic was not molded to Mirella. Rolls of flesh bulged out and spilled over in all directions as she sat down.

"Well, they followed the coordinates your young man gave 'em and they found his plane, all shot to hell like you said."

"And what about the camp?"

"There's a cabin up there, all right. But that's about it."

Dana dropped her head in her hands and massaged her brow. She hadn't expected those men to sit tight for twenty-four hours and wait for the FBI to come, but still she'd hoped for it. She looked up at Mirella again. "What about Billy Loudenberg? Did they pick him up yet?"

"Nobody home at the farm."

"Then check the hospitals for the other guy, Zack. I broke his nose, he probably went to the emergency room last night."

Mirella's eyes shifted. "Yeah, somebody's doin' that."

"Somebody?" Dana pushed away from the table and got to her feet. "Mirella, why isn't this getting any priority?"

"Hey, it's Sunday, and this is a busy office. For a lot of these guys, this is their first Sunday off in months."

Dana's voice rose incredulously. "There's paramilitary nuts running around the countryside with submachine guns, and these guys don't want to give up their day off? Mirella, you drove three hours up here, and it's not even your district."

"That's 'cause you was in trouble, honey. But these guys— all they got is some clowns shot up a plane, and that's nothin' but a property crime. How they gonna justify a full-scale man-hunt when they got no evidence of paramilitary? Shit, they wasn't even wearin' uniforms."

Dana paced the room. She'd wondered about the uniforms herself. All the news stories about the paramilitary movement carried photos of men in camouflage fatigues, but the men on that mountain were wearing T-shirts and blue jeans. One of them even had Reeboks on his feet.

"What about the submachine guns we brought back?" she said, turning on Mirella.

She shrugged. "Gone to the crime lab. But hell—lots of bad guys got those."

"The firing range—and those targets?"

"No sign of 'em."

"But there were chalk lines on the grass—there must be some residue they could test for."

"Ain't no crime to draw on the grass."

"Mirella!—what about the satellite dish on the roof? They must have some kind of communications system in there."

"Yeah, it's called a TV set."

"No—"

"You think they got cable out there in the boonies?"

Dana stared at her until Mirella's eyes dropped to the table. Sharply, she said, "What's going on here?"

"Back off, chile." She slapped her palms on the table and pushed herself to her feet. "I'm a guest here myself, and I'm only tellin' you what they tole me."

Dana's mouth pulled tight and she pointed her arm at the door. "Then go out there and find your host and tell him I want to talk to him. Now."

Andy came back before Mirella did, and he took one look at Dana's face and said, "What happened?"

"Nothing," she said bitterly. "That's what they're doing to catch these guys—nothing. And I can't get a straight answer out of anybody, including my own best friend." She stirred herself and asked, "What about your plane?"

"I arranged for a mechanic to go out there and do what he can to get it airworthy. It'll take a couple days."

The door opened again, and Mirella came in with a thin, ascetic-looking man in tow. She introduced him as Dick Lomax, her counterpart, an Assistant U.S. Attorney in the Scranton office.

Lomax stood with his back stiff against the door. His eyes were so pale they looked opaque in the poor office light.

"Mr. Lomax," Dana said, "perhaps you can explain to me exactly what steps your office is taking to apprehend the men who attacked us."

"I'm not at liberty to do that. We have an ongoing investigation."

"If you mean into our assailants," Dana retorted, "so far I wouldn't call it much of an investigation."

"I mean more than that."

She waited, but his mouth closed as tightly as his face. She looked to Mirella. "What's he talking about?"

"Honey, they been lookin' into these characters for a long while."

"Then go out and arrest them, before they turn their guns on somebody else."

"Nobody's gonna get hurt," Mirella said.

"We need more time to put our case together," Lomax said.

"More time?" Dana burst out. "What is this? Another stand-off like that Freemen thing in Montana? You let them do whatever they want for six months, so no one'll accuse you of excessive force?"

Lomax's pale eyes glinted. "Fuck this," he muttered to Mirella. "*You* deal with her." He grabbed the knob and started to wrench the door open.

Dana stepped into his path. "No, *you* deal with me, Mr. Lomax, or tomorrow I'll hold a press conference and tell the world everything that happened—up on that mountain as well as right here in this office."

He shut the door again. "That cannot happen. We have a grand jury impaneled. You may not talk to anybody about anything."

It took Dana thirty seconds to realize what he was saying, and her eyes flared wide. "You can't stop me."

"It's grand jury information," Lomax said.

"We witnessed it ourselves! You can't throw a grand jury cloak over things we saw and heard on our own."

"We have a serious felony investigation here!"

"Yeah, and we have fifty billion dollars' worth of claims to defend against!"

Mirella's hand was on Dana's arm. "Come on now. You need our back-scratchin' much as we need yours."

Dana flashed hot eyes at her. "What are you doing, Mirella? Double-teaming me?"

"Listen, babe, you don't go along, Lomax here'll slap a court order on you so fast your head'll spin."

"Fine, give me an order," Dana bit out. "And after I violate it and you jail me for contempt, I'll have the whole civil bar picketing Janet Reno's house in twenty-four hours. Maybe then somebody'll realize who the victims are here."

Mirella's eyes went small and shiny like coffee beans. "Wait here." She took Lomax by the elbow and hauled him into the corridor.

Dana flopped into a chair to wait. Andy was sitting at the end of the table with his chin in his hand, watching her.

They came back in two minutes. "Give me one month," Lomax said. "We'll have our indictment by then, and you can spout off all you want about it."

Dana glanced at Andy, but Mirella intercepted the look and made a final pitch. "Hell, chile, you more'n two years away from trial anyways. Ain't no skin offa your back."

Dana shook her head. Mirella didn't understand civil litigation. Most cases were fought and won before trial ever began. Dana knew her real battle wasn't convincing the jury that Pennsteel was blameless, it was convincing all the plaintiffs-to-be. And that battle had to be fought soon.

Mirella stepped close and spoke softly. "I wouldn't be asking you if it weren't important. You have to trust me on this one."

One month. Dana closed her eyes and calculated. It would take her a week, maybe two, to work up the data to confirm Andy's theory about the Skyhawk's route. Another week or two beyond that and she could put together a pretty impressive computer simulation to illustrate the collision. She'd go one better than Ira Thompson's press conference; she'd put on a full-scale presentation with graphics.

"All right," she said finally. "One month." She stood up and leaned over Mirella. "And no extensions. You hear me, honey chile?"

32

By two o'clock they were in a rented red Camry on the turn-pike, heading south. Andy took the wheel and drove in silence while Dana mulled endlessly over the scene with Mirella and Lomax. They said they needed to build their case, but from where she stood, they had an airtight case already: the eye-witness testimony of two credible citizens; the physical evidence of the plane and the guns; and good leads for finding two of the suspects who could almost certainly be flipped to testify against the rest. Yet not only wouldn't they go out and arrest the offenders, they imposed a monthlong gag order on the witnesses. Why the delay and why the silence?

"Got a theory?" Andy asked, reading her mind.

She shifted in her seat to face him. "I have two, and I don't know which one's worse."

"Try 'em out on me."

"Okay, number one: Lomax is out to fry bigger fish than these guys, and for something a lot worse than smuggling guns and shooting up your plane. Maybe they're planning to blow up something, something awful like the Oklahoma City Federal Building. And Lomax needs to catch them in the act. Or at least a lot closer to the act than this."

"Sounds reasonable. What's theory two?"

"There's some kind of cover-up going on, and Mirella and Lomax are part of it."

He cocked an eyebrow. "What are they covering up?"

"Well, for sure they're covering up their half-baked police work today. Mirella lied to me at least twice about what they were doing to investigate the scene and to arrest Billy Loudenberg and the other guy, Zack."

"I don't exactly picture your friend Mirella having ties to a right-wing paramilitary troop."

"No," Dana conceded. "But a cover-up doesn't have to be to conceal a crime; it could be just to conceal somebody's screwup. Maybe Lomax collared these guys before, and without taking the time to figure out what they were up to, he gave them immunity or something. Or say those guns came out of an FBI evidence locker. Pretty embarrassing to the Justice Department if anybody got wind of that."

Andy drove a few more miles in silence, then said, "Can I ask you something?"

"What?"

"If you believe all that—if you believe *any* of that—why didn't you tell them about the film and the burglaries?"

"Because I was afraid our story was already incredible enough. I thought they'd write me off as a nut case if I told them somebody was following me and calling me on the phone and breaking into my house to steal a roll of film." She gave a shrug. "Though it looks like they had me written off from the start."

He cut in, "Calling you on the phone?"

"Yeah, somebody called the office a few times and wouldn't leave his name—when was that?—Thursday. And there were some hang-ups on my home machine Thursday night."

"Oh." Sheepishly, he said, "That might've been me."

"Andy—" she cried, piqued. "Why didn't you just leave a message?"

"I didn't know what your situation was then."

"What situation?"

He reached over and stroked her hand.

Her wedding band again. She buried both hands in her lap. "That was no reason not to leave a message. As of Thursday, we were a lawyer and an expert working together on a lawsuit, and that's all."

"Maybe that's all you were working on," he said with his

dimples popping. "I mighta been working on something else, too."

She gave him an exasperated look. "Why didn't *you* tell the FBI those guys are chasing the film?"

He was watching a slow-moving truck ahead, and he cut out around it and sped ahead before he finally answered. "Because I don't think they are."

"What?"

"Like you said before, it doesn't make any sense. What do they care about pictures of the accident scene? The ATF's got their guns, the FAA's got the tail number off the Skyhawk, the coroner's got the ID of Loudenberg and his kid. There's nothing on the film that can fuck 'em any more than that."

"But if the pictures show the plane was at fault—"

"Big shit. Like you said, who's gonna sue them?"

She threw her hands up. "But then what does *that* mean? A whole different set of criminals broke into my car and house?" She shook her head emphatically. "Maybe that's what life is like up in the Last Frontier, but it's a little far-fetched for Pennsylvania."

"The other day you thought the paramilitary angle was far-fetched."

"Yeah, well . . ." She turned her face to the window. "The other day everything seemed different."

Philadelphia was still fifty miles south when she remembered to check her voice mail. The batteries in the flip phone were dead, but she plugged the auxiliary cord into the outlet under the dash and dialed the office.

About a hundred calls had come in during the forty-eight hours since she'd been gone. Laboriously, she went through each one, fastforwarding through those that could wait and listening closely to those that couldn't. There were several messages from Travis Hunt, each one a little more frantic than the one before, until finally she reached the one she'd been dreading.

"Dana," he mumbled miserably, "I heard from the sound engineer. He ran every filtering program he could on the CVR tape, and I'm sorry, but it's not there. Your voice, I mean. Anyway, sorry."

She groaned out loud.

"What?" Andy said.

Briefly she explained, then pushed replay and handed him the phone and slumped against the seat back. That was it, then. It was her word against Ira Thompson's spin. She'd have to be a witness, and that meant she was out as counsel for Pennsteel. Ironic, really. She and Andy risked their lives this weekend, and all for a case that wasn't even hers anymore.

He listened to Travis's message and handed the phone back. "Let me see if I follow," he said. "Were you looking to prove your conversation with this Sullivan guy, or were you looking to prove that the chopper didn't do a descent?"

"Both. The two stand together."

"Sure. But they also stand apart."

She squinted over at him.

"You don't need the conversation to rule out the descent," he said. "All you need's the recording."

"What?"

"Here's how it works. When you want to do a vertical descent in a helicopter, you do what's called a collective down. You lower the collective lever, which changes the pitch on all the main rotor blades simultaneously. It makes for a pretty distinctive sound."

She sat up straight. "Distinctive enough to be heard on the CVR tape?"

"Hell, yes, that's what I'm trying to tell you."

"So if it's not on there—"

"Then the chopper held its altitude."

"Andy—that's great!" This was something none of the other experts had thought of, and it catapulted her to another idea. "If this maneuver were performed in another JetRanger, you'd be able to hear it on the CVR tape?"

"Yep. Then you could have your sound guy compare it with the CVR tape from the accident."

A minute later she reached Ted Keller's wife, who called him inside from cutting the grass.

"Ted, you ever hear of something called a collective down maneuver?" She sent Andy a quick glance to confirm that she said it right. He nodded.

There was a beat of silence before Keller burst out, "What an idiot!"

"Excuse me?"

"I should've thought of it myself! If Ron did what they're accusing him of, you'd have to hear it."

"Any chance you could take another JetRanger up and—"

"You bet! I'll scrub my morning flight and do it first thing tomorrow."

She sent a dazzling smile to Andy as she disconnected.

They decided to return to the fortieth-floor war room, but Dana wanted to stop at the house first to pack some clothes. They exited the turnpike at Valley Forge, and she pointed the way west and up the hillside road to the house. They parked in the driveway and went in through the front door.

Andy stopped in the hall, rubbernecking to take it all in. "Tell me again," he said. "About how you have to keep working 'cause you have so many bills to pay."

She made a face and started to brush past him up the stairs, but he held her back with a hand on her elbow. "Stay here a minute. Let me check it out first."

While she waited, she went out to the street to collect the mail, and when she came back, she called up the stairs, "All clear?"

"Yeah," came Andy's voice. "Okay if I take a shower?"

"Help yourself."

She went to the kitchen and dropped the mail on the counter. Through the rear windows she could see how dry and brown the lawn was. The level of water in the pool was down three inches, and even the house plants were wilting. One of the showers rushed on upstairs; she pictured Andy in the stream and felt hotter than ever.

She took a cold soda from the refrigerator and poured a few gulps down her throat as she sorted through the mail. Bills, catalogues, a party invitation for Mr. and Mrs. Whitman

Endicott. She tilted the can back again, and when her wedding band clinked against the metal, she went to the kitchen sink and soaped her finger thoroughly and gave a tug. Still stuck. She'd have to go to a jeweler and have it cut off.

She shuffled through the rest of the mail. More catalogues, flyers, a couple marketing videos wrapped in plain brown paper. She picked one up and looked for the company logo on the return address, but there was no address. There was nothing on it but her name, and with a jolt she recognized Whit's handwriting.

She stared at it in astonishment. A Dear Jane letter by video-tape? She never would have expected it from him. Morbid curiosity made her open it and load it in the VCR in the family room.

The video was shot with a handheld camera late Thursday night; the date and time were displayed on the bottom of the screen. A few seconds of grainy static, and Whit appeared. His hair was uncombed and his face haggard, looking as if he just staggered out of bed and was on the verge of collapsing back into it. Dana stood back and crossed her arms. Some wild week he must have had.

But then her breath stopped in her throat and her hands tightened around her arms like blood pressure cuffs. The tape sputtered to an end and still she stood and watched the snow flit across the screen in a stupor of disbelief.

What could she do? *What could she do?* The film was already developed, the Friday morning train had come and gone.

What did they think after her no-show? Did they realize she hadn't gotten the instructions? Or did they follow through on their threat Friday night? No—they must have realized it. They must have tried to communicate with her again.

Of course—the second video. She ran back to the kitchen. The other package was the same: no stamps, no postal cancellation mark. Only her name, handwritten by Whit.

Andy's steps sounded on the back stairs, and she grabbed both videos and ran to the front hall and up the other stairs to the bedroom. She locked the door and flew across the room to the VCR.

The second video was taped Friday night. Whit's hair was plastered to his skull, and his shirt looked as if it had been dunked in water and wrung out by hand. His face was dark, either shadowed by beard stubble or bruised.

Downstairs, Andy was calling, "Dana?"

She didn't dare turn the volume up. She moved next to the TV and put her ear close to the speaker.

"Time is running out," Whit read. His voice was raspy, as if he had a sore throat or a deep thirst. "If the delivery isn't accomplished, these men will kill me. You must follow their instructions precisely.

"Put the item in an eight-by-eleven-inch manila envelope. Take it to the Devon Horse Show fairgrounds Saturday night at seven-fifteen. Come alone; you will be watched at all times. Buy a ticket and take your seat; hold the envelope in your lap."

"Dana? Where are you?" Andy's voice came from the stairs.

"During the intermission, go through the fairgrounds to a shop called 'Horsin' Around.' Inside you will see a table of books for sale. One is entitled *Encyclopedia of the Horse*. Place the envelope inside the bottom copy of the book. Leave at once and take your seat in the stands. Remain there until nine o'clock.

"Follow these instructions precisely and I will be released as soon as the contents have been verified. Dana, do not deviate from these instructions in any way, or I will be killed."

The screen went blank.

She ran for the phone and snatched it up, but no dial tone sounded; the line was disconnected. *Idiot!* she screamed at herself, and slammed it down. She looked around wildly until she spotted her bag, dumped it out on the bed and grabbed her flip phone. The battery was dead, but she had a spare in the closet.

Andy was in the hall. "Dana? Are you in there? What's wrong?"

The battery connected, the phone powered up in her hand, and Whit's voice echoed in her mind: *You must make no attempt to contact the police.*

Standard stuff. Kidnappers probably said it all the time, and most people called the police anyway.

These men will know if you do.

How? Did they have a law enforcement contact? Was that the cover-up? But Mirella couldn't be involved if it were. She adored Whit, she always had.

The consequence will be that you and the children will never see me again.

That was the threat that made her heart freeze up. She couldn't do it, not in the state of their marriage. The girls knew how things were between them—children always knew, no matter how hard the parents tried to hide it. If the worst happened and the threat were carried out—how could she ever face them again? Their daddy would be dead because their mommy wouldn't follow the directions to save him.

"Dana, what's the matter?" Andy rattled the doorknob. "Let me in."

Saturday night had also come and gone, but she knew that the horse show ran through Sunday night. Did they know that, too, and would they go there again and try for another rendezvous? *Do not deviate from these instructions.* But her only hope was that they would deviate themselves.

"Dana, open the door!" He was pounding on it with both fists.

She turned the phone off and unlocked the door.

He stood with his fist raised to pound again. All he wore was a towel around his hips, and his hair was black and spiky from the shower. Slowly, he lowered his arm. "What's wrong? What happened?"

She turned and picked up the envelope of photographs from the bed. "I need the negatives," she said. "And every print you made."

"What for?"

"I can't explain now. Just get me the negatives and the prints."

His expression went petulant, and he folded his arms stubbornly over his chest. "I knew this was gonna happen."

"What?"

"That you'd have some kind of guilt attack once you got

back to the happy family home. So I'm out now, right? Out of the case, out of your bed."

Dana had to clench her fists tight to keep herself under control. "This has nothing to do with you, Andy."

"I can see that he hasn't been gone long. So, I'm just the rebound man, right?"

"Please—" She felt as if something were about to rupture. "Just tell me where the negatives and the rest of the prints are."

"No," he said mulishly. "Not until you tell me what's going on."

And then it did rupture. She flew at him with her fists flailing against his chest. "Give it to me!" she screamed. "Give me the film!"

He grabbed her by the wrists. "Cut it out," he said, gritting his teeth. "Stop playing games with me."

"Me!" She struggled to break free, and he tightened his hold. "You're the one who thinks this is all some rollicking good adventure. I'm the one whose husband's been kidnapped!"

Andy's face went white as she burst into tears. "God, Dana— I'm sorry." Abruptly, he dropped her wrists, and she plunged her face into her hands. He put his arms around her and pulled her to his chest. "Let me help."

She sagged against him, drained, too weak to argue or to deny herself the comfort of his support. She was tired, so tired.

"Please," he whispered.

She tilted her head back and searched his eyes, and slowly she nodded.

33

Andy took the Camry and was back at the house by six-thirty with eight negative strips and a set of five-by-seven prints. Dana slid everything into an unmarked manila envelope and closed the brass clasp.

"They won't be happy when they see that the film's already developed," he said. "They're gonna think you kept a set of prints for yourself."

He was sitting on the foot of her bed, watching the second video again.

"There's not a thing I can do about that."

"You could keep a set of prints for yourself."

"No. I can't take that chance."

She closed herself in the bathroom and took a hurried shower. The mirror was fogged when she stepped out, and she had to rub a spot clear to see herself. Her eyes stared back bleakly, and the harder she looked, the more desolate they became. Where was Whit now? In an underground bunker, penned up in a sweatbox, probably suffering abuse and certainly indignity, and all because of her.

And all for nothing if she surrendered everything.

She threw the bathroom door open. "There's no way they could tell? I mean, there's no kind of signature on the negatives to show how many or what size prints were made from it?"

Andy turned from the screen. "Nope."

She wavered in the doorway, trapped in indecision. "Then

237

maybe I'll keep the eight-by-tens," she said, but a second later bit her lip in uncertainty.

"Good idea," he said. "In fact, it's such a good idea that I already hid a set of eleven-by-fourteens under the floorboards of the car."

"You—what did you say?" But she knew what he said, and exactly how clever and devious and infuriating it was.

"You know the old saying? 'Damned if you do, damned if you don't'?" His dimples bored in. "The way I figure it, if you're damned either way, you might as well do."

She made an exasperated noise and went into her closet for something to wear. Something conspicuous, she decided. They said they'd be watching her, she might as well make it easy for them. She pulled out a halter-top sundress of bright coral-pink and laid it on the bed.

Andy was watching the first video again. "Is he always like this? Sort of twitchy?"

"For God's sake," Dana snapped. "His life's being threatened. Anybody'd be nervous."

"Sorry," he mumbled.

She opened her lingerie drawer, turned her back to him, and pulled her underwear on under the robe.

"What's your take on the drop-off points?" He ejected the cassette from the VCR. "The R5 train and the Devon Horse Show. Any connection?"

"I don't know." She reached for a bra but dropped it when she remembered the backless dress. "The R5's a commuter train into the city."

"Ever take it?"

"I used to, all the time. We go to the horse show all the time, too. My older daughter's horse-mad."

"Uh-huh."

There was something in his tone. She turned around to face him across the bed. "Why?"

"Did your husband know about the film?"

"You're the only one I told."

"Uh-huh," he said again.

"What are you getting at, Broder?" She picked up the dress and went into the closet to change.

"I don't know, I was just remembering something. When I was a kid, maybe twelve years old, I got caught setting brush fires in a neighbor's field. Dead to rights, and no defense but boredom and curiosity. My mother shut me up in my room—it was one of those wait-till-your-father-gets-home scenes, you know?"

She stepped into the dress and fastened the buttons at the strap behind her neck. "Yeah?"

"But I decided I wouldn't wait. I packed my canteen and Swiss army knife and shimmied down the rain gutter and headed for the woods. I snared a rabbit and gobbled up blue-berries and slept out under the stars for three days. It was the most fun I ever had. And by the time the search party came along, my folks were so glad to see me again, nobody ever said a word about any brush fires."

"I'm not following." She reached for the zipper at the small of her back.

"I was just thinking—maybe you'll be glad to see your hus-band again."

She shoved the door open. Andy was standing outside, watching for her reaction.

"Let me get this straight," she said. "You think Whit faked his own kidnapping? So I'd take him back?"

"It's a theory."

"With one small flaw."

"What's that?"

"He's the one who left me."

Her skirt flared wide as she turned away from him and started out of the room.

"Wait—you're not zipped."

Before she could twist away, he had the zipper up and his arms folded around her shoulders. "I'm sorry," he said. "I was an idiot to say anything. But at least I'm not as big an idiot as your husband."

She whirled again, her eyes blazing, but something in his look stopped her from whatever she might have said. He was grinning his usual maddening grin, but behind the dimples there was a wariness, an edge of fear, and it was enough to make her go into his arms.

"Let me go with you," he murmured as they held each other.

"No, they'll be watching me. I have to be alone. Please, Andy. Just wait here for me."

He yielded at last with a breath of agreement against her lips before he kissed her.

The evening's event was a world-class jumping competition, and the parking lot at the Devon Horse Show was filled to capacity. Neighboring homeowners sat in lawn chairs at their curbs holding placards that read, PARK $5. Dana slowed next to an old man in plaid shorts and a sleeveless undershirt. His driveway was already full, but he waved her onto his lawn between a hydrangea bush and a geranium bed and collected his money with a toothless grin.

The light was fading from the sky, the crickets were singing in the grass, and everywhere was the musky scent of horses. The perimeter of the fairgrounds was fenced in on all sides, and a bottleneck was forming where the crowd streamed through the gates. Most of them were dressed casually in shorts and jeans, but for many the evening was a significant social event; they sat in boxes and drank champagne and dressed accordingly, the women in hats and heels, and the men in blazers and natty buff slacks.

Despite the crowd, there was no line at the box office, and Dana hurried toward it as one of the equestrians strode past in gleaming knee-high boots and an elegantly tailored coat. At the window were two grandes dames from the charity committee sponsoring the event, and their silvered heads bobbed together in a private, delicious conversation. Dana cleared her throat twice and finally spoke up. "Excuse me? I'd like a ticket, please."

One of the women turned an appalled look her way. "A ticket? Whatever to?"

"Tonight's show."

The other woman pursed her lips and pointed to a preprinted sign that read SOLD OUT.

"No, I don't want a reserved seat," Dana said. "Only open admission. You sell unlimited open admission tickets, you always have."

"We don't, and we never have," she said through locked jaws. "For the finals, it's reserved seating only."

"You must have something left!"

But the women turned away to resume their discussion.

Dana stumbled back from the window. If she couldn't get into the show, then neither could the pickup man—unless he bought his ticket earlier.

She couldn't take the chance that he didn't. She'd already missed one rendezvous; if anything went wrong this time, it couldn't be because of her.

"Extra ticket, anyone?" she called across the crowd. "I need one ticket."

No one glanced her way. A policeman was directing traffic in the road; he could probably cite her for what she was about to do. She shouted out, "I'll pay a hundred dollars cash for one ticket!"

Suddenly she was besieged by a dozen people waving tickets in her face. She traded with a boy in a Smashing Pumpkins T-shirt, who stuffed the money in his shorts pocket and declared, "Wow! I didn't wanna go to the stupid thing anyway!"

Her seat was in the stadium, three levels up. She squeezed her way up the stairs, past hot dog vendors and caterers bearing willow hampers. "Excuse me, excuse me, please, sorry, thank you," she said as she skirted past fourteen bony knees in the row.

She sat down in her bright pink dress and held the envelope on her lap. The lights were already on in the Dixon Oval, illuminating an elaborate course of jumps and the five groundskeepers raking the dirt smooth in front of each. Another set of stands rose on the other side of the arena. Someone over there could be watching her, confirming that she came alone and brought the envelope. A dozen pairs of binoculars were pointed her way, and she stared at each of them until her vision blurred out of focus. Someone had to be over there, they had to try again tonight, they had to get in despite the sold-out tickets.

The loudspeaker crackled an announcement that propelled the crowd into their seats with an excited buzz. A fanfare of bugles sounded as a color guard of military school cadets marched into the oval. Behind them a procession of hard-hatted riders trotted in on light-stepping horses. The spectators around her were scanning their programs and making careful predictions in the margins. Dana always did the same when she came with Kirsten and Katrina, but not tonight.

Her flip phone was in her bag and her fingers ached so much to take it out and call the girls that she had to dig her nails into her palms to stop herself. Whoever was after the film knew where she lived, what she drove, and who her husband was. But did they know about her kids, and could they trace the call to find them?

Like most trial lawyers, Dana had an uneven base of knowledge. Through her cases she'd become an expert in such unlikely fields as liquor distilling, restoration of Old Masters, and LIFO accounting. In the course of preparing for the Palazzo Hotel trial, she learned enough about electricity to rewire her house and apply for a union card. But she never had a case involving telecommunications, and she didn't know the answers to the questions that were pounding at her. Here she was with an expensive, cutting-edge communications tool, and she was afraid to reach out and touch anybody.

A sustained burst of applause startled her. It was the end of the first half and the start of intermission. The stands emptied and poured into the fairgrounds at the north end of the complex, and she let herself be swept along with them. Dusk had fallen, and the artificial lights were up, and somewhere a bagpipe was braying. The odor of hot grease and Coke syrup drew the crowds ten deep in front of the refreshment stands, but she continued on, to the middle loop of the concourse.

The vendors' booths were built like miniature cottages, scarcely bigger than a little girl's playhouse. The Horsin' Around bookstore was a tiny blue and white cottage with Victorian gingerbread decorating the eaves. Browsers were squeezing themselves through the double Dutch door when she arrived. Clutching the envelope tight at her side, she followed after them.

The shop was the size of a cramped galley kitchen, with merchandise displayed on magazine racks along the two blank walls and on a long table along the wall under the single window. The crowd shuffled in tiny half-steps around the room. Ahead of her were a hearty-voiced woman herding three children along, a young couple holding hands, and an old couple snapping too loudly at each other.

She located the *Encyclopedia of the Horse* in the back row of books stacked on the table along the window wall. It was a coffee-table-sized book, easily bigger than the dimensions of the manila envelope. There were only eight copies, but at forty-five dollars a pop, a sellout before intermission ended was unlikely.

She cast a glance in all directions and quickly slid the envelope between the pages of the bottom copy of the book.

Outside, the loudspeaker crackled again to announce the end of intermission and the beginning of the final jump-off rounds. Dana returned to her seat and stayed there as instructed until the stroke of nine, then got up and left the stands.

There was one more thing she had to do, and she had to do it here, where the kidnappers couldn't have thought to monitor the line. She closed herself into the phone booth beside the box office.

"The O'Donnells, please," she said, and waited for the call to go through.

When her sister's voice came on, her knees almost buckled with relief. "Oh, Karin, thank God you're there."

"Hey, we've been worried—did you know your home phone was broken?"

"Karin—I need you to do something for me."

"Okay, shoot."

"Pack up, check out, take the kids to Mom and Dad's and stay there until I call you. And don't say a word to anybody about where you've gone."

For a moment Karin didn't speak. The show was ending, and

Dana stared blindly at the nameless faces streaming past the phone booth for the parking lot.

"You're serious."

"I'm terrified. I can't explain now, but if there's even the slightest chance that the kids are in danger—"

"Mom and Dad'll be frantic."

"I know, I'm sorry—"

"We'll be there by midnight. Call us then, okay?"

"Karin, thank you."

Dana cradled the phone and sagged against the glass wall. They were safe—the girls at least were safe.

Andy was waiting at the front door when she pulled into the driveway. "Are you all right?" he asked as she came through the door.

"I don't know," she said miserably and started up the stairs. "I don't even know if they were there tonight. They probably weren't. The envelope's probably still sitting on the table."

From the bottom of the stairs he said quietly, "No. They got it."

She had to grab the banister to keep from falling as she turned around to face him. "How do you know that?"

"I was hoping I might be able to spot the pickup man."

"You were there? But—you couldn't have been—the show was sold out."

"Not back by the barns it wasn't." He climbed the stairs toward her. "And all it cost me was five minutes of mucking out stalls."

"What?"

"The best way to go unnoticed is to stop and do a little manual labor. Nobody ever wants to make eye contact with the hired help. But anyway, if I could get in, I'm sure they could. They're the crooks."

"Just once," Dana said, her jaw clenched furiously, "could you do what I ask you to do?"

"I thought I did," he said with a grin. "Twice."

She glared at him. "Well? Did you spot the pickup man?"

"No." The smile faded. "About fifty people went through after you, and by the time I got inside, the envelope was gone."

She turned on the landing and gazed through the Palladian window at the lights winking in the valley and the beam of moonlight bouncing off the black water of the pool. They were there, the kidnappers were there tonight. That meant Whit was still alive, it had to mean that much.

But something else made no sense. "Wait a minute," she said, looking back at Andy. "How'd you get to the horse show? I had the car."

"I took the truck in the garage."

Her face went rigid and she hurtled herself past him and down the stairs and through the house to the garage. She hit the lights, and a scream caught in her throat at the sight of the battered old pickup.

"That's Whit's truck," she choked. "He took it when he left."

"God—I never thought—the keys were in it. And so was the garage door opener."

"They brought it back here. And what better place? If they left it anywhere else, the police would find it and start asking questions."

Andy touched his hand to her back, and the feel of his fingers against her bare skin made her tremble.

"Pack a bag," he said. "We're getting the hell out of here."

Andy backed out of the garage with the headlights off. It was after midnight, and they crept past the Camry and down the mountain lane in total darkness. There was no traffic on the roads until they reached the 202 interchange, where a string of headlights flashed on the highway bridge overhead. The north-bound ramp was a left turn on the far side of the bridge, but Andy suddenly jerked the wheel ninety degrees to the right and roared up the southbound ramp.

"No," Dana said. "It's the other way to the city."

"I know the way. And if you want your friends to know, too, I'll drive straight there."

Her heart clutched. "Are they following us?"

"Not if I can help it."

He stayed in the right lane and held the needle at fifty-five. Traffic was light, but a few cars zoomed up from behind and cut around to pass. Andy kept his eyes moving from one mirror to the other, and as they passed the Great Valley exit he said, "Don't look now, but we might have company."

Dana sucked in her breath and started to twist around in her seat.

"Don't look, I said!"

She winced and kept her eyes to the front. "What do you see?"

"I'm not sure." His gaze flicked briefly to the mirror. "A dark sedan, big, maybe a Lincoln."

"Are you sure it's following us?"

"It's definitely following us. The question is whether it's doing it on purpose. But there's one way to find out."

He stomped the pedal to the floor and wrenched the wheel to the left. A car was in the passing lane, and he cut hard across its path and left the road with a groan of the truck springs and a furious wail of the car horn behind them. Dana's head jarred against the metal roof as the pickup lurched down into the medial strip, bottomed out in the gully, and climbed back up the other side. Another horn wailed at them as they cut into the northbound lane.

"Now you can look," he shouted as he maneuvered into the flow of traffic.

She whipped around. The driver behind them was shaking his fist, but no one was imitating their U-turn. Across the highway a navy-blue Lincoln cruised by in the southbound lane. Innocent or not, it wasn't following anymore.

34

Ten point five square feet. Sixty-eight point twenty-five cubic feet. Almost twelve thousand one-inch cubes of space in the latrine, and Dana's face floated out of reach on every last one of them.

Whit's beard was five days long, it had to be Sunday night, and though he didn't know what time it was, he knew in his bones it was too late. Too late for rescue, too late for regrets, way past time for reconciliation, and no one to blame but himself.

Life doled out opportunities, one to a customer, and all that separated success from failure was what each one did with his chance when it came. He'd had his, and he'd done nothing. The second videotape was a gift, a chance to signal to Dana the identity of the third man, and he blew it, and all because he couldn't remember.

It was insane. He could remember a million other things about Dana, light-years ago—the words they spoke when they first met, the clothes she wore when he first undressed her, the way her hair smelled when he kissed her in the wind on a stormy night. But he couldn't remember a voice that he knew— he *knew*—belonged to someone in her life today. Once he'd known everything about her, but now—somewhere along the way he'd lost track of her. She was like a Christmas card friend he neglected one year; the next year's card came back marked, "Forwarding Address Expired."

He reached for the jug and drank a long swallow of luke-warm water. *Think,* he urged himself. *Remember.* Twelve thousand cubes tumbled through his brain like balls in a bingo cage, and out of all of them one image suddenly sharpened into focus.

It was of glasses raised, light refracted, the good crystal filled with effervescing liquid shooting prisms around the table. The in-laws were there, Karl beaming from ear to ear, and Anna preoccupied with baby Trina squirming on her lap. Karin was there with her ex-husband, and the kids were giggling under the table. The memory camera panned the room and zoomed in on Dana. She was laughing, radiant with happiness, and suddenly Whit remembered. It was the celebration dinner for her partnership election.

But where was he in this joyful scene? The camera turned around on itself and found him sitting with his arms crossed over his chest, forcing a smile and wondering darkly what they all must be thinking about him.

Her partnership was a real cause for celebration. She'd won the respect of her employers, and her financial future was now secure. A first-rate education was guaranteed for the girls; they could build the house they'd been dreaming of.

And all he could think of as he tossed back his champagne was *What about me?*

"Everything's not always about you, Whit!" Dana once hurled at him, but somehow he'd believed there was a limited allotment of good fortune to be meted out per marriage, and that every gold star on Dana's chart necessarily meant a black X on his. That was why he couldn't remember, that was the reason he'd lost track of her over the years. Every memory of her was of success, and another grinding reminder of his own failure.

Stiffly, he stood up and tried to stretch out his cramped muscles. Everything was too late, including Ike and his buddy for their nightly visit.

By now Whit knew that they left him alone during daylight hours. He'd also figured out that he couldn't make himself heard through any amount of shouting, and that there was a chain padlocked around the latrine, so that even when he braced his arms on the walls and kicked both legs, the door wouldn't give. He had to give Ike credit: as hidey-holes went, this one was first-rate.

Not that it mattered much, since his stay was drawing to a close. If Dana made the delivery last night and Ike was true to his word, his release was imminent. If she didn't or Ike wasn't, then a different kind of release awaited him. *The angle at which a man finally lies down . . .*

Voices buzzed outside the latrine, and he sat up tense and strained his ears. A moment later Ike spoke through the overhead speaker.

"Professor, we're going to open the door for your food. Back up into the corner by the john. There will be two guns trained on you. If you make any move toward the door, those guns will be fired." Ike recited the instructions in a drone; he was almost as weary of the routine as Whit was.

This time it wasn't a paper bag that was thrust at him, but a box. Whit felt around the edges and pried up the flap. Inside was the smooth hard sphere of an apple, a sandwich—he took a whiff—of sliced turkey, and two sugar cookies. He recognized it as the standard box dinner peddled at the horse show.

"Did you pick up anything else while you were there?" he shouted at the ceiling. "I mean, I was only wondering."

There was no answer. He bit into the sandwich and wondered if this were his last meal.

At last Ike spoke again through the ceiling. "Professor, we have another statement for you to read." Into his weary tone crept something new. Sympathy? No, worse than that—he was embarrassed.

"My wife didn't show," Whit said flatly.

"No, she came. She followed the instructions."

She came. She followed instructions. He focused so hard on those words he almost missed what Ike was saying next.

"But there's a problem with the item she delivered. It's not in the condition we hoped it would be. That's why we have to ask you to read another message."

Whit leaned his forehead against the wall as Ike went through the drill for the videotaping. Dana came, she followed the instructions, they were giving her another chance, and that meant another chance for him.

Ike recited the same old instructions in the same old drone, but suddenly Whit was hearing another voice in his memory, and he shot to his feet.

Out of nowhere, he remembered the third man.

"I'm ready!" he shouted.

35

Miss Texas threw up the minute she lifted her head from the pillow Monday morning. Travis brought saltines and ginger ale on her breakfast tray, and she was perking up a little until he said he had to get to the office, at which point she threw up again, this time on him. By the time he finished changing, she'd drifted back to sleep. She was so beautiful, sometimes it was hard to believe what came out of her stomach.

He pressed a light kiss on her forehead and went downstairs. There was a burble of voices in the living room, where the decorator was already setting to work with a crew to mount the cornices for the drapes. A new Oriental rug was unfurled over the living room floor, and fabric swatches for the drapes and upholstery lay everywhere. They were doing the living room first, then the dining room, then the family room, no—Travis corrected himself—the keeping room, because the decorator said family room sounded too middle class. By the time all was said and done, the tab would be close to fifty thousand dollars.

Miss Texas said she didn't mind waiting to furnish the place, she didn't have to invite her mother up, she was sure she could do without even though neither of her sisters had. But it suddenly dawned on him: his credit was good, why make her wait? Last week he took out a loan—high interest but small monthly payments—with a balloon in six months. By the time it came due, he'd have his partnership interest to pledge as collateral and could refinance on better terms. "You can invite your whole family and half your sorority if you want, sugar babe," he told her.

"Try to keep the noise down," he said to the decorator as he picked up his briefcase in the hall. "My wife's a little under the weather today."

Everybody was under the weather today. It was another scorcher outside, so hot it felt like Dallas in August during pre-season practice for college football. He backed out of the driveway and cranked up the air conditioner. The weather report came on the radio with a forecast of continued heat and drought, but—the first ray of hope for weeks—with a twenty percent chance of precipitation on Thursday.

He wondered if there'd be any ray of hope at the office today. Saturday's report from the sound engineer was devastating. Despite all the man's cautionary statements and dire predictions, Travis was sure he'd come up with something of Dana's voice on the tape recording. But now—nothing.

He arrived at the office, scooped the mail off his secretary's desk, and rounded the corner to find Brad Martin having a panic attack in his office.

"Oh, my God!" Brad was pacing so rapidly across the tiny room that he seemed literally to be bouncing off the walls. "Did you see this? Did you see what those assholes did to us? What the hell do we do now?"

He clutched a half-shredded newspaper in his hands, and Travis stopped him long enough to pry it from his fingers.

"This isn't my fault," Brad shrieked as Travis scanned the page. "I sent out the press release exactly the way Dana wanted it. If it's anybody's fault, it's hers. She should have known—"

"Get back to work." Travis shouldered Brad out of the office and closed the door. On the front page of the Sunday *Inquirer*, below the fold, was another story about Peter Seferis's class action, this one highlighting Pennsteel's response to the suit. They'd edited out all of Dana's sympathetic remarks about the children at the park that day, but quoted her as saying: "Pennsteel isn't going to roll over for this kind of extortion."

* * *

The rest of the morning's news was no better. The eyewitness interview videotapes were done, but were virtually worthless: although everyone saw the plane and helicopter come down, not a soul saw them come together. And the ad requesting film of the accident had been running for seven days in ten different newspapers without a single response. He couldn't believe it. Probably a hundred video cameras there that day, and not a Zapruder in the crowd.

Travis collapsed miserably against the back of his chair. There was nothing to refute Ira Thompson's theory of the case except Dana's testimony, which meant Jackson, Rieders & Clark had to withdraw. Which meant Travis would lose his XO position on the team and his second chair at trial, not to mention the opportunity to bill another thousand hours before year-end. He'd end up being the Invisible Man of the firm.

He'd end up being passed over for partner, fifty thousand dollars in debt and with a baby on the way.

He spun around to his terminal and pulled up his last message from Dana, Friday night's e-mail. But though he read it through twice again, it still didn't make any sense. Why should he lay off Loudenberg? That was his number one project.

He tried calling her again, but her secretary still didn't know where she was, and when he dialed her home number, he got a recording that the line was out of service. Weird.

One other place she might be: the Batcave downstairs, where the Palazzo team used to hide out when the office got too frantic. He scoured his desk drawers until he found the scrap of paper with the unlisted number of the phone there, but nobody answered when he dialed it, even after ten rings.

When his own phone rang later in the morning, he grabbed for it, hoping for maybe the first time ever that it was Dana and not Miss Texas. But it was yet another woman.

"Hey, Travis," Judy Loudenberg said. "You been keepin' yourself a stranger."

"Oh, hi, Judy. Sorry, it's been real busy down here."

"Too busy to give me a call once in a while?"

"Uh—Judy, I'm not sure that's such a good idea. After the way Bill, Jr., looked at me and all."

"Well, guess what? Billy's went away. Everybody's went away! I got the place all to myself."

"Where'd they all go?"

"Dottie went to her sister's up at Binghamton and took the brat with her. Billy, I don't know where."

"He do that often? Go off without telling you where?"

"His dad always did the exact same thing. Dottie says don't let it worry me, it's just man stuff in the woods. But ann-y-way." Her voice went long and sticky. "Why don't you come on up and see me?"

"Gee, I'd like that, Judy, but I'm so damn busy—"

She interrupted in a singsong: "I know something you don't know, I know something you don't know."

Travis pounced, "About Donny flying the plane?"

But she sang on, "Bill took a trip out of the country last month."

"Where to?"

"I don't know, but he had to get hisself a passport."

"What's that got to do with the accident?"

"Well, that's for you to figger out, isn't it?"

Travis stared at the work piled up on his desk, then at Dana's last e-mail, at the *Inquirer* article on his desk, and finally at the framed photograph of Miss Texas on his credenza.

"You free this afternoon?" he asked.

"No, but real cheap." She giggled. "See ya then."

36

The phone rang inside Dana's head like a pickax against a boulder, and she shot straight up on the cot. Sunlight was streaming into the war room, and Andy was up and dressed and working at the table. "Let it ring?" he asked.

She nodded, though the movement made her head pound. Slowly, she lifted her wrist and squinted at her watch. "Ten-thirty!"

"It was close to dawn before you finally drifted off. I thought you oughta sleep in."

The phone rang on, and she listened with mounting dread. No one knew she was here but her family, and they were under strict orders not to call. Late last night her father whisked them all off to a friend's house on the Chesapeake, where no one would ever think to look for them. She was determined that no one was going to trace phone calls to them either.

At last the ringing stopped. It was a wrong number, she decided, or someone looking for Maria.

She got up and staggered to the rest room and thought of all the work she had to do today. She hadn't spoken to Charlie Morrison since Thursday, and though she might be prohibited from telling him about what happened in Laporte, she needed to tell him everything else they now knew about how the collision occurred. There was bad news to deliver, too: the new lawsuits brought by Peter Seferis and Angela Leoni, the threat by Dan Casella.

Dan Casella. A dim recollection stirred at the thought of his name, and instantly it exploded into full-blown panic.

She burst out of the rest room and ran to the telephone and dialed Bill Moran's office. "He's not in today, Ms. Svenssen," his secretary reported.

"Did he go to meet Dan Casella at Alpine Valley?"

"Well, no, I don't think so. He's taking a long weekend at the shore."

Dana slammed the phone down, then picked it up again and dialed Casella's number, hoping desperately that he and Moran had somehow already connected and worked things out.

"He's not in, Ms. Svenssen," Casella's secretary said.

"Do you know where he is? Or when he'll be back?"

"He had a meeting upstate this morning. And he called a minute ago to say he had to stop at the courthouse before he returns to the office."

Her eyes squeezed shut. "Is there any way I can reach him? What's the number of his car phone?"

"I'm afraid he's not in his own car today."

"Please—if he calls in again, tell him I had an emergency this morning, but I'll meet with him any time, anywhere. Please tell him—don't file."

"I'll tell him," she promised cheerfully.

Dana hung up and ground her fists against her skull. It was too late. Casella had already been stood up at the park; he was already storming to the courthouse to file his complaint against Pennsteel.

She dialed again and reached the Pennsteel offices. "This is Dana Svenssen. It's urgent that I speak to Mr. Morrison."

"Oh, Miss Svenssen. He's been trying to reach you all morning."

Charlie's voice sounded seconds later. "Dana, all hell's breaking loose up here."

"What—"

"There's no time to explain. Can you get up here right away? I need you."

*   *   *

Pennsteel maintained a dozen mills and fabricating plants in aging industrial buildings that belched out black smoke over low-income housing, but its corporate headquarters were set in a bucolic office park. The grounds were green and manicured, park benches sat under every shade tree, and a family of swans circled lazily in a man-made pond. Dana was always struck by the controlled serenity of the setting; it reminded her of a Jane Austen novel, or the grounds of a mental hospital.

It was different today. There were no spaces left in the lot, and she ended up parking the Mercedes on the grass along with dozens of other cars. Voices were shouting some kind of refrain, over and over again in an angry chant, and blue and red lights were swirling in front of the main entrance.

She hiked up the hill. Five police cars were parked on the plaza, and three news-camera vans were parked beside them. A throng of women and children was milling around the fountain in front of the entrance doors. Several were hoisting hand-lettered signs that proclaimed PENNSTEEL HAS A COLD-STEEL HEART and PROTECT OUR CHILDREN FROM CORPORATE CALLOUSNESS.

One man stood strategically between an array of TV news cameras and the open globe sculpture that was the Pennsteel logo. He was elegantly dressed in Armani and Gucci, and he spoke in a voice that was permanently and effectively hoarse as he cried out on behalf of his clients and all those similarly situated. It was Peter Seferis.

Dana clenched her jaw against the pounding in her head and forced her way through the crowd until she could hear what he was telling the reporters. So far as he knew, this protest rose up spontaneously when the parents of the Alpine Valley victims read the callous and insensitive remarks made by Pennsteel after his lawsuit was filed. But though he had no hand in this demonstration, he certainly understood their feelings and endorsed their efforts to express them consistent with their First Amendment rights. Pennsteel must be made to hear, Pennsteel must be made to see, Pennsteel must be made to pay.

That was the chant she was hearing from the crowd: "Pennsteel must pay, Pennsteel must pay." There might have been a

Vietnam-era protester in the group, too, for another voice was crying: "Hey, hey, what d'you say, how many kids did you scar today?"

A force of private security guards stood ten strong to block the entrance to the building, but an elderly secretary was waiting inside the doors behind them, and at her command Dana was admitted through the line. The woman pivoted on her sensible heels and led the way into the elevator, to the top floor, and down a corridor to a pair of oaken double doors. She opened one and stood aside.

It was the Pennsteel boardroom, and a dozen people were seated at the long gleaming table. The secretary took her place at its foot as Charlie Morrison rose and crossed the room to Dana. He gripped her by the elbow and spoke in a low voice. "The shit's really hitting the fan."

"I know, I saw—"

"There's more. The amusement park filed suit today."

She winced. "Charlie, that's all my fault. I should have—"

"Sssh. Let me do the talking."

He led her to a seat beside him. "Gentlemen and Mrs. Dolan, for those of you who haven't met her before, this is Dana Svenssen, from Jackson, Rieders and Clark, our outside counsel."

There were no smiles to greet her. Oliver Dean was presiding at the head of the table with a stern expression, in stark contrast to the benign one he wore in the portrait hanging on the wall behind him. Flanking him at the table were an old man with a dour Quaker face and a nearly-as-old woman with a pheasant-feathered hat perched on her head. Ted Keller was squirming in his seat at the other end of the table, and Tim Haguewood and John Schaeffer were glowering across it. The friendliest face in the room was in the portrait hanging next to Dean's. It was Victor Sullivan, captured in a broad Irish grin.

"Ms. Svenssen," Oliver Dean said. "We've been hearing from Ken Llewellyn, our public relations director."

His gaze moved down the table until it landed on a round-figured man with elaborately blow-dried hair. "One of Haguewood's people," Charlie whispered in her ear.

Llewellyn nodded and not a hair moved on his head. In front of him lay three different colored folders and four pens in perfect order. "I spoke with my contacts at each of the three network affiliates, and they all report the same: they received anonymous phone tips that there would be an organized march on our headquarters today. The protest apparently was triggered by a statement that appeared in Sunday's *Inquirer*, as follows."

He pulled a clipping from his red folder, and the pounding crescendoed in Dana's skull as her own words came back to haunt her: *Pennsteel isn't going to roll over for this kind of extortion. This action is completely inappropriate, as Mr. Seferis well knows.*

The faces around the table went tight with anger. It was only a fragment of what she'd dictated, with all the countervailing sympathetic remarks omitted, but she couldn't deny that she'd said it. She cleared her throat and prepared to confess.

"Yeah, that's right," Charlie said before she could speak. "I approved that press release. What about it? It's the truth."

Dana turned to stare at him. He never approved it, she never even showed it to him.

"You should have run it past Ken," Haguewood said.

"What for? This wasn't some puff piece for community goodwill."

As Llewellyn bristled and Haguewood started to sputter, Oliver Dean intervened. "Perhaps if you shared it with Ken," he said, his eyebrows arched high, "we'd be enjoying more goodwill than we seem to be at the moment."

But Charlie was unrepentant. "There's no way we could have predicted that Seferis would pull this kind of stunt. But we knew for sure that if we made any kind of admission, any kind of conciliatory statement at all, he'd turn it right around and use it against us. Dana wrote us a good tight statement based strictly on the legal considerations of the case, and I backed her up. I still do."

He turned a challenging look on each man in the room, and one by one they looked away, until he came to Oliver Dean, who looked past him to gesture to the secretary at the other end of the table. She rose with a stack of papers and moved behind each seat to distribute them. Dana took hers and did a quick scan. It was Dan Casella's complaint on behalf of the amusement park, not only filed, but already officially served on Pennsteel. He was smart enough not to follow Ira Thompson's lead on venue; he filed with the Court of Common Pleas for Northampton County. Juries might be notorious for doling out cash in Philadelphia County, but Alpine Valley was one of Northampton County's biggest employers: everybody on a jury there would know somebody whose pocketbook was pinched by the park's closing.

The company executives had bigger concerns than venue, though. "Ten million dollars!" John Schaeffer blurted, his index finger running along the closing paragraph of the complaint.

"And that's only damages to date. They're also claiming lost profits at a per diem of twenty thousand. Six months and it'll be close to another four million. Fourteen million at six percent compounded daily." Not surprisingly, these remarks came from Tim Haguewood, head of finance.

"It won't be six months," Charlie said. "It won't even be six weeks. This is a tempest in a teapot."

"Looks more like a hurricane in the tropics to me," Haguewood said, and down the line Llewellyn chortled.

Oliver Dean was still on the second page, and more disturbed by what he saw there than the demand for damages. "It says here that we reneged on our promise to clean up the amusement park." He flicked glances left and right at the two directors beside him, then turned a look of moral indignation on Charlie and Dana. "Did we do that?"

"No, sir. No," Charlie said firmly. "We fully intend to honor the pledge. But we need to get our people in there to do some estimates and calculate the costs. It's nothing but logistics at this point."

"Logistics that are costing us twenty thousand a day," Haguewood said. "Isn't it time somebody got up off their asses?"

Oliver Dean murmured a dismayed, "Tim," but Dana held up a hand. Her head ached so much her vision blurred, but she had to speak up. It was time to take out her sword and fall on it. "Gentlemen, it's all—"

"Well and good," Charlie cut in, "to be second-guessing and pointing fingers. But let's remember one thing. We all agreed the day of the crash that volunteering a cleanup was the way to go. But I haven't seen anybody but Dana step up to the plate. In twenty-four hours after the crash she had six lawyers working full-time on this case. In three days she had a dozen of the top aviation experts in the country onboard. Five days after the accident, she won us the right to make a presentation to the NTSB before they issue any report on the accident."

"And ten days after the accident we get this." Haguewood threw down his copy of Casella's complaint with his lip curled.

Charlie pushed back from the table and got to his feet. "What are we talking about here? A couple of days' delay. What's that come to?" He stood up and snapped his fingers in Haguewood's direction as if he expected him to whip out a calculator and supply the answer. "Maybe a hundred thousand dollars, tops? Do I have to remind you people that eleven days ago Dana got us a jury verdict that saved the company millions of dollars?"

He paced behind the row of chairs. "So what are we going to do? Nickel and dime her to death until we lose the best trial counsel we ever had? Or maybe stop bean-counting long enough to give her the support she needs?"

Tim Haguewood locked his jaw furiously at the barb, but Charlie turned to face the triumvirate at the head of the table. "If we don't reward loyalty with loyalty and back her up in this, then this company is as morally bankrupt as those people out there claim we are."

A nervous throat-clearing sounded from one of the men, and another shifted in his seat, but no one spoke until at last Oliver Dean said, "Points very well taken, Charlie."

But Haguewood had one last volley to fire. "What's the point of supporting her to defend an indefensible case? You all heard the cockpit recording, and regardless of what she says"—a quick jab of his finger at Dana—"there's no way we're going to get around that."

"Yes, there is."

This voice was new to the debate, and everyone's eyes moved in search of it. Ted Keller rose to his feet and stood with military rectitude at the foot of the table. "The JetRanger never dropped its altitude. We can prove it. In fact, we already have."

Dana shot out of her chair. "Ted, you took another Jet-Ranger up this morning? You got the results back from the sound engineer?"

"I did. And he confirms that there's nothing on the accident tape that comes close to the engine sounds on my tape."

"What's this all about?" Dean asked.

Dana turned to him in excitement. "Mr. Dean, we can prove that the helicopter maintained its altitude. We can prove that the plane flew up underneath and crashed into it." She looked to Charlie. "With a few days to work up some visuals, we can demonstrate exactly how and why that happened."

She glanced down the length of the table. "Look, the NTSB has agreed to hear us out, the press is clamoring for information—why don't we do it all in one fell swoop? Why don't we schedule a public presentation, invite the NTSB, the plaintiffs' bar, the newspapers and television stations, and show them once and for all why Pennsteel isn't responsible for any of this?"

The room was silent until the dour Quaker next to Oliver Dean dropped his lower jaw and declared, "Well, by God, why don't we?"

Dean looked to the woman beside him, and the feathers fluttered on her hat as she gave a nod.

"Charlie?" he said.

"Sounds good to me."

"Then let's put it to a vote. All in favor?"

Like the wave at a football game, the hands went up in domino effect around the room, ending finally and reluctantly with Tim Haguewood's.

"I have another suggestion," Dana said. "One that might help us with the six o'clock news tonight." Grimaces appeared as the group remembered the barbarians at their gate. "Let me try to reach Harry Reilly right now and schedule our NTSB presentation, then one of you—maybe Ken?—can go down and announce it to the reporters."

"Excellent idea," Dean said. "But Charlie, why don't you and Dana talk to the cameras on this one?"

"Yes, sir."

The meeting was adjourned.

Within an hour the meeting outside the Pennsteel doors was also adjourned. Dana reached Harry Reilly, and he agreed to assemble his people and hear her out on Thursday. Charlie went downstairs with her and stood stoically by her side as Ken Llewellyn summoned the cameras and reporters. The army of women and children closed in around them, and they booed and catcalled as Dana spoke, until suddenly Peter Seferis realized the microphones were picking up every word and shushed the crowd so that he could hear what the rest of the world soon would.

As silence fell, Dana was saying, "—irrefutable evidence that the helicopter crew was without fault. This terrible tragedy was caused entirely by the reckless flying tactics of the plane's pilot. On Thursday we'll demonstrate to the satisfaction of everyone exactly how this awful event occurred. And we invite you to come. All of you. Everyone here today, and everyone else who's been injured, and every lawyer who's considering litigation on their behalf. Please come and see for yourselves. Find out the facts before you start fixing blame."

The cameras were turned off and packed up, and with their departure the crowd seemed to lose its steam. Seferis left, and soon the mothers were bundling their children into minivans as they realized they still had dinner to get on the table.

As Charlie walked Dana to the door, he said, "You sure wowed us in there today. But are you really that confident we can win this thing?"

"Yeah, I am."

He raised his chin and squinted at her. "Maybe you got some secret weapon you're not telling me about?"

"Maybe I do." She turned at the door and took his hand. "Thank you for what you did today, Charlie. You really went out on a limb for me, and you know I didn't deserve it."

"I don't know anything of the kind." Gruffly, he reached

around her and opened the door. "Besides, it's me who should be thanking you. You handed me a golden opportunity today."

"How's that?"

"This race for Vic's job? It's pretty much narrowed down to me and Haguewood. Did you notice the two old birds sitting beside Ollie?"

"Uh-huh."

"They're the two swing votes on the board. And unless I miss my bet—they just swung my way."

37

Travis stopped in Montrose for a couple six-packs and some hoagies and chips, and Judy Loudenberg almost swooned on the stoop of her trailer when he suggested a picnic.

"Got a favorite spot?" he asked her, but it turned out she was a town girl, and after two years of wedded bliss, she had never ventured farther from the trailer than her in-laws' house. It was too hot to go tramping very far, so they ended up eating on a bedsheet in the shade of the barn.

"You're the sweetest man," she declared while olive oil dripped from her chin. "I knew it the first time I seen you. He looks like he knows how to treat a lady, I said."

"Said to who?" Travis gulped.

"My own self, you silly. I said, there's a man who'd bring a girl candy and flowers now and then. Maybe a little piece of jewelry or sumpin'. Tell her she's pretty once in a blue moon."

"Doesn't Billy do any of those things?"

"Huh. About never. Only one thing he ever wanted to do with me, and these days he don't even wanna do that no more." She peeked under her lashes at him and tried a suggestive smile. Her two front teeth protruded; he could see where the enamel was pitted and stained.

"These days? You mean, since the accident?"

"Nah, even before. Like he's got some big trouble or some-thin'. Mr. Big Shot. Can't even tell me about it, it's such a big deal."

"You think it's got anything to do with where he went off to?"

"Beats me." She stuffed the rest of the hoagie in her mouth, and washed it down with a swallow of beer.

Travis forced his hand out to touch her hair. It felt like a Brillo pad. "I bet you know a lot more than you let on."

"I betcha you do, too," she snickered, and plastered her mouth against his.

He'd already polished off his own hoagie, but the taste of onion and oregano in Judy's mouth almost made him gag. He held his breath and tried to kiss her back without parting his lips enough to let her tongue slither in. This had nothing to do with Miss Texas, he had to remind himself. This was only work, and Miss Texas always said he didn't need to tell her about work.

Judy flopped back on the sheet, and Travis popped open another beer for her.

"So what's the story on Bill Senior going out of the country?"

"I dunno." She took a swig. "Some kind of business, Dottie said. He needed a passport, like I toldja."

"True Value business?"

"No, you silly!" She hooted and slapped his knee. "He had some other business goin'. With partners and deals and stuff. Billy, too."

"Maybe that's what's been on Billy's mind. Having to carry on his dad's business."

"Maybe." She tilted the can to her mouth for a long swallow. Suddenly she giggled, making beer spew from her nostrils, then levered up and ground her mouth against his. Again he held his breath and gave himself another pep talk: James Bond never hesitated to woo a woman in exchange for intelligence, and he never puked his guts up over it, either. F. Lee Bailey might have done the same thing in his better-looking days; Johnnie Cochran probably still did.

Over the course of the next hour, Judy couldn't decide which she wanted more—to fool around or get drunk—so every time she came at him, Travis thrust another can of beer at her. She got up once to go around the barn to pee, and when she came back she didn't have any pants on, only a shirttail that didn't quite reach. But she didn't seem to expect him to do anything about it, so he just handed her another beer. She drained it and flopped back on the sheet with her legs spread open. A minute later she was dead to the world.

"Judy," he whispered, touching her shoulder. "Judy?"

She snorted and rolled over and rooted her face in the ground.

Slowly, he eased himself up and stepped lightly around the barn and crossed the field to the trailer. He started in the bedroom. The dresser drawers were built into the wall, and he went through each one. On Billy's side there was underwear, socks, a couple hunting knives, T-shirts, work shirts, blue jeans. Basically the same on Judy's side, except for some tattered bras and bikini underpants. No letters, no photos, no documents. Nothing under the bed—it was built on a platform.

The same was true in the kitchen and living room. No papers of any kind except an out-of-date *TV Guide*.

An open field stretched from the trailer to the Loudenberg farmhouse. Travis looked both ways, then sprinted across the field to the sagging front porch.

The door was locked. He went around back, but that door was locked, too. He circled the house and pressed his face to the screen of every window. Nothing in there but an empty house—living room and dining room in the front, divided by a flight of stairs, kitchen and washroom in the back.

The screen on one of the living room windows buckled as he leaned against it, and he peered in at the catches. One was unhooked. He grabbed the bottom of the screen and jiggled it until the other catch came loose and the whole screen slid to the ground. Praying he'd have as much luck with the window, he braced his hands against the sides of the frame and pushed up. Luck was with him. It wasn't locked, and it squeaked up far enough for him to shimmy through.

He landed in a roll on a braided rag rug in the middle of the living room. There was a magazine rack by the easy chair. He thumbed through it, but there was nothing in it but back issues of *Field and Stream*. He went through the dining room, past the table covered with wilting funeral flowers, and into the kitchen.

A few envelopes sat among the clutter on the counter, and he thumbed through them, but found only sympathy cards and oil and electric bills, both past due.

Each tread squeaked under his feet as he went upstairs. At the landing there was a bathroom with rust-stained fixtures and linoleum peeling off the floor. One bedroom contained a double bed under a patchwork quilt. The next was probably the daughter's room, done up in pink gingham. The last one must have been Donny's. It held a twin bed and a plain-fronted chest of drawers.

Travis searched through every drawer and closet, under beds and behind furniture. Somewhere, there had to be a piece of paper that explained the source of Loudenberg's inheritance or documented his trip out of the country or even just alluded to his business ventures. Except there wasn't.

A panicked sweat broke out over his body. If he didn't find something—if he didn't *do* something to turn this case around in a big way, today, he could kiss his partnership goodbye. He'd have to default on his balloon loan, the bank would get a judgment lien on the house, and Miss Texas would go home to her mother before she'd make a move down.

"Travis?"

He stumbled to the bathroom window. Still wearing nothing but her shirttails, Judy was wandering around the side of the barn.

He went to the sink and splashed two handfuls of cold water on his face, then opened the medicine cabinet in search of some aspirin or something.

"Travis, where are you?"

No time. He slammed the mirrored door shut, and the whole cabinet rocked loose in the wall.

Funny. He opened the door again. Where there should have been screws anchoring the cabinet to the wall, there were only a couple of bent-over nails. He pried them back and pulled the cabinet out.

"Travis?"

He jumped to the window with the cabinet in his hands. Judy had her pants on now. In another minute she'd come looking for him. He hurried back to the sink and was starting to lift the cabinet back into place when he saw the bag taped to the wall stud. He pulled it free and stared through the hazy plastic in astonishment.

There was another bag in the toilet tank, this one double-wrapped in plastic, and a third behind the plumbing access panel for the tub. There was no time to count it, but there was no question it was more than fifty thousand dollars.

He barreled down the stairs. Through the dining room window he saw Judy peering into the open window of his car. He snatched a handful of flowers out of the funeral spray and let himself out the back door. He strolled around the house and across the field with his hands behind his back.

"So," he called. "Sleeping Beauty finally woke up."

"Where'd you run off to?" Judy demanded, hands on hips.

He produced the pilfered bouquet with a flourish. "Just picking you some flowers."

Her mouth dropped open for one stunned moment before she flung her arms around him. "You are the sweetest man, Travis Hunt!"

"Never too sweet for you," he said, and holding her in a one-armed hug, he dropped the bundles of cash through the window onto the floor of his car.

38

It was after four when Dana left Pennsteel and started the drive back to Philadelphia. Almost twenty hours since she made the drop-off at the horse show—Whit could be free by now, and the worst of this nightmare would be over.

The thought was enough to hold her headache at bay, and she passed the hour's drive with an hour of telephone calls. First, to Dan Casella to beg for forgiveness and schedule a meeting the next morning; then to Bob Kopec, an environmental specialist at Harding & McMann, to hire him as co-counsel to oversee the park cleanup project. Next she called Norm Wiecek at UAC and filled him in on Thursday's presentation to the NTSB. Predictably, he moaned that it was a terrible idea to go public with any kind of evidence so soon, it would only end up backfiring on them, and besides—how could they possibly put it together in three days? Dana spent fifteen minutes trying to reassure him before she dialed Don Skelly at Geisinger.

"Hot damn," he crowed at the news. "That'll be the biggest show in town. Where you planning on holding this shindig?"

"I was about to ask you if we could use your auditorium again."

"What d'ya know? I was about to offer it."

"Set it up for me, Don?"

"You betcha."

Dana was mired in rush hour traffic on the expressway into the city before she remembered to check in with Celeste, who'd already left for the day. But Dana's voice mail held a message from Mike Pasko at Pennsteel.

"Ms. Svenssen, I apologize for my delay," he said when she reached him. "But my usual sources refused to share any information about their investigation. In fact they refused even to confirm that there *was* an investigation."

"I was afraid of that," Dana said.

"But of course, that alone tells us something."

"What?"

"There must be an informant."

A horn wailed before she realized she was drifting across the center line, and she hurried to cut the wheels back to the right. If Lomax had an informant placed in the paramilitary troop, he'd have to protect him; he'd have to make sure no one aroused the militia's suspicion that they were under investigation. It made perfect sense.

"One other piece of information," Pasko went on. "The investigation isn't being run by the FBI or the BATF. The DEA's calling the shots on this one."

The Drug Enforcement Agency? That made no sense at all.

Whit's pickup was parked in a space reserved for one of Dana's vacationing partners, and when she pulled into her usual space, Andy climbed out of the cab.

"Hi." She fell in step beside him toward the elevator. "Everything go okay at the photo lab?"

"Yeah."

There was something in his voice. She stopped, and a fresh wave of dread crashed over her at the look on his face.

"What is it?"

"I stopped by your house on my way back." He held up something in his hand. "There's another video."

"Dana—" Whit had to clear his throat and say it again. "Dana . . ." From lack of use or thirst or maybe illness, his voice was failing him badly.

The date and time display at the bottom of the screen showed that it was recorded only a few hours ago. Whit was still alive only a few hours ago. Dana held tight to that thought as she stood frozen before the video cart in the war room.

"You know what the problem is. These men can't release me so long as there's a risk that you haven't fully complied with the demand. Therefore, my stay here must continue indefinitely, until they can feel certain of your compliance. If you go to the police, or if the item surfaces in any way, they will know it, and I will be killed.

"Dana . . ." She held her breath as Whit lowered the script and spoke directly to the camera. "I love you."

Her breath came out in a sob. Andy tried to put his arms around her, but she threw him off and lunged for the rewind button. She watched the tape again with her fist in her mouth and tears welling in her eyes. *Indefinitely,* they said. *Until they could be sure.* When would that be? Trial was at least two years away.

She ran to the worktable and shuffled through the papers until she found the stack of eleven-by-fourteen-inch prints. She never should have held them back. They knew. Somehow they knew. She dashed to the door, and her hand was on the knob before Andy spoke.

"Aren't you forgetting these?"

In one hand he held a long narrow box and in the other a cylindrical roll of papers.

"What's that?"

"The slides I made this afternoon, and the blowups."

She hadn't realized, and she went back and grabbed them. This time she had the door open before he said, "And aren't you forgetting something else?"

It hit her like a punch in the stomach. She didn't know where to take them. She fell back against the door. The photographs spilled out of her hands, and as she started a slow slide to the floor, she cried, "There's nothing I can do to save him."

Andy caught her under the arms and held her. "Sssh. We'll save him. We just have to find another way."

"There's no way," she moaned against his shoulder. "Even if I knew where to go—they'd never believe we haven't held something back."

"We have to figure out who they are and why they're doing this."

"We know who they are."

"Do we?"

She pulled back and stared at him.

" 'If you go to the police, they will know it and I will be killed,' " he quoted.

Her eyes flared wide. "We went to the police yesterday, and he's still alive today."

"Which means they don't have a clue what happened up there. Dana, I think I was right before. The kidnappers don't have anything to do with those guys up at Laporte."

But she didn't want to believe that, not when there was a more hopeful thought. "No, it means they're only making empty threats."

"Well, your husband takes them seriously enough. I mean, jeez, he's still as jumpy as he was in the first tape."

She looked at him blankly.

"You know—the way his hand and face sort of twitch?"

Dana pushed him back so hard he had to rock on his heels to catch his balance. "Where is it?" she cried. "The first tape? I need to see the first tape!"

She found it on the TV cart and loaded it in the VCR. Whit's grainy face appeared again, and his raspy voice spoke.

"Dana, I'm being held by a group of armed men who mean me no harm but who will be compelled to kill me if you fail to comply with their demands. You know what they want."

"There!" She hit rewind and watched Whit's left hand as he spoke. His index finger was crooked, and his nail tapped a tooth, then lifted to scratch his head.

Dana backed away from the screen with her hands over her mouth.

"What is it?" Andy said. "What's wrong?"

"He's talking to me—he's using our secret code to talk to me!"

"A secret code? Dana!" he shouted. "That's great!"

"No—that's what's wrong." She covered her face with her

hands as the tears spilled out of her eyes. "I can't remember it. I can't remember any of it."

She played the tapes one after the other, again and again into the night. Andy dozed on his cot across the room, and so she watched with the volume off and her hands clenched tight. *Think,* she pleaded with herself. *Remember.*

"Dana, I'm being held by a group of armed men who mean me no harm but who will be compelled to kill me if you fail to comply with their demands." His left index finger, crooked. "You know what they want." The nail tapping against a tooth. "Put the item in an eight-by-eleven—" The finger rose to his hair and scratched.

There—that was a reference to hair, a description of someone's hair, she was almost certain of it. He was describing someone's hair. But what did teeth have to do with hair? It didn't make sense.

It would never make sense. It was only a game, a silly lovers' pastime. Instead of talking baby talk to each other, they'd talked spy talk. It was never meant to survive the semester.

But somehow Whit still remembered.

It was impossible. She was the one who kept mental files of birthdays and telephone numbers; she was the one who could recite by heart the Federal Rules of Civil Procedure and all the verses to the "Twelve Days of Christmas." Whit was the one who couldn't remember the PIN for their ATM card or the names of their next-door neighbors after five years. How could he remember the code when she couldn't?

She turned away from the screen in despair.

Don't think about Whit. The words were an incantation she used to ward off the unhappiness as their marriage soured, but she'd obeyed them too well. She'd forgotten the Whit she once knew, she'd forgotten their courtship, she'd even forgotten what he looked like then. How could she ever hope to remember a complex system of signals that went back twenty years?

She watched each tape once more in sequence, but it was no use. All she could do was follow the kidnappers' orders. She wouldn't go to the police; she wouldn't disclose the film, not to anyone.

She switched off the TV and lay down on a cot, but she couldn't switch off her brain. Every time she closed her eyes, the videos played again behind her eyes, faster and louder until Whit was screaming at her: *If you fail to comply with their demands—the children will never see me again—time is running out—do not deviate—I will be killed!*

Abruptly, she sat up and swung her feet to the floor. Andy was asleep across the room, and his skin shone white in the faint light that glowed through the windows. She stole across the concrete floor toward him and stood watching as his chest rose and fell with the rhythm of his breaths. He slept the way Travis Hunt did, like a child, the peaceful sleep of the unburdened conscience. It was hypnotic, the gleam of his skin in the moonlight, the sound of his breath in the silence.

"Andy," she whispered.

He stirred and rolled toward her. "Hmm?" he mumbled. "You want me to help you remember?"

"No." She dropped to her knees beside him. "I want you to help me forget."

His eyes flashed open, and he reached out and pulled her onto the cot.

39

Whit dozed with the scent of old roses in his nostrils, a sweet and musky fragrance redolent of the sachet-lined drawers of an old Southern lady. He dreamt of pale pink buds unfolding in silken layers and drifting, sighing onto snowy white damask. Softly, Dana laughed and floated above the petals as her wedding dress billowed in the breeze. Her hair was her bridal veil, and it rippled in lush waves and pooled around the naked soles of her feet. She lifted her hands to her headpiece and plucked another pink bud from the crown of roses. Again the petals wafted from her fingers, and again the sweet musk of antique roses filled his head. He reached out, but his hands were clumsy and useless, and the petals slipped from his fingers. Dana's laughter died; the scent began to fade. "No!" he cried, and he stretched, yearning toward her. But he couldn't reach her, and when he looked down, he saw he had no hands.

He woke with a violent jolt. His body was wedged between the toilet and the wall, and his hands had gone numb, pinned under his rib cage. He twisted around and sat up, but still his breath came in hard, shallow draws. Stupid dream. Nothing in the latrine smelled of roses, least of all his own body. In fact, if he didn't soon have a shower, he'd start hacking off body parts himself.

He rubbed his hand over his beard, but there was little point in measuring time now. Ike made it clear his release wasn't imminent, and Whit knew he couldn't even count on dying anytime soon, not so long as the food and water kept on coming. The biggest danger was that he'd perish of boredom. He'd memorized every square tactile inch of the latrine; he'd thought every thought of Dana he could bear to think; and every time he tried to force his mind to another place, it landed at the last place he wanted it to: on Stegner's *Angle of Repose*.

All summer long, when it might still have done some good, he couldn't force his mind to the project to save his soul; now, when it was pointless, it was all he could think about. He wished he could take a page from the book and give up trying the way the two principal characters did. Ah, yes, he remembered: that was where the scent of roses came from. Stegner employed the rose as a metaphor for Oliver and Susan's marriage: it was a brief, lovely bloom, when they could still see a world of promise and hope in each other, followed by a quick fade when the disappointment took root and they couldn't sustain their love any longer.

Whit stood up and stretched, and for the first time in twenty years he wondered why they couldn't. Because it wasn't possible, or because they gave up trying? The angle of repose that they ultimately found together—was it something worth striving for, or was it nothing more than the place where they finally gave up the struggle of trying for something better? If the latter, he'd been misreading Stegner for twenty years.

He sat down hard on the edge of the toilet while ideas whirled through his mind like dervishes. He was all wrong about *Angle of Repose*: it wasn't about the quiet dignity of learning to live with disappointment; it was about two people making the biggest goddamned mistake of their lives. Repose wasn't the destiny of man, and Oliver and Susan shouldn't have settled for it. They leaned together like intersecting lines, a false arch, Stegner called it. "For lack of a keystone," he wrote, "the false arch may be as much as one can expect in this life."

He was saying it right there, all along he was saying it— *expect more, do not settle for less, never give up looking for the keystone.*

Ike's voice crackled through the speaker in the ceiling, and Whit squeezed his eyes to shut out the noise. *Not now. Don't interrupt me now. Can't you see I'm finally working after twenty years?*

"Professor, I'd like to apologize for this turn of events," Ike was saying. "It was never our intention to hold you this long. I hope you can understand that."

Whit didn't answer. He was too busy trying to contain the thoughts in his brain.

"You've earned my respect, Professor. To tell the truth, I didn't expect you to conduct yourself with much in the way of fortitude, but you've surprised me."

Shut up. Go away. Can't a man get any peace and quiet around here?

"I'm aware of your discomfort. We may not be able to arrange other accommodations for you, but I would like to improve your situation to whatever extent we can, consistent with the demands of security. So I put it to you, Professor: what can we do to make you more comfortable?"

Whit squinted up at the ceiling as the words began to penetrate.

Ike repeated, "Professor, isn't there something we can do for you?"

Whit stumbled to his feet. "Yes!" he shouted. "There is! Bring me paper—a pen—and a light to write by!"

He stared upward, waiting for the answer, hoping for it as if his life depended on it. He strained his ears. Was that a whispered consultation he was hearing? What were they doing? *Damn it, answer me!*

"I think that can be arranged," Ike said at last.

40

"What time is it?" Dana murmured.

Daylight was lifting over the Delaware and funneling down the east-west streets of the city and into the windows of the office building. She and Andy lay on the cot, their naked bodies spooned together.

"Only five-fifteen. Go back to sleep."

"I can't, I have so much work— Oh, Andy! I forgot to tell you, we're making a presentation to the NTSB on Thursday. I've got the computer simulators coming in, and I need you to work with them and with Diefenbach to put together some visuals on the collision path."

"Okay. Sure."

"And I'll need you there to answer questions, maybe even do part of the presentation. I don't know—I can't use the accident photos, so I'll have to figure out—"

"*Dana*—I said okay. Would you please relax?"

"Mmm. Remind me how."

His arm tightened around her waist and he nuzzled her neck. "Do you ever think about quitting?"

"My job? More and more all the time. Why?"

"There's this cabin I have my eye on." Softly, he brushed his lips against her ear. "It's in the Alaska Range, north of McKinley, on the shore of a glacial lake that's the sharpest shade of turquoise you ever saw. Twenty miles to the nearest neighbor, and you can only get there by plane. Seaplane in the summer, then in the winter the lake freezes up so solid you could land a 727 on it. You come out of the cabin and you can count fifty mountain peaks at your doorstep."

She opened her eyes and rolled over to face him. "Why are you telling me this?"

"I don't know, I've been thinking a lot about it. Maybe I'd like to buy it and live there." He shifted his weight, and the next words came more quietly. "Maybe you'd like to come with me."

Her breath expelled in a short, astonished burst. "To Alaska?"

"Hey, it's a great place. You gotta see it."

"But what would I do there?"

"They got lawyers in Alaska, too, you know."

"What kind of clients would I represent? With no roads, and twenty miles to the nearest neighbor? What kind of cases?" She laughed. "Grizzly bear disputes?"

"I thought maybe you had enough of clients and cases and working in a system that's broken. And lying awake all night with an ulcer burning through your stomach."

She reached over and touched the side of his face. "You're right. Maybe I have had enough. But Andy—I can't just run off with you."

"Why not? We work pretty well together, you know." He grinned as he fondled her breast. "And the sex ain't bad either."

She worked her hand behind his neck and pulled his mouth to hers for a kiss. "I'm crazy about you, Andy, you know that. But there're too many differences between us."

He pulled back with a scowl. "Age difference, you mean. Listen, you're the one hung up on that, not me."

"No, not just age. I mean—what about my children?"

He tried to conceal it, but she saw it in his face: he'd forgotten about them, and it took him a second to respond. "Bring 'em along. Kids love it up there."

"And then what happens?"

"What d'you want, a script?" he complained. "Can't we just take it as it comes? Do we have to plan every little detail?"

"You don't," she said. "You're practically at the start of your life; you can be open to everything. But I'm halfway into mine. I can't pull out of it without knowing what's ahead."

"Come on, where's your spirit of adventure? Is this the same lady who busted a guy's nose and hid out in the wilderness all night?"

She laughed and kissed him again. "All right. Let's say I pack up my kids and go with you and we give it a try. And five years from now the adventure's over and we call it quits. You'll be thirty-five with a world full of options and opportunities before you. But I'll be forty-five, washed-up in the law, with two teenagers who either already resent me for taking them away from their father or come to resent me for taking them away from you. And that'll be the rest of my life—alienated from my children, stuck in a second-rate career, maybe single forever."

He sat up on the cot and folded his arms over his knees. "So what're you saying? That I have to marry you before you'll come with me? God."

She shook her head. "I couldn't marry you if you wanted me to. Because then I'd have to worry about your children." He looked at her blankly, and she said, "The ones you'll never have if you saddle yourself with me."

"We could have our own."

"No, we couldn't. My tubes are tied. See? Your babymaking years are still ahead of you, but mine are long over."

"I don't even know if I want kids."

"Oh, Andy." She sat up and wrapped her arms around him. "Don't you see how that only proves my point?"

He shook loose and flung himself to his feet. "Hey, remind me never to try arguing with a lawyer again."

He stalked off toward one of the bathrooms, and she got up wearily and went to the other one. She brushed her hair, and as she stood at the sink and brushed her teeth, part of Whit's signal came back to her. His fingernail tapping on a tooth, then lifting to his head and scratching. He was describing someone's hair, but how did teeth tie in? Sharp, biting—hardly descriptors for hair. Hair would be described as long, short, brown, blond. She opened her mouth and spat out a foam of toothpaste.

Or white.

"Andy!" She burst out into the war room. "White hair—the kidnapper has white hair!"

He was pouring a pot of water into the coffeemaker, and the stream stopped in midair as he stared at her.

"Wait a minute." He slammed down the coffeepot and picked up the cylinder of enlarged prints. "Wait one fucking minute."

He unrolled a blowup of the wreckage as it lay entangled on the roller coaster. The steel gridwork appeared in sharp detail as the rescue workers scaled it. He pointed. "There."

One of the firemen climbing up the roller coaster had a full head of bright white hair. On his coat was the insignia of a fire company in Allentown.

"One of the firefighters?" She stared at the man's face. It was unlined, which meant his hair was either dyed or prematurely white. Either way, it was his most distinctive feature.

Andy made a little frame of his fingers to isolate the man's face until nothing appeared of the wreckage or the roller coaster. "I could crop this and take it up to the fire station. Show it around, see if I can get a name."

He looked at her with the question written on his face. Last night she'd resolved to follow the kidnappers' orders strictly and hope that much alone would win Whit's release, but she knew it was a resolution born only out of failure. Now she'd broken at least part of the code, and if she could do something, anything, to find out who these men were, she had to do it.

She reached for Andy's hand and squeezed it. "Yes," she said. "Thank you."

He gazed at her hand as it lay in his. "It's still two years till trial, right? At a minimum."

"Right," she said, puzzled.

"Well, I can plan at least that far ahead." A slow grin spread across his face. "And I'm planning to be around."

She put her hands on his face, a thumb beside each dimple. "Good plan," she said.

* * *

Dana scheduled a team meeting for ten o'clock, but at ten-ten only the two paralegals and Brad and Katie were in the conference room. Even Travis was absent.

"Anybody hear from Lyle?" Dana asked.

"Out sick," Brad said.

"What about Sharon?"

"This is her day off," Katie said.

Dana gazed despondently around the table. Fewer than forty-eight hours to put together a major presentation, and she was down to a skeleton crew. Even if they worked around the clock, it would be impossible to pull this off.

Travis burst in mumbling an apology and quickly took his place at the table.

"All right," Dana opened. "Everyone knows about Thursday's presentation?"

They all nodded.

"Most of the experts are flying in today. We've got tonight and tomorrow to put together a trial-quality presentation. I'm afraid this will have to be a full-court press."

They nodded again, grimly, and Dana doled out the assignments. The computer simulation people were already on a plane from Boulder, and Brad would work with them. Travis would work with Ted Keller and the acoustic engineer on the sound-spectrum analysis of the two CVR tapes. Katie would take charge of the documents they'd use as exhibits and handouts, and supervise Luke with the videos and photographs. Maria was in charge of logistics: she would arrange for the facilities and equipment, and transportation and lodging for the experts. As for Dana, she would spend the next two days constructing her opening and closing statements and her narration to the demonstrative aids.

"What about your telephone conversation with Sullivan?" Travis asked. "You planning to mention it?"

"Yes."

Brad Martin's face contorted with alarm. "But you don't need to! We've got the engine sounds now to prove the helicopter didn't drop altitude."

"And that's good, persuasive evidence," she agreed. "To the

NTSB and Ira Thompson and the handful of other people who understand it. But the audience will be full of people who don't understand anything more than what they think Vic said. I have to let them know they're wrong."

"You do that," Brad said wildly, "and somebody'll file a motion the next day to disqualify us as counsel for Pennsteel."

"Probably," she said. "We've got good grounds to fight it. But if we lose, we lose."

"After all we've done and all we've been through the last ten days? Look—" Brad shot a desperate look at Travis, but when no help was coming from that quarter, he struggled to bring his voice under control. "All I'm saying is, why force the disqualification issue now? You keep the lid on your conversation with Sullivan, and we can hold on to this case at least through next year."

"If we spend the next year defending a few hundred copycat suits, Pennsteel will exhaust its entire ten-million-dollar deductible before we ever get to trial. Even if we win every case, Pennsteel still loses."

She pushed back from the table and moved to the door. "Trial might be two years away, but this case is going to be won or lost on Thursday."

Her phone rang incessantly through the rest of the day, mostly lawyers rattling their sabers and reporters angling for a quick and dirty preview of Thursday's disclosures.

"Hold my calls please, Celeste?" she said after she fended off the fifth.

She returned to work, but before she could make any headway on her presentation, the experts began to trickle in. The computer programmers, all gripping state-of-the-art laptops in their hands; John Diefenbach lugging more reams of radar printouts; the aerodynamicist; the visibility expert. Dana greeted each with a five-minute update, then turned them over to Celeste, who stowed them in separate conference rooms to make their phone calls and review their notes before the full-team meeting at five.

She was back at her desk again, and trying again to make a

good start on her opening when the phone rang again, three times without a pickup. Celeste was away tending to another of the arriving experts. Irritably, Dana picked up.

"Dana Svenssen," she snapped.

Hesitantly a voice said, "Mrs. Endicott?"

"Yes. Who's this?"

"This is Jerome Allen?"

"Yes?"

"I cut your grass?"

"Oh! I'm sorry, I wasn't thinking—" She tried to remember when she'd last paid his bill. "Is there a problem?"

"No, ma'am. I mean—well, yeah—I been kinda worried about Whi—Mr. Endicott?"

It struck her then—it was his voice on the answering machine last week. So, Jerome the lawn man was Whit's fellow babe hound. Carousing made stranger bedfellows than she'd thought.

"We been readin' together a couple nights a week, and well—he never showed up the last couple times, and your phone's out, and I was wonderin' if he be sick or somethin'?"

"You've been reading together," Dana repeated.

"Yeah, well, not exactly. I mean, I can't read so good. But Mr. Endicott, he be a big help to me. No point in teaching 'bout books, he says, if there's nobody can read 'em. He got me this book, and we been goin' through it—"

She stumbled to her feet. "Whit's been tutoring you?"

"Yes, ma'am. So—is he all right or what?"

Tears swam in her eyes. "Jerome—I'm so—sorry," she stammered. "I didn't realize—I mean, I didn't know you two had an appointment, or I would've called you myself. You see, Whit—had to go out of town unexpectedly."

"Oh. But he's okay, then?"

"Yes," she choked. "He's fine."

"Any idea when he'll be back?"

She had to take a deep breath before she could answer him. "Not definitely. But soon, I hope."

"Okay. Well, thanks, Mrs. Endicott. Sorry I bothered you."

He disconnected, and she stood listening to the dial tone buzz in her ear before she finally sat down and hung up. Why didn't Whit tell her about this? But in two beats she answered her own question. Because she was never around, and when she was, they talked only about the girls or the house. She never asked him about himself, because she was always too afraid of what he might answer.

She looked up as Travis tapped on her door.

"Hey, I thought you oughta know," he said. "Katie just left. Her husband came and took her to the hospital."

"Oh!" She forced herself to come alert. "The baby?"

"Yeah."

"What hospital?"

"Bryn Mawr."

She jotted it down on a piece of paper, the same page that listed Katie's name beside a half-dozen work assignments. "We'll have to replace her," she said heavily. "Though God only knows who Austin'll send me this time."

"Don't worry about it. I'll pick up her end."

"Thanks, Travis," she said with a weary smile, and turned back to the terminal.

"Scary stuff, this baby business," he said behind her.

She glanced over her shoulder, and his expression made her slowly wheel her chair around. "Travis, are you . . . ?"

"Well, you know—" His face showed an uncertain grimace. "—you can't marry Miss Texas and drag her north and not give her a baby."

"Oh, Travis!" she exclaimed, and jumped up to give him a hug.

Long after he was gone, Dana sat at her desk in a daze. It seemed a lifetime since her last pregnancy and childbirth, and in fact it was a lifetime—Katrina's. She turned to look at her baby girl's face in the portrait on her credenza, and suddenly, with no more trigger than that, her mind was spiraling into a memory she hadn't relived for years, of Katrina's birth, which was also nearly Katrina's death.

The contractions started at dawn on a Thursday morning. Dana assumed she had the luxury of time—Kirstie's delivery had taken thirty-two hours from start to finish. While Whit called the doctor and packed her bag, she prepared and labeled Kirstie's lunches and put a big pot of soup on to simmer, then went upstairs and laid out three coordinating outfits for Kirstie to wear to nursery school, all the way down to socks and underwear. The sitter arrived at eight, but Dana decided to wait until nine, when the office opened. She had an appellate brief due in three days and couldn't leave it unfinished.

But there was more behind her delay than that. There was a kind of feminine heroism in carrying on in the face of childbirth; it was the modern yuppie take on the peasant women who used to squat by the fields to give birth. How long she waited to call the doctor, how far dilated she was by the time she arrived at the hospital, whether she did it without drugs, and best of all, in a birthing room with only a midwife in attendance—all of these were points to be scored in the maternal Olympics.

Whit kept a hand on her belly and timed the contractions while she spent half an hour on the phone with the word-processing people going over the revisions to the last draft of the brief. "We better go," he warned when she finished that call, but she pressed down the switch hook and dialed the paralegals to give them the instructions for filing and service. Only one more call, to let Cliff Austin know what was going on. She started to dial, but Whit bellowed an exasperated "Now!" and jerked so hard on the telephone wire that the plastic connector splintered in the jack.

"All right," she muttered irritably and got to her feet.

At once she felt a pressure like a ten-ton weight on the floor of her pelvis. No, it couldn't be—it took thirty hours to reach the second stage of labor with Kirstie, and she'd barely passed three.

She dared not tell Whit, he was already angry enough at the delay. "I think I'll sit in the back" was all she said as he helped her to the car.

The pressure was unbearable, and she couldn't find a position that would ease it. It was a thirty-minute drive to the hospital, and she knew what the books said: the second stage of labor lasts an average of fifty-five minutes for a first baby, and twenty minutes for subsequent babies. But it was impossible, it had to be, it couldn't come this fast.

"Whit," she cried through bloodless lips. "It's crowning."

His face froze in the rearview mirror. They were on a rural road, no more than halfway to the hospital. He pulled off to the shoulder and closed his eyes for a second's deliberation. Her membranes ruptured as he jumped out, and he flung the door open to a gush of amniotic fluid. The urge to bear down was overpowering; there was nothing she could do to hold it back, even when she felt the perineum rip. Whit blanched, but somehow forced himself to get between her legs, and he was there to guide the head through the tearing tissue. The shoulders followed in an easy slide, and at the moment she thought the worst was over, he groaned, "Oh, God, no."

She propped up on her elbows. The baby was a bruised shade of blue, and Whit was unwinding the cord from her neck.

A cry strangled in her throat, and she watched in horror as he got the cord free and worked his fingers into the baby's mouth to clear it of mucus. Still she lay, a tiny, inanimate shape between Dana's legs.

Whit's eyes flicked up, dark with dread, and Dana began to sob in giant heaves. They'd lost their baby, their much-loved and planned-for baby, and it was all her fault, hers alone, and she prayed her heart would burst with the agony that swelled it.

But Whit bent over and covered the baby's blood-streaked face with his mouth and breathed softly, once, and again and again. Dana fell silent, watching, afraid to breathe herself lest it rob them of their air. When at last he lifted his head, the baby's cries filled the car.

The neonatologist declared her to be perfect, and by the end of the day she'd nursed twice and gone to sleep a rosy shade of pink. Dana had some stitches taken and was ready to go to sleep herself when Whit came into her room to say good night.

He still looked shell-shocked, and his hands trembled when he touched her, but they'd been rock-steady when it mattered. He saved two lives that day, Katrina's and hers both. When he bent to kiss her, she grabbed his face between her hands. "I love you, Whit Endicott," she said fiercely, tears streaming down her face. "Do you hear me? I love you!"

Celeste had to speak her name twice before Dana blinked and looked up.

"Another one of your experts arrived. I put him in 48C."

"Okay, thanks."

Except for Andy, all of the experts had already arrived. Dana took the stairs up two flights and cracked open the door of the conference room.

"Are you all right?" He grabbed her by the hand and pulled her inside. "I've been trying to reach you all day."

"Why? Did something happen?" She felt a surge of hope. "Did somebody recognize the white-haired man?"

"No." He pushed the door shut behind her. "Nobody knows him. I must have talked to fifty guys, and they all say he's never worked out of that station. But one of them spotted something else."

He opened a folder on the table and took out a photograph. It was a blowup of the white-haired firefighter, cropped to show only his face and the heavy black coat with the company insignia on the yoke. "Take a look."

Dana followed his finger. The man's coat was hanging open, and under it he was wearing suit pants and a white shirt. "Funny way for a fireman to dress," she murmured.

"No, look at this." Protruding from the man's shirt pocket was a round black case with a thin cylinder extending upward.

"What is it?"

"I should have recognized it myself," he said. "It's a gas tank charge."

Her knees buckled and she sat down hard on a chair. "What does—how does it—"

"There's a magnet here on the side. You clamp it onto a fuel tank, stick a blasting cap in the cylinder here and a time-delay firing device into the bracket on the front. Then get the hell out of the way."

"The second explosion—"

"Yeah. The tank in the JetRanger was probably still intact.

And look where the guy was." He unrolled the original photograph that showed the man's position on the roller coaster, three cross grids below the JetRanger. "He was headed straight for the chopper."

Dana stared at the photos. "We always assumed the fire spread, that it sparked into the other tank, and that's what caused the second explosion."

"Yeah, it could have happened that way. And nobody'd have any reason to suspect anything else." He held up the photograph. "Unless maybe somebody snapped a picture of it."

"Andy," she gasped. "People were killed—"

"I know."

She felt suddenly cold. It wasn't evidence of the angle of impact or militiamen or even submachine guns that she caught on Kirstie's camera. It was evidence of murder.

"After he planted the charge and was back on the ground, he must've looked up," he said. "He saw you taking pictures from the Ferris wheel. But the timer was already activated, there was nothing he could do to shut it off. So he followed you through the park and tried to rip the camera off your shoulder. And when that didn't work, he figured out who you were—"

Numbly she said, "I was on the news that night. It wouldn't have been too hard to find out."

"Dana," he said urgently. "These people have already killed once. Maybe they didn't intend to, but they intended everything they've done since then. We can't fool around with this anymore. You gotta call the cops before they come after you."

She shook her head in bewilderment. "That's what I don't understand. I'm the one who had the film. Why did they take Whit when they could have taken me?"

"I guess you haven't given them an opening."

But she'd endured enough vulnerable moments over the last week to know that wasn't so. There had to be another reason.

"Let's back up," she said. "Why did this guy plant the explosive? What was he looking to destroy? The guns?"

"Coulda been. He didn't necessarily know they'd been thrown clear of the wreckage."

"But even so, did he really think he could wipe out all traces?

All the metal pieces, the steel stampings—some of that would have to survive the fire. Wouldn't he know that?"

Andy lifted a shoulder. "Maybe."

"So let's focus on what he *did* destroy."

"That's easy. The blade strikes on the skids of the Jet-Ranger. All the evidence of the angle of impact. The cause of the whole fucking collision." He made an exasperated noise. "But Loudenberg caused it, so that brings us right back where we started."

"Who knew that an hour after the crash?"

He squinted. "I'm not following you."

But Dana's thoughts were moving too far and too fast for her to back up and explain them now. She visualized the wreckage as she'd filmed it, before the second explosion, while it was still smoldering on top of the roller coaster. Nobody knew then who or what caused the collision. With causation unknown, who stood to lose the most?

Not the Loudenberg family, with no assets and no insurance. And not Pennsteel, whose deductible was steep at ten million but not astronomical. But United Aviation Casualty, its primary insurer, had an almost certain exposure for the next ninety million, and Geisinger Underwriters was on the hook for everything else, for all damages in excess of a hundred million dollars—in a case where demands in the billions had already been tossed out. The same Geisinger that just spent three hundred million dollars building a palatial new hotel and conference center.

She remembered the three men as she met them in the music hall the day after the accident. Charlie Morrison was popping Rolaids, and Norm Wiecek was pulling a gloomy face, and all the while Don Skelly beamed affably, cracked jokes, and sprang for coffee but not lunch.

Skelly was notified of the accident within minutes after it happened. From King of Prussia he could have a man there within the hour. His words at the diner last Saturday echoed in her mind: *I'm not worried on this one,* he'd said. *With no physical evidence, you gotta look to the common sense of the thing.* She'd thought of him that day as a curious mix of savvy veteran and good ol' boy, company man and everyman, but what else was in his mix? Conspirator? Saboteur? Murderer?

"Dana, I mean it," Andy was saying. "Call your friend Mirella if you want. But call somebody."

She looked over at the phone. What could she tell Mirella? If she named Don Skelly, the FBI would pay him a visit and Whit would be dead within the hour. If she didn't name Skelly, all they would do was step up their investigation of the militiamen, the obvious choice but a dead end that would do nothing to save Whit.

She shook her head. "I can't."

"What if they kill you?"

But she knew she wasn't in any danger, and now she knew why. She was on Skelly's side, working to exonerate the Penn-steel crew and to shield Geisinger from its billion-dollar exposure. He needed her to be alive and well and working hard. It was the film he wanted destroyed, not her.

"No, Whit's the one in danger. Andy, I have to find him." Desperately she said, "I have to make myself remember."

"You gave it your best shot."

She closed her eyes and slowly shook her head. "Not my best."

41

They spread out one of the sleeping bags on the concrete floor
between two steel support posts and sat on it cross-legged as if it
were a picnic cloth. Andy poured a glass of wine and held it out
to her.

Dana hesitated. "I should keep my mind sharp."

"It's that sharp mind of yours that's been standing in your
way. Let it go dull for once."

"Why don't you just pump me up with sodium Pentothal?"
she said, but she took the glass and poured the wine down her
throat.

"Okay. Tell me again what brought on this flashback today."

"One of my associates went into labor, and another one told
me his wife's pregnant, and I started thinking how long ago it
was for me, and suddenly it was all there, in living color."

He tipped the bottle into her glass again. "Then let's start at
the beginning and see what triggers what."

This time she sipped more slowly. "Just like that, huh?"

"Okay, let's try it this way," he said with his dimples boring
in. "I'm Barbara Walters. Dana, tell us about the first time you
saw Whit."

She sputtered a laugh that made a fine mist of wine spray
out. "Well, Barbara, it was my sophomore year at Penn. He
was a teaching assistant in the English department, and I took
his fall semester class in American Literature. No, wait." She
stopped and stared into the wine. "No, that's not right. Isn't

that strange—that's when I first *met* him. I forgot that I first *saw* him . . ."

. . . the spring of her freshman year. She was working part-time at Le Bus, a mobile kitchen housed in an old school bus that served as a gourmet alternative to the greasy spoon lunch wagons that parked on every other campus corner. With her hair pinned up under a Phillies cap, she tossed pasta salads and made sandwiches on whole-grain bread while the customers lined up on the sidewalk and shouted their orders through a little sliding school bus window. She'd worked there all year, in bikini top and shorts during the dog days of September, in parka and mukluks during the frozen days of January.

It was in March that she began to notice a new face among the lunchtime customers. His head floated six inches above the crowd and he never wore a coat, only a pair of leather gloves and a muffler wrapped twice around his neck. He had shaggy brown hair that swept over his brow and required much head-tossing to keep off his face, but there was something about his eyes, something about his voice. . . .

"Who is he?" she asked, and speculation flew down the length of the bus. He was an Oxford don on sabbatical. No, he was this year's poet-in-residence. No, you're all wrong, take a look at the guy's build, he's gotta be one of those Montana novelists. Only one thing was certain: he had something to do with the English department.

"Okay," Andy said. "So you mooned over him awhile at the lunch bus."

Dana gave him a look and held her glass out for a refill.

"When did you actually talk to each other?"

Not until the fall, in an old Humanities building at Thirty-fourth and Walnut. Sophomore year, Am Lit, in a musty second-floor classroom. She pictured the corridor and tried to put herself in it, moving down the hall, scanning the doors with the room numbers stenciled onto the opaque glass. An empty classroom appeared to her right, and she took a step in and gazed around. Was this the one? She couldn't remember.

The next classroom was smaller and stuffier but no more familiar, and a mist of tears came into her eyes. She'd never be able to remember the code, because she couldn't even remember the room where it all started.

Andy reached over and squeezed her hand. "It's the first day of classes," he said. "You've got your books in your arms, and you're walking down the hallway. . . ."

No, running, for she was late, embarrassingly so, since as a sophomore she was expected to know the way to everything. A voice floated out as she scanned the doors for the room number. "Dana Svenssen," he said once, then repeated, "Dana Svenssen?"

She crashed through the door, shouting, *"Here!"*

And there she was, in the classroom. The windows were open, and sunlight streamed in through the leaves of the elm tree outside. Birds were singing in its branches, and a car honked at the traffic light below. The battered desks, the chalk dust—this was it.

He was calling the roll at the front of the room. Twenty years of age and expression peeled away, and there he sat as she first knew him: a big man, unexpectedly rugged, with a bony face full of angles and planes and hidden meanings. Shadowed eyes at once penetrating and impenetrable. A firm mouth, now curving into a smile.

"So you are," he said as the class tittered. He pointed to an empty chair. "I wonder if you'd mind being *there*."

By this time she realized that the instructor of Twentieth Century American Literature was also the Byronesque mystery man at Le Bus about whom she'd fantasized for the last six months. Blushing furiously, she hurried to her seat.

For the rest of the hour she tried to conceal her embarrassment by studiously avoiding eye contact with the instructor. But as he spoke, in a voice she already secretly knew, it made her imagine he was somehow speaking to her alone, and suddenly it was as if the room cleared and no one was there but the two of them. Before she realized what she was doing, she looked his way, and at the same moment he looked hers.

Her eyes welled up at the memory. There'd been enough moments of instantaneous sexual attraction in her life, but that day in class was the only time she ever felt *this*. It was a force so strong they could hear each other's heartbeats across the room.

Andy cleared his throat. "The code. When did you start using the code?"

The spring semester. One day Whit kept her after class on a pretext, and as soon as the door was closed behind the last student, he caught her in his arms and asked her to come to his room that night. But she pretended to make an issue of it, protesting that her classmates would grow suspicious, their affair would be revealed, if he singled her out like that again. "What am I supposed to do?" he complained. "Pass you a note?"

Her eyes lit up. "No, not notes. Signals."

It was a primitive code at first. A tug on the left earlobe meant yes, on the right, no. But as the semester progressed, they invented ways to expand and refine it. Times and places started to figure into their signals, and they practiced on the rest of the class. *The redhead in the third row, second chair, is writing a letter to her boyfriend,* Dana would signal him, and Whit would call on the redhead to share her thoughts with the group. *The guy in the first row, last seat, doesn't have a clue what you're talking about,* and Whit would say, "Mr. Conway, how does Twain's use of water imagery differ from Melville's?" Once, wickedly, she said, *I'm not wearing any underwear,* and it was Whit's turn to sputter and turn red in the face.

"Okay, whoa, stop," Andy said. "This business about describing other people. Go over that again."

"Well, hair color—I already figured that out. He points to something a particular color, then scratches his head."

"But what about this third row, second chair signal?"

Dana drank another glass of wine and squinted hard to visualize it. The desks in the classroom were arrayed in five rows of five, and dimly she remembered a finger count—three fingers resting on the chin meant third row, followed by two meant second chair.

"All right!" Andy crowed, and he jumped to his feet and went to the VCR and loaded a tape. It was on the final video that

Whit gave that signal. Three fingers laid on his chin, followed by one.

"Third row, first seat. Right?"

Dana bit her lip. "I think so."

"Okay, and right after that comes hair color. Brown. So we're talking about somebody with brown hair who sat front and center in your class?"

"That's it?" Dana rose unsteadily from the floor. "I'm supposed to remember one person out of a class of twenty-five from twenty years before? He's out of his mind!"

She turned and gazed out across center city and over the Schuylkill to West Philadelphia where the Penn campus lay hidden under a canopy of trees. Because of the river, only a few streets went through from center city to the campus—Chestnut, Walnut, South Street past Franklin Field, site of the famous Penn Relays and the not so famous Quaker football games.

Football. The city lights began to blur. She closed her eyes and the picture that came into focus in her mind was of the boy in the center front seat in Am Lit class. Jason Carraway—a big bashful boy with fuzzy brown hair and the best throwing arm the Quaker offense had ever seen. He had high hopes of playing professionally after college, but before the first scout ever put in an appearance, Jason was exposed in a cheating scandal and jumped off the roof of Franklin Field. Poor, doomed Jason—of course she remembered!

But her thoughts pulled up short. Jason had been dead for almost twenty years. There was no way he was involved in the explosion of the wreckage or Whit's kidnapping.

"Anything make sense?" Andy prompted her.

"Only if he's being held captive in a football stadium."

She dropped to the floor, and the room tilted and her head swam at the movement. It was all too obscure. Remembering the code was no help at all; even when she knew what Whit was saying, she couldn't understand him. She reached for the wine, but the bottle was empty.

"Let's try another one," Andy said. "Here's a signal he gave on all three tapes." He squatted in front of her and lifted his hand, thumb and index finger together, and the circle tilted twice.

"Oh, that one's easy," she said. "That was the signal for me to meet him for a drink at the Rathskeller."

"What the hell's that?"

It was a dimly lit basement-level pub where Penn grad students used to drink beer and talk politics and get laid. It reeked indeterminately of beer and urine and marijuana, and in the back was a unisex rest room that was the most renowned such facility on campus. Couples hooked up and disappeared into the bathroom, later to return mussed and glazed, and always in under ten minutes.

Dana and Whit eschewed the bathroom and spent their evenings in a dark corner absorbed with books and poetry and each other, but she couldn't deny that they left the Rathskeller a little more aroused for their observation of the others. She remembered walking to Whit's apartment, holding hands in the moonlight as they murmured and laughed together. They scuffed their soles on the pavement, pressed their noses to shop windows, stopped to point out the stars, anything to prolong the delicious anticipation—until at last one of them would break into a run and pull the other in a wild headlong gallop inside and up the stairs. They'd roll into bed and laugh until they were breathless. Sides heaving, eyes still leaking tears of hilarity, they'd turn to each other and suddenly go sober. Whit would reach out and touch his thumb to the ridges of her lips and, wide-eyed, she would draw it inside, sucking deep—

"This isn't helping," Andy cut in. "Back up to this Rathskeller joint."

Yes, the Rathskeller was easy to remember, for that was where they played out one of the worst scenes of their relationship.

It was Dana's twenty-first birthday, and they were to meet at the Rathskeller for her first legal drink. She arrived early and decided to surprise him. Jubilantly, she flashed her ID and ordered two frosty mugs of beer, then positioned them untouched on their table while she waited for him.

It was March of her senior year. She was bound for law

school, he was applying for faculty positions, they were in love and mostly living together, but he'd never once mentioned what would happen after May. For her, the future always loomed ahead, beckoning her on and pointing out the path and whispering urgently in her ear: Where are we going? What's going to happen next? Visualize it, plan for it, make it happen. While for Whit and every other young male of her acquaintance, the future was a dim and distant specter that never spoke at all. When a young woman said *love*, she meant the rest of their lives together; a young man said *love* and meant a very intense now. Whit said he loved her, and she believed him, but when he said he wanted her forever, she knew that forever existed only a semester at a time.

The frost was melted and trailing like tears down the sides of the mugs by the time Whit finally came through the door. "Dana, look who's here," he called, and brought his friend Jack Lucas to the table. "Perfect, you already ordered," he said, and then compounded his oversight by grabbing one mug and sliding the other one to Jack.

"Here's to Harvard and Professor Whit Endicott!" Jack crowed, and clinked his mug against Whit's before they both tilted them back and drained half the contents.

"Excuse me?" Dana said.

Whit threw an arm around her and kissed her, while Jack explained, "That man, who at the moment is pawing you so indecorously, is today the recipient of a letter, typed on official department stationery, mind you, postmarked Cambridge, Mass., signed by the chairman of the English department—"

"Whit, you have an offer from Harvard?" she asked, and he nodded with his eyes aglow.

For the last six months they'd pored over law school catalogues together, and they'd celebrated as each acceptance letter arrived. They were all in now—from Penn, Columbia, Georgetown, and Michigan—and Dana was delaying her decision only until she saw how Whit's prospects materialized in the same cities. Boston was never on the list. At least not on any list he'd ever shared with her.

"I didn't realize," she said to Jack, a face-saving way of

saying *I didn't know, Whit never told me, I guess we don't mean that much to each other after all.*

"Who could've guessed?" Jack laughed. "I mean, he hasn't published, he never writes anything but derivative bullshit, but the damn fools still want him!" He leaned over and slapped Whit on the back.

Whit at least had the good grace to go sober. "Dana, I meant to—" he began. But he stopped and gave her one of their secret signals instead, and got up and headed for the bathroom.

She sat stunned as Bruce Springsteen wailed, *"Baby, I was born to run"* on the jukebox. If ever she wanted crude sex in the Rathskeller bathroom, it was not tonight.

"Excuse me, Jack," she said, and rose from the table. "I'm late for study group at the library."

She grabbed her coat, and the moment she was through the door, she broke into a run, so hard and fast that the tears dried on her cheeks before they could freeze in the cold night air.

Nothing kills love faster than the suspicion that it's no longer returned. A half hour later Dana had her clothes out of Whit's apartment and back in her room at the dorm. An hour later the phone started to ring, and she let it, and two hours later when he arrived at the dorm, her friends did as she asked and told him she hadn't been back.

She holed up in her room for a week while she typed the application forms, solicited another round of faculty recommendation letters, and ran up long-distance telephone bills to every level of faculty and administration she could tap. It took all of her powers of persuasion, but at the end of the week a slot about to be awarded to someone on the wait list was given to her instead.

The next day she emerged from the dorm, and Whit ambushed her before she'd gone a hundred feet on Locust Walk.

"Dana, where have you been?" he shouted, running up with his coat flapping loose. "I've been out of my mind!"

"Oh, hello, Whit," she said without stopping.

"Look, I would've explained everything the other night if you'd only come back to the john like I asked. I never applied to Harvard. Not officially. Basically it was an unsolicited offer. I didn't mention it to you because I wasn't really considering it. I mean, it's an honor; anybody would have to get excited about it. But I've decided to stay on here at Penn."

"That's wonderful, Whit," she said, still moving in long-legged strides across campus. "The department will be so pleased."

"I have an hour free," he said. "I'll help you move your things back to my place."

"Thanks, but I'm staying on in the dorm."

"Dana, don't do this."

"What's the point, Whit? School ends in six weeks."

"But that's what I'm trying to tell you! We don't have to end when the semester does."

"No, I'm afraid we do. You see—I've accepted Stanford Law."

She left him standing on the green with his jaw hanging open. "Stanford?" he shouted after her. "That was never on your list."

She turned and met his eyes.

"Oh, I get it," he said, suddenly bitter. "This was your hole card, wasn't it? Your secret escape hatch for the day I let you down."

She tossed her head and walked on, and this time he didn't follow.

The semester ended, she received her diploma and smiled for her parents' camera, she even spent a few bikini-clad weeks on the beach that summer, but through it all an air of unreality persisted. They didn't really break up, he wasn't really settling into Cambridge already, she wasn't really packing her bags for Palo Alto. The truth to her during those months was like the future to a young man: a silent, spectral figure it was easy to close her mind to.

Reality hit her like a cold hard rain the moment she stepped off the plane into the California sunshine. It was over, he was gone, and the rest of her life stretched before her in a blank white void. She moved listlessly through her classes, impassive and all but inanimate, while the pain grew inside her like a hidden cancer. She longed for him every day and dreamt of him every night and cursed the stupid pride that drove them a continent apart. But that same stupid pride kept her from picking up the phone and calling him.

One day in October, four weeks into the fall semester, she was sitting in torts class, shoulder-to-shoulder with a hundred others, when the rear doors of the lecture hall crashed open. Her head swiveled back along with the rest of the class, and she froze to her seat when she saw Whit.

"Yes?" the professor said. Whit, desperately scanning the sea of faces, didn't answer him, and Dana couldn't open her mouth to speak. "Can I help you?" the professor snapped.

Wild-eyed, Whit called, "Dana? Dana, are you here?"

She found her voice at last, enough to let out a giddy squeal of delight. The aisles were clogged all around her, so she jumped up on the long curving desk, skipped across twelve feet of books and papers, and hurled herself into space at the end of the row. Whit caught her there, and it was three days before he let her go.

Later he tried to tell her—he ran into one of her friends who decided to tell him the story of her all-out campaign to get into Stanford, and he knew then it wasn't a hole card but a last-ditch effort to save herself, what a fool he'd been, it was all his fault—but she'd hushed him with a finger to his lips.

"You came for me," she said. "Nothing else matters."

"I don't believe it," Andy said. "You never squealed in your life."

He spoke in a light, teasing tone, hoping to make her laugh and dispel some of the horror in her eyes. But it was too late. Her head was spinning and her stomach was roiling and the tears were streaming down her face. For years she'd been forcing herself to forget these things. *Don't think about Whit. . . .* The refrain became her mantra, but not because she didn't love him—because she loved him so much that watching that love fade was more than she could endure. The only way to bear the loss was to forget what it was that she lost.

Whit, where are you? She buried her face in her hands and her shoulders heaved as she sobbed. In a bar under a football stadium, held captive by a white-haired man and the ghost of Jason Carraway? She needed to find him, she needed to open an escape hatch for him, but she didn't have a hole card; she wasn't holding any cards at all.

Oh, Whit, I want to find you, I want to listen to you and understand everything you say. Please, give me one more sign.

Andy stooped beside her and tried to coax her to the cot, but she shook him off and curled herself into a ball on the floor and let the memories of Whit wash over her like the tides.

Give me one more chance to come for you.

42

The white-haired man drove up the curving lane and parked once more at the edge of the parking lot where the lights didn't penetrate the perimeter of darkness. As before, he pulled a cap over his hair and looped the rucksack over his shoulder before he stepped out of the car. This was the seventh consecutive night he'd come here; the drill was a familiar one.

But tonight would be his last visit, and so tonight the drill was a little different. He opened the trunk and lifted out a shovel, then unlocked the storage compartment in the floor and took out the Glock 17. He snapped a new magazine into the butt, clicked the baffle tube to the muzzle, then slid it into the custom-fit holster below the back of his neck.

At the tree line he strapped on the goggles and crossed the open field to the back of the fence. The weather had been so hot and dry for so long that the night couldn't wring enough moisture out of the air even to make dew. The grass crunched under his feet like peanut hulls.

He picked the padlock on the gate and checked the trip wire. No one had entered the site since he himself the night before. Though everything else had gone wrong with this mission, nothing about the site could be faulted. For seven days it had remained inviolate.

But he understood that it couldn't remain so indefinitely, just as he understood why his contact had at last ordered that the mission be aborted. For his own part, he'd seen the end coming for forty-eight hours, ever since he retrieved the envelope and confirmed that the film had been developed. The situation could no longer be contained. Any number of people might have seen the photos by now, and there was no way to silence them all. The only course was to cut their losses and move on.

He regretted it, though. During his years in Special Forces, it was often his duty to terminate others, friend or foe or by-stander, but never before was he required to kill someone who'd earned his respect as much as this one had.

At the edge of the excavation he looked down at the latrine. The turquoise fiberglass showed as a dull brackish green under the sepia cast of the goggles. A thin curving line of orange marked the outline of the door where it faced the solid wall of earth. The professor had his light on.

He fitted the shovel through the straps of his pack and climbed down the ladder to the bottom of the pit. The ground was hard and dry, digging would be difficult, but he found a likely spot behind the latrine and set to work.

The professor called out to him, but there was no time to chat. He worked steadily until, at a depth of three feet, the shovel clanged against solid rock and he decided to end it there. Al-though six feet was the standard, it wasn't necessary here: in a month's time the entire floor of the pit would be covered with a foot of concrete. He finished out the corners of the rectangle and stood back to appraise his work. A pit inside a pit. It was like a Chinese box. He looked at his watch. Almost time now.

"Ike? Is that you?" the professor called again. "Don't be shy now. Feel free to speak right up."

The white-haired man chuckled. The professor had been a real revelation. His sense of humor never flagged, and he'd shown as much mental stamina as most of the professional sol-diers he'd known. Resourcefulness, too—he nearly escaped that first night. In a different site he would have succeeded.

There. A slight vibration from the receiver in his pocket. The wire at the gate had been tripped, as he expected.

"I wasn't expecting you here," he called out. "I thought we were supposed to meet in twenty minutes in the park."

Tobiah was climbing backward down the ladder. He was

dressed all in black, and with his dark skin would have been invisible to anyone without night-vision goggles. A useful attribute. It was one of the reasons the white-haired man had recruited him, both for Special Forces and later for the corporate world.

Tobiah turned slowly at the base of the ladder with his gun in his hand. "Hands on your head, sir," he said.

The white-haired man dropped his jaw. "Tobe—what the hell—"

"I'm sorry, sir. I have my orders. Hands on your head."

"Orders to kill me, Tobiah?" he asked as he folded his hands over the back of his skull.

"The only thing linking us to the explosion is your face in the photos."

"Ahh. So if you can't destroy the photos, you can at least destroy me. Is that about the size of it?"

"I'm afraid so, sir."

He smiled. "This is my own doing. I trained you too well. I wouldn't be so expendable if you weren't there coming up right behind me. I suppose you have my job now?"

Tobiah gestured with the gun for him to back up, to the side of the pit where the earthen wall would absorb whatever sound the silencer didn't.

The white-haired man obeyed, taking careful steps backward with his hands balanced on his head. "We could take off, you and me, Tobe. I hear they're hiring in Liberia. Lots of opportunities there for a guy like you. We could leave the boss to stew in this by himself."

"I thought of that, sir, I did," Tobiah said, pushing forward.

"But . . . ?"

"But I asked myself what you'd do in this situation. And I figured you'd go for the promotion."

The white-haired man threw his head back and roared, and Tobiah laughed along with him. With his neck bent back, it was an easy reach to the butt of the Glock. Tobiah was still laughing as the nine-millimeter bullet cracked into his skull above the left ear. Too high and offside, he chastised himself, and he delivered another shot directly between the eyes before Tobiah hit the ground.

He stood a moment over the body and mourned him. He was a fine soldier, one of the best he ever had the privilege of commanding. He had only one flaw, really, one that grew worse instead of better over the years, and that was his trust in his superior. A fatal flaw, as things turned out.

He rolled him into the grave and backfilled it, then hid the shovel behind a stack of steel beams. It would make for a nice little bonus for the first construction worker back on the job when work resumed.

He unpacked the rucksack and picked up the transmitter connected to the speaker on the roof of the latrine.

"Professor, we're going to open the door now to give you your food. You will back up into the corner by the john. There will be two guns trained on you as the door is opened. If you make any move toward the door—"

"Those guns will be fired," the professor said. "Yeah, yeah, get on with it, will you, so I can get back to work?"

The white-haired man smiled and unlocked the heavy chain around the latrine. The professor was on his knees, using the lid of the toilet as a desk. He barely glanced up as the jugs and boxes were handed in and the chain locked again.

But a minute later the professor's voice rose out of the latrine. "What did I do to deserve all this?"

"I suggest you ration it carefully, Professor. You see, I won't be coming to visit you anymore. I don't expect anyone will, not for at least a week. Pace yourself, and you'll have enough food and water to last you till then."

"And what's this?" the professor shouted. "Now you're giving *me* videos?"

"That's for you to watch if you manage to make it out of here alive, Professor."

"Talk about anticipation. I can hardly wait."

The white-haired man climbed out of the pit and pulled the ladder up after him, then padlocked the gate behind him. As he trotted to his car, the sepia glow of his watch read 0300. Four hours to get to Kennedy and catch his flight to London.

In forty-eight hours he'd have a new name and a new home in the jungles of Africa. Same hair, though. It would be so rare there—who knows? They might make him a god.

43

Wednesday morning came, too soon. Dana opened her eyes and watched the hot gray sun beat down through a steamy canopy of clouds. Andy appeared through the same kind of haze on the other side of the war room. He was packing up his papers, and faintly she remembered that he was due at Geisinger this morning to work with the simulation team. In twenty-four hours they'd be making their presentation to the NTSB and the world, and she didn't have a clue what she was going to say.

They parted on the landing of the fire stairs before Dana headed up and Andy down.

"Good luck today," she said.

"You, too. See you at the hotel tonight. And be careful, okay?"

The sky remained a ponderous gray all morning, and Celeste arrived at her desk wilted and panting and complaining of the unbearable humidity outside. The coffee cart made its rounds with nothing but cold sodas on its shelves, and a system-wide e-mail went out warning everyone to stop fiddling with their thermostats; the air-conditioning couldn't be pumped any higher than it was.

Dana slogged away at her desk, struggling through three drafts of an opening speech, then three more of a closing, but nothing seemed to click, and by afternoon she'd scrapped them all. She blanked the screen and stared at it so long she could almost imagine she was falling through it into some kind of void.

She gave a start as Clifford Austin announced himself with a dry cough in the doorway.

"I heard a rumor—" he began, and came in and seated himself.

"Sorry, Cliff, I can't talk. I'm under the gun here."

"—that you engaged Bob Kopec as your co-counsel for the environmental problems at Alpine Valley."

"That's right."

"The last time I checked our firm's attorney roster, Kopec's name wasn't on the list."

Her mouth pulled tight as she realized his purpose. "Yeah, and if you ask me, Bill Moran's name shouldn't be on the list either. You said he had time for this, Cliff, but he never bothered to return my calls, and he stood up our opposing counsel—"

"We don't earn our fees by sending work to other firms, Dana. You had no business going outside with this. And you'd better bring it back."

She stared at him. "This is my case," she said with cold fury. "And I'll handle it in the way that best serves my client's interests. If you try to interfere one more time, if you make any more threats—I'll leave this firm tomorrow and I'll take my client with me."

Austin sat so still for so long that Dana could almost imagine that Charlie's joke came true and rigor mortis was complete. But at last he said, "Now who's making threats?"

"It's not an empty one. You know Charlie Morrison won't keep his business here if I go."

Austin leaned back and watched her through slitted eyes. "The client is Pennsteel Corporation, not Charlie Morrison. I wonder how tight a hold you'd have if he were gone. And I wonder how soon he'd be gone if the board knew everything that we know about him."

Her eyes flashed. "You do that, and Charlie'll sue you for slander. And I give you one guess who his lawyer will be."

An uncertain tap sounded on the door, and they looked over to see Travis shifting from foot to foot on the threshold.

"We'll discuss this another time."

Austin rose stiffly and headed for the door, and Travis almost fell over his feet getting out of the way. He turned to Dana with a look of pure panic on his face. "What's going on?"

She raked her fingers through her hair. "More of the same. Nothing for you to worry about."

But his expression made it plain he was going to worry with or without her permission.

"What are you doing here?" she asked. "I thought you were working with the team out at Geisinger."

"I had to come back for something."

"How's it going out there?"

He shrugged. "The way this thing is shaping up for tomorrow? I don't know. Between the computer simulations and the sound engineering, it comes off as nothing but high-tech speculation."

Dana kneaded her forehead.

"I mean, it's plausible and all," he said. "But I don't see how we back it up. Thompson's gonna say, sure, it coulda happened this way, but it also coulda happened a dozen other ways. If only we had something more."

It was what she'd been struggling against all day. There was a crater-sized hole in their case, and it wasn't going to be filled with her own self-serving testimony about the conversation with Vic. The photographic evidence of the blade strikes was what it would take, and that was the one piece of evidence she couldn't use.

"I know, I'm probably worrying for nothing." He pulled the door open. "You'll pull something out of your hat, like you always do."

"Do I?"

"Hey, I almost forgot why I came by. Katie had the baby this morning. Little girl. Seven pounds, two ounces."

Dana leaned back. "Oh—how wonderful! Are they both—"

"Doin' fine. I sent flowers from the team."

"You're a prince, Travis Hunt."

"Yeah, well." He blushed. "I figured the queen was too busy to do it herself."

* * *

Late in the afternoon the overhanging clouds went from vaguely ponderous to openly threatening, and an excited buzz spread through the corridors that it might actually rain tonight. It was like a snowfall in Miami. Secretaries poured into empty window offices, and lawyers dropped in on each other on pretexts just to get a different view as the heavy black clouds billowed and blew across the sky.

Dana gave up trying to work against the beehive hum of voices around her, and she slipped downstairs to the war room, where at last in the quiet hours of the evening she was able to concentrate on her speech. She finished a rough draft by eight o'clock and telephoned the team at Geisinger to see if they'd had equal success.

Andy took the call. "We got trouble," he said.

"What now?"

"Diefenbach won't sign off on my reconstruction of the plane's flight path."

"But it ties in with his radar hits."

"Yeah. The problem is the long stretches in between where there aren't any hits. He says the only reasonable assumption is that the plane flew straight and level at two thousand feet, because that's what a reasonably prudent pilot would do."

"There wasn't anything reasonable or prudent about what Loudenberg was doing."

"I know that. Problem is, Diefenbach doesn't."

She felt sick with frustration. Andy's reconstruction made so much sense—she could close her eyes and picture the Skyhawk at fifteen hundred feet trailing the JetRanger a thousand feet above it, and suddenly going into a climb as the mountain approached.

"Andy! The photo of my daughter, the one with the Skyhawk in the background—"

"Forget it," he said. "You use the photos and they'll know you can identify the bomber. They'll go after you for sure."

Storm clouds were tumbling across the sky outside, and a wind kicked up and blew debris sideways past the windows.

"Dana?"

"Yes, of course, you're right," she said. "I'll come out there and talk to Diefenbach myself."

"Don't expect any miraculous conversions."

"I'll be there in half an hour."

She hung up and went to the worktable to gather up the photos: the eleven-by-fourteens, the slides, and the blowups.

Outside, the clouds opened up at last and released a wall of water that hit the plate-glass windows with a resounding boom. The rain pelted against the simmering rooftops of the city and steam hissed up like a million vaporous spirits all rising from their graves at once.

She found a plastic bag in the makeshift kitchen and packed the photos in it for the trip to Geisinger, then searched for another plastic bag to cover the suit she would wear tomorrow. The rain hammered against the windows and echoed in a deafening roar across the empty floor, so loud she almost didn't hear the scrape of shoe leather on the floor outside.

Her eyes darted to the door as the key left in the dead bolt started to turn.

She lunged across the room and snatched the key out. She could hear the slide of metal in the tumblers of the lock. Someone was trying to pick the dead bolt.

It was impossible. No one knew she was here but Andy, and he was twenty miles away. No one but the Palazzo team even knew she had access to this space.

She ran for the phone and dialed the security desk in the lobby, and through ten rings she could hear the grate of metal as it pried at the tumblers of the lock.

She'd never seen the security desk unmanned, night or day, but no one answered the phone tonight. She hung up and her eyes moved wildly through the room in search of some kind of weapon, even just a pair of scissors, but the only thing that came close was the paper cutter on top of the photocopier by the door. She looked up at the unfinished ceiling, with the utility cables and junction boxes running between the beams, and all the useless knowledge of electricity she'd acquired during the Palazzo case came back to her in a rush.

She reached behind the copier and pulled out the plug, then

laid the cord across the paper cutter and sliced the handle through the insulation and wire. Carefully, she held the cut end of the cord against the blade and stripped off the plastic sheathing. Two wires were exposed inside: the silver-colored neutral wire and the copper-colored hot wire. She peeled back the insulation and left six inches of the hot wire protruding.

The pick was still scraping at the lock, and when she peered at the dead bolt, she could see the tumblers starting to move. She took a breath, inserted the hot wire into the lock, then dropped to her knees and plunged the plug into the outlet.

From the other side of the steel door came a bloodcurdling scream.

She waited with her heart pounding inside her ribs, straining her ears for any sound outside the door, but the rain was beating so hard the glass rattled in the windows, and after ten minutes she couldn't hear anything. She got up and crept back to the phone and dialed the security desk again.

"I'm awful sorry I was away, miss," the apple-cheeked old man said after he slid his ID under the door and she opened it to him. "Somebody made a prank call and I had to go all the way up to forty-two for nothin'."

Dana came out with her briefcase and the two plastic bags. "No problem," she said. "I was just a little spooked by the storm. Would you mind walking me to the garage?"

"Be happy to."

She pushed the call button for the elevator.

"Wouldja take a look at this?" the guard exclaimed.

She turned back. He was pointing to the door, where the metal was scorched black around the dead bolt.

"Looks like somebody took a blowtorch to it," he said, flabbergasted.

"Construction workers," she muttered, and stepped into the elevator.

He rode with her to the garage and saw her safely behind the wheel of her Mercedes before he gave a little salute and got back on the elevator again.

She locked the doors and took a deep, steadying breath before she turned the ignition key. The engine started with a muted growl that was familiar and reassuring. She backed out of the space and was heading up the exit ramp when a black sedan screeched out of nowhere and blocked her path.

The doors flew open and two men jumped out and ran at her with their raincoats flapping and their left hands raised.

Gasping, Dana threw the car in reverse and stomped on the gas, and it squealed backward thirty feet across the concrete floor, until the rear bumper bashed into a steel post and the engine stalled. The men ran toward her, and when they slammed their hands against the windshield, she squeezed her eyes shut and screamed out loud.

A gentle rapping sounded on the passenger door, and she opened one eye to see Mirella Burke's face at the window. Dana blinked in astonishment and looked back to the windshield. Each of the men was holding an FBI shield to the glass.

"You gonna let me in?" Mirella yelled. "The way you drivin' I sooner be in there with you than out here in harm's way."

Dana's breath came out in a shudder as she pressed the unlock button. Mirella opened the door and the springs rocked and groaned as she lowered herself into the seat.

"You kinda techy tonight," she said.

Dana clenched the wheel to keep her hands from shaking. "What the hell is this?"

"We been tryin' to find you for close to three hours. Finally I say she ain't gonna go off and leave that fancy car here all night, so let's jest wait here. Course now I see you don't think so highly of this car after all."

Dana turned on her with her eyes blazing. "Would you please tell me what's so goddamned important you had to ambush me like this?"

"Whoa, honey, cool your jets. I'm here for your sake, not mine." A smile spread over her face. "We got our indictment this afternoon. Just in the nick of time for any certain lawyer who might be puttin' on a show tomorrow, if you get my drift?"

Dana got it, and her relief was instantly surpassed by her exhilaration. "Mirella!" she exclaimed. "You mean I can go public with the paramilitary connection?"

A puzzled look came into Mirella's exotic eyes. "Go public all you want," she said. "But you best get your facts straight. They ain't no paramilitaries. They's drug dealers."

Dana stared at her.

"See for yo'self." Mirella reached into the voluminous folds of her raincoat and came out with a sheaf of papers.

Dana ran her eyes down the first page. *United States of America v. Carlos Reyes, Nestor Santiago,* and another twenty names she'd never seen before. What struck her first was the name of the court—the United States District Court for the Eastern District of Pennsylvania. Scranton and Montrose were in the Middle District.

She turned on Mirella. "This is your case, isn't it? Lomax was only acting as your stooge."

"Ain't much of an act with him."

"You were lying about everything—"

"Withholdin' information, precious."

Dana skimmed the list of defendants. "Billy Loudenberg—he's not on here."

"No, we made ourselves a private arrangement with young Billy."

Slowly Dana said, "He's your informant."

"Po' boy couldn't take it no more after his daddy and brother got kilt. He came to us next day and signed a full confession."

"But what . . . ?" Dana riffled through the pages of the indictment but couldn't find what she was looking for. "What is it they were doing?"

"Distributing marijuana, cocaine, and other controlled substances. With a little sideline in illegal assault weapons."

"I can't believe it—"

"The dead boy, Donny, he's the one got 'em into it. He was a small-time pusher in his high school, and he met a few higher-ups and introduced 'em to his daddy. So the old man cuts a deal and plows up his thirty acres of wheat and plants some marijuana. Turns a nice profit on it, too. But he had his eye on somethin' bigger. He took up flying, and that got him into the regional distribution business. Then he hooked up with some of the big boys in New York and Miami. By the end, he was running a couple million dollars' worth of guns and drugs up and down the East Coast."

"Those men in the woods—who shot up Andy's plane—"

"You stumbled onto one of their depots, honey. Them boys was there waitin' on a drop, Billy and Zack, along with three of the boys outta New York. You lucky you came out of there breathin'."

Dana gaped at her, then burst out, "Then why in God's name did you let them get away?"

"Reyes and Santiago was the ones we wanted. If we'da brought in Billy and Zack, they woulda gone underground faster than a mole with a cat on its tail."

"But didn't Billy name them in his confession?"

"Shore he did. But you know how long it would take one of you high-priced lawyers to tear him to pieces on the witness stand? We needed more than a crooked farm boy's word on it."

"And now you have more?"

"Yes, ma'am. The luck turned our way for once."

"And my way, too, I guess," Dana murmured.

"Well, I guess so," Mirella said indignantly. "After I been sittin' here waitin' on you all night."

"Oh, Mirella, thank you."

She leaned over to give her a quick hug, but Mirella reeled her in and clasped her against her pillowy bosom. "Now you wanna tell me what's goin' on that made you jump out of your pasty white skin tonight?"

"I sure do," Dana said. "Can you meet me tomorrow afternoon?"

Mirella squinted at her for a long moment before she nodded. "All right. I s'pose I can wait that long. Meanwhile—" She glanced back at the steel post rising out of the trunk of the Mercedes. "—you need a lift anywheres?"

Dana left her battered car in the garage, and the FBI agents drove her to King of Prussia through the pounding rain. As soon as the bellhop in the Geisinger Center Hotel showed her to her room, she called Andy in his.

"Jesus!" he exploded. "It's after eleven, I've been going crazy!"

"I know. I'm sorry."

"Are you all right?"

"Yes, I'm fine."

He hesitated. "Can I come to your room?"

"Please," she said. "Right away. And bring John Diefenbach with you."

44

Whit closed his notebook and leaned back as the rain beat a tattoo against the fiberglass shell of the latrine. Twenty years of stalling and grousing and writing tripe were undone in two days' work. His book was as good as finished. A month or two to flesh it out, and the manuscript would be done.

"For lack of a keystone," Stegner wrote, "the false arch may be as much as one can expect in this life. Only the very lucky discover the keystone."

Well, he'd discovered it all right, though it was stretching it to call himself lucky at the moment. But as he drew a drink of water from the jug, he toasted himself and made a vow: if he made it out of this hellhole alive, he'd find another keystone, one that would bring Dana back and hold her to him for the rest of their lives.

He tossed down the water and unwrapped tonight's ration of food. A week, Ike said, before he could expect to be found. The food and water might last, but the charge on the flashlight never would. He reached to turn it off.

Darkness fell and the storm seemed to roar even louder. He got to his feet and stretched as high as the ceiling allowed, then shifted his weight from one foot to the other. One corner of the latrine suddenly lurched. He caught his hands on the walls to steady himself as one side began to sink. The earth was washing out below.

Finally. Now he might be able to blow this joint. He braced

his hands against the side walls, raised his feet, and kicked with every ounce of strength he could muster against the door. It didn't give, but the latrine began to sway, then pitch, and suddenly he was scrambling for balance as it toppled backward into the mud.

His head struck against the base of the toilet, and he clawed himself up in a daze and reached for the flashlight. When he switched it on, he saw that the latrine was lying on its back, with the door above him. He planted his feet against it and kicked hard, but it still didn't give. He fell back panting.

A drop of water splashed on his head, and he shone the flashlight up. The speaker that sat on the roof all week must have come loose in the fall, because now the light was shining through the air vents. And about as easily the water was pouring in.

Another drop fell, and it burst and splattered on his head like the detonation of a tiny bomb.

45

Thursday morning the rain was still gushing out of the sky and battering against the trees and windows and roadways. After sixty days of heat and drought, the ground was baked too hard to absorb it, and the runoff flowed in torrents down the hillside to form a pond at the base of the Geisinger drive. A steady line of traffic was turning into the complex, and each car splashed through the flooded intersection as if it were swimming a moat to the castle.

Dana watched the traffic from the window outside the fifth-floor auditorium. It was half an hour until the scheduled ten o'clock conference, but the news crews were already setting up their cameras and the seats were filling up rapidly. Despite the weather, most of the Philadelphia bar seemed to be turning out for the event. Every time the elevator chimed, the doors opened to deliver another load of spectators, and there was a familiar face in each load.

The next time the doors opened, the familiar face was Charlie Morrison's. "Dana," he called, and strode down the corridor with his hands thrust deep in the pockets of his sopping raincoat. "How's it look for today?"

"Good, I think. Though the only thing that matters is what *they* think." She gave a pointed nod toward the auditorium.

"Well, whatever they think—you've done a hell of a job, and I really appreciate it. And I hope I'll have a lot of opportunities to show you how much."

She smiled. "I hope so, too, for your sake, Charlie."

A door slammed down the hall and her back went stiff as Don Skelly approached.

"Hey, Morrison, stop dripping on my brand-new carpet," he said, and stopped to light a cigarette.

Charlie cracked a smile. "You got more serious water problems than me, Don. Your storm drains are all backed up on the road. And it looks like you're building the world's biggest swimming pool over there." He pointed to the excavated foundation of the west tower.

"Yeah, I see it," Skelly grumbled. "But you won't be laughing if it turns out the construction delays were caused by the steel fabricator." He turned to Dana. "Hope you'll represent us if we end up suing Pennsteel's ass over this."

"I have a conflict," she said tightly.

The elevator chimed again and Norm Wiecek came out with his head drooping.

"Damn, there's my worser half," Skelly said, and took another drag of his cigarette as he went off to greet him.

Charlie was watching Dana. "You having some kind of trouble with Skelly?"

She gave a grim nod. "I'll fill you in later, okay? I have to go in and get ready."

"Yeah, sure. Break a leg."

She opened the rear door of the auditorium and strode down the aisle. The members of the computer simulation crew were at the foot of the stage, working at three different terminals that would project onto the giant movie screen. A man was leaning over the operator at one of the terminals, but he straightened as Dana approached.

She gave a start. "Andy?"

His hair still wasn't gray, but his suit was, and with a striped tie and crisp white shirt, he looked nothing like the devil-may-care teen dream she'd come to know over the past week. He seemed capable and sober, a professional.

"You look great," she said after a stunned moment.

"You, too, for a lady who got maybe two hours' sleep."

She lowered her voice. "Diefenbach still onboard?"

"Totally," he said, and pointed with his chin to another terminal, where Diefenbach stood nodding at the images on the monitor.

"Then it was worth it."

He looked over his shoulder, then took her hands in his. "Jeez, you're freezing. Are you all right?"

"I'm a little nervous, I guess." She cast her eyes over the rest of the team working at the front of the room. "Have you seen Luke?"

"In the booth with the sound engineer the last time I saw him."

She ran up the stairs and ducked behind the curtains to the sound booth in the wings. Luke's head was visible through the glass, hovering between the engineer's and Travis Hunt's. She tapped on the glass and beckoned him outside.

"Would you find a slide projector and set it up in the projection booth?" she asked when he came out.

The young man scrunched up his face at her. "What for? We don't have any slides."

"We might."

He shrugged and set off.

When she turned around, Travis was watching her through the glass. His eyes darted away.

Dana glanced at her watch. Two minutes to ten. Voices were swelling to a dull roar in the auditorium, and when she looked out through the curtain, she saw a standing-room-only crowd. One by one she called the roll: the team of NTSB investigators sitting front and center, with Harry Reilly and Jim Cutler both tending solicitously to a man between them who must have been a member of the Safety Board; her own people serving as a buffer behind them; and behind them Peter Seferis and his mothers' brigade, Ira Thompson, Dan Casella, Angela Leoni, and a hundred strangers' faces.

Oliver Dean and the Three Amigos were down front, with Charlie on Dean's right, and Haguewood and Schaeffer jockeying for room behind them. Another man was speaking earnestly to Dean on his left, and Dana was startled to see Clifford Austin. But a moment later she knew his game: he was there to whisper in Dean's ear. He had enough sense, she hoped, not to repeat his slander against Charlie, but she could easily imagine Clifford Austin poisoning her own well, commenting sadly on her many feuds inside the office and convincing Dean that it was her team and not her who put this program together, and that those kinds of resources were available only at a big full-service firm like Jackson, Rieders. A quick, bitter resentment flared within her.

It was extinguished the moment she looked behind the Pennsteel contingent and saw Don Skelly sitting with a self-satisfied smirk on his face. The sight of him made her tremble with fear and disgust. Three people killed, dozens injured, Whit held hostage—all so Skelly could protect Geisinger's balance sheet and preserve this heap of steel and concrete.

She looked away from him to see Mirella Burke barreling down the aisle in a caftan that flapped behind her like bats' wings, and in that moment Dana made her decision. Before the day was over, she'd find a way to expose Skelly, and she'd do it here in front of Mirella and a hundred other witnesses.

Luke passed behind her with a slide projector, and Dana called to him in a whisper. "Wait a minute." She reached into her briefcase and tucked the box of slides under his arm. "Keep quiet about this, okay?" she said. "I'll let you know if I decide to use them."

"Okay," he said, and hurried to the projection booth in the back of the room.

"Dana," somebody called from across the stage. "It's ten o'clock."

She stepped out onto the stage and the buzzing dwindled and died as she took her place behind the podium. From here the crowd looked vast and hostile, hundreds of eyes squinting in suspicion, hundreds of mouths poised for debate.

"Good morning," she said into the microphone, and closed her ears to the electronic feedback. "I'd like to thank the National Transportation Safety Board for sending its representatives here today and for giving Pennsteel this opportunity to present the results of its investigation. And I thank all the rest of you for being here as well.

"Thirteen days ago Pennsteel's corporate helicopter and a privately owned light plane collided in midair over the Alpine Valley amusement park. I was there that day, as I know some of you also were. It was the worst catastrophe I ever hope to see in my lifetime.

"None of us knew then what caused this terrible tragedy. None of us could have known—that day or many yet to come. But many fingers were pointed, and not coincidentally, they were all pointed at the deepest pocket available: Pennsteel. No one rushed to judgment against the impecunious party, but there was a virtual stampede to judgment against Pennsteel.

"Under these circumstances, Pennsteel had no choice but to conduct its own investigation and find out for itself what caused the collision. Twelve days ago we began that process, and now, here today, we know the answer.

"We know now that this awful disaster was no act of God. To paraphrase one of my colleagues who's here in the room today, this calamity was brought about by an act of extreme recklessness and callous disregard for human safety. It was that reprehensible.

"Twelve people are dead and dozens more are injured, and all because the pilot of the Skyhawk deliberately engaged in a dangerous and deadly maneuver. It was the aviation equivalent of tailgating, but worse—because he was doing it in a way intended to render the plane invisible to the helicopter crew, so that they never had a chance to protect themselves from him.

"Most of you have heard my colleague theorize that the helicopter caused the accident by dropping five hundred feet in altitude in the space of about fifteen seconds. The radar doesn't support that view, nor do any of the eyewitnesses. But he bases his theory on the helicopter's cockpit voice recording. You've heard it, of course, Mr. Reilly; I imagine everyone in this room has. But I wonder how many of you have really listened to it? Because what the recording actually proves is that the helicopter did *not* lose altitude before the collision."

Reilly leaned over to whisper to Cutler, who was shaking his head. Three rows back Ira Thompson was sitting in a fog with his tie flipped over his shoulder and his glasses pushed back on his head.

"I'm going to ask a pilot to speak on this issue. Andrew Broder, helicopter and light plane pilot, and also aeronautical engineer. His CV has been provided to you already, Mr. Reilly, and it's available at the door for anyone else who's interested. Mr. Broder?"

She stepped back into the wings as Andy tightened his tie and took the microphone. "Could I have the first screen please?" he said.

The lights went down in the auditorium, and the movie-sized screen on the stage lit up with the first computer simulation.

"This is the cockpit of the JetRanger," Andy said as an animated pilot dropped into the seat and assumed the controls. "To make a descent in this craft, sufficient to travel the vertical distance hypothesized here, the pilot must execute a maneuver known as a collective down." The animated figure reached for the lever and lowered it.

"This changes the angle of attack of the main rotor blades. Which in turn decreases lift and power." The simulation zoomed out of the cockpit to an exterior view showing the helicopter in profile as the rotor blades turned and the craft began to drop.

"The result sounds like this."

The engineer flipped a switch in the sound booth, and out of all sixteen speakers in the auditorium came the high-pitched whine of the engine as the simulation zoomed back into the cockpit. The pilot repeated the maneuver, and the pitch of the whine dropped two octaves.

"That recording was made Monday morning," Andy said. "In the same model JetRanger descending from two thousand feet mean sea level to fifteen hundred feet in fifteen seconds. Now we'll listen to the recording made before the collision. The voices have been suppressed; the engine and rotor noise has not."

The second recording was played, and the high-pitched whine never altered until the sounds of the collision screamed out.

The lights came up, and as Dana stepped up to the podium she did a quick survey of the audience. Jim Cutler was taking furious notes, Dan Casella was stroking his chin, Don Skelly was sitting with his hands holding his elbows as if he were about to burst at the seams with delight. But Peter Seferis was jumping to his feet with a scowl on his face.

"Cute trick," he called out. "Taking Sullivan's voice off the tape. But you won't be able to erase the evidence at trial so easily."

"Evidence of what, Peter?" Dana asked.

"Of—you know—what Sullivan said! You can play all the games you want with engine sounds. The man said what he said."

The audience buzzed in support.

"Are you referring to this?" Dana said. "Roll the tape please."

Vic Sullivan's voice came out of the speakers this time. "Hey, I see where we are. Coming up on that amusement park, I can see the roller coaster, whaddya call it, Alpine Valley."

At the podium, Dana leaned over and spoke into the microphone, and her reply resonated out of the same speakers. "No kidding! Give a wave to the ground, Vic. My kids are there on a field trip today."

Ira Thompson sat up straight and let his glasses fall into place over his eyes.

"Whaddya know," Vic's voice boomed. "Hey, Ron, set this baby down. Let's go cruise for a couple of blondes."

Angela Leoni's dark eyes darted to Dana, and across a hundred feet she mouthed, "Jesus."

"Victor Sullivan was speaking to me on the telephone immediately before the collision," Dana said. "Luke, would you show the first slide, please?"

The house lights went down again, and an image filled the screen, of the backs of two little girls with their pale blond hair tied up in pigtails.

"Ladies and gentlemen, these are the blondes Mr. Sullivan was referring to."

A hush fell over the audience for a moment, then suddenly the crowd was roaring with laughter. Harry Reilly went red in the face, and even Dan Casella grinned. Peter Seferis flopped back in his seat.

"Mr. Reilly, your laboratory's examination of the CVR has probably revealed a short in the wiring that prevented the recording of incoming transmissions on Channel 4." One of the NTSB investigators nodded, which meant that Ted Keller had guessed right. "I've prepared a transcript of the entire conversation as best I can recall my side. Copies are available at the back of the room."

Maria stepped forward from the back and held up a stack of papers in her hand. A half-dozen people went back immediately for their copies.

"Now that we've demonstrated what *didn't* happen," Dana said. "Let's take a look at what *did* happen."

Another simulation was projected on the screen. This one was a three-dimensional cutaway showing the relative positions of the helicopter and the plane in the air.

"The grid on the left side of the screen shows the altitude," she explained. "These numbers are based upon three different sources of data gathered and analyzed by radar expert John Diefenbach. That data and Mr. Diefenbach's CV are available at the door. As you can see, the JetRanger is flying at twenty-five hundred feet, and the Skyhawk is at fifteen hundred as we begin tracking them. Proceed please?"

The simulated image moved into the cockpit of the Jet-Ranger and gave the audience a you-are-there view through its windshield and out to the rolling terrain beneath it.

"The compass in the corner of the screen indicates the helicopter's heading," Dana said. "You can see it's holding steady until—" Appearing on the screen ahead was a simulation of houses and streets and lawns. "—a residential neighborhood approached. In order to avoid a direct flyover, the helicopter turned twelve degrees north." The compass heading changed, as did the image through the windshield: the roller coaster of Alpine Valley appeared ahead.

There was a sudden lurch of the cockpit on the screen, and a second later a streak of white outside the right window. "Freeze that, please," Dana said, and when the image held, it was recognizable as the right wing of the Skyhawk, pitched upward into the main rotor of the helicopter. "Proceed," she said, and there was a burst of orange as the fuel tank exploded in the wing.

The audience gasped as the rotor came off and the helicopter went into a spiral to the ground. The last thing they saw were the rails of the roller coaster zooming in before the screen went blank.

"Put us in the plane now, please," Dana said before the buzzing in the audience could grow too loud.

Another you-are-there view appeared, this one behind the controls of the Skyhawk. Through its windshield, the rear of the JetRanger was visible ahead and to the south, but with the same altitude and heading. Abruptly it pitched its nose down, and the audience watched the ground surge up before the plane leveled off at fifteen hundred feet. Seconds later it climbed again, back to almost twenty-five hundred feet. Again the helicopter appeared through the windshield at eleven o'clock high.

"Mr. Broder, from a pilot's point of view, would you explain what appears to be happening here?"

At a podium on the other side of the stage, Andy turned on a second microphone. "The flight route indicates that the Skyhawk was attempting to avoid radar detection. For much of its path, it flew at fifteen hundred feet, which is too low in this terrain to be detected on radar. This is a fairly common practice, known variously as terrain-flying or scud-running. But what the Skyhawk also did was fly so close to the JetRanger that it came inside the same radar footprint."

The room was in darkness, it was impossible to see anyone's expression, but a frenzied whispering began. The simulated Skyhawk dove again, and this time the ground seemed to come up to meet it. A chorus of *ooohs* sounded from the audience. Abruptly the simulation showed the nose pitching upward.

Andy explained, "The pilot lost sight of the rising terrain, and when he reached the mountain, he went into a steep climb." The simulation pitched the view upward, and the JetRanger ahead disappeared off the top of the screen. "So steep he almost lost lift and went into a stall. To keep out of a stall, you bring the nose down and increase applied power, as you see the pilot doing now by depressing the throttle."

"What you can't see now," Dana said, "is the relative position of the helicopter. And unfortunately, neither could the pilot of the Skyhawk. Could you give us a cutaway view at this point, please?"

The image rotated outside the cockpit of the plane and pulled back until both craft were visible. The helicopter was almost directly above the plane.

"Oh, God," came a voice out of the darkness.

"Put us back inside the plane, please?"

The simulation returned the audience to the cockpit of the Skyhawk. The view turned to look upward to the left and to the right. In each direction the wings blocked the sky.

Andy continued, "The pilot's been tailing the helicopter for miles, but now he can't find it. He lost his bearings when he pulled up over the mountain and now he's looking in all directions but he can't see it. He figures there's only one way to find out where it is."

The computer image pitched the nose upward, and a collective gasp sounded as the audience realized the inevitability of the next scene. The JetRanger appeared huge and ominous in the sky overhead. The plane tried to pitch down, but too late. The propeller blade sliced through the right skid of the helicopter, and the prop was torn off as the second blade struck the skid. The right wing tilted up and struck against the main rotor of the helicopter. The fuel tank explosion was simulated again, and this time the blast took up the entire screen.

They ran through two more simulations, from different perspectives, each one ending the same, until at last Dana said, "Lights up, please."

Ira Thompson was on his feet before the darkness ended. "Bill Loudenberg isn't here to defend himself," he shouted, his voice ringing through the auditorium. "But someone ought to speak up on his behalf. What you're saying about him is an abomination! He was a licensed pilot with a flawless record. He was a family man with deep roots in his community. There's no plausible reason for him to do what you're accusing him of."

Dana gripped the sides of the podium as she waited for the audience reaction to die down. "Yes, Ira," she said. "Bill Loudenberg was all the things you mentioned. He was also a drug trafficker."

A quick sharp silence, and pandemonium broke out. Photographer's bulbs were flashing, reporters were breaking for the aisles, Ira Thompson was shouting outraged denials.

"Mrs. Burke?" Dana called into the microphone. "Perhaps you'd be willing to speak to this question?"

Mirella's slanted eyes went narrow, but slowly she heaved herself to her feet.

"Assistant U.S. Attorney Mirella Burke," Dana said, introducing her.

The room went quiet. "Late yesterday," Mirella said, "a federal grand jury returned an indictment against twenty-eight members of a conspiracy to import and distribute controlled substances and illegal assault weapons. Two of the members of that conspiracy, now deceased, were William A. Loudenberg and Donald L. Loudenberg, his son. Both are alleged to have been actively involved in the transport of illegal drugs and weapons through the instrumentality of a Cessna 172 Skyhawk aircraft, registered to William A. Loudenberg, of Montrose, Pennsylvania."

Mirella took her seat again as Dana announced, "Copies of the indictment are available at the back of the room."

This time there was almost a stampede on Maria as she held up the papers at the door.

Dana waited five minutes for order to be restored before she spoke again. "We expect to present testimony at trial about the flying practices of pilots involved in the drug trade. We understand that a common practice is to follow a legitimate craft so closely that the radar detects only a single presence, effectively rendering the drug runner's plane invisible on radar screens and thus undetectable by law enforcement authorities. This, we believe, is what William Loudenberg was doing at the time of the collision."

"You believe?" Thompson bellowed. "You understand, you expect? This is rank speculation! The radar doesn't support your theory, and neither do any of the eyewitnesses. I've been through the same radar data myself a hundred times, and it doesn't bring you up to the point of collision. It can't get us that close, and neither can you."

A babble started to build as others agreed or disagreed or advanced their own theories. Dana gazed out over the podium as their voices swelled. Thompson was clever to turn her own language back against her. He was also right. She might have disproved his theory, but she hadn't proved her own, either; all she did was illustrate it.

"I *can* get us that close," she said finally. "Luke?"

Andy's head swiveled and his eyes burned into her from across the stage.

"Bring up the next slide please," she said.

"Dana!" Andy hissed.

The lights went down and the slide went up, and there it was for all the world to see: the helicopter and plane entangled on top of the roller coaster.

"This is no simulation," she said. "These are actual photographs of the wreckage taken before the second explosion obliterated it. You'll note the parallel slices on the skid of the JetRanger. These were made by the propeller blades of the Skyhawk as we demonstrated earlier. This is the actual proof of the angle of impact. Next slide, please?"

The next photograph showed the plane over the mountain behind Katrina. "And this is the actual proof of the climb we simulated over the mountain."

Andy crossed the stage and stood behind her, and the room fell eerily silent as the slides flashed on the screen, one after the other in a relentless procession. The only shots held back were those that showed the white-haired man climbing the framework of the roller coaster.

"Where did these photos come from?" It was Thompson's voice again, rising out of the darkness.

"I took them myself, Ira."

The lights came up, and the voices of the crowd crescendoed wildly.

As she waited for the noise to die down, Dana searched out

Don Skelly, hoping to read the guilt in his eyes, but he sat in the audience with a big grin plastered on his face. A chill slithered up her back at the sight of him.

On the other side of the auditorium, Travis got up from his seat and ran up the aisle. An image came suddenly to her mind, of Travis as he must have run as a football star years before. He galloped up the steps to the projection booth, and Dana watched in horror as her mental image morphed into something else. *He reminds me a little of that football player at Penn,* she once told Whit. *Oh, yeah, Jason Carraway,* he'd said.

She jumped as Andy touched her elbow. The audience was quiet again, and waiting for her to speak.

"Mr. Reilly, we have a set of these photographs for you and your team, and also a copy of our computerized simulation. If anyone else would like copies of the photos or an opportunity to view the simulation again, please contact my office to make arrangements. Can I answer any questions at this time?"

Reilly and Cutler were huddling with members of their team. Ira Thompson sat in a seeming daze, but Dan Casella caught her eye and gave a nod that told her he at least was persuaded. The mothers' brigade had a hundred questions but they were turning them all on Peter Seferis, who was trying to squeeze past their knees on his way to the aisle and out of the room.

Travis came out of the projection booth, and Dana's eyes tracked him back to his seat. It was impossible. No matter what pressures he was battling, he was her good right hand; he could never be involved in something like this.

"Then I thank you all for coming," she said into the microphone. "You can pick up packets of information at the door on your way out."

But another voice hissed at her as she left the stage: who else but Travis knew to look for her on the fortieth floor last night?

46

A hundred voices began to clamor as she hurried behind the curtains. The most urgent one was at her elbow.

"Now they know you kept the photos," Andy said as they cut behind the screen. "And since you held back the incriminating ones, they have to know that you figured out what happened. Dana—"

"Andy, I paid too much for those photos not to use them today, when it mattered." He shook his head desperately, and she reached out and touched his arm. "It's all right. I know who they are now."

His eyes opened wide, but before he could ask more, Charlie Morrison was strolling backstage with his hands in his pockets, the picture of relaxed confidence. "That was incredible—Dana, you blew them away!"

"It was all Andy's doing," she said, and Charlie turned his congratulations on him.

But Andy could barely respond. His eyes were fixed on Dana, while hers were on Mirella Burke and Angela Leoni as they made their way across the stage.

"Charlie, do me a favor?" Dana asked.

"I guess I owe you about a thousand."

"Ask our people to stay. There's something I need to discuss with them. Wiecek and Skelly, too."

"You bet," he said, and took off.

Andy's eyes shot a question, but she shook her head at him

334

as Angela teetered up on her stiletto heels. "You did great, Dana! And you know somethin'? Frankie's kids are doin' really great, too. I don't think we need to go too much farther with this thing. A few thousand bucks apiece and we're gone."

"Not a dime, Angela."

She made a little face as if to say *You can't blame a girl for trying.* "All right, then, be a hard-ass. But come on down to the lobby bar and let me buy you a drink, okay? For old times' sake."

Dana didn't reply; she was gazing past her to Don Skelly as he strode across the stage with his bantam chest thrust out.

"What a show!" he said, whistling through his teeth. "You blew me away! And those photos! Who woulda guessed it?"

Dana felt a cold hatred grip her heart so hard it made her toes go numb. "Don—I want you to meet Mirella Burke."

Skelly was amazing. He showed nothing more than a gleam in his eye as he pumped Mirella's hand. "Pleased to meetcha—nice work catching them druggies."

"Dana." Angela was tugging on her sleeve. "You comin' for that drink or not?"

"Sorry, Angela, I have another meeting. Give me a rain check?"

A second's hurt flicked over her face. "Yeah, all right," she said, and wobbled away on her perilous heels.

"What's this about another meeting?" Skelly said.

"In the auditorium, Don, if you don't mind hanging around a little longer?"

"Nothin' I'd like better."

Dana watched him stride past Angela and cut through the curtains. If anyone could co-opt Travis, it would be Skelly. He was the deadliest adversary she'd ever known.

"Guess I'll keep Angie company," Mirella said, and started to follow after her.

"No!" Dana blurted, and Mirella turned with her eyebrows arched. "Please stay. I have to talk to you."

Mirella tilted her chin up and squinted her eyes.

Andy said, "Dana, what's going on?"

Before she could answer him, Mirella heaved a sigh and said,

"She's got something to tell me she thinks I need to know. But Dana, honey, I already know all about it."

Dana's expression went blank. "You do?"

"But I got somethin' to tell you. Give the kid a break. He did the right thing in the end. And where would we all be if he didn't?"

"Mirella, what are you talking about?"

"Travis Hunt, who'dja think? That sweet boy out there shakin' in his boots 'cause he's afraid Miss Prissy Prim Proper here is gonna burn his ass. Okay, so he crossed a line—but he knows it, and if he hadn'ta come to us with the money, you never woulda had the indictment today."

Dana threw a look at Andy, but he was as baffled as she. "Mirella, I don't know what the hell you're talking about!"

"Oh." She blinked. "Lord, I spilt the beans for nothin'."

"Tell me!"

"All right, all right." She heaved another sigh. "Travis got a little too gung ho tryin' to please you on this case. He broke into the Loudenberg farmhouse looking for some evidence to help you out. But what he found was the evidence we been waitin' for, that Billy Loudenberg's been lookin' for and never could find. Close to a hundred thousand dollars cash that we traced right back to Reyes and Santiago."

"He—he brought it to you?" Dana stammered.

"First thing Tuesday morning. Then came in and did his duty before the grand jury yesterday afternoon."

Dana pressed her palms to her temples. "That's it? He didn't—"

Brad Martin stuck his head around the screen. "Dana? Everybody wants to know how long they're supposed to wait out here. What shall I tell them?"

"Sorry, I'll be right out."

"Wait a minute," Mirella said. "What were you fixin' to tell me?"

"Go have a seat, Mirella. You can all hear it together."

Mirella looked askance, but walked off the stage with her caftan billowing behind her.

Dana started for the sound booth to find Luke, but Andy caught her by the arm.

"I have to do this, Andy," she said, shaking him loose. "Don't try to stop me."

"I wasn't going to," he said. "Give me the slides. I'll run the projector for you."

She gazed at him as he stood waiting, tense and solemn, then took them out of her bag, the five she'd held back, and tucked them into his palm.

He leaned in close. "Be careful," he breathed against her lips before he kissed her.

She waited a minute, then stepped out on the stage and stood at the podium again. The group was gathered in the first three rows, the Pennsteel officers, Wiecek and Skelly, Mirella Burke and the Jackson, Rieders team. Cliff Austin was still at Oliver Dean's side, still angling for Pennsteel's business, but Dana didn't care anymore. Let him poach Pennsteel away from her. After today, she didn't care if she ever represented another client for the rest of her life.

In the back of the room she saw the square of light from the projection booth, and when Andy's silhouette passed through it, she began to speak.

"Thank you all for staying. I have a matter of grave concern to discuss with you. You've all realized of course that I concealed the photographs of the wreckage until today. There's something else I've been concealing. It's something that sent me into hiding for most of the past week, something that somebody wants so badly they broke into my car and my house and kid—" She had to stop and clear her throat. "—kidnapped my husband."

A rumble of surprise rolled like thunder through the group. Charlie Morrison's jaw dropped, and next to Mirella, Travis's eyes went wide. Don Skelly was staring with hooded eyes.

"Good Lord, what is it?" Oliver Dean called out.

"There were two catastrophes at Alpine Valley that day," she said. "The first was the midair collision, and we showed you the cause of that this morning. The second catastrophe was the explosion that killed three firefighters and injured dozens of others. What I'm about to show you is the cause of that explosion. Andy?"

The lights went down, and in the next instant the white-haired man was projected life-sized on the screen beside her. The first shot showed him scaling the framework of the roller coaster with the other rescue workers, but the view zoomed in closer and closer as Andy clicked through the rest of the slides. The final shot was of his shirt.

"That's a gas tank charge in his pocket," Dana said.

Silence held tight through the room as the lights came up again. She looked from the faded image of the saboteur to Don Skelly, where he sat unflinching in the audience.

No one spoke until Charlie called out, "What are you saying, Dana?"

She took a breath. "This man deliberately blew up the wreckage to destroy evidence of the cause of the accident. He spotted me photographing the scene after he'd already set the charge. Ever since, he and his confederates have been trying to get the film, any way they can."

"You sayin' they took Whit?" Mirella demanded.

Tears welled in Dana's eyes. "Yes, they—" She broke off as her throat closed up, and she had to duck her head and squeeze her eyes shut.

Oliver Dean rose to his feet and spoke to the projection booth. "Would you go back two or three slides?"

Andy clicked back until the full face of the white-haired man returned to the screen.

"Look here, Charlie," Dean said. "Isn't he that security man of yours? That fellow Pasko?"

Slowly, Dana raised her head. *Pasko—Michael Pasko? Pennsteel's security director?*

Charlie got to his feet and squinted hard at the screen. "I don't know," he said, mystified. "You could be right, Ollie."

Dana looked back to Don Skelly, whose expression showed nothing but curiosity aroused.

It hit her then, so hard she had to grip the podium to keep from swaying on her feet. *Michael Pasko, a good man in a crisis,* Charlie said. *Use him,* he said.

"Let me get Mike on the horn," Charlie was saying now as he made his way to the aisle. "I'll call him down here and we'll get to the bottom of this right now."

A pounding started in Dana's ears as Charlie strode up the aisle and exited at the rear of the auditorium. Mirella was on her feet now, too, but all Dana could do was stare at the faces in front of her as they let Charlie go without a backward glance. None of them saw, no one could see it but her. Mirella's lips were moving, but the pounding in Dana's head swelled to a roar so loud it drowned out everything else.

"Excuse me a moment," she said.

She left the stage and walked stiff-legged up the aisle and through the door at the rear. Charlie was in the corridor, punching the elevator call button with a hand wrapped in gauze bandages. An image flashed in her mind of the dead bolt on the war room door, blistered and charred by the surge of electricity. Who else knew about the war room on the fortieth floor? The man who paid the rent on it every month.

He turned around at the sound of her heels on the floor. "Ahh, Dana, always here when I need you," he said.

"Hurt your hand, Charlie?" she asked.

He thrust the bandaged hand into his pocket. "Yeah, burned it on the barbecue last night. Listen, Pasko's on his way, but meanwhile I got another crisis brewing back at the office. Cover for me, will you?"

She walked the length of the hallway toward him. "No, Charlie. I won't. Not this time. Not ever again."

His lips went white as she drew closer. The elevator doors opened behind him, and his eyes slid left and right as he backed into it.

The only thing Jason Carraway was more famous for than football was cheating. Whit knew the whole story of Charlie's expulsion from the firm, and he'd never understood her unwavering refusal to believe that Charlie could have destroyed the documents. *His career was on the line,* he said once. *A lot of guys'll do desperate things when their back's against the wall.*

Dana broke into a run as the elevator doors began to close.

"Where's Whit?" she screamed. "What have you done with my husband?"

The doors snapped shut on Charlie's bloodless face, and she threw herself against them, pounding her fists, shrieking, "Where is he? What have you done with him?"

Angela Leoni stuck her head out of the telephone booth down the hall. "Dana, what's the matter?" she called.

Dana ran to the windows at the end of the corridor. Charlie was in the parking lot, sprinting bareheaded through the rain. He scrambled into his Porsche and peeled out of the lot, shooting up geysers of water as he raced down the drive.

She let her head fall against the glass, but the cool surface couldn't penetrate the fevered workings of her mind. Her instincts about people were better than this, she'd thought, but she was wrong about Skelly, she was wrong about Travis, and she was wrong about Charlie. Charlie Morrison, her old friend and loyal client, whose career was on the line, who knew about the collision within two minutes, and who dispatched Mike Pasko within five, to destroy all evidence whether it was favorable to Pennsteel or not, because he wasn't willing to take a chance on not.

She stared blindly through the teeming rain. Charlie Morrison, a nice guy who finally got to finish first, but it was all a simulation. He lied and cheated to try to climb his way up at Jackson, Rieders, and he did the same at Pennsteel; the only difference was that now he was good at it; now he fooled everyone.

Angela was speaking beside her, but nothing penetrated. Dana was blind, deaf, and dumb. And if Whit were dead, she only wished that she could be dead, too.

But she wasn't blind after all. Somewhere a light flashed and it cut into her brain like a laser. She pressed her face to the glass and looked for it again. Where was it? Where did it come from? She was sure she saw it.

There. Another flash, and long enough this time for her to trace the line of light back to its source, at the bottom of the excavation for the west tower.

Another flash, and this time she tracked it to a turquoise latrine lying on its side in the mud. A disreputable bathroom in the back of a basement-level watering hole.

The Rathskeller.

"Whit!" she cried.

The fire door banged behind her as she bolted down the steps and through the lobby and outside. She ran through the parking lot with her heels splashing through the puddles, then over the sodden grass to the chain-link fence around the construction site. The gate was on the far side, and she raced for it so fast her feet slid out from under her and she landed in the mud. She hauled herself up and ran on.

A length of chain secured the gate to the fence, and there was a padlock holding the two ends together. She twisted the lock and jerked hard, and when it didn't open she grabbed two handfuls of the chain and pulled with all her strength, but it wouldn't break.

She kicked off her shoes and jumped at the chain-link fence, catching on with both hands and one toe wedged between the links, and pulled herself up, arm over arm to the top. A pipe railing ran along the upper edge, and the cut ends of the wire protruded in a jagged line above it. Her jacket snagged and ripped as she heaved herself over the top, but she landed on her feet on the ground.

On the far side of the pit the latrine was lying on its back, door side up, in half a foot of rising water.

"Whit!" she yelled. "Whit!" But the wind whipped up her words and blew them away into the rain.

She found the ladder and dragged it to the edge of the pit and lowered it over the side. The rungs were slippery against the glossy nylon of her hose, and six feet from the bottom she lost her footing and toppled to the ground. She sprawled on her back and rolled up, spitting mud and water.

"Whit!" she cried, slogging through the mud to the latrine. "Whit, are you in there?" She fell to her knees and put her mouth to the crack of the door. "Whit—Whit, are you there?" The rain and the tears mixed on her cheeks as she strained to hear.

"Dana," came the rasping voice at last. "Is that you?"

He was there. She threw herself against the latrine and shouted through the crack. "Oh, God, Whit—I'll get you out. Hold on, please, Whit, hold on."

"Dana, there's a chain—"

"I know, I see it. But it's padlocked."

"The latrine's narrower at the top. Work the chain up from the middle, it'll slide off."

Water was streaming from her hair into her eyes, and she pushed it back and stumbled to her feet. She grabbed the heavy length of chain and tugged it toward the roof. It moved a few inches and stopped, hooking on a protrusion on the side, and she worked her fingers under it until she could get the chain over the bump, then she tugged with both hands again. It inched up, over the midsection of the latrine, and finally, toward the end, slipped off clean.

She got a muddy grip on the handle and jerked hard, and Whit burst out, beard-stubbled, sopping wet, and blinking hard against the light.

"Dana!" He reached for her, and they fell together to the ground.

"Oh, Whit!" she cried, clutching her arms around him. "Are you all right? I was so afraid I lost you!"

Other voices carried to them through the storm, and they looked up to see a crowd gathered at the edge of the pit. Angela was teetering through the mud in her high heels, and behind her Mirella's caftan whipped like the wrath of God in the wind. Travis was bracing the ladder from the top as Andy scrambled down the rungs and vaulted to the ground.

"They're coming for us," Dana said.

"You came for me," Whit said. "Nothing else matters."

He tucked her beneath him to shield her from the rain, and in the shelter of his own body he leaned down to kiss her.

"Dana," he whispered when their lips parted. "I finished my book."

Her eyes fluttered open in confusion, but then they lit like a beacon and shone up at him through the storm.

"Oh, Whit!" she squealed, and flung her arms tight around him.

47

The rain tapered off before nightfall, and by Friday morning the storm water had drained off the roadways and soaked into the earth and refilled the water tables. Overnight the dedicated green space around the Geisinger complex was green again.

Dana took a whiff of the air as she stepped out of her car. It smelled fresh and clean, renewed. She was dressed casually today, in a black linen shift and espadrilles, and the bashed-in trunk of the car was packed full with shorts and swimsuits and beach towels. A one-hour meeting, and then she was off, to gather up the children and settle in for two weeks' glorious repose at the shore.

Travis was waiting outside the auditorium when she got off the elevator, and he barely raised his head to mumble a greeting as she handed him the video. It was hard to tell who was more ashamed, Travis for what he'd done, or Dana for what she thought he'd done. He took off at once for the projection booth.

"Dana—a word?"

She turned to see Clifford Austin coming down the hall. Back again, still angling for the Pennsteel account, or maybe to gloat that he was right about Charlie Morrison all along.

"What is it, Cliff?"

"First of course I want to tell you how enormously impressed we all were with your presentation yesterday." He pulled himself up straight and haughty before her. "And now that we realize the personal strains you were under—"

"Thank you, Cliff. If you'll excuse me—"

"No, wait." An anxious edge creased his voice. "I know we've had our disagreements from time to time. But you must know I've always had the highest regard for you. Last night the executive committee asked me to let you know how much we all value you as one of us. And how important it is that you should remain happily in the firm."

"I see." A faint smile came to her lips. Oliver Dean was a loyal man; he'd obviously resisted Austin's pitch. "Well— thank you for passing along the message." She opened the door and left him standing confounded behind her.

Don Skelly rose to greet her as she came in the auditorium. "Hey there, Dana."

"Morning, Don. Thanks for letting us use your place again today."

"Hey, any time. Most of the Pennsteel boys put up here in our hotel last night. You keep this up, Geisinger'll end up *making* money off this case."

Andy was waiting for her backstage. He was wearing the old familiar blue jeans and sport coat; his spiffy new suit from yesterday was too mud-splattered for a repeat performance today. He started toward her but stopped at a distance of four feet.

"How's your husband?"

"Good. A little dehydrated, so they kept him overnight for observation, but he'll be out today."

"He's a lucky guy."

"I know. He could have died in there."

A lump traveled down his throat. "That's not what I meant."

"Oh, Andy." She bit her lip against the feeling that swelled inside her. "I'm so sorry."

He took a step toward her and reached out to brush his knuckles against her cheek. "It's my own fault. I'm the one who helped you fall in love with him again."

But she shook her head. "I was always in love with him. You helped me remember why."

A hollow look came into his eyes, and she caught his hand against her face and kissed the well of his palm. "You're very special to me, Andy Broder. What happened between us is going to be a precious memory for the rest of my life."

His eyes fell shut, and when he opened them again, they showed a rueful resignation. "Is it okay if I keep in touch?" he asked. "Maybe drop you a Christmas card once a year? I don't want to lose track of you."

"I'd like that." She took his hand and held it clasped between both of hers. "And maybe you could send me some photos now and then?"

"Of what?"

"Your wife and kids, for instance." He gave a little smile, and she went on, "The first helicopter you buy for your charter company."

His dimples bored in as the smile went to a grin.

Voices sounded from the auditorium, and Dana turned and stepped out to the podium. Oliver Dean was there, front and center, with the two remaining Amigos and most of the Pennsteel board. Norm Wiecek and Don Skelly sat separately with a few of their own board members. Some of her own people were there, too—Lyle, Brad, Maria. Even Cliff Austin came down the aisle to sit with the Jackson, Rieders contingent.

Dana turned off the microphone; these were her people, and this news should come to them in her own voice.

"Charlie Morrison was arrested by the FBI last night as he was boarding an Air Jamaica flight to Kingston."

A whisper shot through the auditorium.

"My husband identified Charlie as one of his kidnappers along with Michael Pasko and Tobiah Johnson. Johnson's body was found last night in a shallow grave in the excavation. Pasko apparently fled the country Tuesday night, but he left behind a videotape. The FBI has the original. We were given a copy. Travis, would you roll it please?"

The auditorium went dark and a bigger-than-life-sized image of the white-haired man appeared on the screen behind her. He was seated behind a desk; the background had already been identified as his own office at Pennsteel.

"Professor Endicott," he said, speaking to the camera with a smile. "If you're watching this, it means you survived, and I salute you. You showed more grit than I, for one, ever expected to see from you. I figure you've earned an explanation for your ordeal. This is it.

"My name was Michael Pasko, and I enjoyed a distinguished career with the United States Army, Special Forces, before Charlie Morrison hired me to be Director of Security and Special Services for Pennsteel Corporation.

"One of Mr. Morrison's greatest concerns over the last few years has been the spiraling cost of litigation. It's become clear to him that when a corporation is sued, it can't win, even if it ultimately wins the trial, because it still has to pay the enormous costs of its defense. A corporation wins only when it can stop the lawsuit from being filed. My mission was to develop early intervention techniques to achieve that goal.

"When the Palazzo Hotel fire broke out, I was on the first plane to San Diego, but I arrived too late. Although Pennsteel was found to be without fault, the litigation ended up costing the company three million dollars in defense costs. And all of that money came out of the insurance deductible, which came out of Morrison's budget.

"He was aiming for a significant promotion within the company, and his budget was under strict scrutiny from the board of directors. He was determined that nothing like the Palazzo debacle would happen again.

"When he received word of the JetRanger collision, he sent me to the park to eliminate any forensic evidence that might be used to launch another round of lawsuits against Pennsteel. I determined that the fastest way to do that was to blow up the remaining fuel tank. It was never my intention, nor Morrison's, to endanger human life in the process. This was an unfortunate transactional cost.

"But more unfortunate still is the fact that I did not observe your wife photographing the mission until it was too late. I followed her in an effort to get the camera; if her reflexes were a little slower, none of the rest of this ever would have happened.

"I reported to Morrison, and his instructions were clear: obtain and destroy the film; do not harm the woman. A simple enough mission. I enlisted my lieutenant, Tobiah Johnson. We expected the matter to be concluded within a day.

"Nothing went as expected. The film didn't turn up in the car or house. Morrison searched her office himself, but the film wasn't there either. I proposed your kidnapping, Professor, but even that was doomed from the start, because your wife had already developed the film.

"Today I was ordered to terminate you and abort the mission. After long consideration I've decided to disobey that order. Please don't imagine I'm being entirely altruistic here. It's obvious to me that I'm scheduled to be the next fatality. I've decided not to let that happen. It seems to me you deserve as much.

"You notice I said my name *was* Michael Pasko. By the time you watch this tape, it won't be, so tell the FBI not to bother searching under that name. You might tell them to focus on Charlie Morrison instead. I suggest they begin with the safe in my office. I recorded every conversation I ever had with Morrison, and all the tapes are there.

"That's it, then. Good luck to you, Professor."

The video sputtered to an end, and Travis came out of the booth as the house lights rose over a dazed audience.

"Miss Svenssen," Oliver Dean began, and cleared his throat and began again. "Miss Svenssen, these tapes he mentioned— is it true?"

"Yes," she answered from the podium. "The FBI recovered them late last night. The conversations appear to be genuine. And completely incriminating."

The board members shook their heads as they tried to absorb the information. Tim Haguewood called out, "So what does all this mean for Pennsteel?"

"I'm afraid Pennsteel has exposure for all the damages resulting from the second explosion," she said. "And since it was caused by an intentional act, there's a significant exposure to punitive damages as well."

That comment launched a new round of buzzing.

"It's ironic, isn't it?" Oliver Dean said. "We weren't responsible for this awful disaster, but now, thanks to Charlie, we are."

"You may be," she corrected him. "It's not a clear-cut liability, and you have a substantial defense. Charlie's actions were criminal and certainly way outside the reasonable scope of his duties. He was acting on his own private motive: he wanted Vic's job. If he'd murdered Vic to clear the way for himself, no court would hold Pennsteel liable for it. Is this any different?"

"Not legally, perhaps," Dean said. "But morally? One has to wonder."

Dana's eyes searched out Travis and found him sitting alone three rows behind the rest of her team. She could see that he was sick with anxiety over his future in the firm. He'd gone too far, he'd crossed a line, but to her mind Clifford Austin was more accountable for it than he was. Eight years ago Charlie Morrison was just another Travis Hunt with his back against a wall. If anyone had taken him in hand the way she intended to take Travis, none of this would have happened.

"You may be right, Mr. Dean," she said finally. "If there are things going on inside the company that led Charlie to do what he did, they should be fought. But that doesn't mean you shouldn't fight against forces outside the company, too.

"Because Charlie was right about this much: businesses are being held hostage to the cost of litigation. You can't win even when you win, and there are too many people out there who know that fact and exploit it. Give them an easy payoff, and you might as well be paying ransom to a kidnapper."

"Then what are we supposed to do?"

The question came from Haguewood, but she turned to Oliver Dean and the other board members with her answer. "Don't pay the ransom on these lawsuits. Assert your defenses. Fight back."

"Will you, Miss Svenssen?" Oliver Dean called out. "Fight back for us? Or is it true what I've been hearing, that you're leaving your firm and perhaps even the practice of law?"

She lowered her eyes to the podium and silence fell through the room. A smile began to curl on Haguewood's mouth as the seconds crawled by, while across the aisle, Travis sat white-faced, barely breathing as he waited for her answer.

A door opened and closed softly, and Dana looked up from the podium. Whit stood in the back of the auditorium with his arms folded, watching her. He was clean-shaven now, and on his gaunt face was an expression she hadn't seen for years, but one she remembered as clearly as yesterday: a look of wonder, that she existed and was his.

"I have some serious disagreements with the management of my firm," she said finally. "But when I joined the partnership, I saw it as a kind of marriage—not always perfect, but always permanent. We have a lot of problems that have to be resolved, but I intend to be there to resolve them." Travis sagged back with relief, sprawling his bulk over both armrests. "And I'll become managing partner myself if that's what it takes to resolve them." A few rows in front of Travis, Cliff Austin's spine went rigid. "So the answer, Mr. Dean, is no, I'm not leaving, and yes, I will stay on and fight for Pennsteel, if you want me."

From the back of the room Whit spoke to her across two hundred seats, and she didn't even need hand signals to understand him now.

Oliver Dean turned to the board members around him. "All in favor?" he said, and the ayes had it.

She scanned down the balance of her agenda, then closed her notes. "I know you have a lot of questions about everything that's happened in the last two weeks, but if you'll allow me, I'd like to turn the podium over to someone who can answer them far better than I. He's the man who led our investigation, and if and when these cases go to trial, I hope he'll agree to be our principal testifying expert. Andrew Broder."

Andy stepped up to the podium as Dana ran down the steps and up the aisle to the back of the auditorium.

"What do we know about this gas tank charge?" someone called to the stage.

Andy's eyes tracked Dana as she went into Whit's arms, then he turned to answer the question.

ACKNOWLEDGMENTS

Angle of Impact was inspired by a real aviation disaster: the midair collision of a helicopter and a small plane over the Philadelphia suburbs on April 4, 1991. Most Philadelphians can vividly recall the horror of that day. But anyone involved in the aftermath of the tragedy will recognize that the accident described in the book is purely fictitious and bears no resemblance to the actual event beyond the fact of a midair collision.

However, it was through my own involvement in the aftermath that I had the good fortune to work with J. Denny Shupe and James H. Rodman, Jr. As lawyers, pilots, and all-around aviation experts, Denny and Jim probably have the knowledge and experience possessed by Dana Svenssen, Andy Broder, and their entire team of experts, combined. I am deeply grateful to them for their valuable time in reviewing the manuscript and for their invaluable advice in correcting technical errors. Any that remain are no fault of theirs.

My thanks go also to my agent, Jean Naggar, for her friendship and steadfast support; to her associates, Joan Lilly and Jennifer Weltz, for their insights and suggestions on early drafts; and to Joe Blades, editor and gentleman, for his enthusiastic and thoughtful treatment of this work.

Finally, I am grateful to my flight instructor, John A. Mignone, who died too soon, but doing what he said he loved best—flying. John, I wish you calm winds and clear skies forever.

A Conversation with Bonnie MacDougal

Q: Bonnie, we know that you practiced law for sixteen years before embarking on your writing career. Would you give us a thumbnail sketch of your experience as an attorney?

A: I spent most of my career with a major Philadelphia law firm. I was a litigator, which is a ten-cent word for a corporate trial lawyer, and I specialized in complex civil and commercial cases, typically big ones that often turned into full-court battles, with armies of lawyers on each side and files that took up floors instead of drawers. I handled securities fraud, products liability, trademark infringement, mass tort—the gamut of high-stakes lawsuits.

Q: At which point did you decide to walk away from the courtroom and into a life of (fictional) crime?

A: Actually, the fiction came first. All my life I wanted to be a novelist, and I went to college and majored in English with that end firmly in mind. But those dreams started to fade as graduation and reality loomed, and I decided I really ought to earn a living instead. I went to law school, then spent a frenetic decade establishing my practice and starting my family. There was little time to think about writing.

But in the late Eighties, a fascinating case came my way. A young professional with impeccable credentials had confessed to an inexplicable crime: he'd taken several million dollars from a client's account, but not for himself. Instead, he'd moved it to another client's account. I was intrigued by the psychology of his motivation and the complex relationships he had with the two clients. During the course of the long litigation that followed, I started to spin out what-if scenarios in my mind, full of alliances and conspiracies that bore no resemblance to reality but made me want desperately to write again. It took me several years—now I was juggling writing along with work and family—but ultimately I completed my first novel, *Breach of Trust*.

I left the active practice of law after the sale of that book, for two reasons. First, I'd gotten the germ of the idea for *Angle of Impact*, but by that time my practice was too all-consuming to allow any time for writing. And second, because I'd become so dissatisfied with the current state of lawyering. I'm not alone: Probably a hundred lawyers have told me how they envy me my escape. But that's not to say I don't sometimes miss it. In my new solitary life as a writer, I often long for the teamwork, the synergy, the exciting ways my colleagues and I used to brainstorm and spark ideas off each other. For that reason I still do some occasional consulting work, and I wouldn't rule out a return to a more active practice at some point in the future.

Q: You don't have a recurring protagonist in your novels—which raises (at least) two questions. First, why did you choose not to create a continuing central character? And how much are your heroines reflections of you personally or other women attorneys you've known?
A: I decided not to write a traditional series for the same reason I decided to become a litigator: I'm too easily

bored. As a litigator, each new case required me to learn all about a new business or product or technology, and that challenge forced me to stay fresh and to keep my edge. If I'd had to do the same kind of work over and over again, I would have gone stale very quickly. As a reader, I've seen this happen to many series authors, and I've also watched some of them attempt to escape with a non-series book that seldom enjoys the same success.

What I've done instead is to create a fictitious Philadelphia law firm—Jackson, Rieders & Clark—with each book following a different lawyer in that firm. This allows me to revisit past characters from time to time, as when Dan Casella from *Breach of Trust* pops up as Dana Svenssen's opposing counsel in *Angle of Impact*. But because I haven't limited myself to a single protagonist, I feel freer to conjure up different moods and create different textures for each novel. Jennifer Lodge in *Breach* is young and naive, and that story was filtered through her rather wide-eyed viewpoint. Dana Svenssen in *Angle* is older, at the top of her form, but besieged by all kinds of stresses in her professional and personal life; the pace of this book is meant to reflect the frenzied state of her life. The protagonist in my current project is yet a different kind of woman; she's secretive and scheming, haunted by her past and weighed down with years of guilt and regret. And so this book has a darker tone than what I've done before.

Despite their differences, each of these characters does bear at least a passing resemblance to me. They all practice the same kind of law in the same kind of firm as I did; and they're all struggling with the same pressures and conflicts that I did. Dana Svenssen comes closest to me in the kind of work she does, but, unfortunately, farthest in how well she does it, since she's better and more successful than I ever was. That was part of the challenge—and fun—of creating her. I wanted to portray a woman in the kind of position of power that we still only see men occupying. I see her as a true postfeminist heroine: she doesn't worry about the glass ceiling because she's already shattered it.

Q: As you write in your acknowledgments page in **Angle of Impact,** *this novel was inspired by a real-life aviation disaster. Would you tell us about that tragic event in 1991—and about your personal involvement in the aftermath? We'd also be interested in learning more about how you departed (rather substantially) from the specifics of that event.*

A: A corporate helicopter and a small charter plane collided in midair over an elementary school in suburban Philadelphia. Seven people were killed—four pilots; a U.S. Senator who was the charter passenger; and two little girls on the playground—and many others were horribly injured. The accident was deeply disturbing to me. My own children had been on their own school playground at the time, and the idea that death could have come raining out of the sky on them was too awful to contemplate.

But soon I had no choice but to contemplate it, because my firm was hired to represent the owner of the helicopter, and I became a member of the litigation team. It was a role that gave me a front-row seat on an amazing effort by the lawyers and forensic experts to determine the cause of the accident and attempt to defend against the onslaught of lawsuits that followed it.

Those two elements—the searing emotional horror of the accident and the intellectual challenge of reconstructing its cause—led me to write *Angle of Impact*.

But I must add that those two elements are the only aspects of the real-life tragedy that can be found in the novel. Beyond the fact of a midair collision, the fictional accident is entirely a product of my imagination and bears no resemblance to the actual events.

Q: *Is it true that you enrolled in flight school as part of your research for* Angle of Impact*?*
A: Yes. Although I learned a lot during the course of the real-life case, I wasn't sure I had enough expertise to write knowledgeably on all the details I'd hoped to include in the book. So in addition to doing a lot of library research, I went to aviation ground school and learned as much as I could about the principles of flight. I also had my instructor take me up in the kind of plane I'd decided to put in the book. A terrible irony is that he was later killed in that plane. Because of that, I haven't proceeded past ground school certification. At this point, frankly, I'm not sure I ever will.

Q: Wallace Stegner's **Angle of Repose** *features prominently in one of your* **Angle of Impact** *subplots. You've gone on record as a devotee of Stegner. Why are Stegner and his novel so significant to you?*
A: Stegner was a great writer, probably the leading literary voice of the modern American West, but what

draws me to him is how he wrote about marriage. More than any other male writer I know, he rendered meaningful explorations of men and women and how they lived together. *Angle of Repose,* a particular favorite of mine, is the story of a failed marriage between a successful career woman (in the nineteenth century, no less!) and a good man whose own career is a disappointment. I saw obvious parallels between this couple and Dana and Whit in *Angle of Impact* (Whit is an English professor who's about to perish because he hasn't published), and so I decided that Whit would be attempting to write a book about Stegner. But I didn't want my characters to share the unhappy fate of Stegner's and simply resign themselves to a failed marriage; I made them fight for their marriage, and in the process, rediscover what it was that made them fall in love in the first place.

Q: Earlier you alluded to your "current project." Without resorting to any spoilers, could you comment briefly on that novel?
A: A young woman lawyer with a secret past marries a man who decides to run for Congress. Both a legal thriller and a political drama, the story follows the course of the campaign as well as a high-profile custody battle in which the lawyer finds herself forced onto the wrong side of the case. And weaving through the story are several seemingly unrelated murders, all of women who worked for the same government agency thirty years ago. . . .

Looking for a new angle?

Win an autographed copy of
Bonnie MacDougal's next exciting thriller!

Coming in the summer of 1999:
another ingenious, unstoppable novel
from the author of *Angle of Impact*.

**And you can get a special preview...
and maybe an autographed copy!**
Starting on April 1, as long as supplies last, we'll
mail out free sample chapters of Bonnie MacDougal's
new novel to those who complete the coupon below
and mail it in. Your coupon must be received by
Ballantine Books no later than March 1, 1999.

In July 1999, we'll give away 500 autographed,
hardcover copies to names selected from those
who wrote in!

What are you waiting for? Write in to win!